Nancy Drew

Drew

DIARIES™

"If you look close enough, there are always clues."

–Nancy Drew

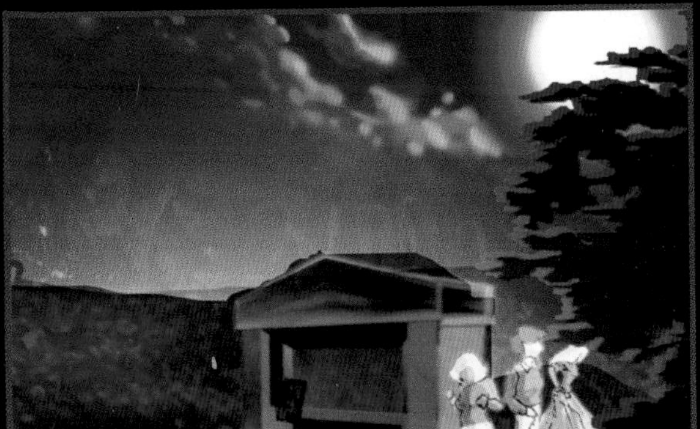

PAPERCUTZ

NANCY DREW GRAPHIC NOVELS AVAILABLE FROM PAPERCUTZ

2 GRAPHIC NOVELS BY STEFAN PETRUCHA & SHO MURASE
Nancy Drew
DIARIES
The Demon of River Heights
Writ in Stone
BASED ON THE SERIES BY
CAROLYN KEENE

"The Demon of River Heights" and "Writ in Stone"

NEW STORY! FULL-COLOR GRAPHIC NOVEL
NANCY DREW
#1
BASED ON THE SERIES BY CAROLYN KEENE
PAPERCUTZ

"The Demon of River Heights"

NEW STORY! FULL-COLOR GRAPHIC NOVEL
NANCY DREW
#2
BASED ON THE SERIES BY CAROLYN KEENE
PAPERCUTZ

"Writ in Stone"

NEW STORY! FULL-COLOR GRAPHIC NOVEL
NANCY DREW
#3
PAPERCUTZ

#3 "The Haunted Dollhouse"

NEW STORY! FULL-COLOR GRAPHIC NOVEL
NANCY DREW
#4
PAPERCUTZ

#4 "The Girl Who Wasn't There"

NEW STORY! FULL-COLOR GRAPHIC NOVEL
NANCY DREW
#5
PAPERCUTZ

#5 "The Fake Heir"

NEW STORY! FULL-COLOR GRAPHIC NOVEL
NANCY DREW
#6
PAPERCUTZ

#6 "Mr. Cheeters Is Missing"

NEW STORY! FULL-COLOR GRAPHIC NOVEL
NANCY DREW
#7
PAPERCUTZ

#7 "The Charmed Bracelet"

NEW STORY! FULL-COLOR GRAPHIC NOVEL
NANCY DREW
#8
PAPERCUTZ

#8 "Global Warning"

NEW STORY! FULL-COLOR GRAPHIC NOVEL
NANCY DREW
#9

#9 "Ghost In The Machinery"

NEW STORY! FULL-COLOR GRAPHIC NOVEL
NANCY DREW
#10

#10 "The Disoriented Express"

NEW STORY! FULL-COLOR GRAPHIC NOVEL
NANCY DREW
#11

#11 "Monkey Wrench Blues"

See page 175 for more NANCY DREW graphic novels!

NANCY DREW graphic novels are available at booksellers everywhere.

NANCY DREW graphic novels are $7.95 each in paperback and $12.95 each in hardcover. NANCY DREW DIARIES

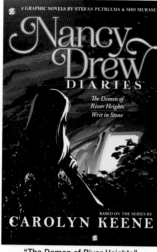

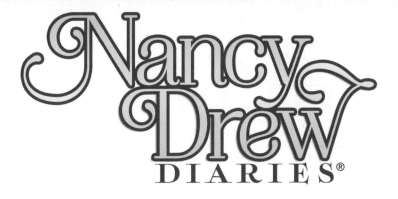

DIARIES®

#1 "The Demon of River Heights"
and
"Writ in Stone"

Based on the series by
CAROLYN KEENE
STEFAN PETRUCHA • Writer
SHO MURASE • Artist
with 3D CG elements by RACHEL ITO

PAPERCUTZ™
New York

STEFAN PETRUCHA — Writer
SHO MURASE — Artist
with 3D CG elements by RACHEL ITO
BRYAN SENKA — Letterer
CARLOS JOSE GUZMAN
SHO MURASE
Colorists
DAWN K. GUZZO — Production
BETH SCORZATO – Production Coordinator
MICHAEL PETRANEK — Associate Editor
JIM SALICRUP
Editor-in-Chief

ISBN: 978-1-59707-501-5

Copyright © 2005, 2014 by Simon & Schuster, Inc.
Published by arrangement with Aladdin Paperbacks,
an imprint of Simon & Schuster Children's Publishing Division.

Printed in Korea
April 2016 by We SP Co., LTD.
79-29, Soraji-ro,
Paju-Si, Gyeonggi-do, 10863

Distributed by Macmillian
Third Printing

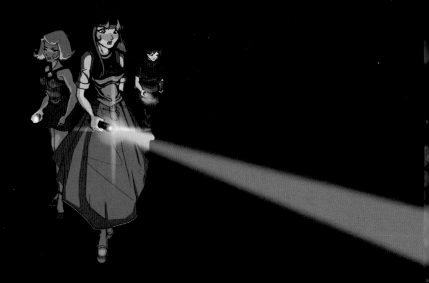

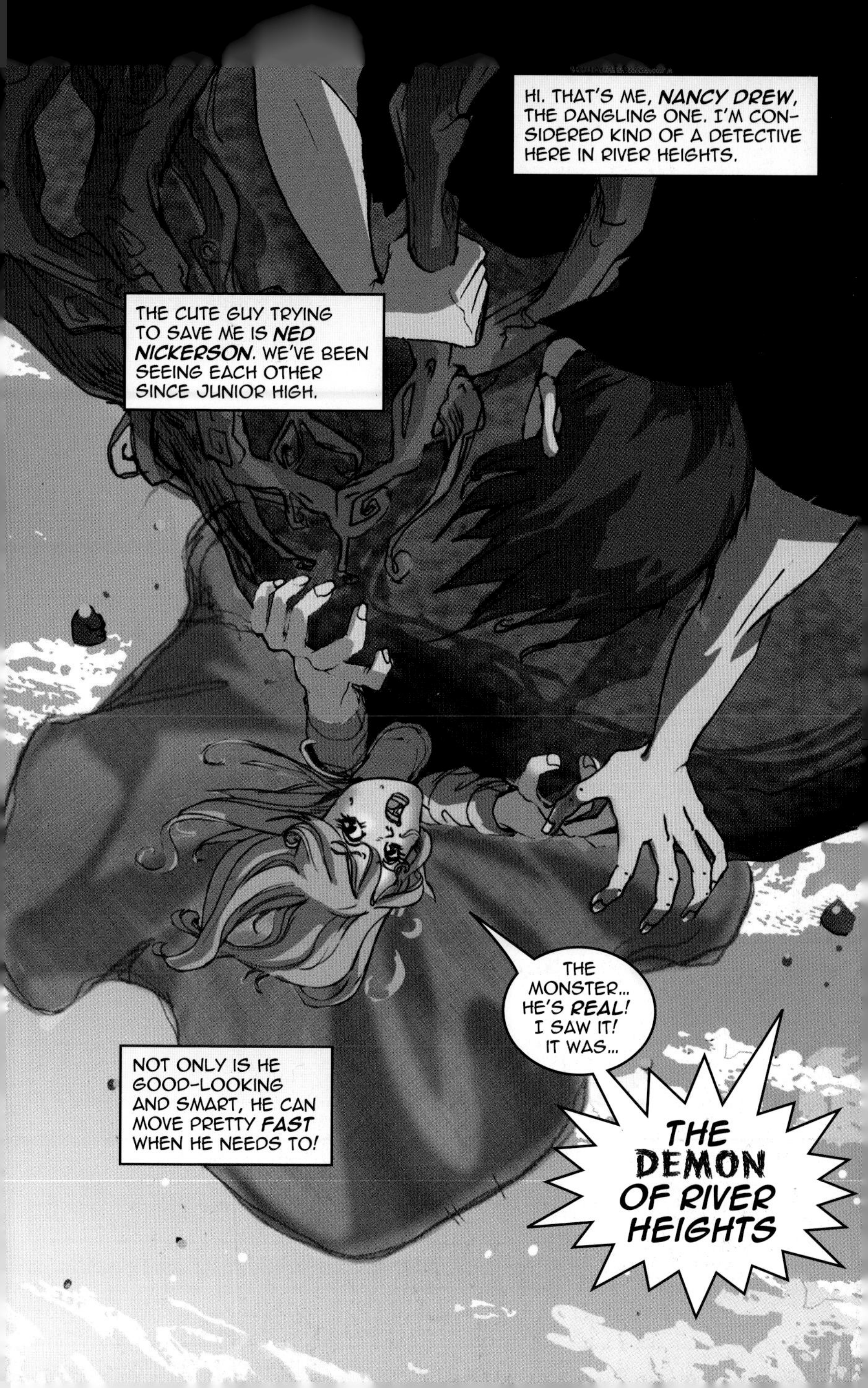
HI. THAT'S ME, NANCY DREW, THE DANGLING ONE. I'M CON-SIDERED KIND OF A DETECTIVE HERE IN RIVER HEIGHTS.
THE CUTE GUY TRYING TO SAVE ME IS NED NICKERSON. WE'VE BEEN SEEING EACH OTHER SINCE JUNIOR HIGH.
THE MONSTER... HE'S REAL! I SAW IT! IT WAS...
NOT ONLY IS HE GOOD-LOOKING AND SMART, HE CAN MOVE PRETTY FAST WHEN HE NEEDS TO!
THE DEMON OF RIVER HEIGHTS

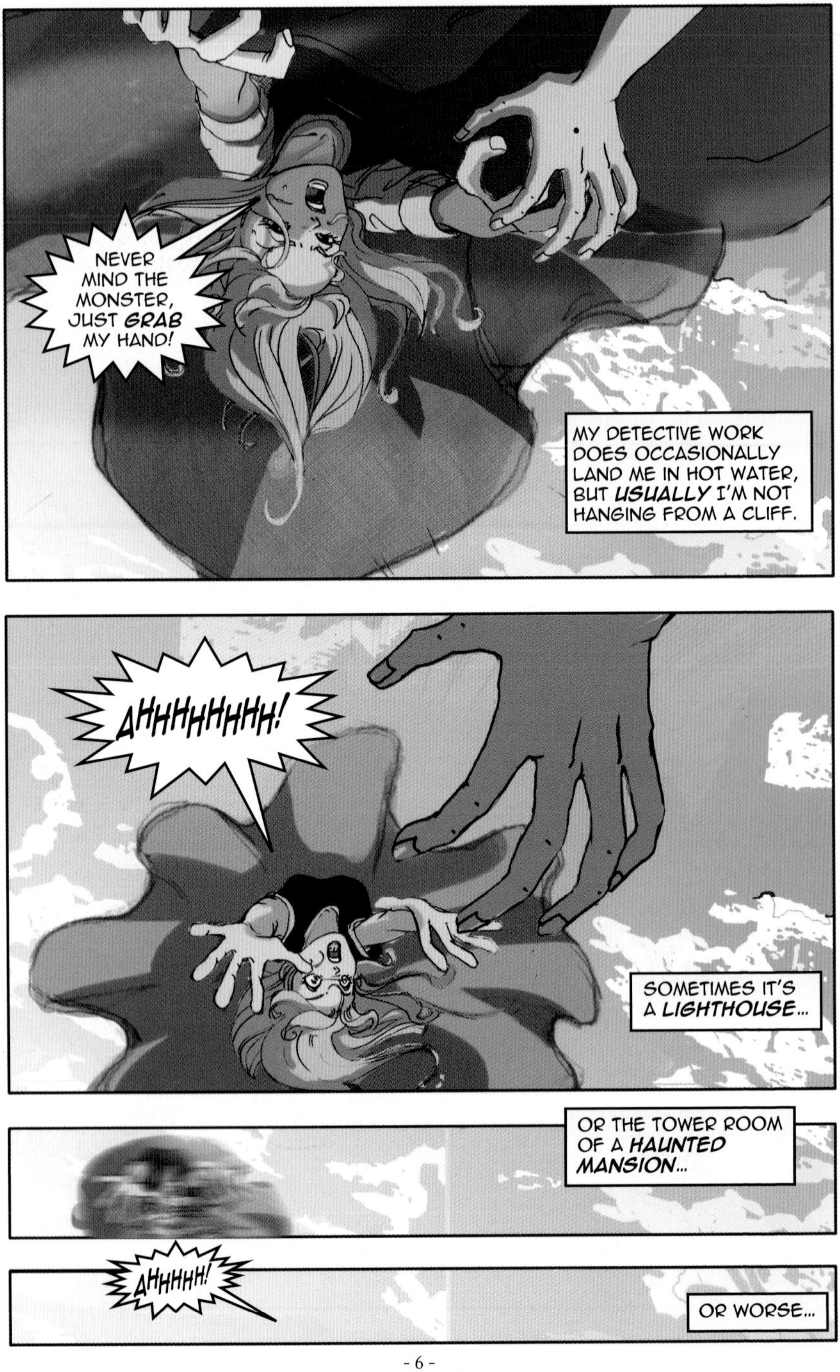

NEVER MIND THE MONSTER, JUST GRAB MY HAND!
MY DETECTIVE WORK DOES OCCASIONALLY LAND ME IN HOT WATER, BUT USUALLY I'M NOT HANGING FROM A CLIFF.
AHHHHHHHH!
SOMETIMES IT'S A LIGHTHOUSE...
OR THE TOWER ROOM OF A HAUNTED MANSION...
AHHHHH!
OR WORSE...

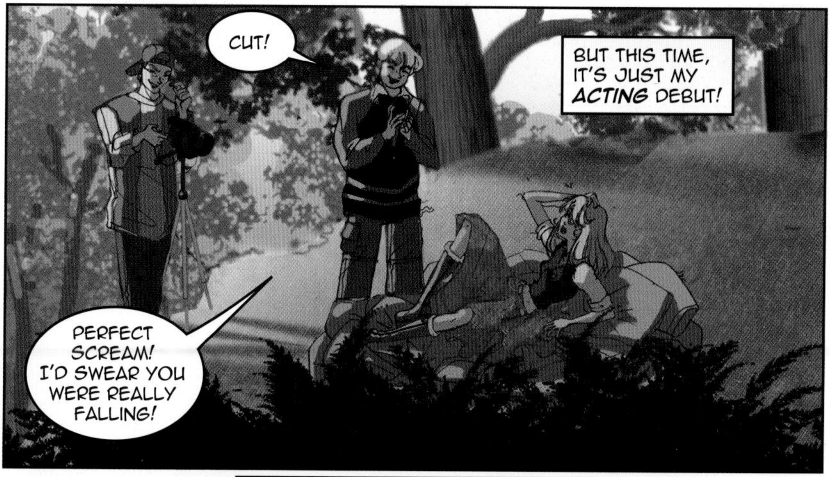
BUT THIS TIME, IT'S JUST MY ACTING DEBUT!
CUT!
PERFECT SCREAM! I'D SWEAR YOU WERE REALLY FALLING!

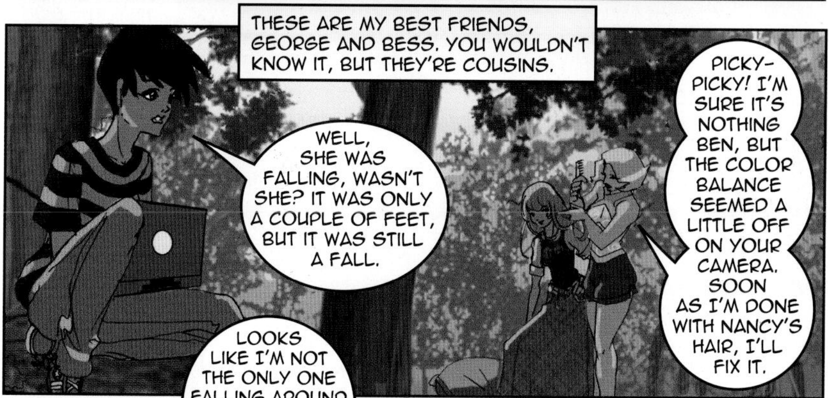
THESE ARE MY BEST FRIENDS, GEORGE AND BESS. YOU WOULDN'T KNOW IT, BUT THEY'RE COUSINS.
WELL, SHE WAS FALLING, WASN'T SHE? IT WAS ONLY A COUPLE OF FEET, BUT IT WAS STILL A FALL.
PICKY-PICKY! I'M SURE IT'S NOTHING BEN, BUT THE COLOR BALANCE SEEMED A LITTLE OFF ON YOUR CAMERA. SOON AS I'M DONE WITH NANCY'S HAIR, I'LL FIX IT.
LOOKS LIKE I'M NOT THE ONLY ONE FALLING AROUND HERE. THEY'RE BOTH PRETTY TAKEN WITH BESS.

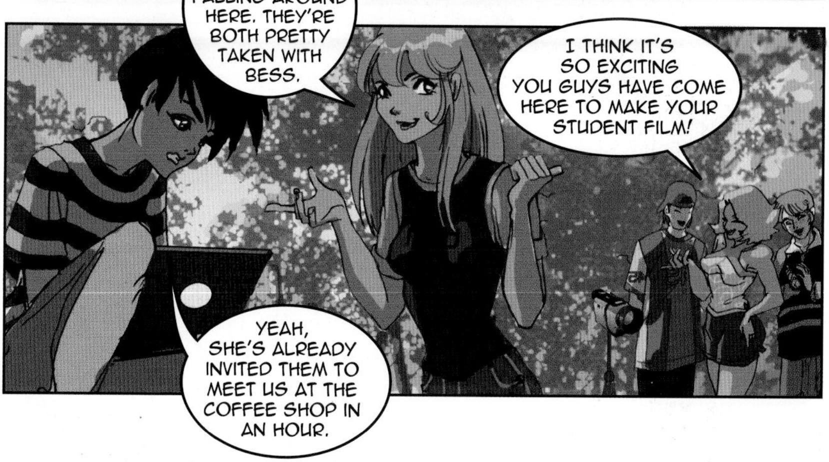
I THINK IT'S SO EXCITING YOU GUYS HAVE COME HERE TO MAKE YOUR STUDENT FILM!
YEAH, SHE'S ALREADY INVITED THEM TO MEET US AT THE COFFEE SHOP IN AN HOUR.

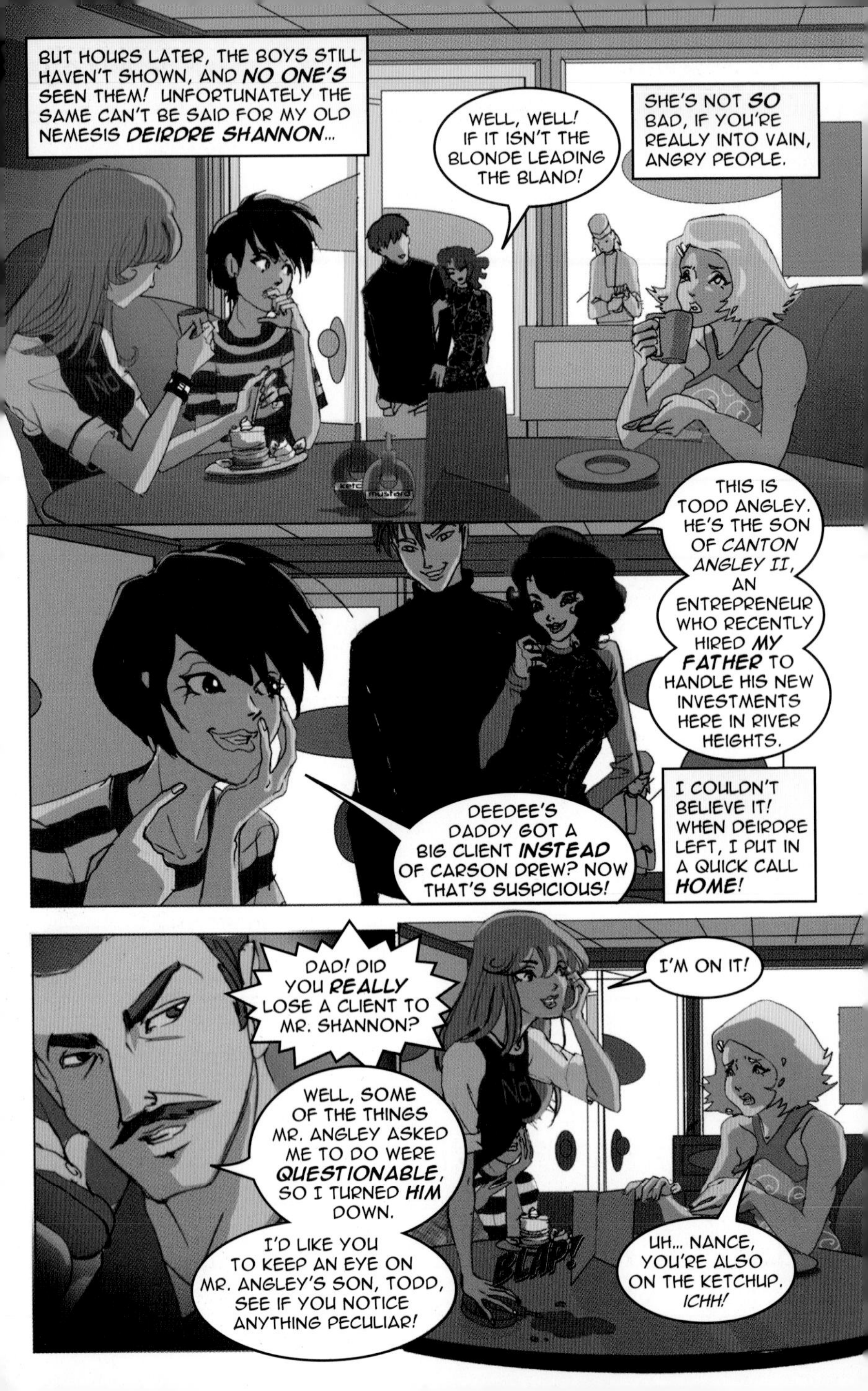

BUT HOURS LATER, THE BOYS STILL HAVEN'T SHOWN, AND NO ONE'S SEEN THEM! UNFORTUNATELY THE SAME CAN'T BE SAID FOR MY OLD NEMESIS DEIRDRE SHANNON...
WELL, WELL! IF IT ISN'T THE BLONDE LEADING THE BLAND!
SHE'S NOT SO BAD, IF YOU'RE REALLY INTO VAIN, ANGRY PEOPLE.
THIS IS TODD ANGLEY. HE'S THE SON OF CANTON ANGLEY II, AN ENTREPRENEUR WHO RECENTLY HIRED MY FATHER TO HANDLE HIS NEW INVESTMENTS HERE IN RIVER HEIGHTS.
DEEDEE'S DADDY GOT A BIG CLIENT INSTEAD OF CARSON DREW? NOW THAT'S SUSPICIOUS!
I COULDN'T BELIEVE IT! WHEN DEIRDRE LEFT, I PUT IN A QUICK CALL HOME!
DAD! DID YOU REALLY LOSE A CLIENT TO MR. SHANNON?
I'M ON IT!
WELL, SOME OF THE THINGS MR. ANGLEY ASKED ME TO DO WERE QUESTIONABLE, SO I TURNED HIM DOWN.
I'D LIKE YOU TO KEEP AN EYE ON MR. ANGLEY'S SON, TODD, SEE IF YOU NOTICE ANYTHING PECULIAR!
BLAP!
UH... NANCE, YOU'RE ALSO ON THE KETCHUP. ICHH!

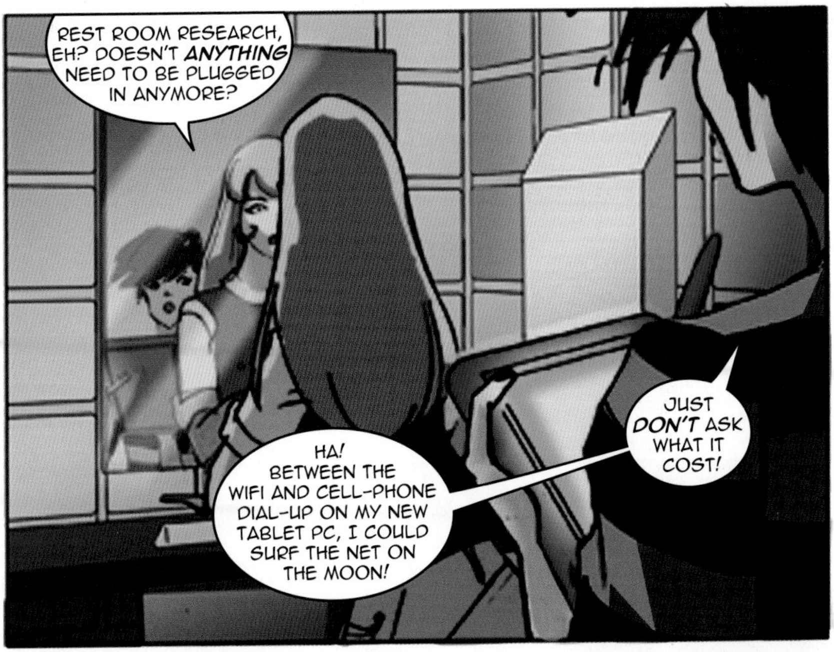
REST ROOM RESEARCH, EH? DOESN'T ANYTHING NEED TO BE PLUGGED IN ANYMORE?
HA! BETWEEN THE WIFI AND CELL-PHONE DIAL-UP ON MY NEW TABLET PC, I COULD SURF THE NET ON THE MOON!
JUST DON'T ASK WHAT IT COST!

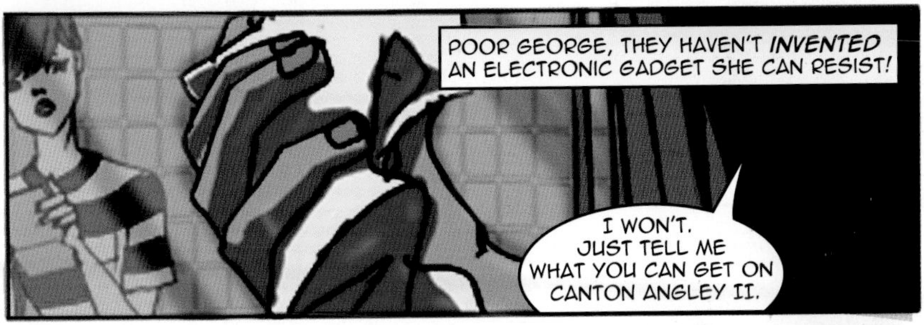
POOR GEORGE, THEY HAVEN'T INVENTED AN ELECTRONIC GADGET SHE CAN RESIST!
I WON'T. JUST TELL ME WHAT YOU CAN GET ON CANTON ANGLEY II.

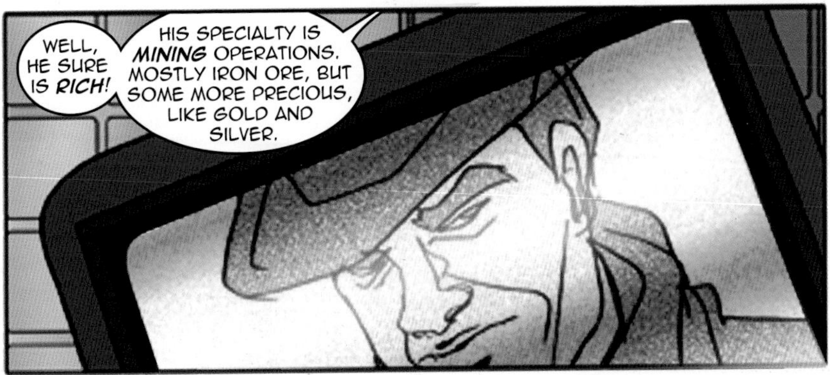
WELL, HE SURE IS RICH!
HIS SPECIALTY IS MINING OPERATIONS. MOSTLY IRON ORE, BUT SOME MORE PRECIOUS, LIKE GOLD AND SILVER.

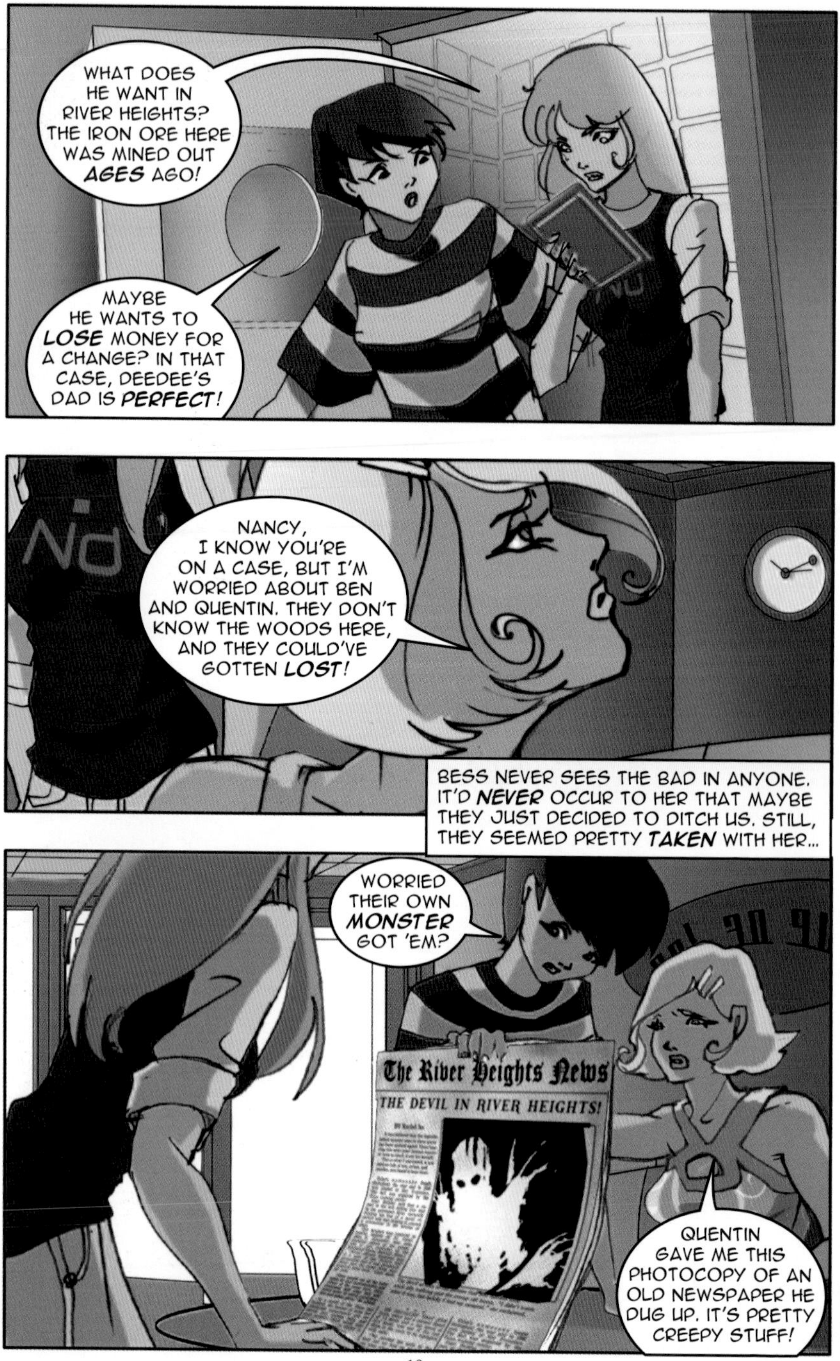
WHAT DOES HE WANT IN RIVER HEIGHTS? THE IRON ORE HERE WAS MINED OUT AGES AGO!
MAYBE HE WANTS TO LOSE MONEY FOR A CHANGE? IN THAT CASE, DEEDEE'S DAD IS PERFECT!
NANCY, I KNOW YOU'RE ON A CASE, BUT I'M WORRIED ABOUT BEN AND QUENTIN. THEY DON'T KNOW THE WOODS HERE, AND THEY COULD'VE GOTTEN LOST!
BESS NEVER SEES THE BAD IN ANYONE. IT'D NEVER OCCUR TO HER THAT MAYBE THEY JUST DECIDED TO DITCH US. STILL, THEY SEEMED PRETTY TAKEN WITH HER...
WORRIED THEIR OWN MONSTER GOT 'EM?
The River Heights News
THE DEVIL IN RIVER HEIGHTS!
QUENTIN GAVE ME THIS PHOTOCOPY OF AN OLD NEWSPAPER HE DUG UP. IT'S PRETTY CREEPY STUFF!

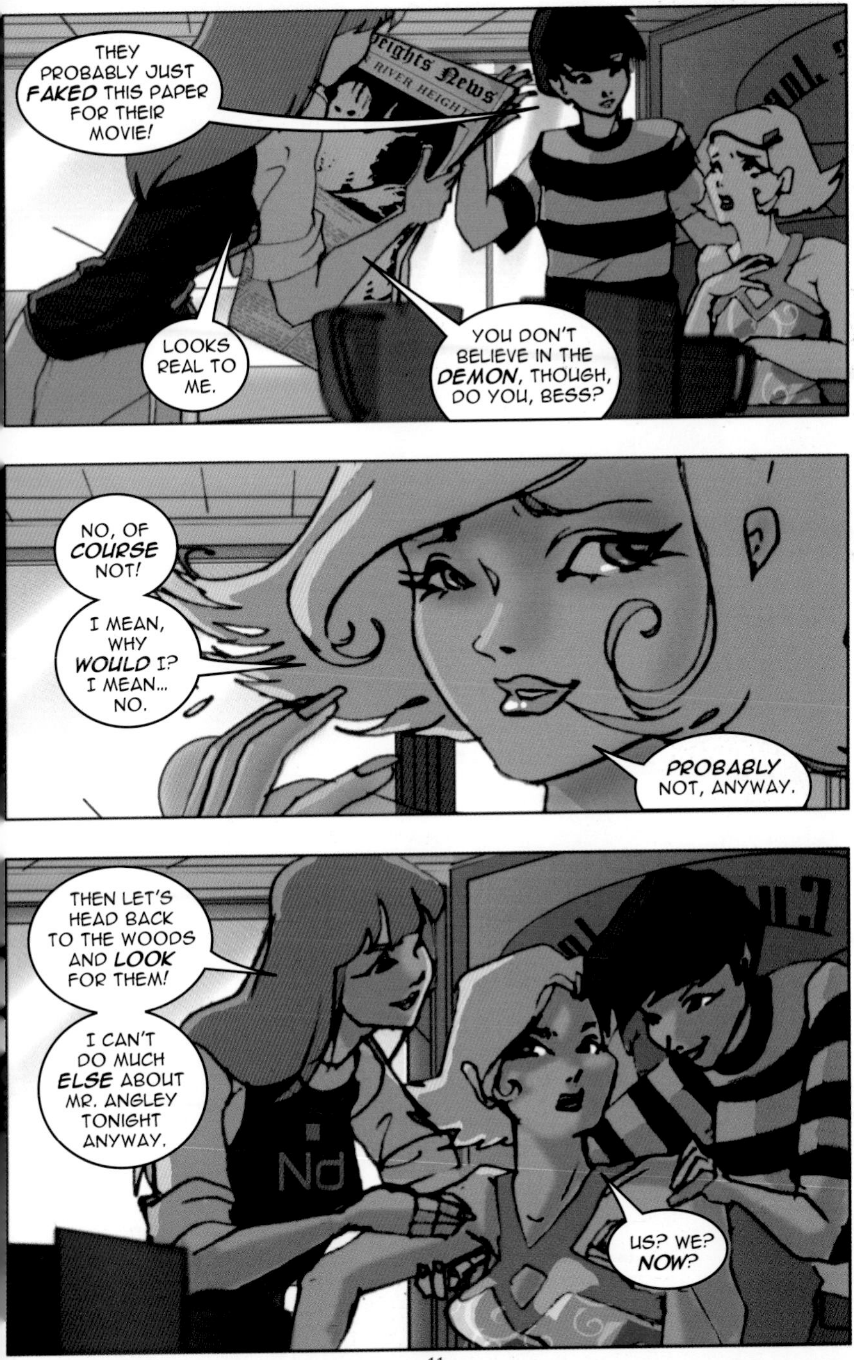
THEY PROBABLY JUST FAKED THIS PAPER FOR THEIR MOVIE!
LOOKS REAL TO ME.
YOU DON'T BELIEVE IN THE DEMON, THOUGH, DO YOU, BESS?
NO, OF COURSE NOT!
I MEAN, WHY WOULD I? I MEAN... NO.
PROBABLY NOT, ANYWAY.
THEN LET'S HEAD BACK TO THE WOODS AND LOOK FOR THEM!
I CAN'T DO MUCH ELSE ABOUT MR. ANGLEY TONIGHT ANYWAY.
US? WE? NOW?

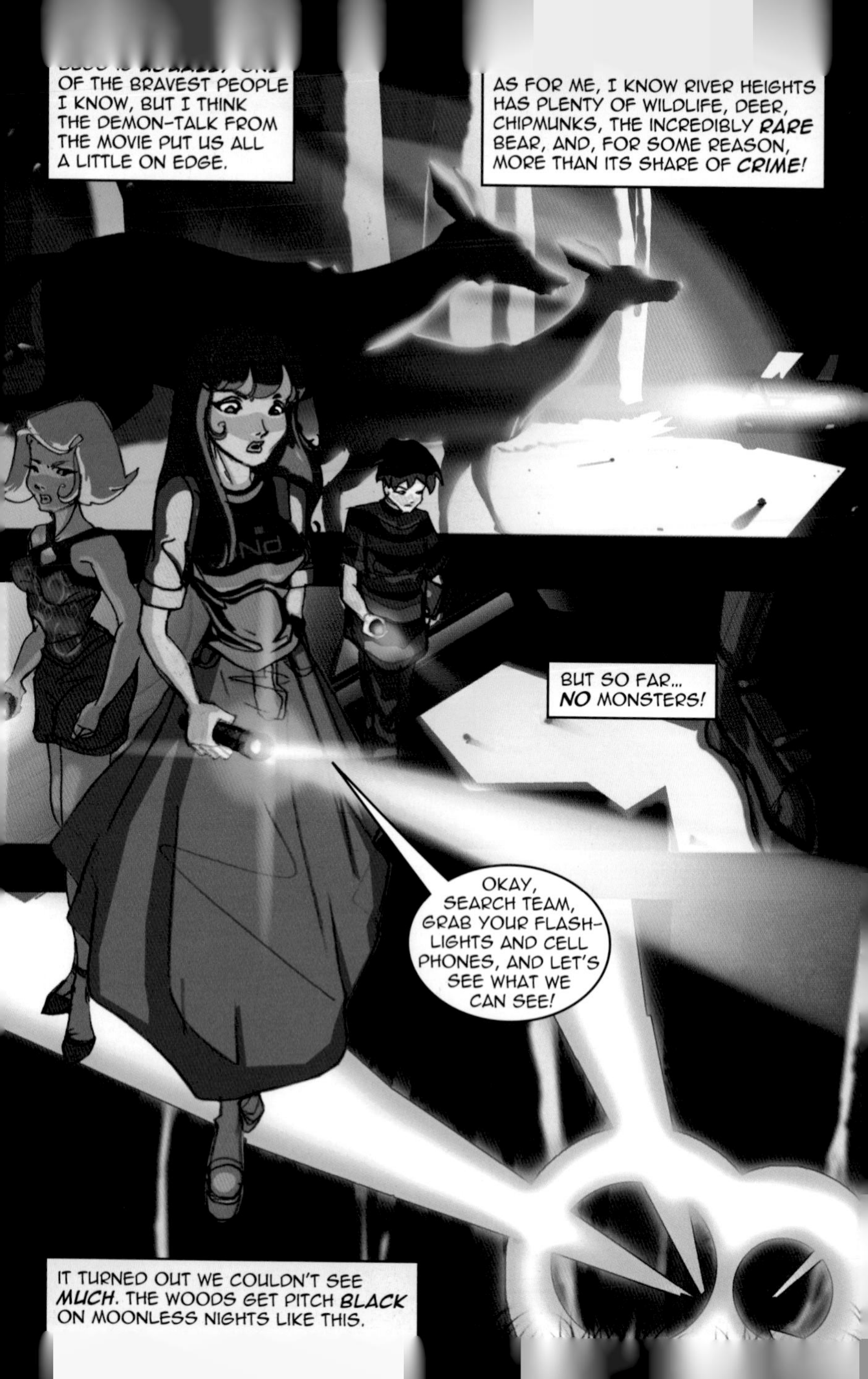
OF THE BRAVEST PEOPLE I KNOW, BUT I THINK THE DEMON-TALK FROM THE MOVIE PUT US ALL A LITTLE ON EDGE.
AS FOR ME, I KNOW RIVER HEIGHTS HAS PLENTY OF WILDLIFE, DEER, CHIPMUNKS, THE INCREDIBLY RARE BEAR, AND, FOR SOME REASON, MORE THAN ITS SHARE OF CRIME!
BUT SO FAR... NO MONSTERS!
OKAY, SEARCH TEAM, GRAB YOUR FLASH-LIGHTS AND CELL PHONES, AND LET'S SEE WHAT WE CAN SEE!
IT TURNED OUT WE COULDN'T SEE MUCH. THE WOODS GET PITCH BLACK ON MOONLESS NIGHTS LIKE THIS.

BUT WE *FINALLY* GOT TO THEIR FAKE "MONSTER'S LAIR" SET WHERE BEN AND QUENTIN SAID THEY'D BE SHOOTING NEXT.

THEY'RE NOT HERE! MAYBE *WE* SHOULDN'T BE EITHER?

I'M WITH BESS FOR A CHANGE!

I KNOW THAT CAVE IS MADE OF STYROFOAM, BUT IT LOOKS A *LOT* CREEPIER AT NIGHT!

I HADN'T WALKED ALL THAT WAY TO LEAVE WITHOUT CHECKING SOME *DETAILS*.

DETAILS ARE THE MOST IMPORTANT THING IN DETECTIVE WORK.

HM... THESE BRANCHES WERE *BROKEN* RECENTLY. THEY PROBABLY WENT *THIS* WAY.

AND, CARRYING ALL THAT *HEAVY* EQUIPMENT IN THIS *SOFT* DIRT, I BET THEY LEFT SOME...

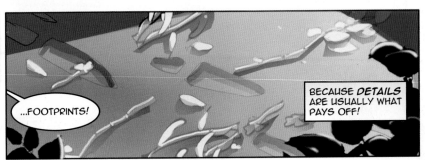

...FOOTPRINTS!

BECAUSE *DETAILS* ARE USUALLY WHAT PAYS OFF!

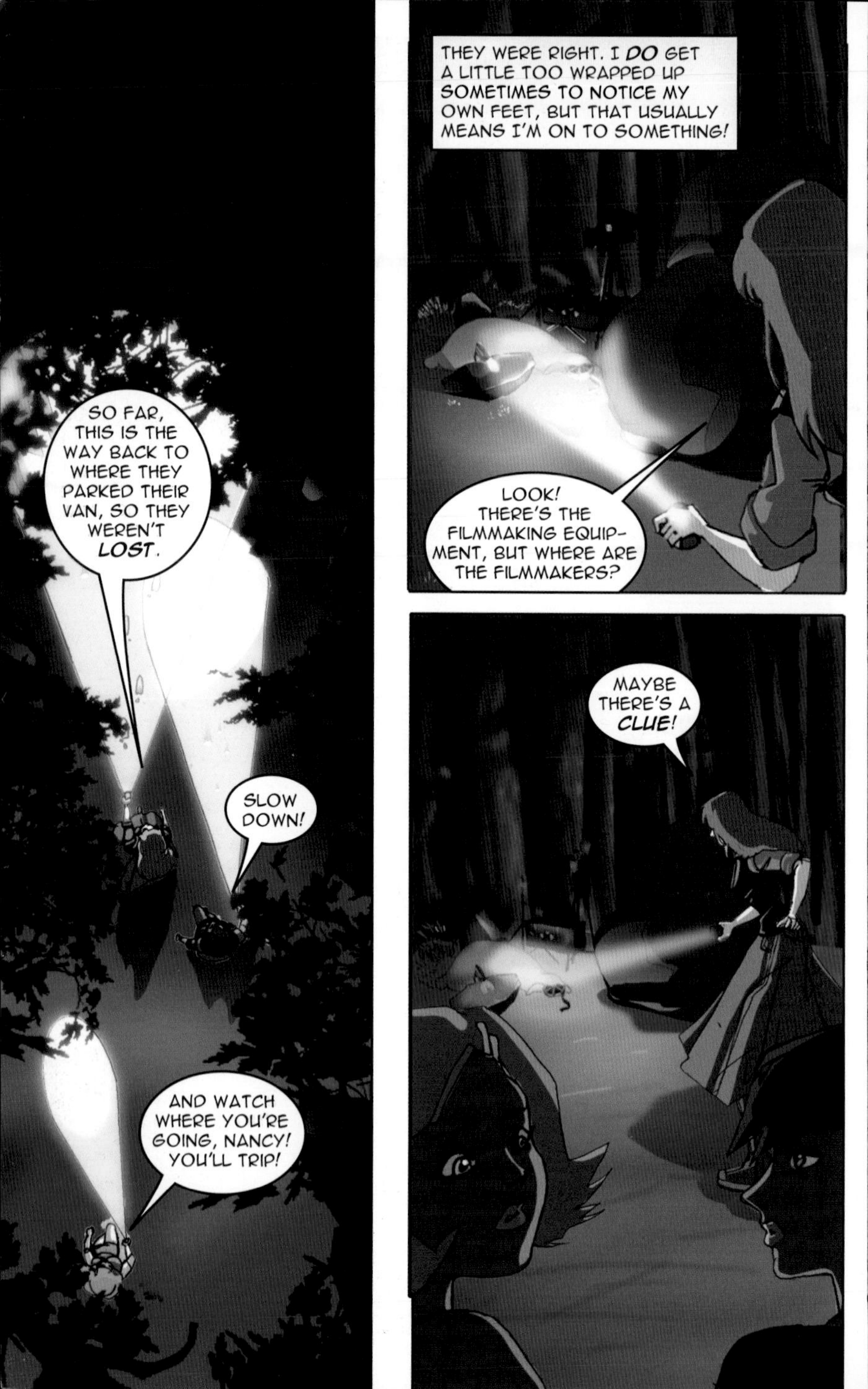
SO FAR, THIS IS THE WAY BACK TO WHERE THEY PARKED THEIR VAN, SO THEY WEREN'T LOST.
SLOW DOWN!
AND WATCH WHERE YOU'RE GOING, NANCY! YOU'LL TRIP!
THEY WERE RIGHT. I DO GET A LITTLE TOO WRAPPED UP SOMETIMES TO NOTICE MY OWN FEET, BUT THAT USUALLY MEANS I'M ON TO SOMETHING!
LOOK! THERE'S THE FILMMAKING EQUIPMENT, BUT WHERE ARE THE FILMMAKERS?
MAYBE THERE'S A CLUE!

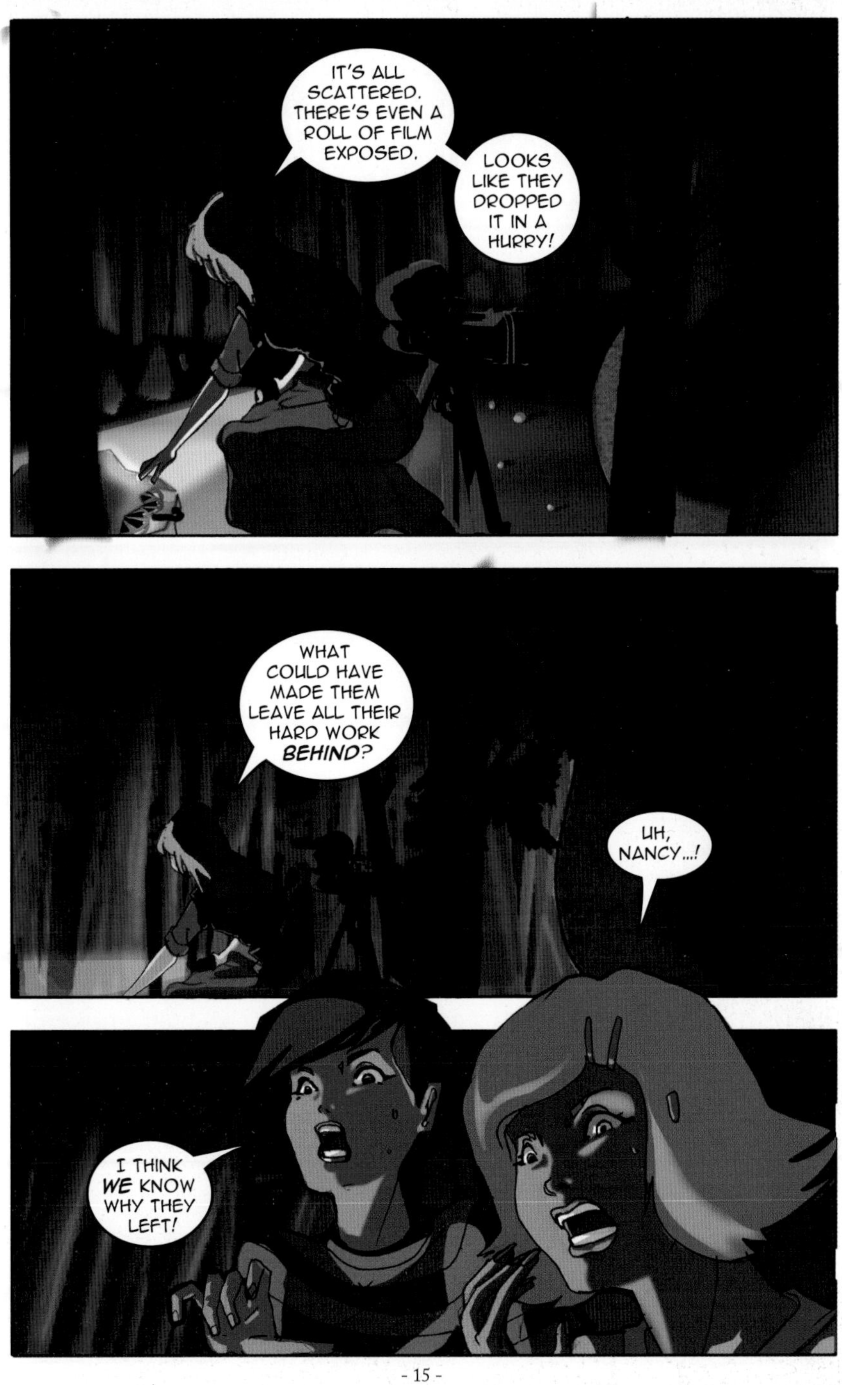
IT'S ALL SCATTERED. THERE'S EVEN A ROLL OF FILM EXPOSED.
LOOKS LIKE THEY DROPPED IT IN A HURRY!
WHAT COULD HAVE MADE THEM LEAVE ALL THEIR HARD WORK BEHIND?
UH, NANCY...!
I THINK WE KNOW WHY THEY LEFT!

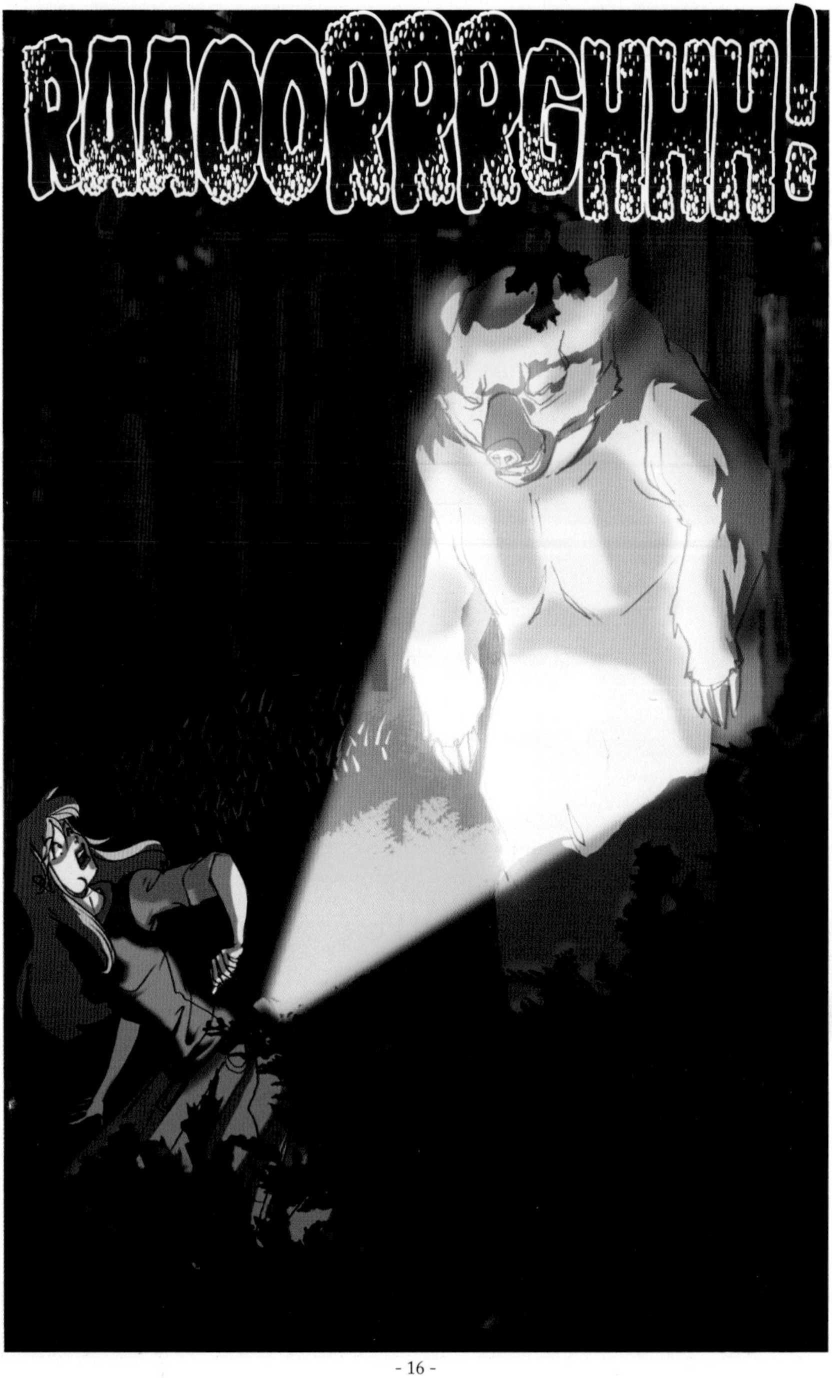
RAAOORRRGHHH!

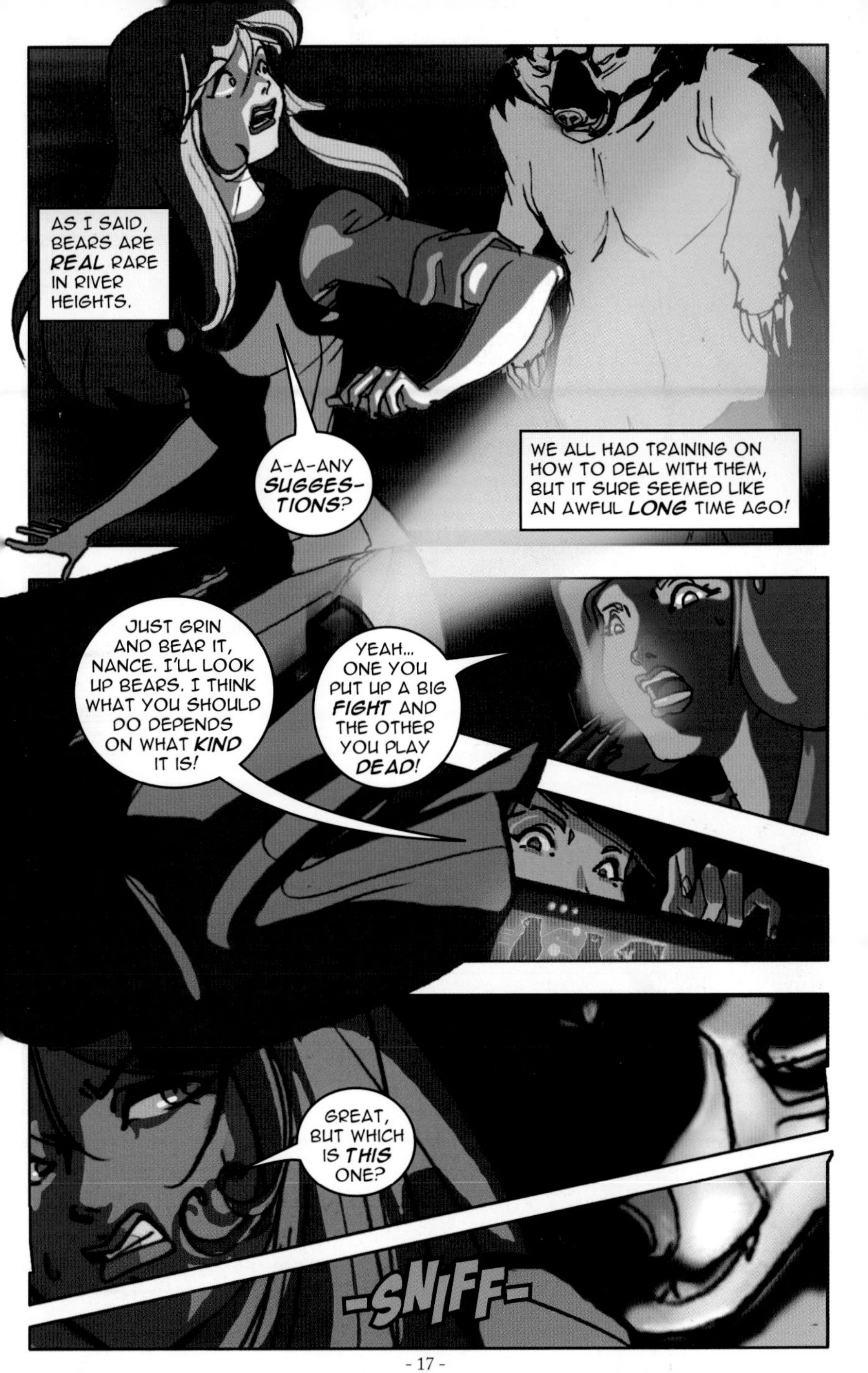
AS I SAID, BEARS ARE REAL RARE IN RIVER HEIGHTS.
A-A-ANY SUGGES-TIONS?
WE ALL HAD TRAINING ON HOW TO DEAL WITH THEM, BUT IT SURE SEEMED LIKE AN AWFUL LONG TIME AGO!
JUST GRIN AND BEAR IT, NANCE. I'LL LOOK UP BEARS. I THINK WHAT YOU SHOULD DO DEPENDS ON WHAT KIND IT IS!
YEAH... ONE YOU PUT UP A BIG FIGHT AND THE OTHER YOU PLAY DEAD!
GREAT, BUT WHICH IS THIS ONE?
-SNIFF-

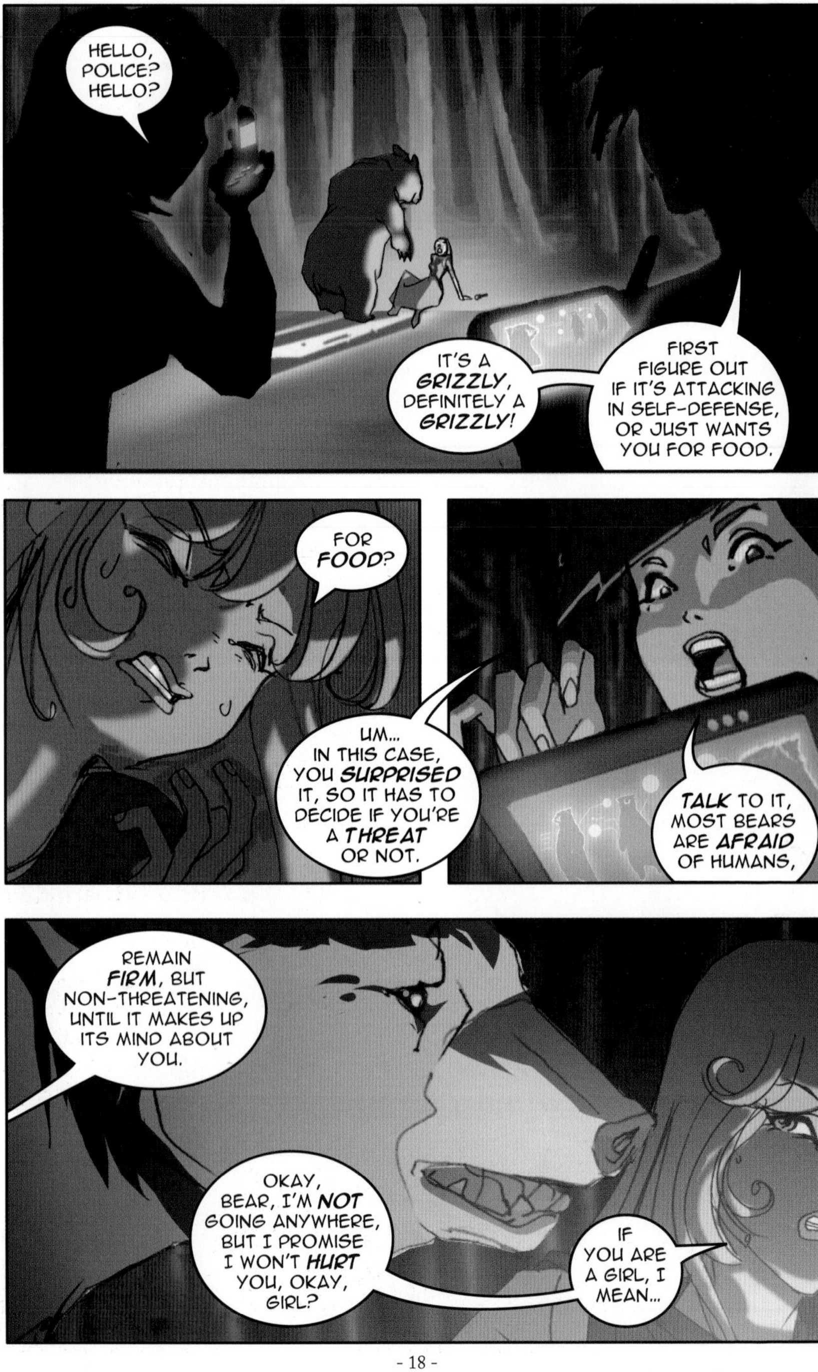
HELLO, POLICE? HELLO?
IT'S A GRIZZLY, DEFINITELY A GRIZZLY!
FIRST FIGURE OUT IF IT'S ATTACKING IN SELF-DEFENSE, OR JUST WANTS YOU FOR FOOD.
FOR FOOD?
UM... IN THIS CASE, YOU SURPRISED IT, SO IT HAS TO DECIDE IF YOU'RE A THREAT OR NOT.
TALK TO IT, MOST BEARS ARE AFRAID OF HUMANS,
REMAIN FIRM, BUT NON-THREATENING, UNTIL IT MAKES UP ITS MIND ABOUT YOU.
OKAY, BEAR, I'M NOT GOING ANYWHERE, BUT I PROMISE I WON'T HURT YOU, OKAY, GIRL?
IF YOU ARE A GIRL, I MEAN...

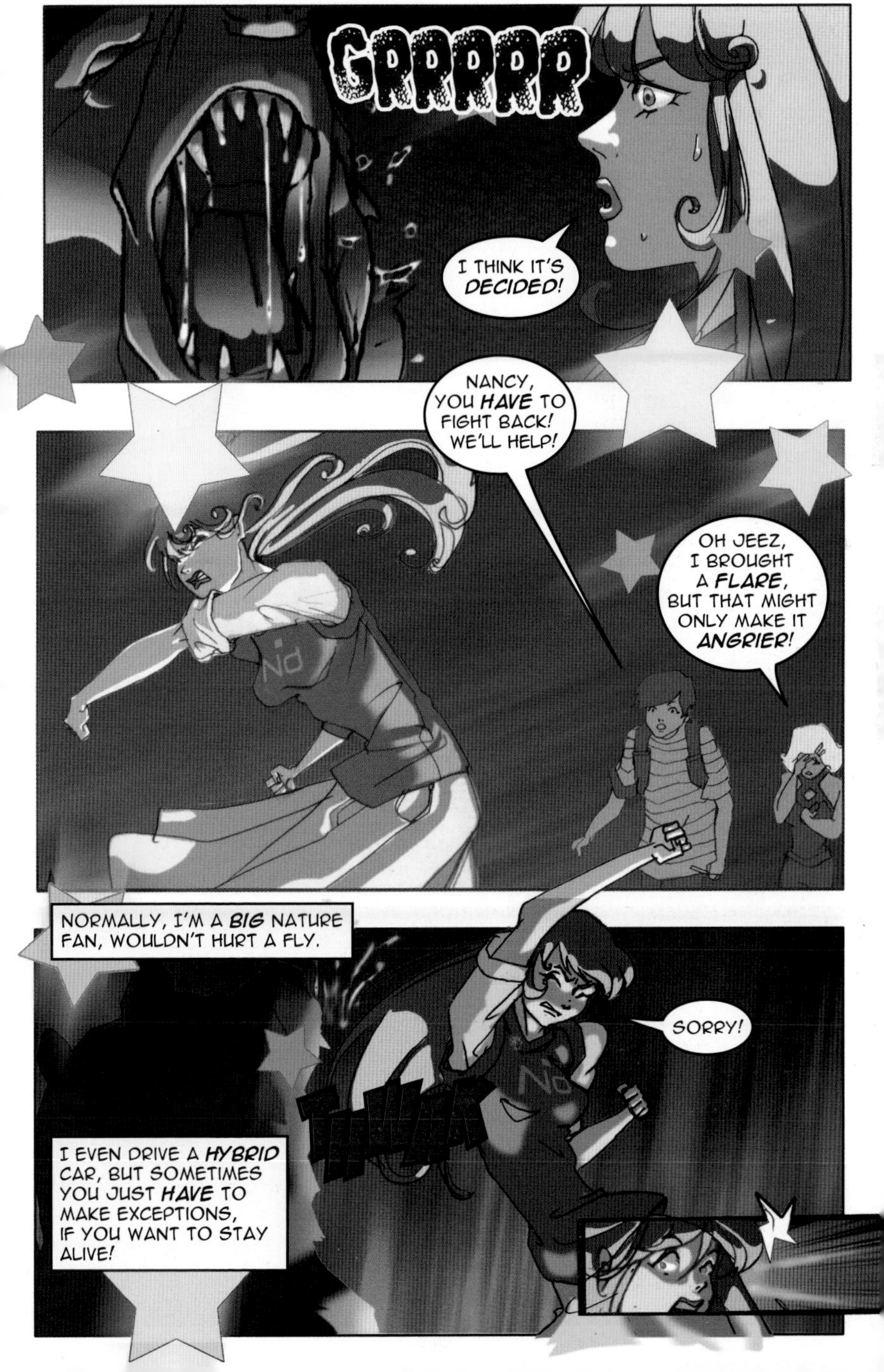
GRRRRR
I THINK IT'S DECIDED!
NANCY, YOU HAVE TO FIGHT BACK! WE'LL HELP!
OH JEEZ, I BROUGHT A FLARE, BUT THAT MIGHT ONLY MAKE IT ANGRIER!
NORMALLY, I'M A BIG NATURE FAN, WOULDN'T HURT A FLY.
SORRY!
I EVEN DRIVE A HYBRID CAR, BUT SOMETIMES YOU JUST HAVE TO MAKE EXCEPTIONS, IF YOU WANT TO STAY ALIVE!

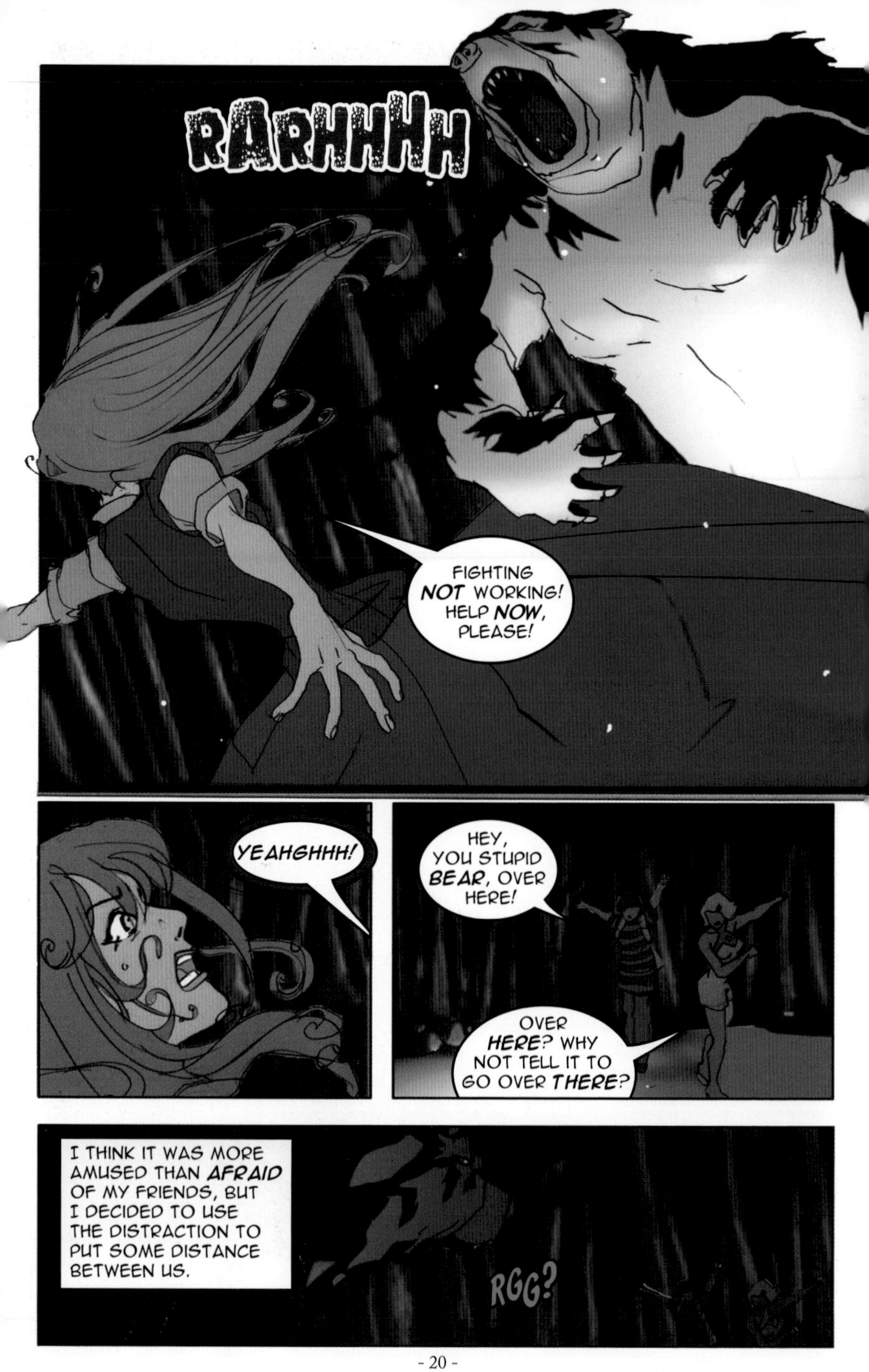
RARHHHH
FIGHTING NOT WORKING! HELP NOW, PLEASE!
YEAHGHHH!
HEY, YOU STUPID BEAR, OVER HERE!
OVER HERE? WHY NOT TELL IT TO GO OVER THERE?
I THINK IT WAS MORE AMUSED THAN AFRAID OF MY FRIENDS, BUT I DECIDED TO USE THE DISTRACTION TO PUT SOME DISTANCE BETWEEN US.
RGG?

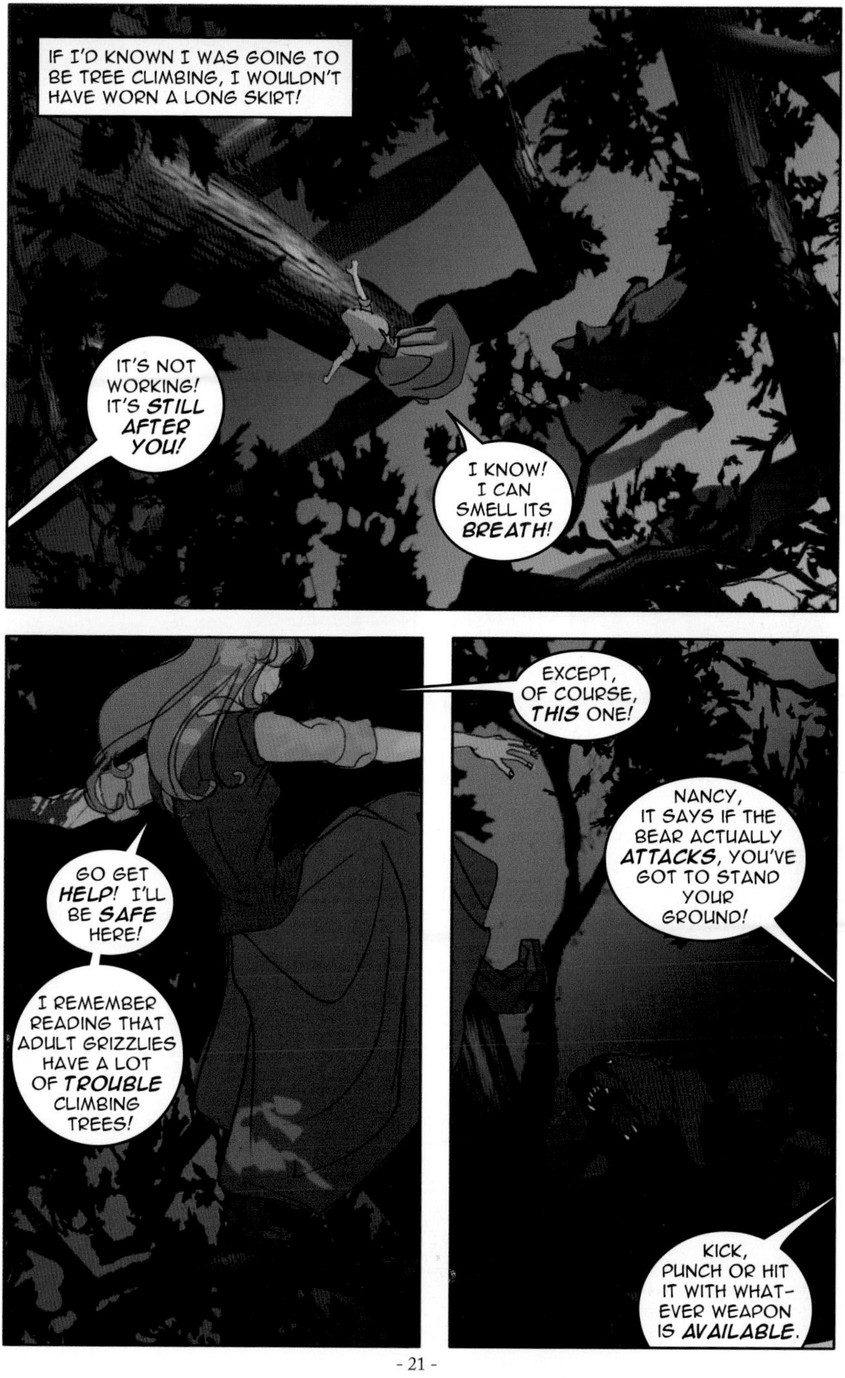
IF I'D KNOWN I WAS GOING TO BE TREE CLIMBING, I WOULDN'T HAVE WORN A LONG SKIRT!
IT'S NOT WORKING! IT'S STILL AFTER YOU!
I KNOW! I CAN SMELL ITS BREATH!
GO GET HELP! I'LL BE SAFE HERE!
I REMEMBER READING THAT ADULT GRIZZLIES HAVE A LOT OF TROUBLE CLIMBING TREES!
EXCEPT, OF COURSE, THIS ONE!
NANCY, IT SAYS IF THE BEAR ACTUALLY ATTACKS, YOU'VE GOT TO STAND YOUR GROUND!
KICK, PUNCH OR HIT IT WITH WHAT-EVER WEAPON IS AVAILABLE.

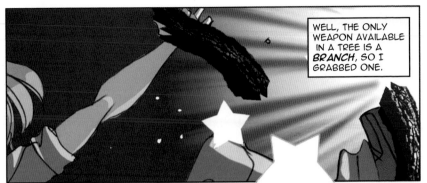

WELL, THE ONLY WEAPON AVAILABLE IN A TREE IS A *BRANCH*, SO I GRABBED ONE.

I WOULDN'T SAY I'M TERRIBLY *STRONG*, BUT YOU'D BE SUR-PRISED WHAT YOU CAN DO WITH YOUR ADRENALINE PUMPING.

I'M *SURE* I WASN'T HURTING IT MUCH, BUT I THINK I MADE IT JUST *UNCOMFORTABLE* ENOUGH TO GIVE UP.

YOU *DID* IT!

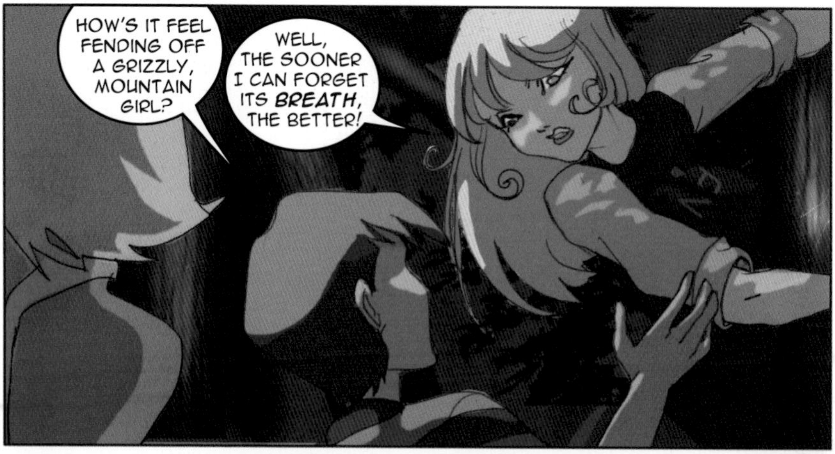
HOW'S IT FEEL FENDING OFF A GRIZZLY, MOUNTAIN GIRL?
WELL, THE SOONER I CAN FORGET ITS BREATH, THE BETTER!

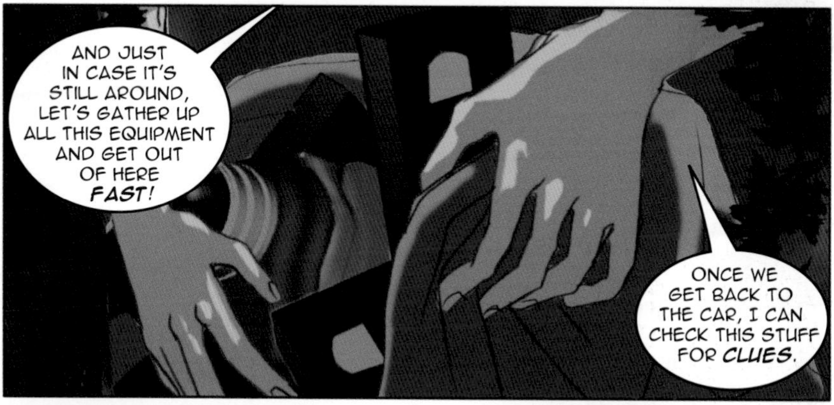
AND JUST IN CASE IT'S STILL AROUND, LET'S GATHER UP ALL THIS EQUIPMENT AND GET OUT OF HERE FAST!
ONCE WE GET BACK TO THE CAR, I CAN CHECK THIS STUFF FOR CLUES.

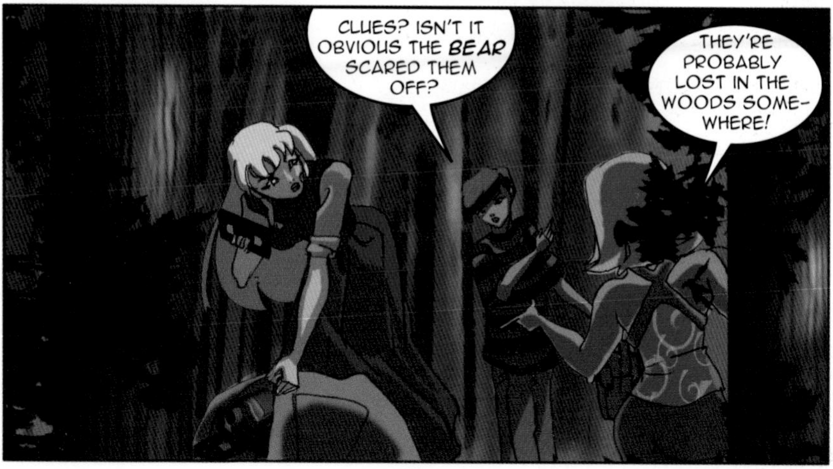
CLUES? ISN'T IT OBVIOUS THE BEAR SCARED THEM OFF?
THEY'RE PROBABLY LOST IN THE WOODS SOME-WHERE!

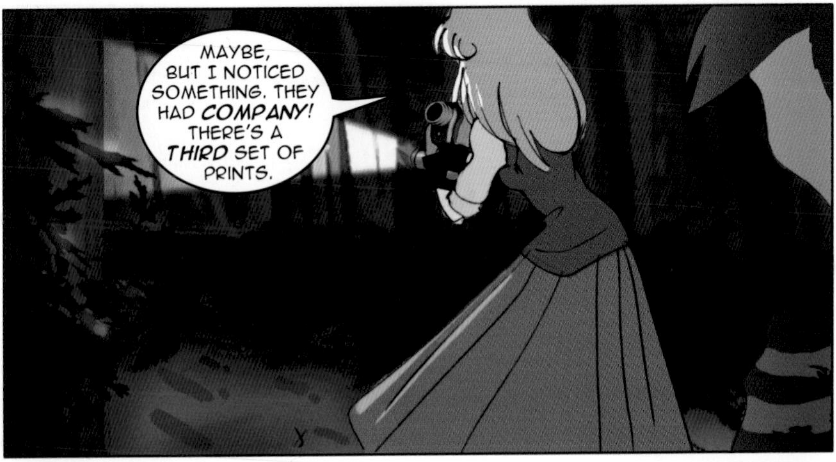
MAYBE, BUT I NOTICED SOMETHING. THEY HAD COMPANY! THERE'S A THIRD SET OF PRINTS.

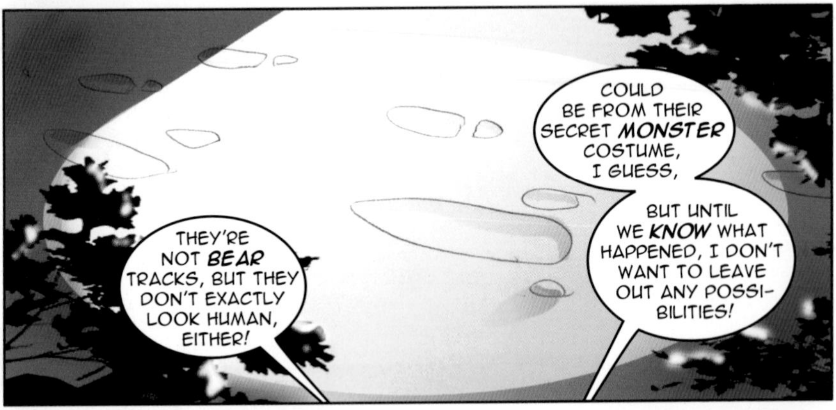
THEY'RE NOT BEAR TRACKS, BUT THEY DON'T EXACTLY LOOK HUMAN, EITHER!
COULD BE FROM THEIR SECRET MONSTER COSTUME, I GUESS,
BUT UNTIL WE KNOW WHAT HAPPENED, I DON'T WANT TO LEAVE OUT ANY POSSI-BILITIES!

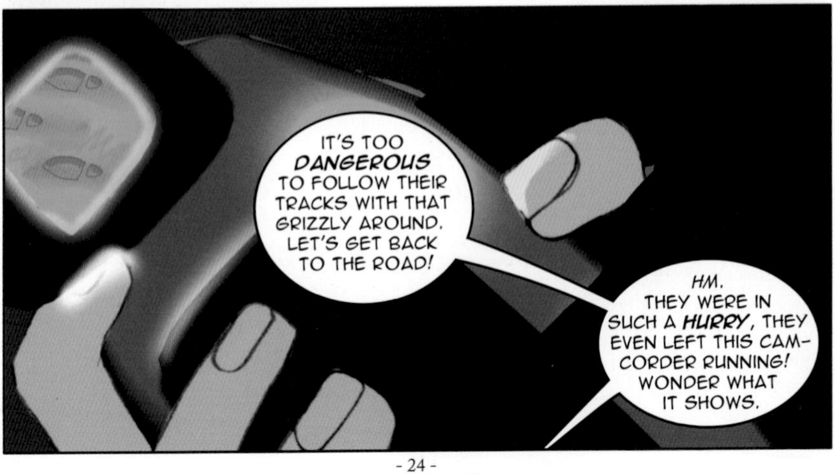
IT'S TOO DANGEROUS TO FOLLOW THEIR TRACKS WITH THAT GRIZZLY AROUND. LET'S GET BACK TO THE ROAD!
HM. THEY WERE IN SUCH A HURRY, THEY EVEN LEFT THIS CAM-CORDER RUNNING! WONDER WHAT IT SHOWS.

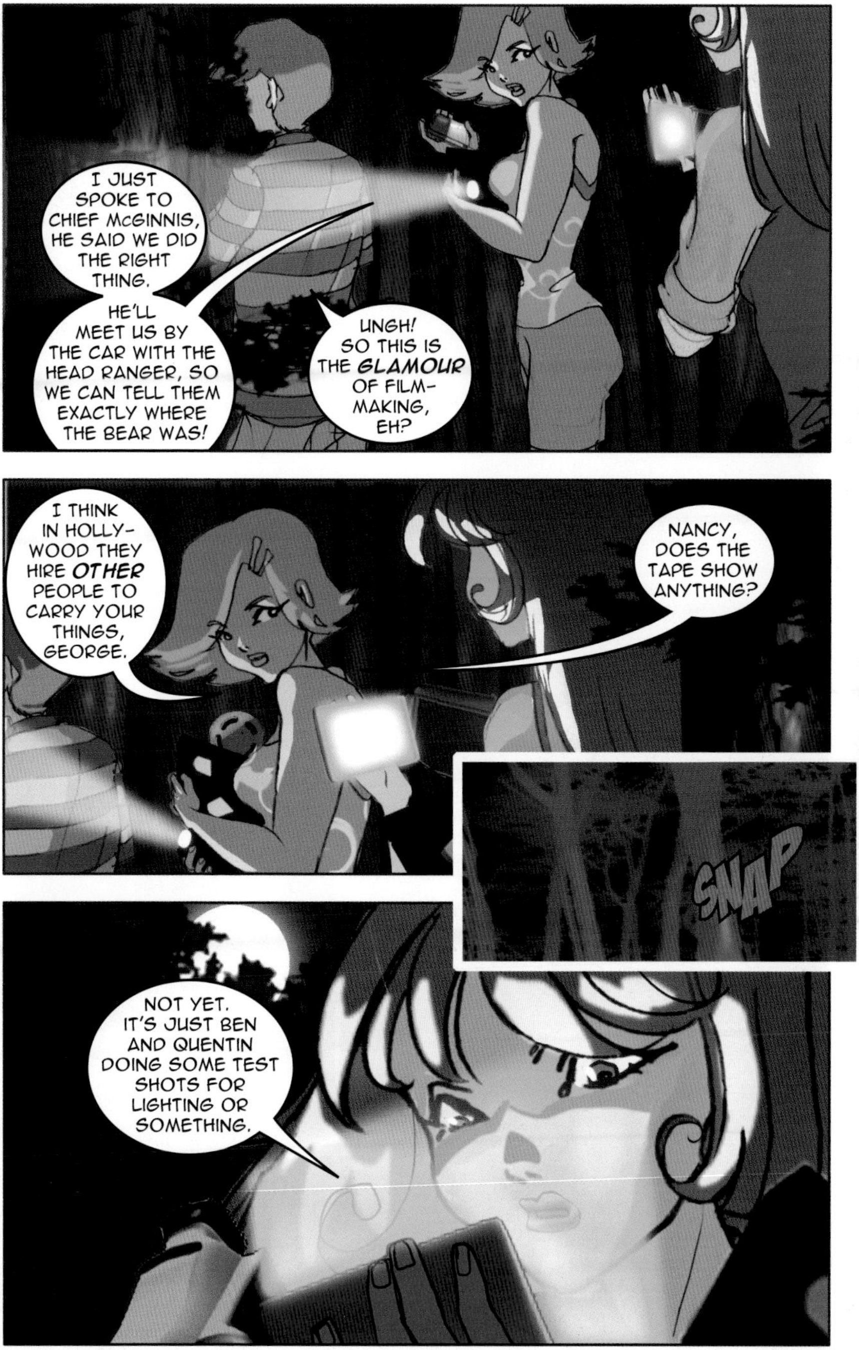
I JUST SPOKE TO CHIEF McGINNIS, HE SAID WE DID THE RIGHT THING.
HE'LL MEET US BY THE CAR WITH THE HEAD RANGER, SO WE CAN TELL THEM EXACTLY WHERE THE BEAR WAS!
UNGH! SO THIS IS THE GLAMOUR OF FILM-MAKING, EH?
I THINK IN HOLLY-WOOD THEY HIRE OTHER PEOPLE TO CARRY YOUR THINGS, GEORGE.
NANCY, DOES THE TAPE SHOW ANYTHING?
SNAP
NOT YET. IT'S JUST BEN AND QUENTIN DOING SOME TEST SHOTS FOR LIGHTING OR SOMETHING.

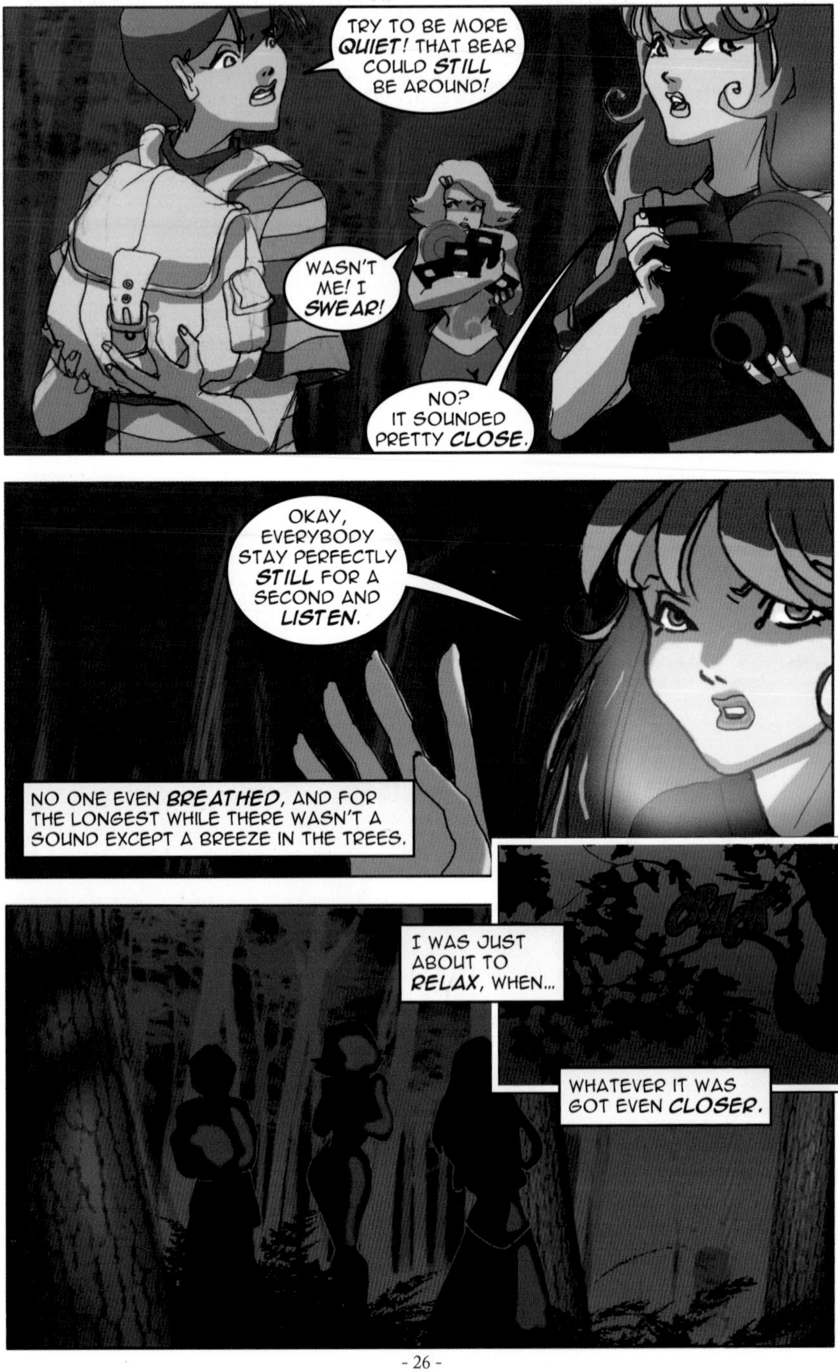
TRY TO BE MORE QUIET! THAT BEAR COULD STILL BE AROUND!
WASN'T ME! I SWEAR!
NO? IT SOUNDED PRETTY CLOSE.
OKAY, EVERYBODY STAY PERFECTLY STILL FOR A SECOND AND LISTEN.
NO ONE EVEN BREATHED, AND FOR THE LONGEST WHILE THERE WASN'T A SOUND EXCEPT A BREEZE IN THE TREES.
I WAS JUST ABOUT TO RELAX, WHEN...
WHATEVER IT WAS GOT EVEN CLOSER.

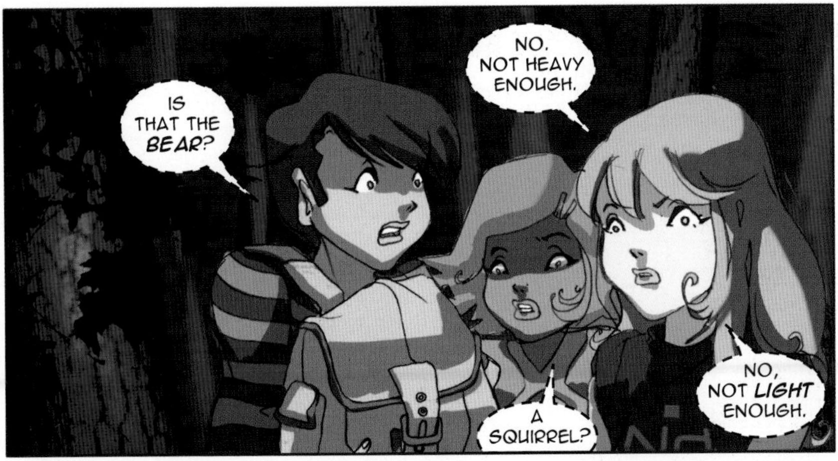
IS THAT THE BEAR?
NO. NOT HEAVY ENOUGH.
A SQUIRREL?
NO, NOT LIGHT ENOUGH.

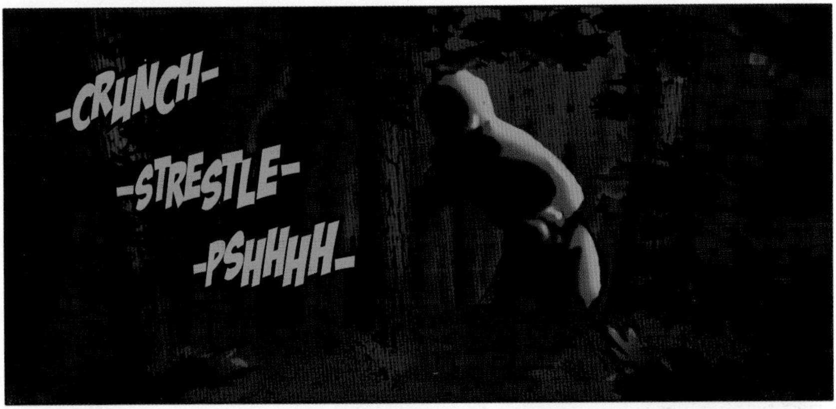
-CRUNCH-
-STRESTLE-
-PSHHHH-

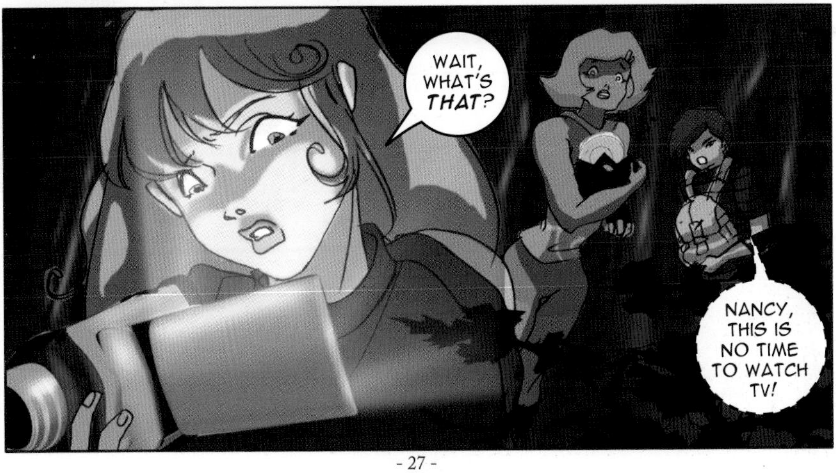
WAIT, WHAT'S THAT?
NANCY, THIS IS NO TIME TO WATCH TV!

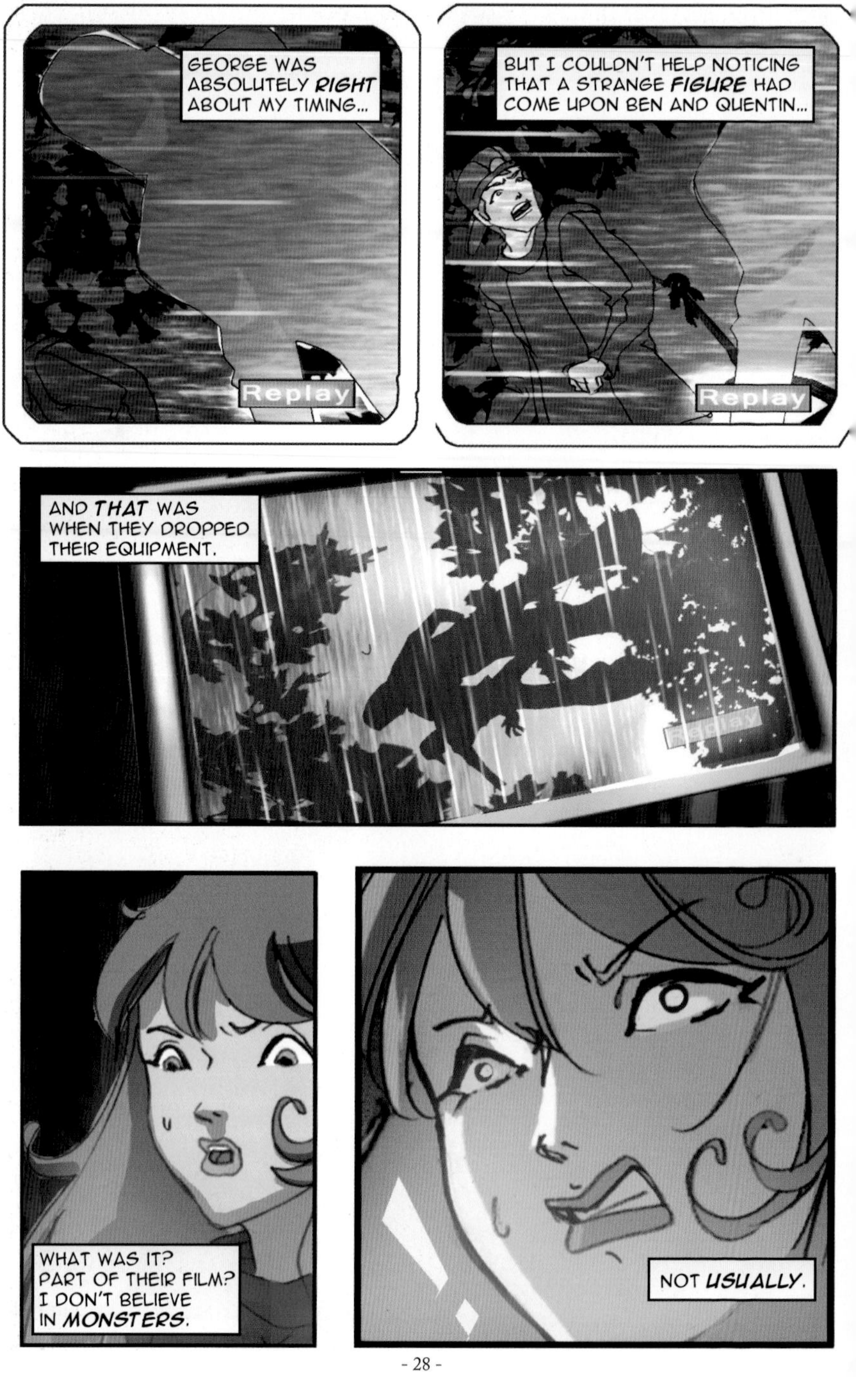
GEORGE WAS ABSOLUTELY RIGHT ABOUT MY TIMING...
Replay
BUT I COULDN'T HELP NOTICING THAT A STRANGE FIGURE HAD COME UPON BEN AND QUENTIN...
Replay
AND THAT WAS WHEN THEY DROPPED THEIR EQUIPMENT.
Replay
WHAT WAS IT? PART OF THEIR FILM? I DON'T BELIEVE IN MONSTERS.
NOT USUALLY.

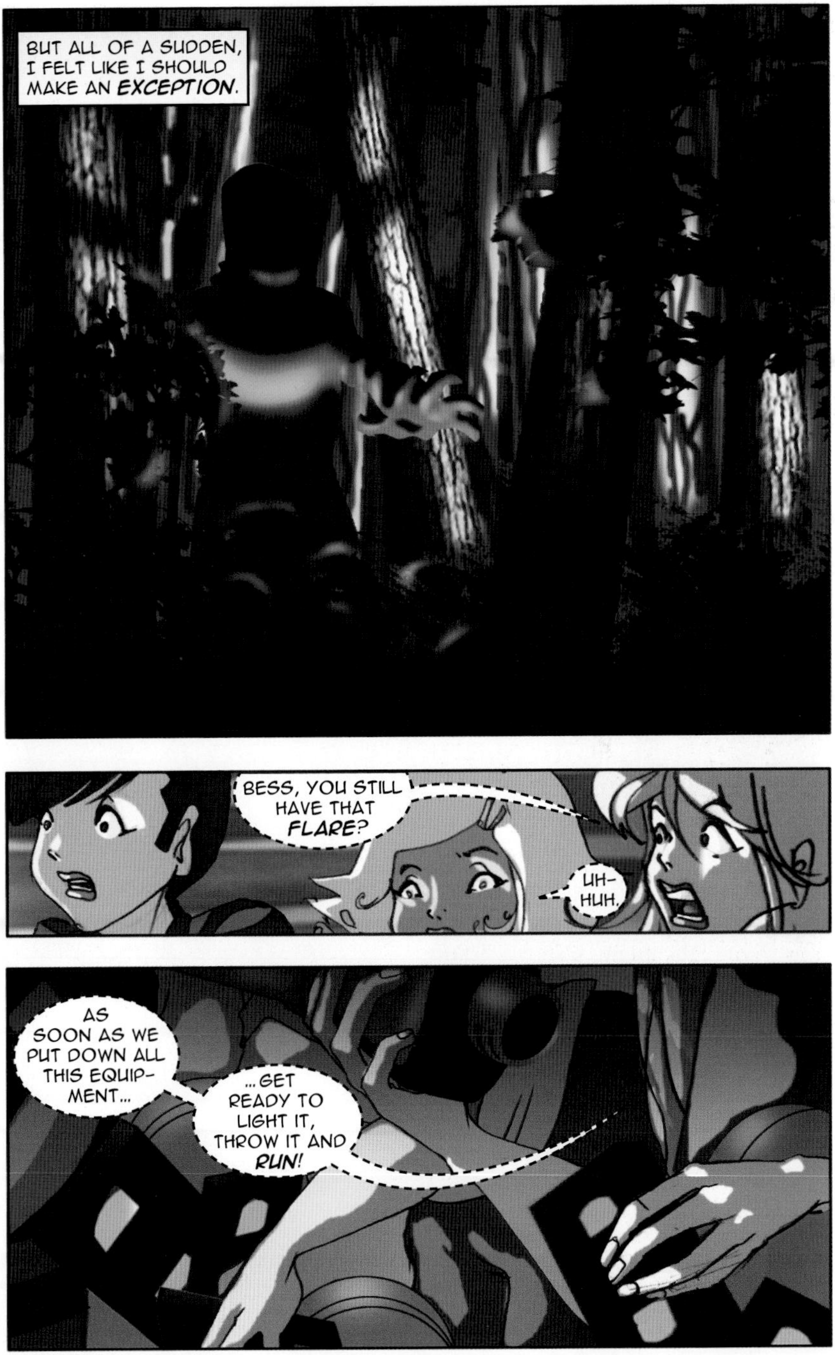
BUT ALL OF A SUDDEN, I FELT LIKE I SHOULD MAKE AN EXCEPTION.
BESS, YOU STILL HAVE THAT FLARE?
UH-HUH.
AS SOON AS WE PUT DOWN ALL THIS EQUIP-MENT...
...GET READY TO LIGHT IT, THROW IT AND RUN!

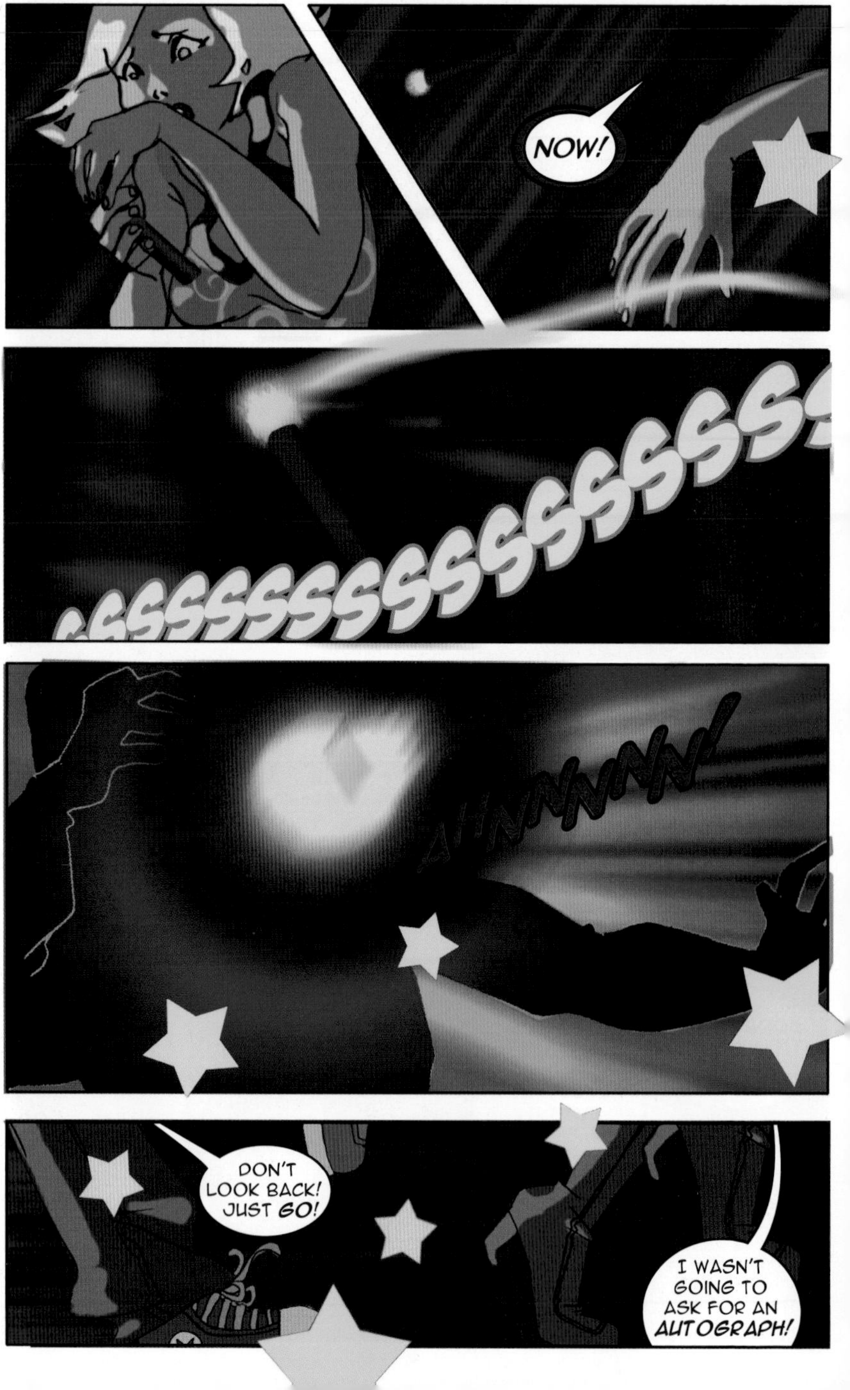
NOW!
SSSSSSSSSSSSSSSSSSSSSS
AHNNNNNN!
DON'T LOOK BACK! JUST GO!
I WASN'T GOING TO ASK FOR AN AUTOGRAPH!

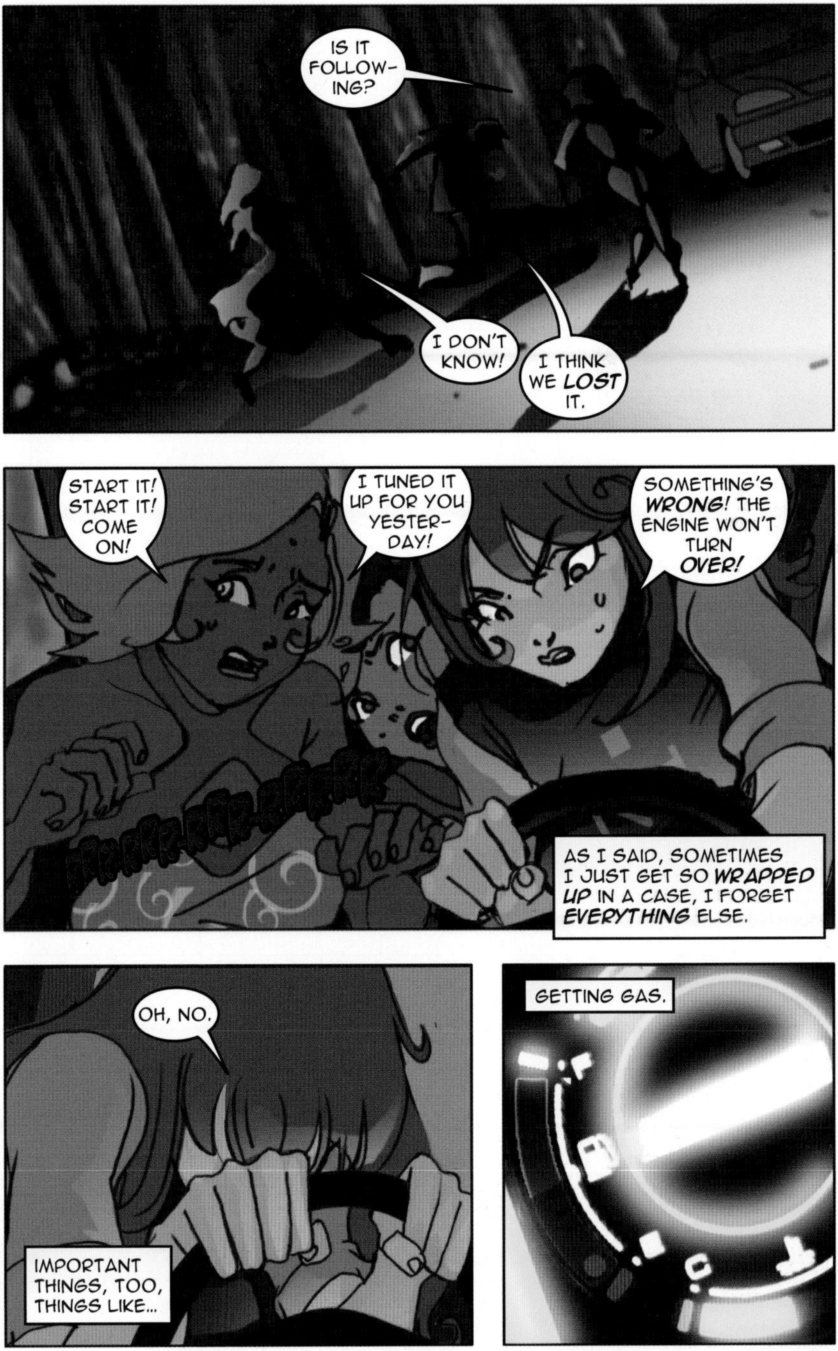

IS IT FOLLOW-ING?
I DON'T KNOW!
I THINK WE LOST IT.
START IT! START IT! COME ON!
I TUNED IT UP FOR YOU YESTER-DAY!
SOMETHING'S WRONG! THE ENGINE WON'T TURN OVER!
AS I SAID, SOMETIMES I JUST GET SO WRAPPED UP IN A CASE, I FORGET EVERYTHING ELSE.
OH, NO.
IMPORTANT THINGS, TOO, THINGS LIKE...
GETTING GAS.

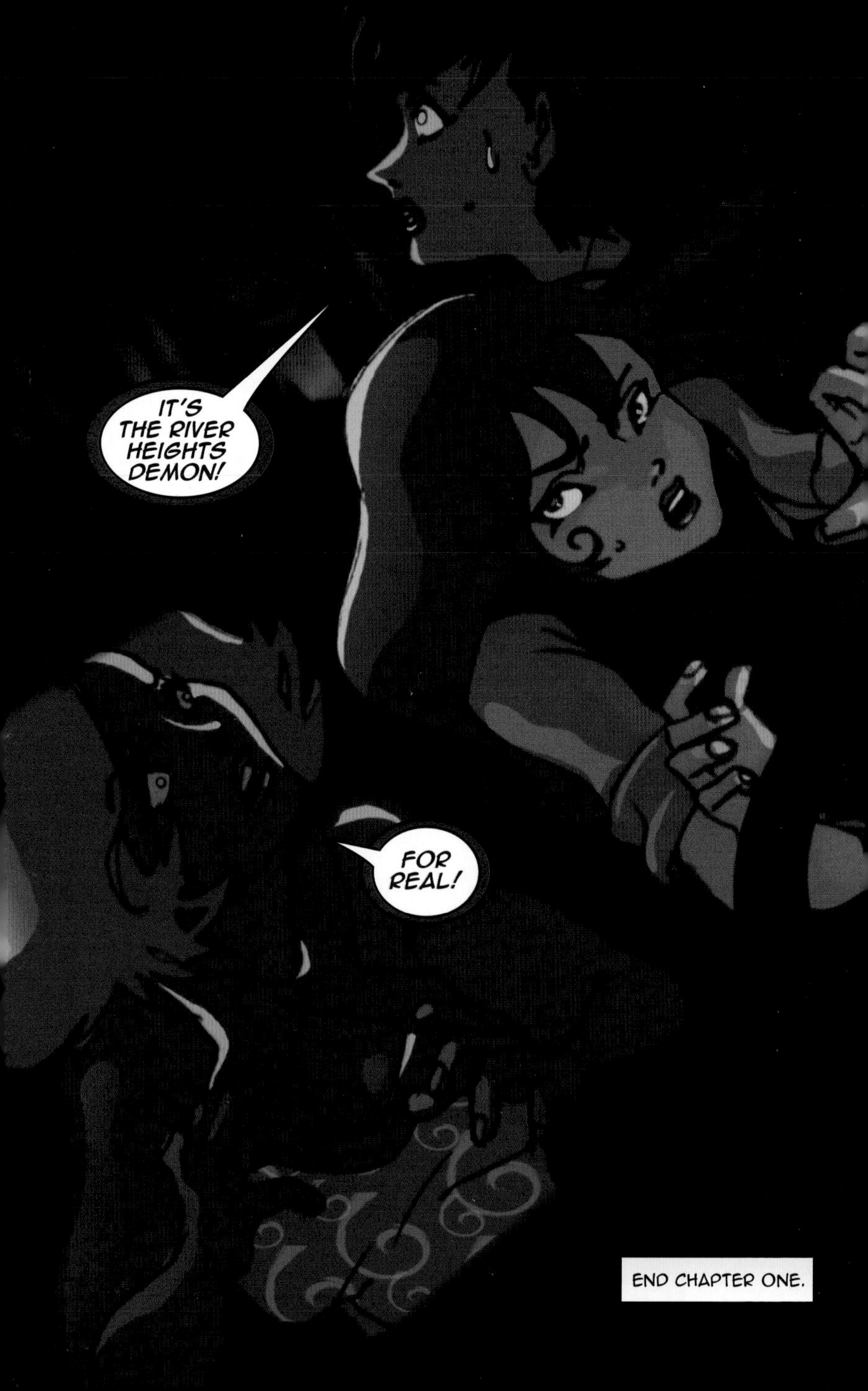
IT'S THE RIVER HEIGHTS DEMON!
FOR REAL!
END CHAPTER ONE.

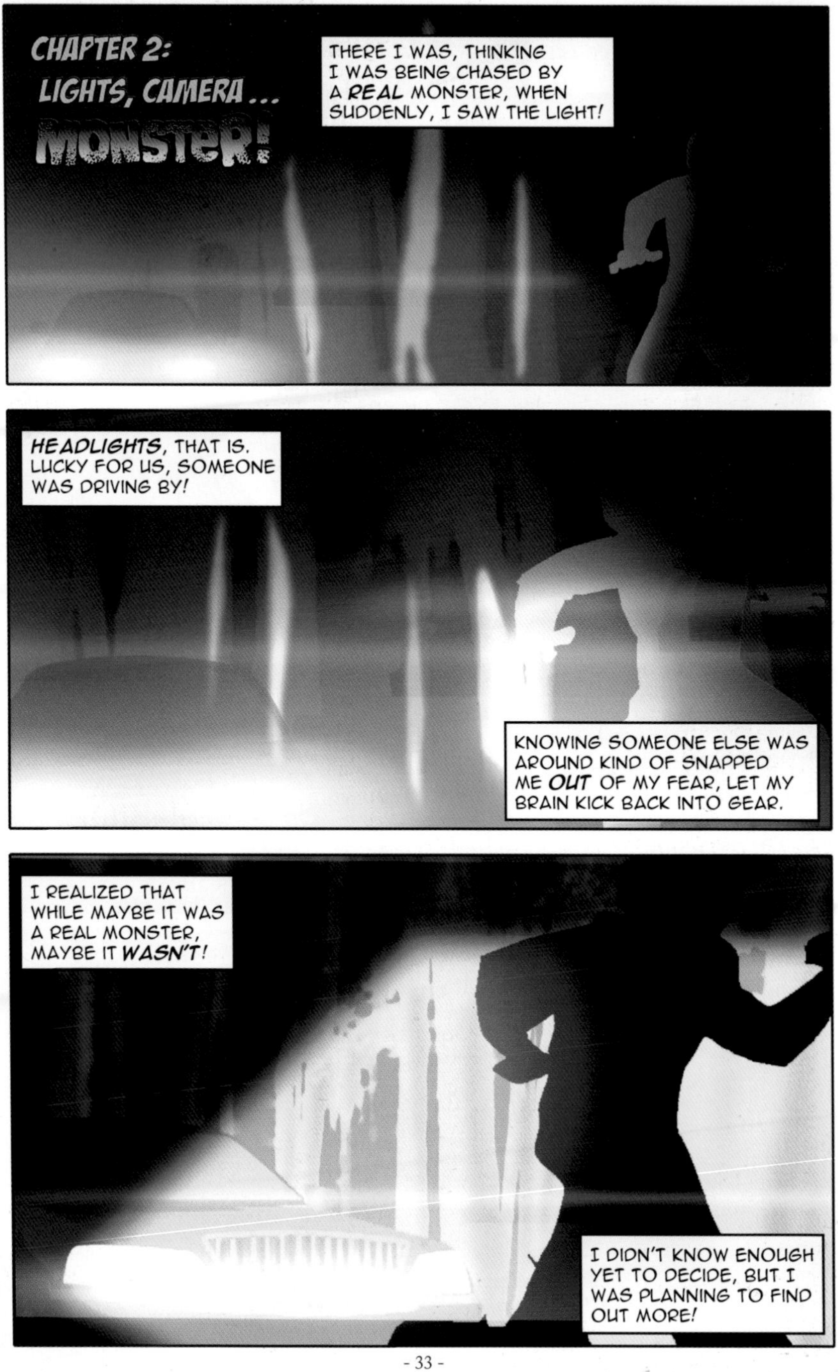
CHAPTER 2:
LIGHTS, CAMERA ...
MONSTER!
THERE I WAS, THINKING I WAS BEING CHASED BY A *REAL* MONSTER, WHEN SUDDENLY, I SAW THE LIGHT!
HEADLIGHTS, THAT IS. LUCKY FOR US, SOMEONE WAS DRIVING BY!
KNOWING SOMEONE ELSE WAS AROUND KIND OF SNAPPED ME *OUT* OF MY FEAR, LET MY BRAIN KICK BACK INTO GEAR.
I REALIZED THAT WHILE MAYBE IT WAS A REAL MONSTER, MAYBE IT *WASN'T*!
I DIDN'T KNOW ENOUGH YET TO DECIDE, BUT I WAS PLANNING TO FIND OUT MORE!

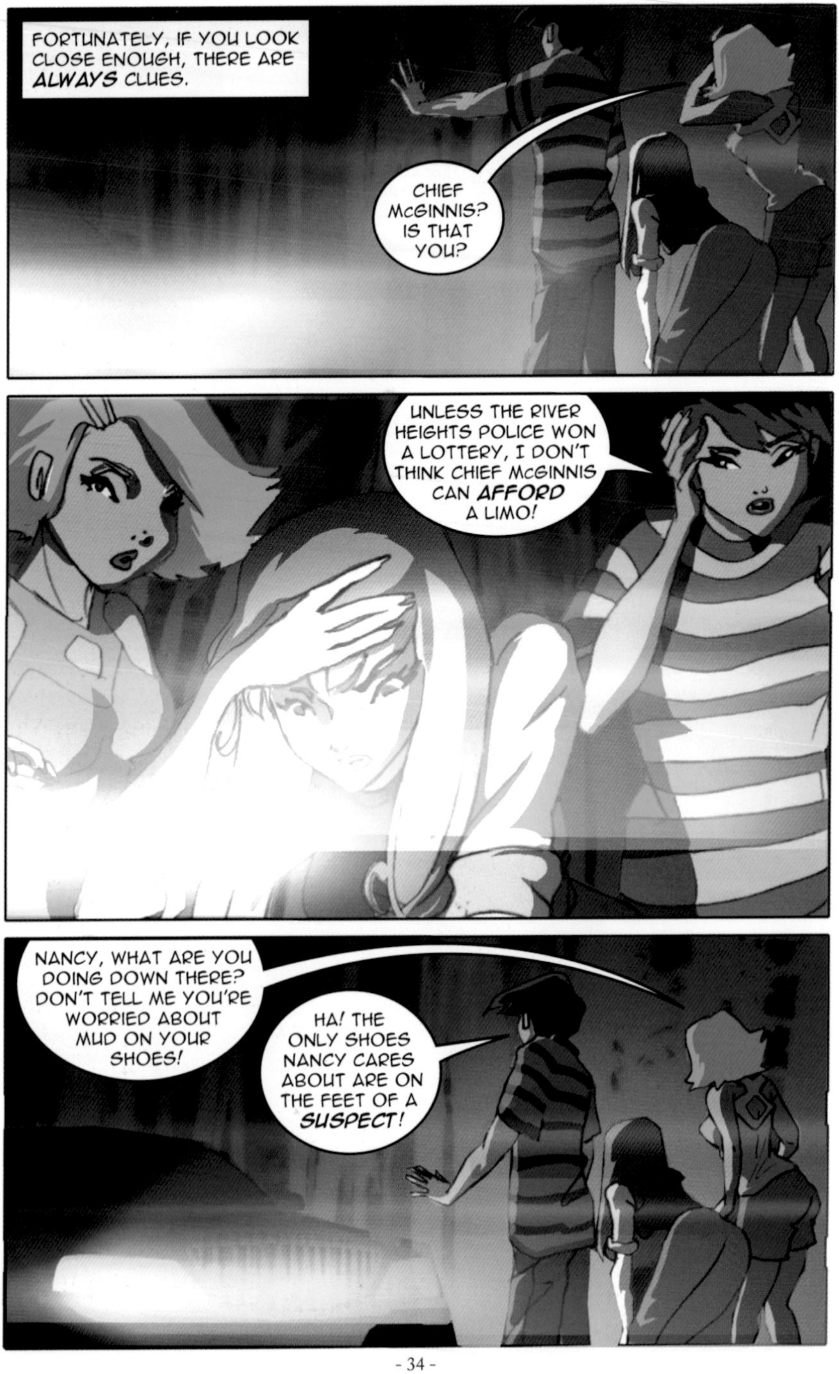

FORTUNATELY, IF YOU LOOK CLOSE ENOUGH, THERE ARE *ALWAYS* CLUES.
CHIEF McGINNIS? IS THAT YOU?
UNLESS THE RIVER HEIGHTS POLICE WON A LOTTERY, I DON'T THINK CHIEF McGINNIS CAN *AFFORD* A LIMO!
NANCY, WHAT ARE YOU DOING DOWN THERE? DON'T TELL ME YOU'RE WORRIED ABOUT MUD ON YOUR SHOES!
HA! THE ONLY SHOES NANCY CARES ABOUT ARE ON THE FEET OF A *SUSPECT*!

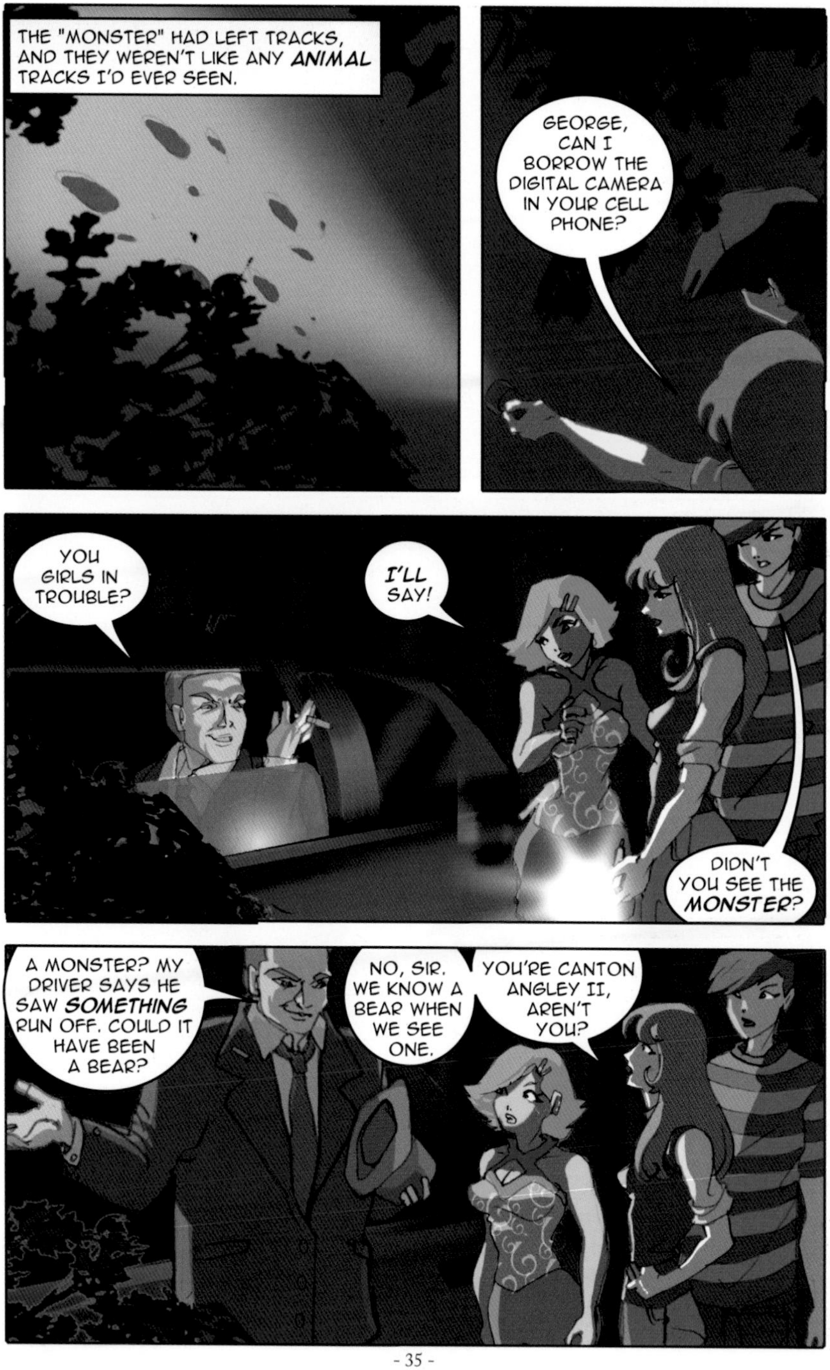

THE "MONSTER" HAD LEFT TRACKS, AND THEY WEREN'T LIKE ANY *ANIMAL* TRACKS I'D EVER SEEN.
GEORGE, CAN I BORROW THE DIGITAL CAMERA IN YOUR CELL PHONE?
YOU GIRLS IN TROUBLE?
I'LL SAY!
DIDN'T YOU SEE THE *MONSTER*?
A MONSTER? MY DRIVER SAYS HE SAW *SOMETHING* RUN OFF. COULD IT HAVE BEEN A BEAR?
NO, SIR. WE KNOW A BEAR WHEN WE SEE ONE.
YOU'RE CANTON ANGLEY II, AREN'T YOU?

YOU HAVE ME AT A DISADVANTAGE, YOUNG LADY. YOU KNOW ME, BUT I DON'T KNOW *YOU.*

I'M SORRY, I'D HEARD YOU WERE INVESTING IN RIVER HEIGHTS. I'M NANCY DREW. THESE ARE MY FRIENDS, BESS MARVIN AND GEORGE FAYNE.

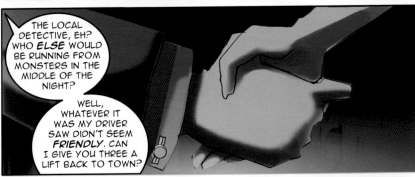

THE LOCAL DETECTIVE, EH? WHO *ELSE* WOULD BE RUNNING FROM MONSTERS IN THE MIDDLE OF THE NIGHT?

WELL, WHATEVER IT WAS MY DRIVER SAW DIDN'T SEEM *FRIENDLY.* CAN I GIVE YOU THREE A LIFT BACK TO TOWN?

I'LL SAY!

ONE AT A TIME, GIRLS!

I COULD CERTAINLY UNDERSTAND HOW RELIEVED THEY WERE TO BE GETTING AWAY FROM THAT THING. I WAS, TOO.

BUT THAT DIDN'T MAKE ME ANY *LESS* SUSPICIOUS OF OUR "RESCUER."

SO, MR. ANGLEY, WHAT SORT OF BUSINESS ARE YOU GOING TO OPEN IN RIVER HEIGHTS?

ARE YOU GETTING OUT OF MINING? I MEAN, EVERYONE KNOWS ALL THE ORE'S TAPPED OUT AROUND HERE.

I'D RATHER *NOT* DISCUSS THAT, ESPECIALLY SINCE I'M NO LONGER USING YOUR *FATHER* AS MY ATTORNEY.

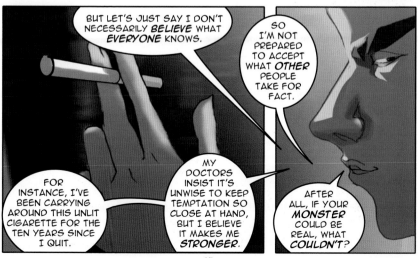

BUT LET'S JUST SAY I DON'T NECESSARILY *BELIEVE* WHAT *EVERYONE* KNOWS.

SO I'M NOT PREPARED TO ACCEPT WHAT *OTHER* PEOPLE TAKE FOR FACT.

FOR INSTANCE, I'VE BEEN CARRYING AROUND THIS UNLIT CIGARETTE FOR THE TEN YEARS SINCE I QUIT.

MY DOCTORS INSIST IT'S UNWISE TO KEEP TEMPTATION SO CLOSE AT HAND, BUT I BELIEVE IT MAKES ME *STRONGER*.

AFTER ALL, IF YOUR *MONSTER* COULD BE REAL, WHAT *COULDN'T*?

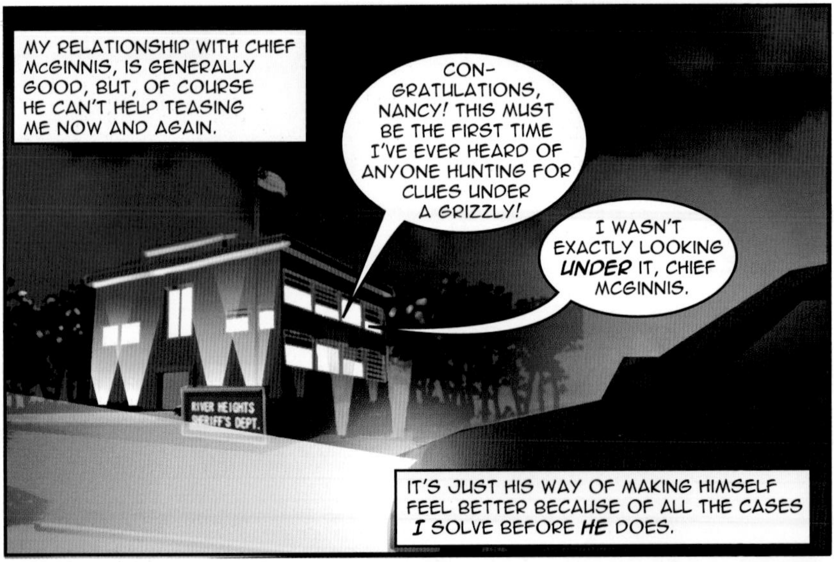
MY RELATIONSHIP WITH CHIEF McGINNIS, IS GENERALLY GOOD, BUT, OF COURSE HE CAN'T HELP TEASING ME NOW AND AGAIN.
CON-GRATULATIONS, NANCY! THIS MUST BE THE FIRST TIME I'VE EVER HEARD OF ANYONE HUNTING FOR CLUES UNDER A GRIZZLY!
I WASN'T EXACTLY LOOKING ***UNDER*** IT, CHIEF MCGINNIS.
RIVER HEIGHTS SHERIFF'S DEPT.
IT'S JUST HIS WAY OF MAKING HIMSELF FEEL BETTER BECAUSE OF ALL THE CASES ***I*** SOLVE BEFORE ***HE*** DOES.

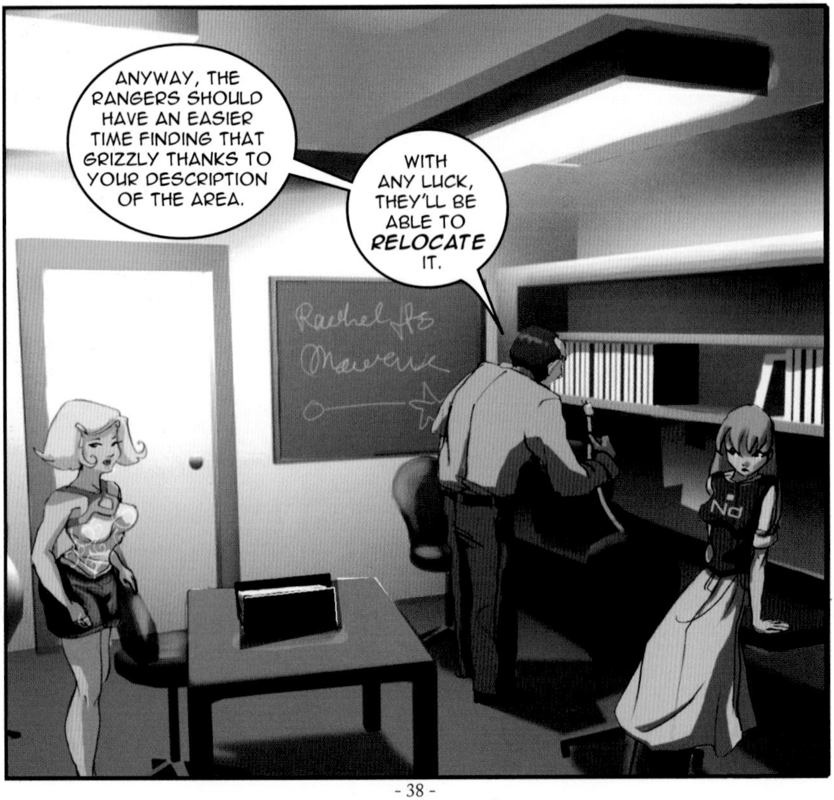
ANYWAY, THE RANGERS SHOULD HAVE AN EASIER TIME FINDING THAT GRIZZLY THANKS TO YOUR DESCRIPTION OF THE AREA.
WITH ANY LUCK, THEY'LL BE ABLE TO ***RELOCATE*** IT.

BUT WHAT ABOUT THIS *FOOTPRINT*? WHAT ABOUT THE MONSTER AND THE MISSING FILM STUDENTS?

YOU SHOULD HAVE SOME OF YOUR MEN OUT THERE, *SEARCHING*!

YEAH! WHAT SHE SAID!

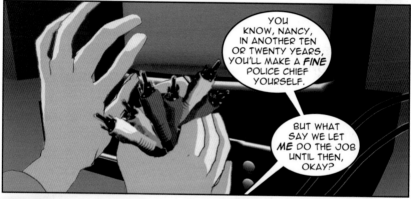

YOU KNOW, NANCY, IN ANOTHER TEN OR TWENTY YEARS, YOU'LL MAKE A *FINE* POLICE CHIEF YOURSELF.

BUT WHAT SAY WE LET *ME* DO THE JOB UNTIL THEN, OKAY?

BUT...

PLEASE. YOU *KNOW* I RESPECT YOUR OPINION BUT YOU WERE PRETTY SPOOKED BY THAT BEAR. *ANYONE* WOULD BE!

AND LISTEN TO THE WAY YOU'RE TALKING!

THE MONSTER AND THE MISSING FILM STUDENTS! SOUNDS LIKE THE NAME OF A BAD MOVIE, DOESN'T IT?

WELL, THAT'S EXACTLY WHAT I THINK THIS IS, A *BAD* MOVIE!

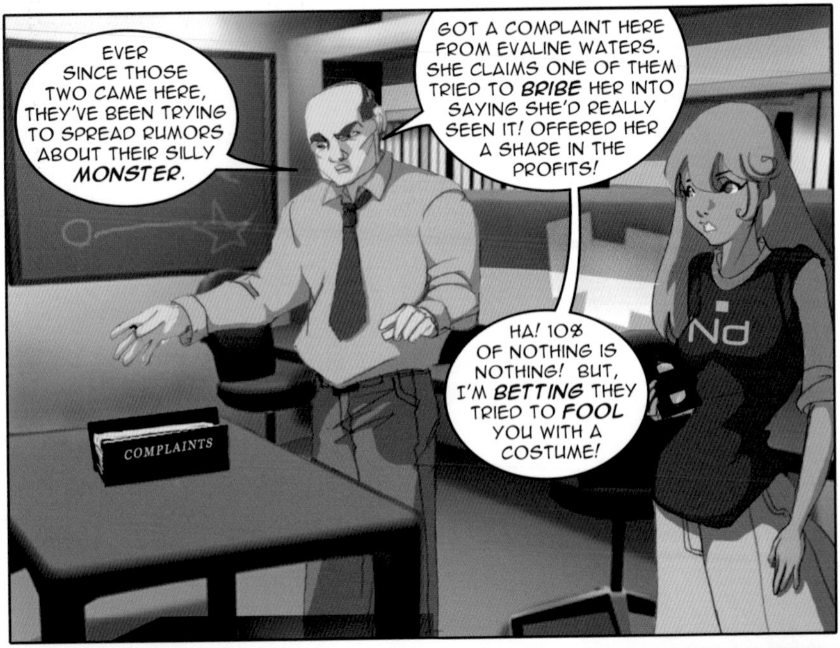
EVER SINCE THOSE TWO CAME HERE, THEY'VE BEEN TRYING TO SPREAD RUMORS ABOUT THEIR SILLY MONSTER.
GOT A COMPLAINT HERE FROM EVALINE WATERS. SHE CLAIMS ONE OF THEM TRIED TO BRIBE HER INTO SAYING SHE'D REALLY SEEN IT! OFFERED HER A SHARE IN THE PROFITS!
HA! 10% OF NOTHING IS NOTHING! BUT, I'M BETTING THEY TRIED TO FOOL YOU WITH A COSTUME!
COMPLAINTS
ND

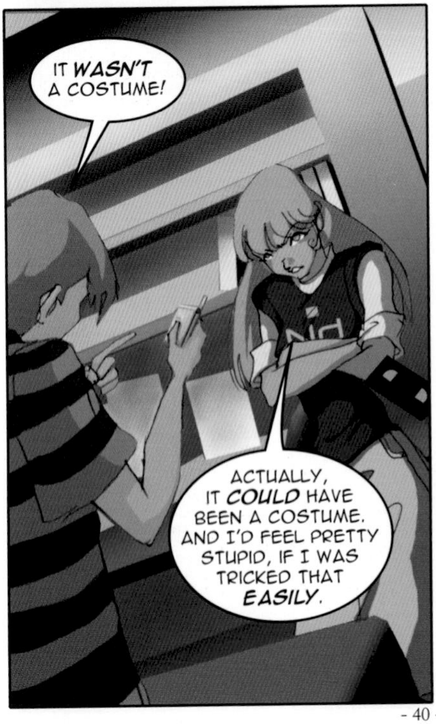
IT WASN'T A COSTUME!
ACTUALLY, IT COULD HAVE BEEN A COSTUME. AND I'D FEEL PRETTY STUPID, IF I WAS TRICKED THAT EASILY.

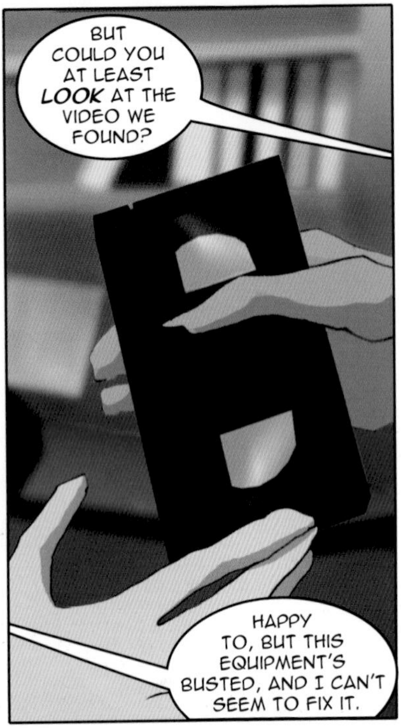
BUT COULD YOU AT LEAST LOOK AT THE VIDEO WE FOUND?
HAPPY TO, BUT THIS EQUIPMENT'S BUSTED, AND I CAN'T SEEM TO FIX IT.

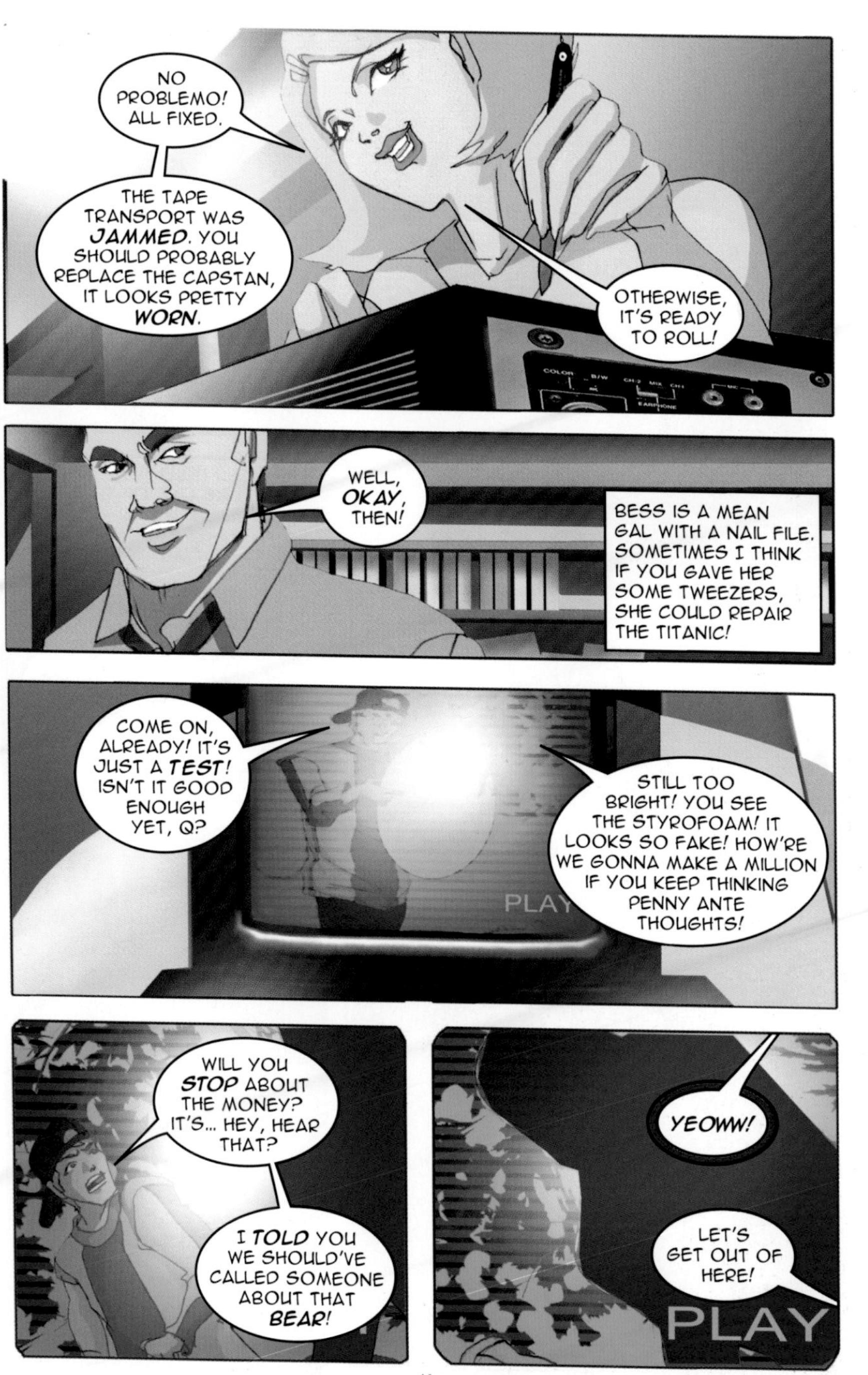
NO PROBLEMO! ALL FIXED.
THE TAPE TRANSPORT WAS JAMMED. YOU SHOULD PROBABLY REPLACE THE CAPSTAN, IT LOOKS PRETTY WORN.
OTHERWISE, IT'S READY TO ROLL!
COLOR
B/W
CH-2
MIX
CH-1
EARPHONE
MIC
WELL, OKAY, THEN!
BESS IS A MEAN GAL WITH A NAIL FILE. SOMETIMES I THINK IF YOU GAVE HER SOME TWEEZERS, SHE COULD REPAIR THE TITANIC!
COME ON, ALREADY! IT'S JUST A TEST! ISN'T IT GOOD ENOUGH YET, Q?
STILL TOO BRIGHT! YOU SEE THE STYROFOAM! IT LOOKS SO FAKE! HOW'RE WE GONNA MAKE A MILLION IF YOU KEEP THINKING PENNY ANTE THOUGHTS!
PLAY
WILL YOU STOP ABOUT THE MONEY? IT'S... HEY, HEAR THAT?
I TOLD YOU WE SHOULD'VE CALLED SOMEONE ABOUT THAT BEAR!
YEOWW!
LET'S GET OUT OF HERE!
PLAY

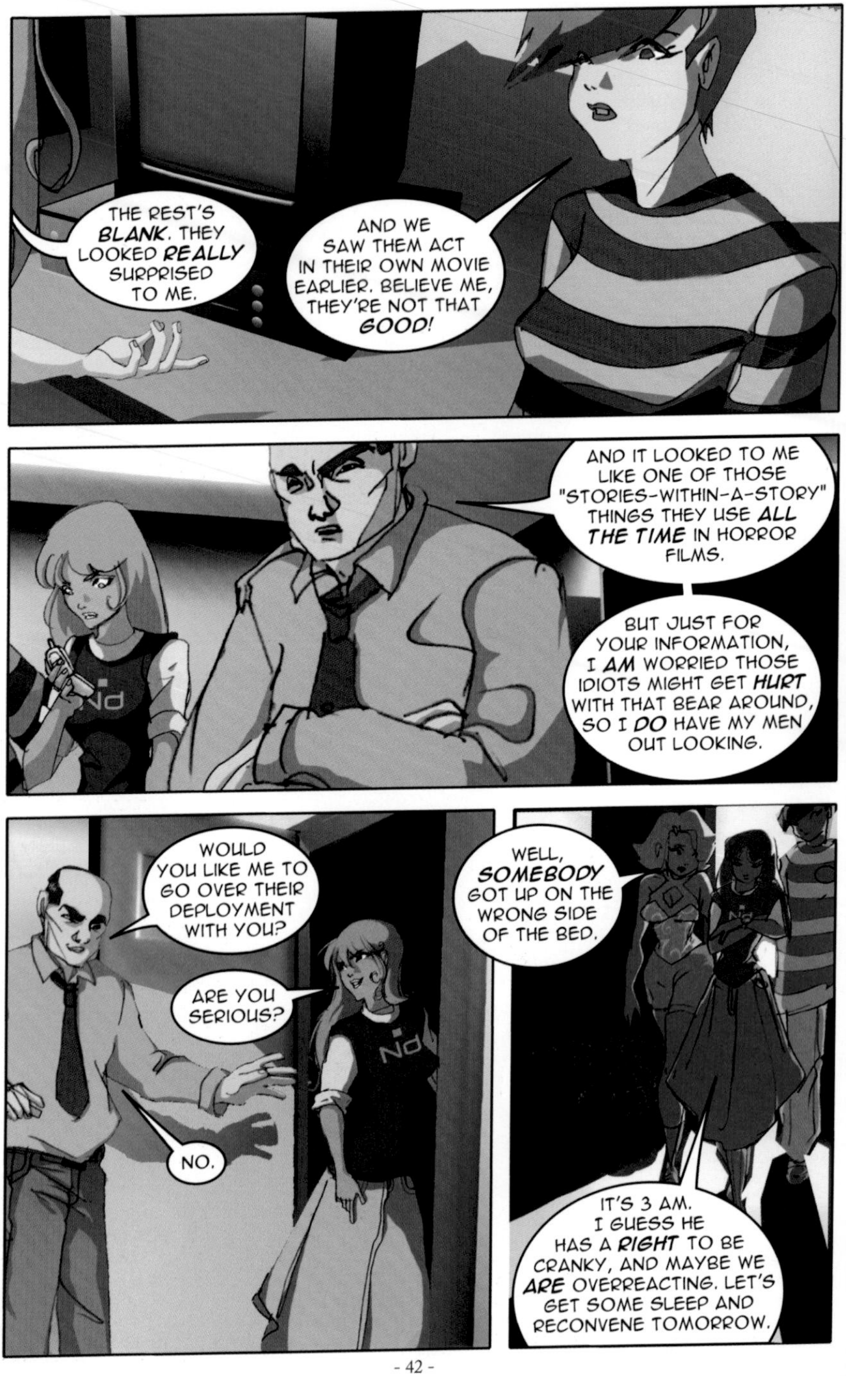
THE REST'S BLANK. THEY LOOKED REALLY SURPRISED TO ME.
AND WE SAW THEM ACT IN THEIR OWN MOVIE EARLIER. BELIEVE ME, THEY'RE NOT THAT GOOD!
AND IT LOOKED TO ME LIKE ONE OF THOSE "STORIES-WITHIN-A-STORY" THINGS THEY USE ALL THE TIME IN HORROR FILMS.
BUT JUST FOR YOUR INFORMATION, I AM WORRIED THOSE IDIOTS MIGHT GET HURT WITH THAT BEAR AROUND, SO I DO HAVE MY MEN OUT LOOKING.
WOULD YOU LIKE ME TO GO OVER THEIR DEPLOYMENT WITH YOU?
ARE YOU SERIOUS?
NO.
WELL, SOMEBODY GOT UP ON THE WRONG SIDE OF THE BED.
IT'S 3 AM. I GUESS HE HAS A RIGHT TO BE CRANKY, AND MAYBE WE ARE OVERREACTING. LET'S GET SOME SLEEP AND RECONVENE TOMORROW.

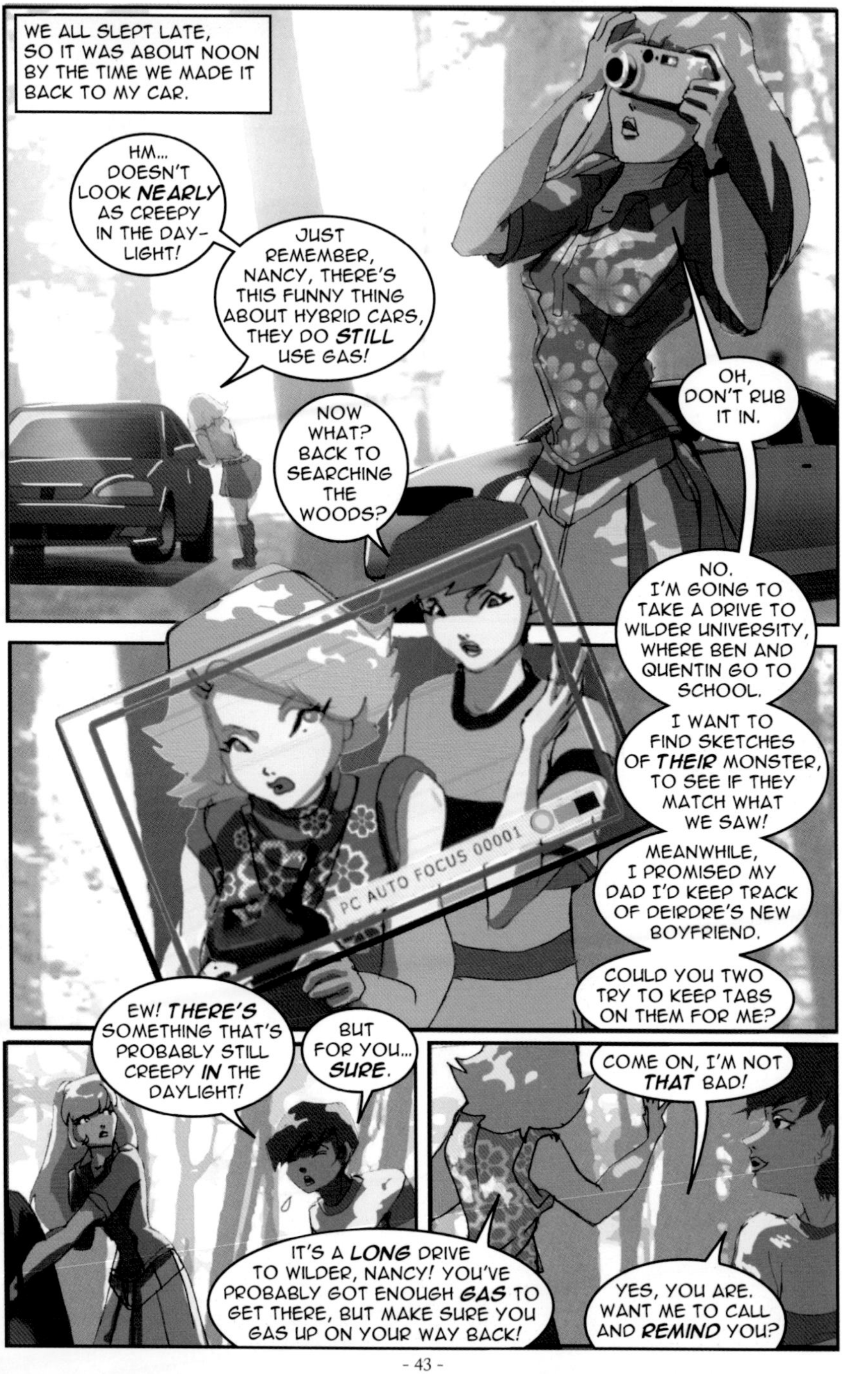
WE ALL SLEPT LATE, SO IT WAS ABOUT NOON BY THE TIME WE MADE IT BACK TO MY CAR.
HM... DOESN'T LOOK NEARLY AS CREEPY IN THE DAY-LIGHT!
JUST REMEMBER, NANCY, THERE'S THIS FUNNY THING ABOUT HYBRID CARS, THEY DO STILL USE GAS!
OH, DON'T RUB IT IN.
NOW WHAT? BACK TO SEARCHING THE WOODS?
NO. I'M GOING TO TAKE A DRIVE TO WILDER UNIVERSITY, WHERE BEN AND QUENTIN GO TO SCHOOL.
I WANT TO FIND SKETCHES OF THEIR MONSTER, TO SEE IF THEY MATCH WHAT WE SAW!
PC AUTO FOCUS 00001
MEANWHILE, I PROMISED MY DAD I'D KEEP TRACK OF DEIRDRE'S NEW BOYFRIEND.
COULD YOU TWO TRY TO KEEP TABS ON THEM FOR ME?
EW! THERE'S SOMETHING THAT'S PROBABLY STILL CREEPY IN THE DAYLIGHT!
BUT FOR YOU... SURE.
COME ON, I'M NOT THAT BAD!
IT'S A LONG DRIVE TO WILDER, NANCY! YOU'VE PROBABLY GOT ENOUGH GAS TO GET THERE, BUT MAKE SURE YOU GAS UP ON YOUR WAY BACK!
YES, YOU ARE. WANT ME TO CALL AND REMIND YOU?

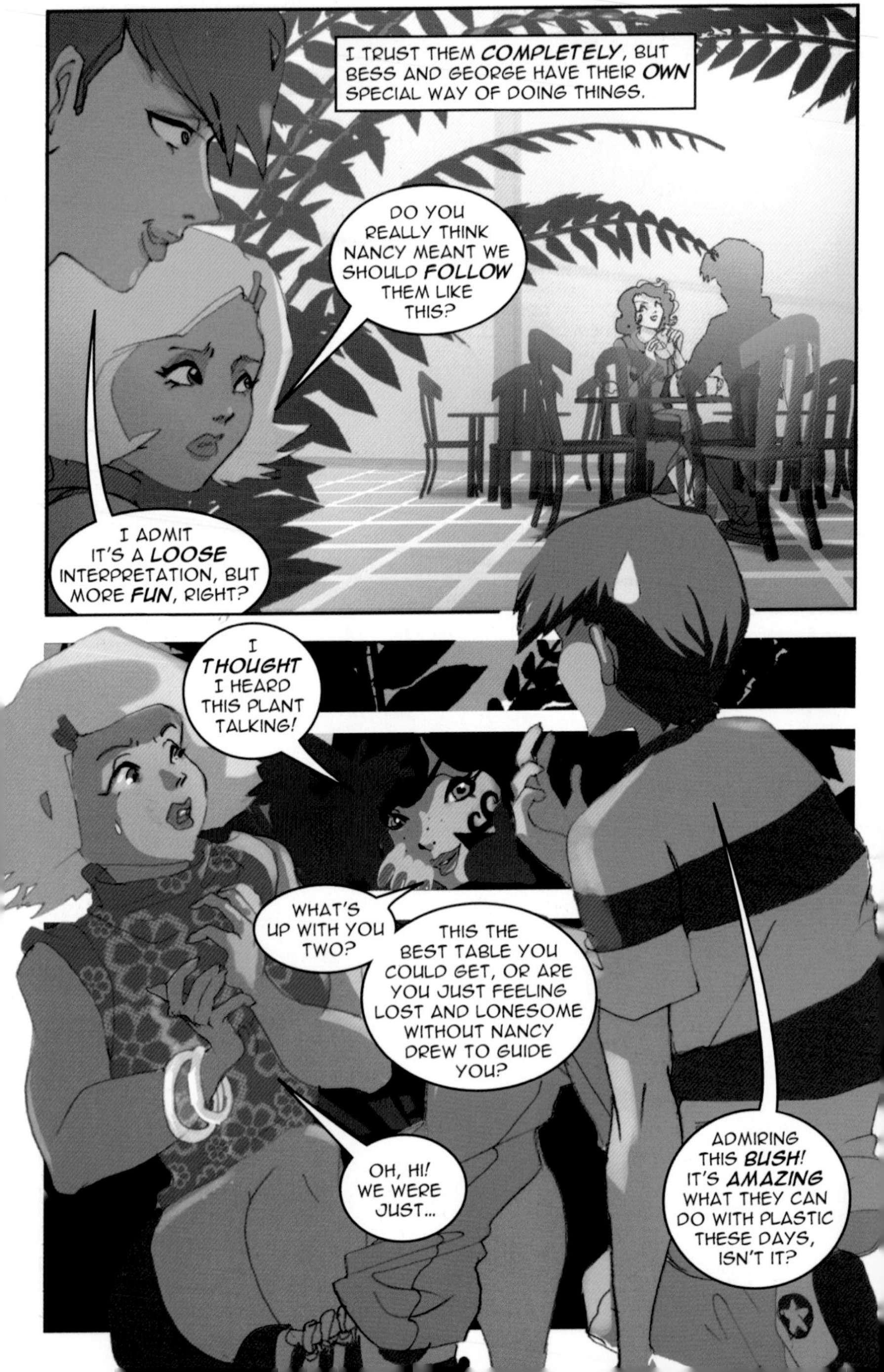
I TRUST THEM COMPLETELY, BUT BESS AND GEORGE HAVE THEIR OWN SPECIAL WAY OF DOING THINGS.
DO YOU REALLY THINK NANCY MEANT WE SHOULD FOLLOW THEM LIKE THIS?
I ADMIT IT'S A LOOSE INTERPRETATION, BUT MORE FUN, RIGHT?
I THOUGHT I HEARD THIS PLANT TALKING!
WHAT'S UP WITH YOU TWO?
THIS THE BEST TABLE YOU COULD GET, OR ARE YOU JUST FEELING LOST AND LONESOME WITHOUT NANCY DREW TO GUIDE YOU?
OH, HI! WE WERE JUST...
ADMIRING THIS BUSH! IT'S AMAZING WHAT THEY CAN DO WITH PLASTIC THESE DAYS, ISN'T IT?

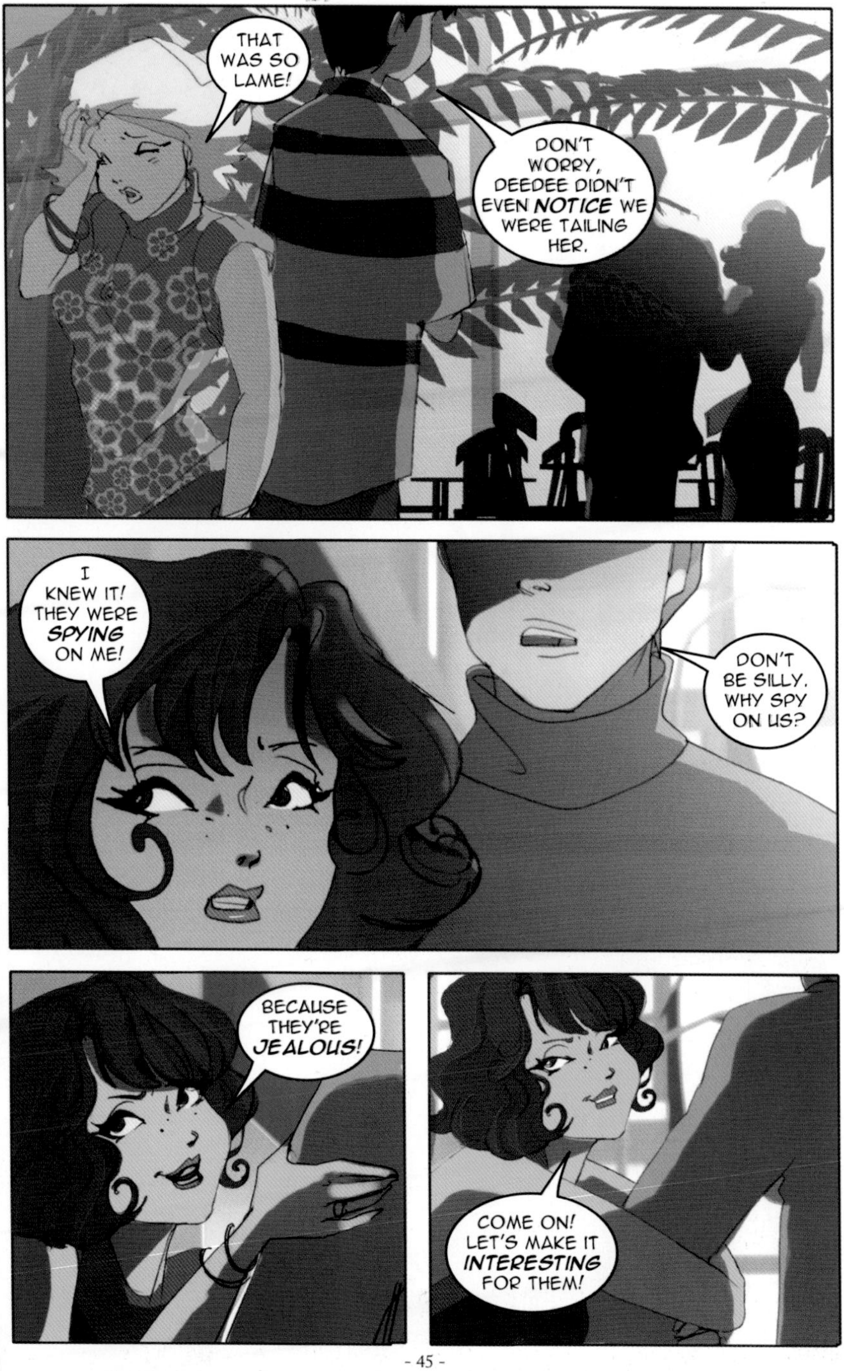
THAT WAS SO LAME!
DON'T WORRY, DEEDEE DIDN'T EVEN NOTICE WE WERE TAILING HER.
I KNEW IT! THEY WERE SPYING ON ME!
DON'T BE SILLY. WHY SPY ON US?
BECAUSE THEY'RE JEALOUS!
COME ON! LET'S MAKE IT INTERESTING FOR THEM!

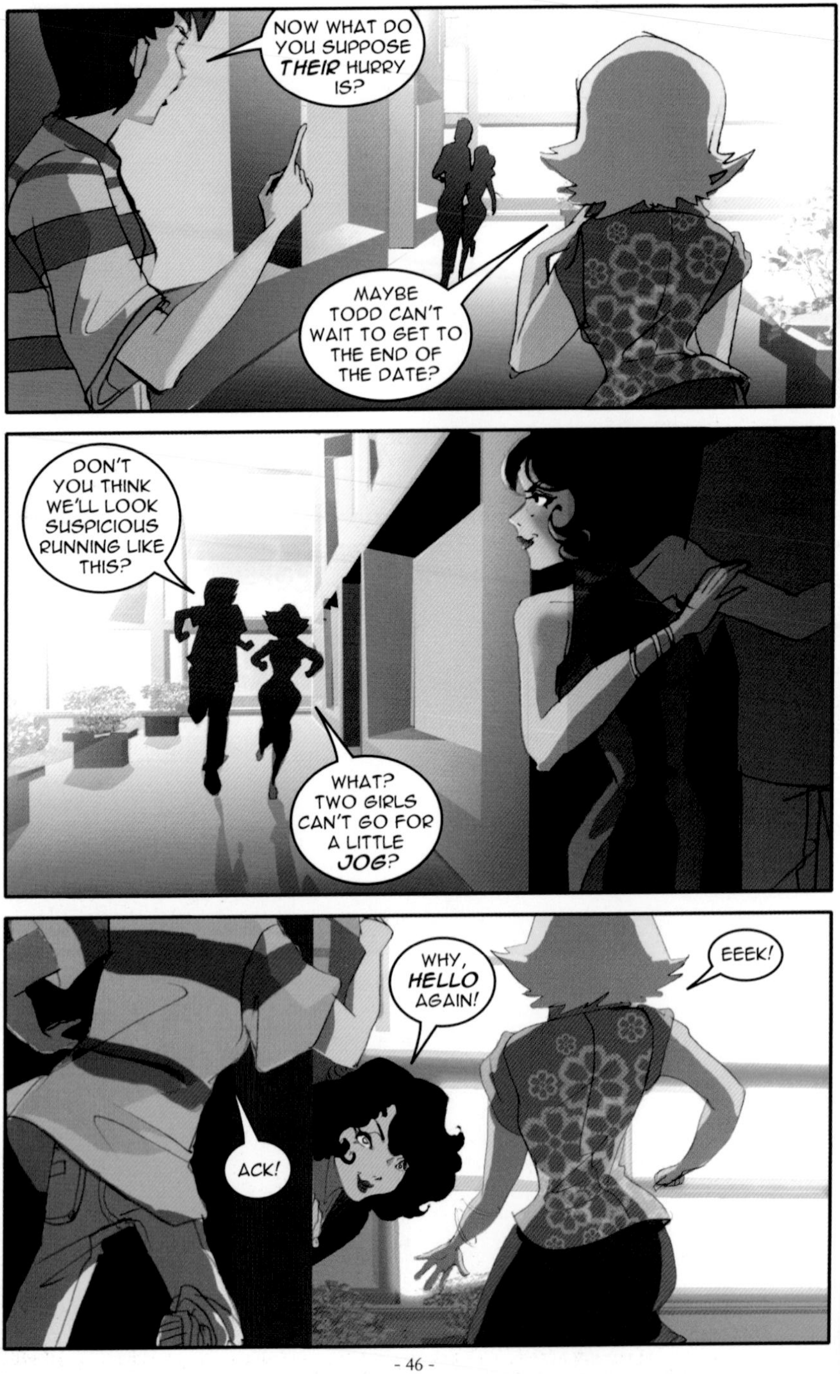
NOW WHAT DO YOU SUPPOSE THEIR HURRY IS?
MAYBE TODD CAN'T WAIT TO GET TO THE END OF THE DATE?
DON'T YOU THINK WE'LL LOOK SUSPICIOUS RUNNING LIKE THIS?
WHAT? TWO GIRLS CAN'T GO FOR A LITTLE JOG?
WHY, HELLO AGAIN!
EEEK!
ACK!

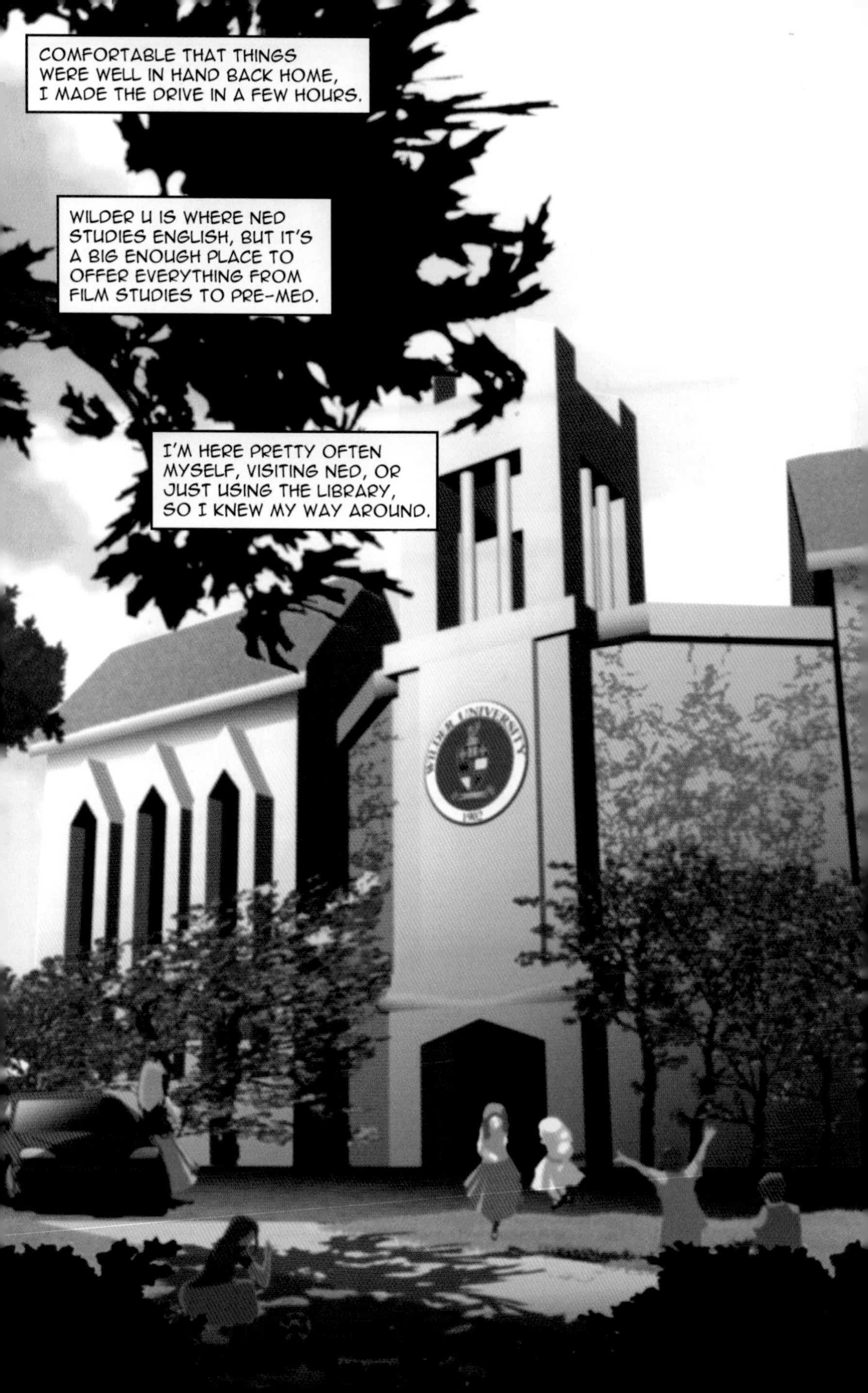
COMFORTABLE THAT THINGS WERE WELL IN HAND BACK HOME, I MADE THE DRIVE IN A FEW HOURS.
WILDER U IS WHERE NED STUDIES ENGLISH, BUT IT'S A BIG ENOUGH PLACE TO OFFER EVERYTHING FROM FILM STUDIES TO PRE-MED.
I'M HERE PRETTY OFTEN MYSELF, VISITING NED, OR JUST USING THE LIBRARY, SO I KNEW MY WAY AROUND.
WILDER UNIVERSITY

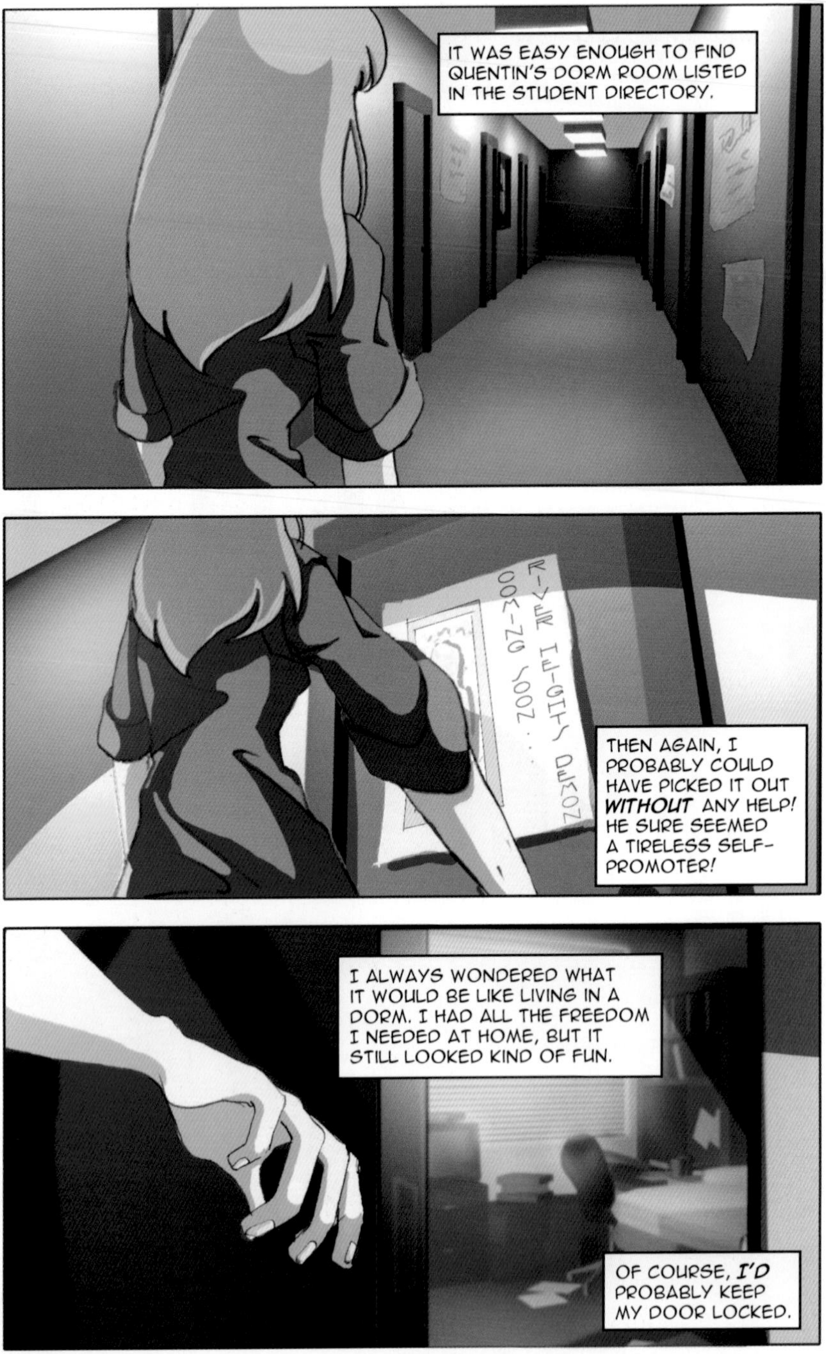
IT WAS EASY ENOUGH TO FIND QUENTIN'S DORM ROOM LISTED IN THE STUDENT DIRECTORY.
RIVER HEIGHTS DEMON
COMING SOON...
THEN AGAIN, I PROBABLY COULD HAVE PICKED IT OUT *WITHOUT* ANY HELP! HE SURE SEEMED A TIRELESS SELF-PROMOTER!
I ALWAYS WONDERED WHAT IT WOULD BE LIKE LIVING IN A DORM. I HAD ALL THE FREEDOM I NEEDED AT HOME, BUT IT STILL LOOKED KIND OF FUN.
OF COURSE, *I'D* PROBABLY KEEP MY DOOR LOCKED.

ONCE I WAS INSIDE, IT DIDN'T LOOK LIKE DORM LIFE WAS SO MUCH FUN AFTER ALL. MOSTLY, IT LOOKED *MESSY*.

TOP SECRET

LIKE THE SIGN ON THE DOOR, IT WASN'T TOO DIFFICULT TO FIGURE OUT WHERE THEY KEPT THEIR NOTES.

IF THEIR MONSTER DESIGNS LOOKED LIKE THE THING WE SAW IN THE FOREST, IT WAS A PRETTY SAFE BET CHIEF McGINNIS WAS RIGHT, AND THE BOYS WERE JUST USING US TO PROMOTE THEIR FILM.

MONSTER DESIGN

A QUICK PEEK COULD SOLVE THE WHOLE CASE!

HEY! WHAT ARE YOU DOING HERE?

MONSTER DESIGN

UNLESS, OF COURSE, I GOT *CAUGHT*.

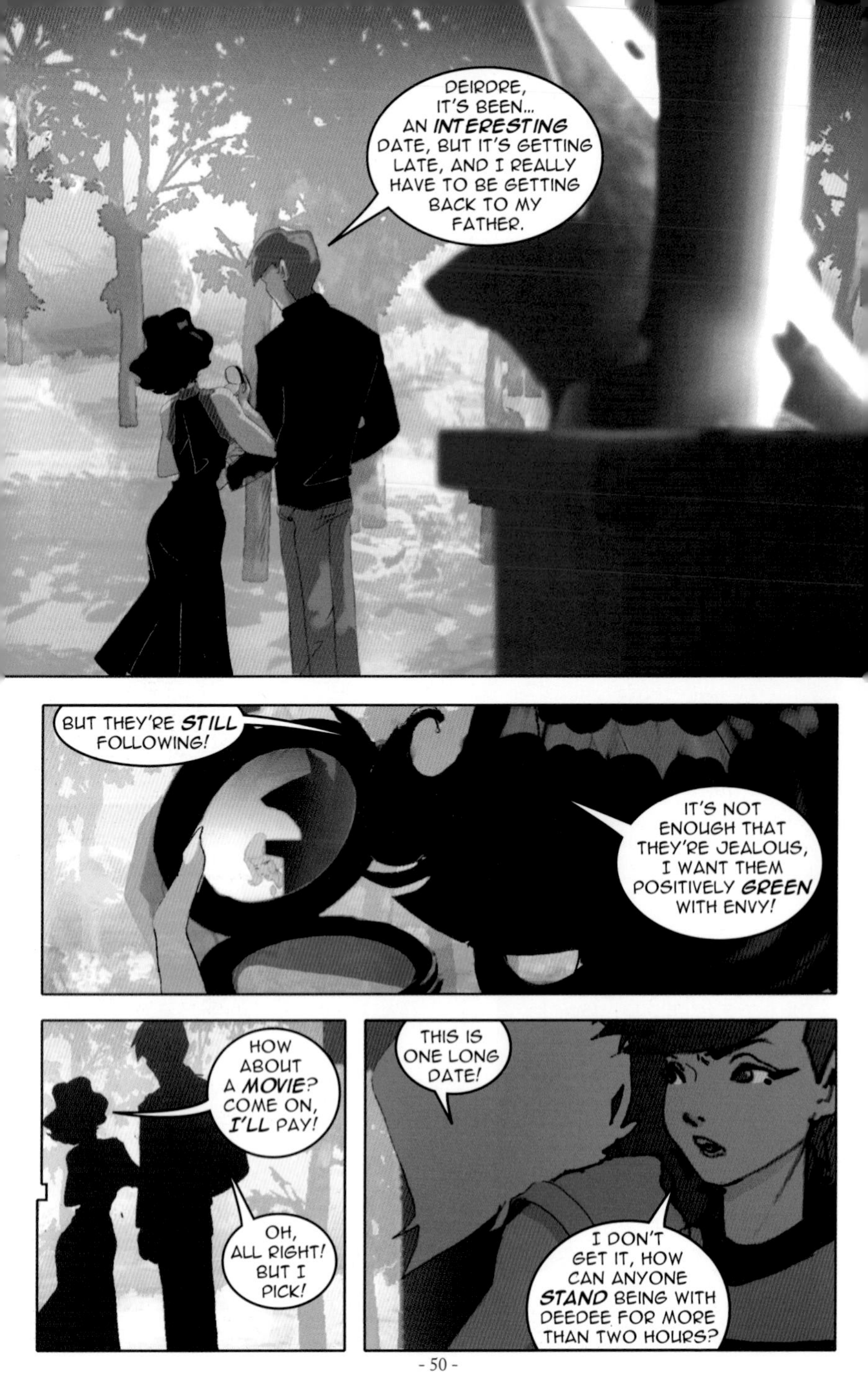
DEIRDRE, IT'S BEEN... AN INTERESTING DATE, BUT IT'S GETTING LATE, AND I REALLY HAVE TO BE GETTING BACK TO MY FATHER.
BUT THEY'RE STILL FOLLOWING!
IT'S NOT ENOUGH THAT THEY'RE JEALOUS, I WANT THEM POSITIVELY GREEN WITH ENVY!
HOW ABOUT A MOVIE? COME ON, I'LL PAY!
OH, ALL RIGHT! BUT I PICK!
THIS IS ONE LONG DATE!
I DON'T GET IT, HOW CAN ANYONE STAND BEING WITH DEEDEE FOR MORE THAN TWO HOURS?

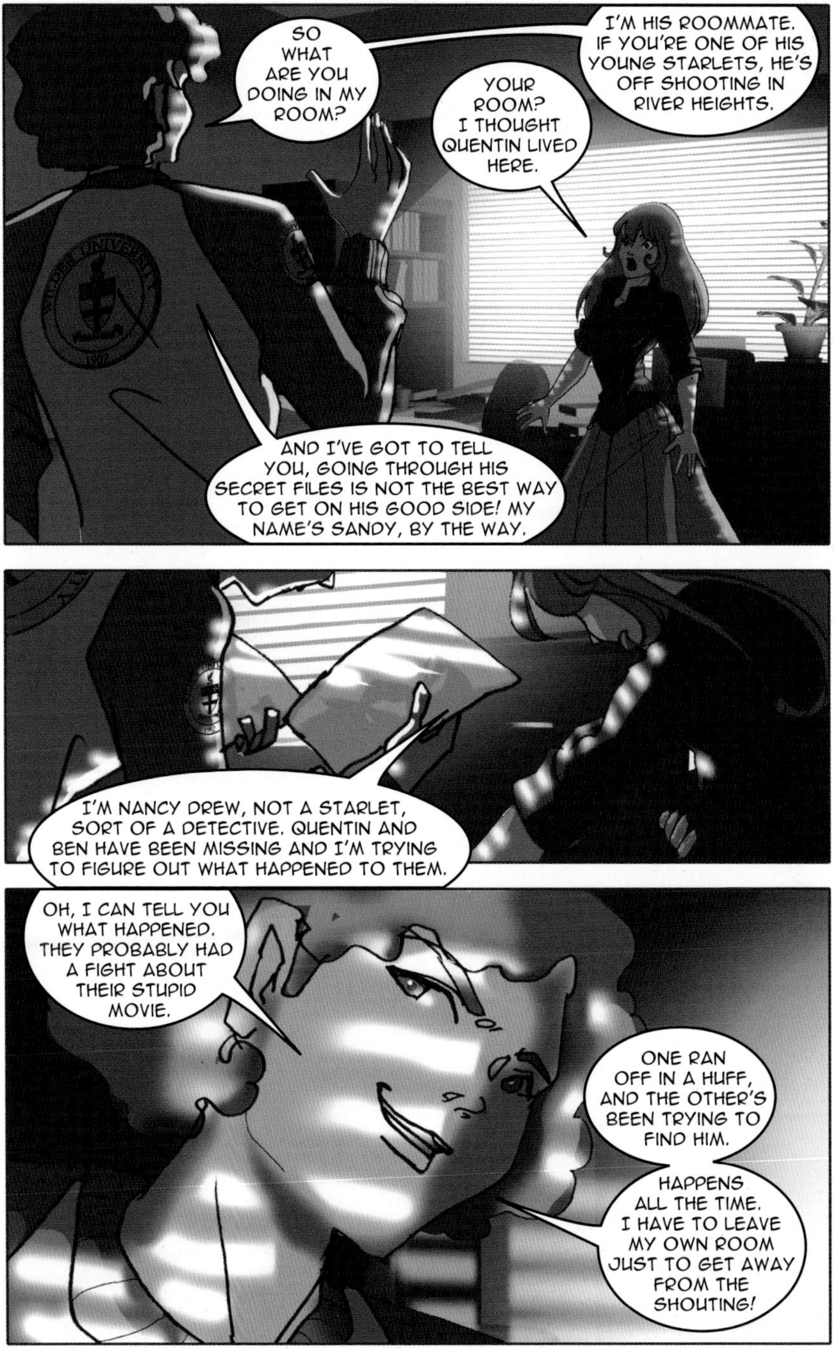
SO WHAT ARE YOU DOING IN MY ROOM?
YOUR ROOM? I THOUGHT QUENTIN LIVED HERE.
I'M HIS ROOMMATE. IF YOU'RE ONE OF HIS YOUNG STARLETS, HE'S OFF SHOOTING IN RIVER HEIGHTS.
AND I'VE GOT TO TELL YOU, GOING THROUGH HIS SECRET FILES IS NOT THE BEST WAY TO GET ON HIS GOOD SIDE! MY NAME'S SANDY, BY THE WAY.
I'M NANCY DREW, NOT A STARLET, SORT OF A DETECTIVE. QUENTIN AND BEN HAVE BEEN MISSING AND I'M TRYING TO FIGURE OUT WHAT HAPPENED TO THEM.
OH, I CAN TELL YOU WHAT HAPPENED. THEY PROBABLY HAD A FIGHT ABOUT THEIR STUPID MOVIE.
ONE RAN OFF IN A HUFF, AND THE OTHER'S BEEN TRYING TO FIND HIM.
HAPPENS ALL THE TIME. I HAVE TO LEAVE MY OWN ROOM JUST TO GET AWAY FROM THE SHOUTING!

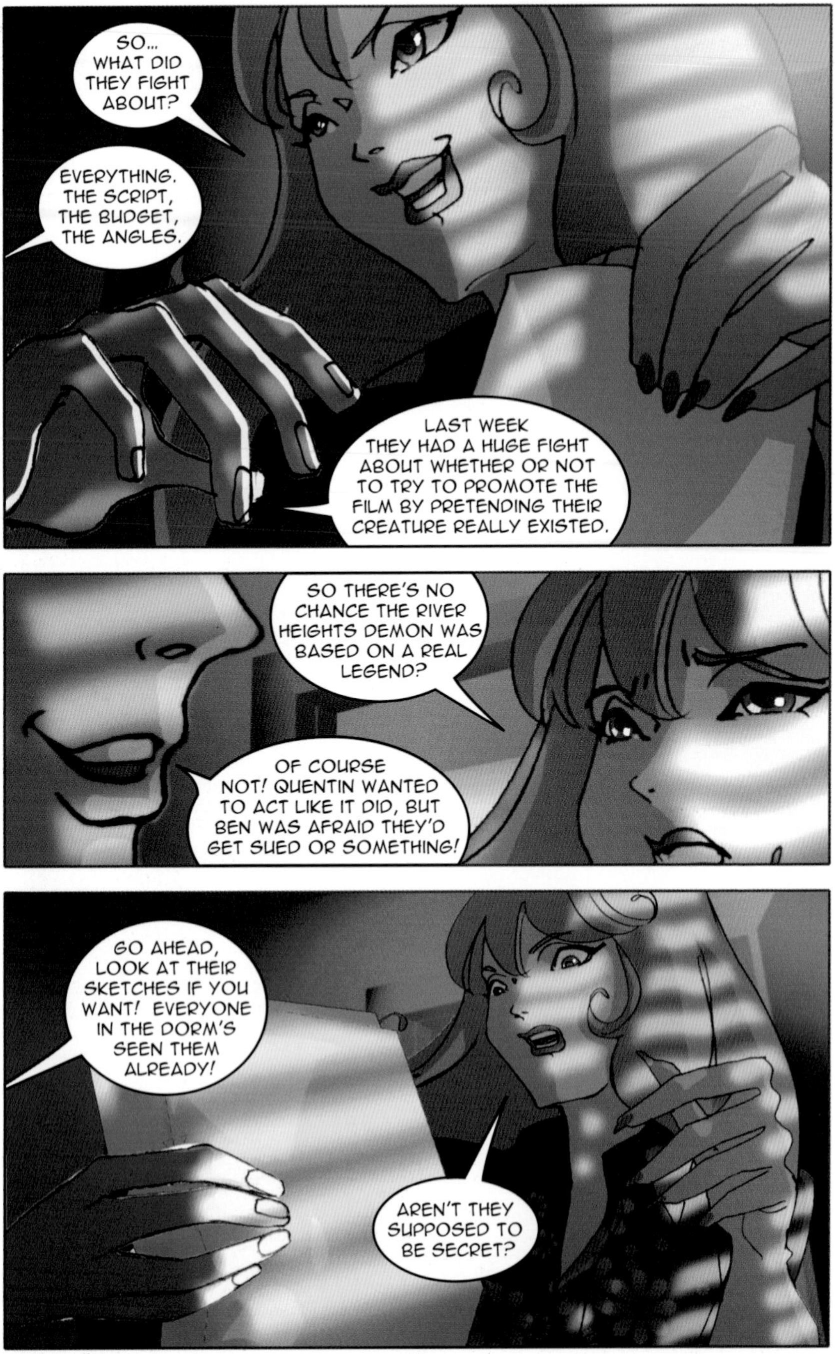
SO... WHAT DID THEY FIGHT ABOUT?
EVERYTHING. THE SCRIPT, THE BUDGET, THE ANGLES.
LAST WEEK THEY HAD A HUGE FIGHT ABOUT WHETHER OR NOT TO TRY TO PROMOTE THE FILM BY PRETENDING THEIR CREATURE REALLY EXISTED.
SO THERE'S NO CHANCE THE RIVER HEIGHTS DEMON WAS BASED ON A REAL LEGEND?
OF COURSE NOT! QUENTIN WANTED TO ACT LIKE IT DID, BUT BEN WAS AFRAID THEY'D GET SUED OR SOMETHING!
GO AHEAD, LOOK AT THEIR SKETCHES IF YOU WANT! EVERYONE IN THE DORM'S SEEN THEM ALREADY!
AREN'T THEY SUPPOSED TO BE SECRET?

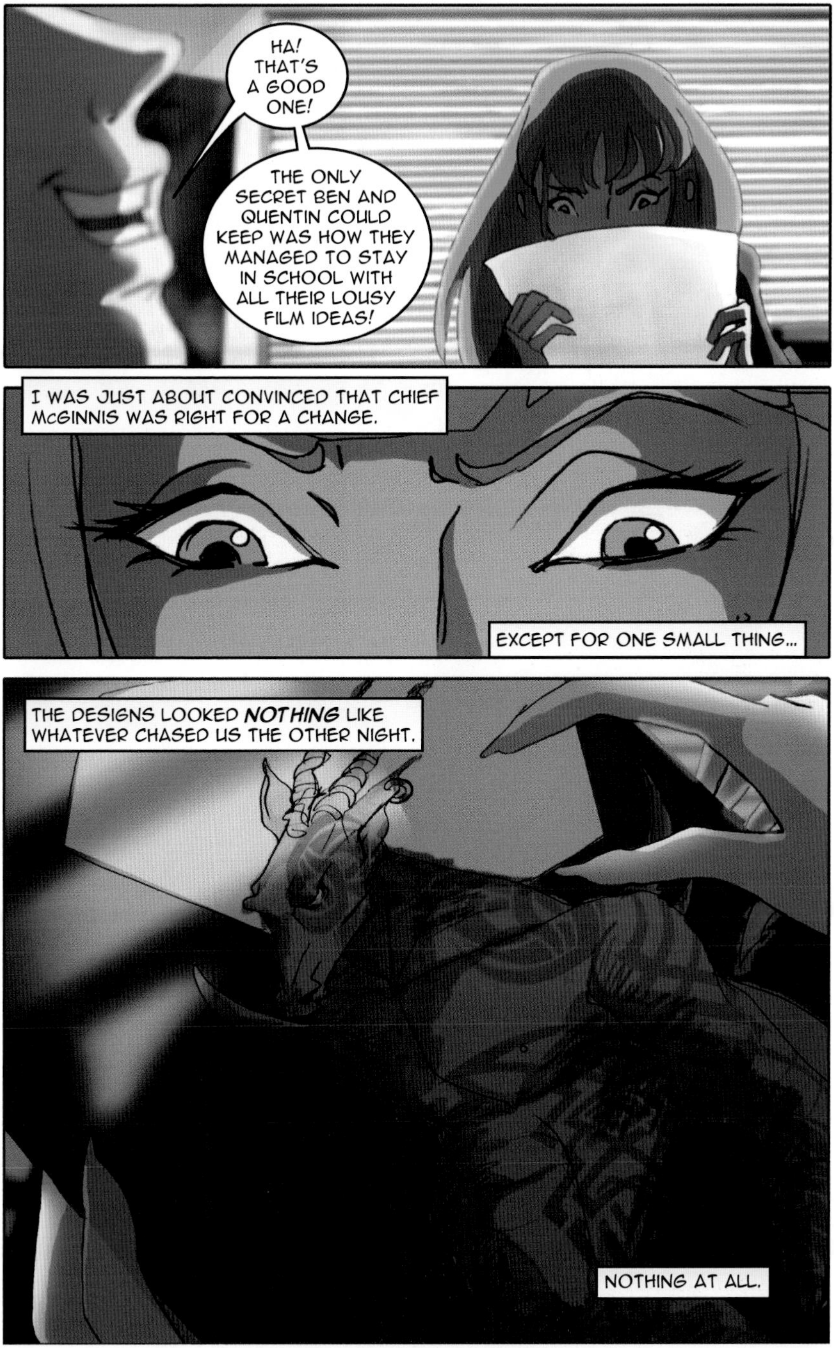
HA! THAT'S A GOOD ONE!
THE ONLY SECRET BEN AND QUENTIN COULD KEEP WAS HOW THEY MANAGED TO STAY IN SCHOOL WITH ALL THEIR LOUSY FILM IDEAS!
I WAS JUST ABOUT CONVINCED THAT CHIEF McGINNIS WAS RIGHT FOR A CHANGE.
EXCEPT FOR ONE SMALL THING...
THE DESIGNS LOOKED ***NOTHING*** LIKE WHATEVER CHASED US THE OTHER NIGHT.
NOTHING AT ALL.

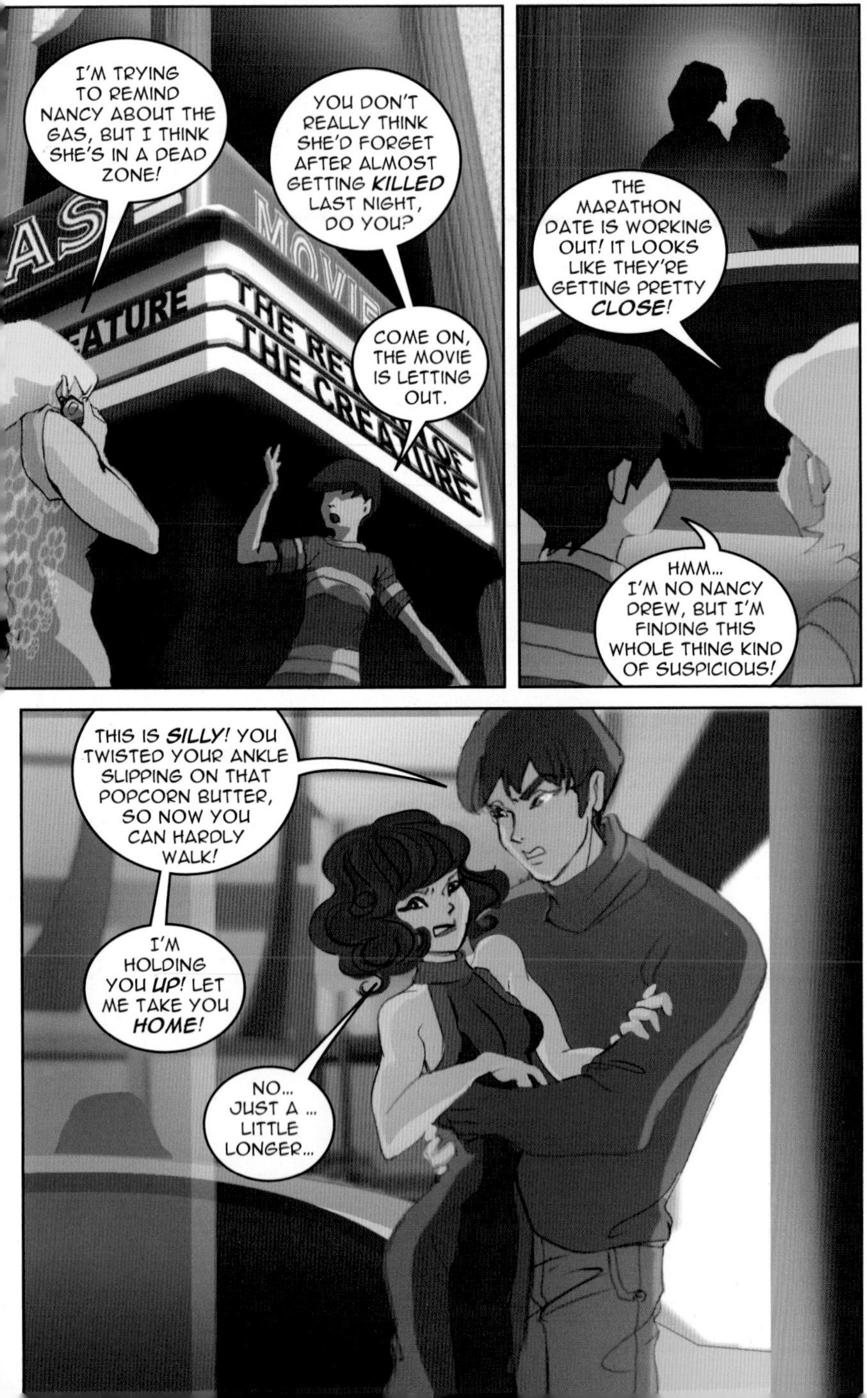
I'M TRYING TO REMIND NANCY ABOUT THE GAS, BUT I THINK SHE'S IN A DEAD ZONE!
YOU DON'T REALLY THINK SHE'D FORGET AFTER ALMOST GETTING KILLED LAST NIGHT, DO YOU?
FEATURE
THE RETURN OF THE CREATURE
COME ON, THE MOVIE IS LETTING OUT.
THE MARATHON DATE IS WORKING OUT! IT LOOKS LIKE THEY'RE GETTING PRETTY CLOSE!
HMM... I'M NO NANCY DREW, BUT I'M FINDING THIS WHOLE THING KIND OF SUSPICIOUS!
THIS IS SILLY! YOU TWISTED YOUR ANKLE SLIPPING ON THAT POPCORN BUTTER, SO NOW YOU CAN HARDLY WALK!
I'M HOLDING YOU UP! LET ME TAKE YOU HOME!
NO... JUST A ... LITTLE LONGER...

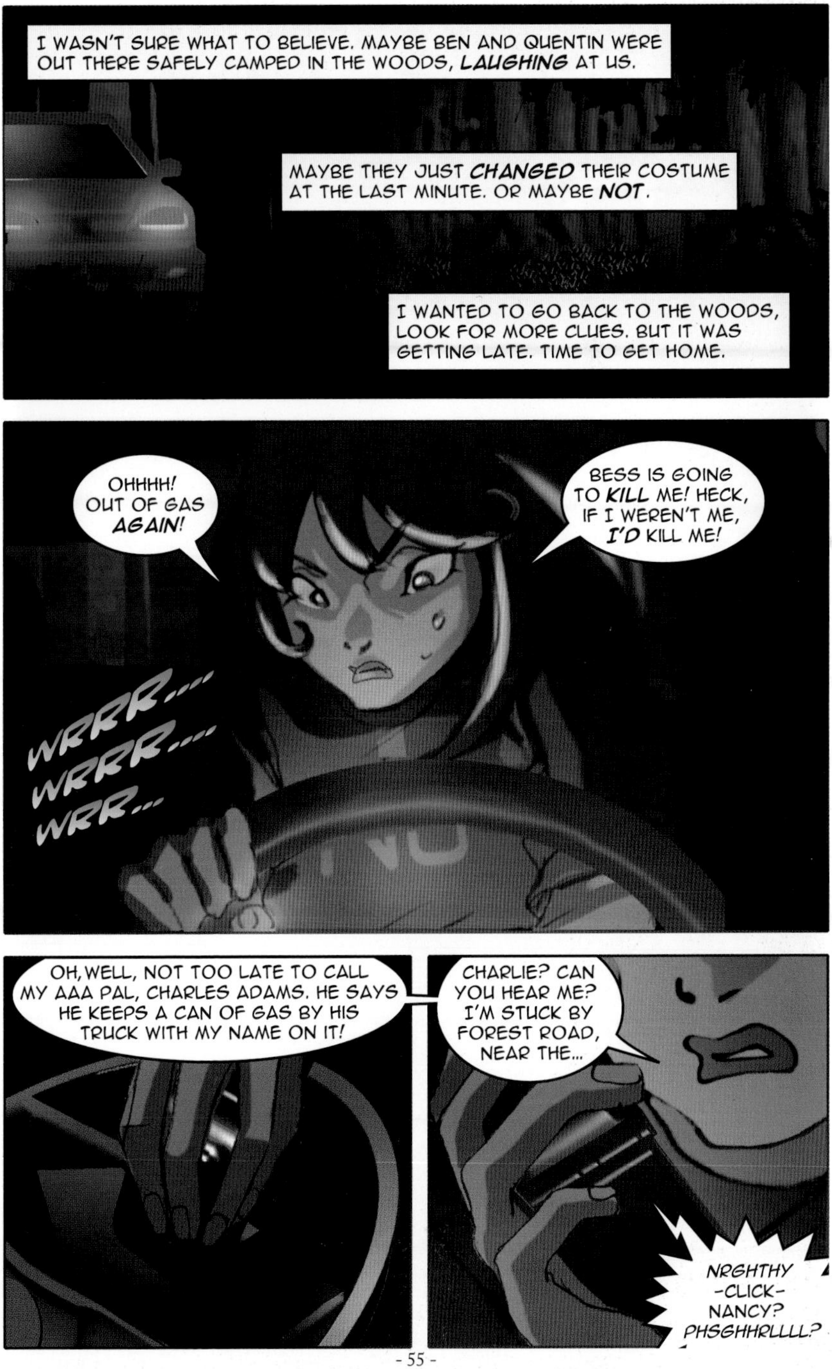
I WASN'T SURE WHAT TO BELIEVE. MAYBE BEN AND QUENTIN WERE OUT THERE SAFELY CAMPED IN THE WOODS, LAUGHING AT US.
MAYBE THEY JUST CHANGED THEIR COSTUME AT THE LAST MINUTE. OR MAYBE NOT.
I WANTED TO GO BACK TO THE WOODS, LOOK FOR MORE CLUES. BUT IT WAS GETTING LATE. TIME TO GET HOME.
OHHHH! OUT OF GAS AGAIN!
BESS IS GOING TO KILL ME! HECK, IF I WEREN'T ME, I'D KILL ME!
WRRR.... WRRR.... WRR...
OH, WELL, NOT TOO LATE TO CALL MY AAA PAL, CHARLES ADAMS. HE SAYS HE KEEPS A CAN OF GAS BY HIS TRUCK WITH MY NAME ON IT!
CHARLIE? CAN YOU HEAR ME? I'M STUCK BY FOREST ROAD, NEAR THE...
NRGHTHY -CLICK- NANCY? PHSGHHRLLLL?

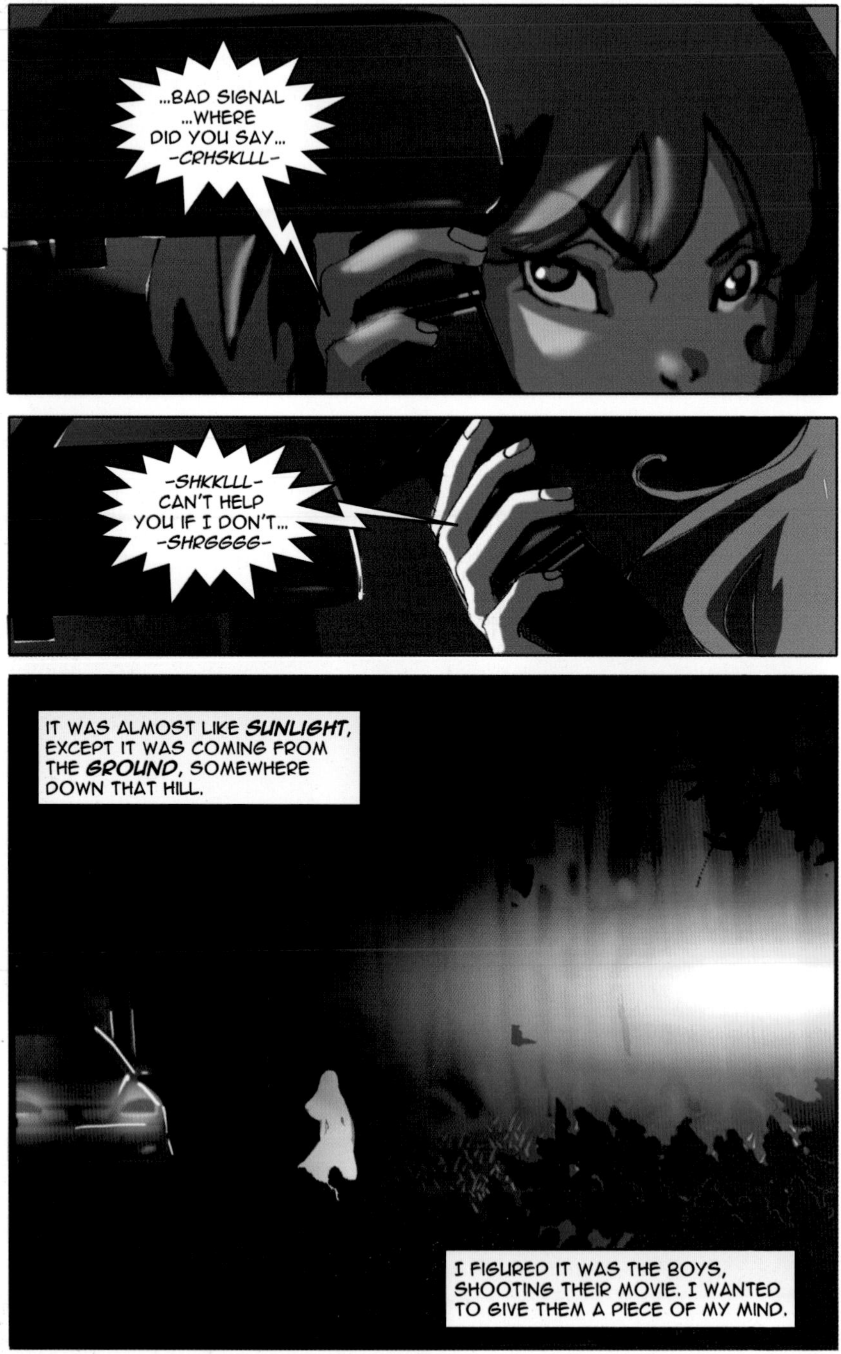
...BAD SIGNAL ...WHERE DID YOU SAY... -CRHSKLLL-
-SHKKLLL- CAN'T HELP YOU IF I DON'T... -SHRGGGG-
IT WAS ALMOST LIKE SUNLIGHT, EXCEPT IT WAS COMING FROM THE GROUND, SOMEWHERE DOWN THAT HILL.
I FIGURED IT WAS THE BOYS, SHOOTING THEIR MOVIE. I WANTED TO GIVE THEM A PIECE OF MY MIND.

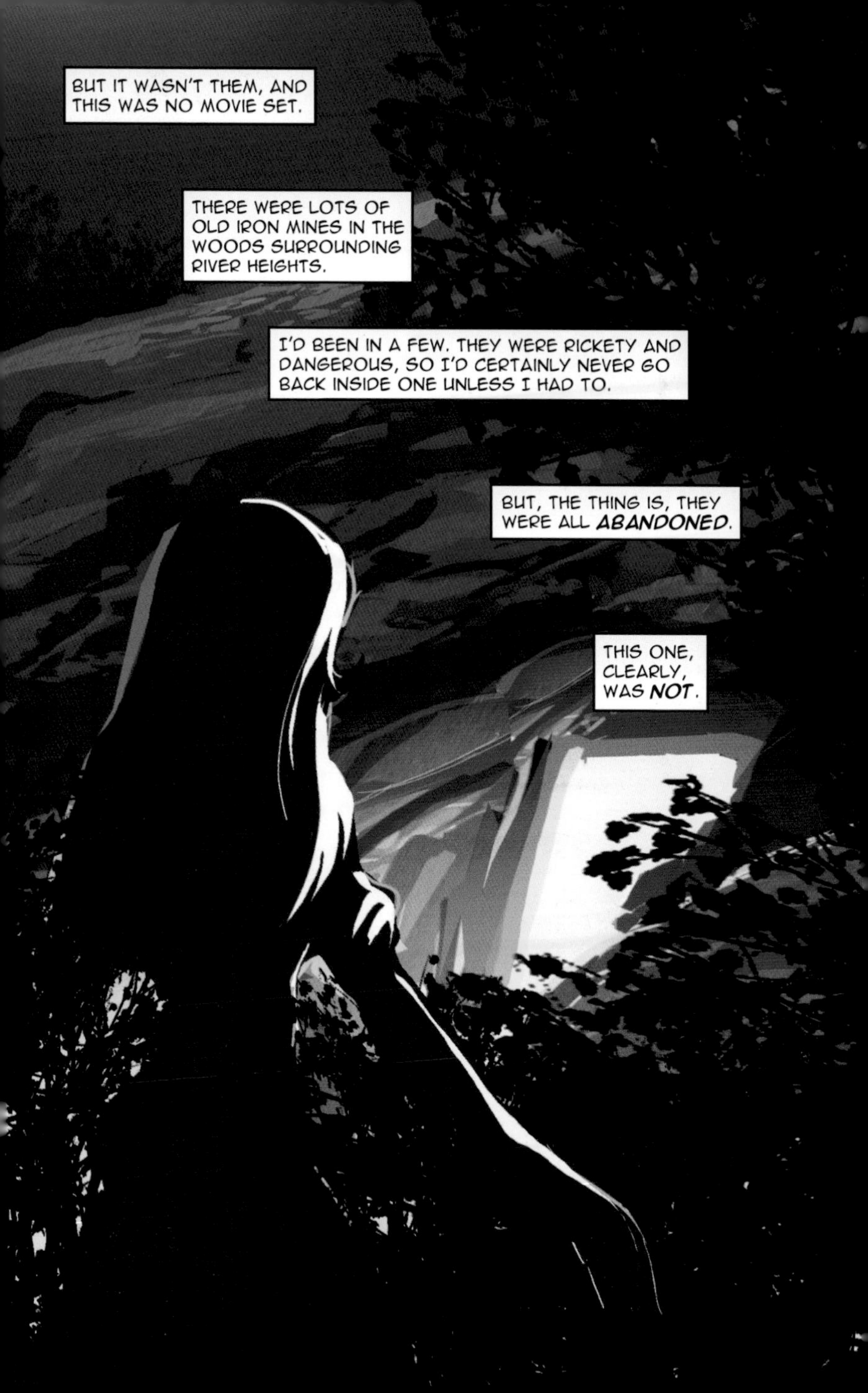
BUT IT WASN'T THEM, AND THIS WAS NO MOVIE SET.
THERE WERE LOTS OF OLD IRON MINES IN THE WOODS SURROUNDING RIVER HEIGHTS.
I'D BEEN IN A FEW. THEY WERE RICKETY AND DANGEROUS, SO I'D CERTAINLY NEVER GO BACK INSIDE ONE UNLESS I HAD TO.
BUT, THE THING IS, THEY WERE ALL ***ABANDONED***.
THIS ONE, CLEARLY, WAS ***NOT***.

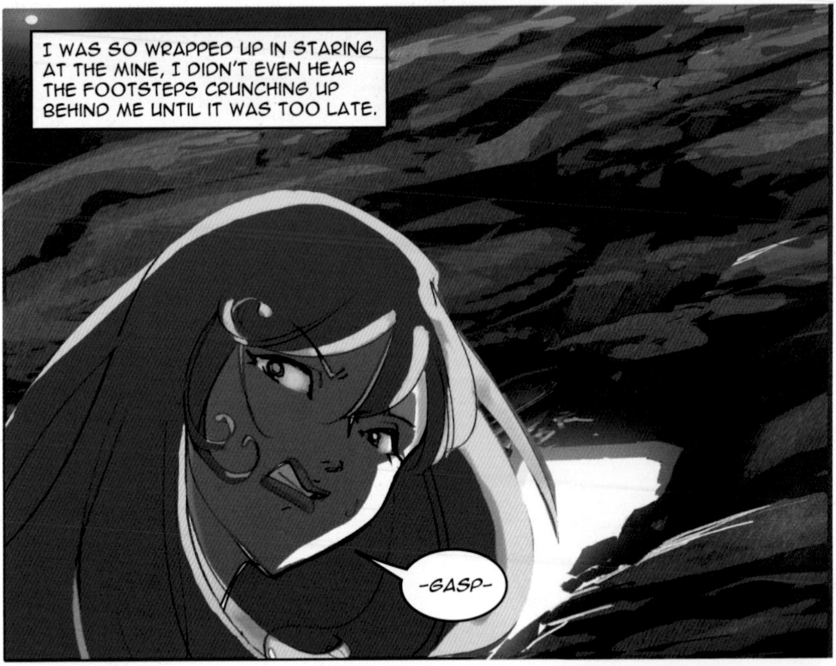
I WAS SO WRAPPED UP IN STARING AT THE MINE, I DIDN'T EVEN HEAR THE FOOTSTEPS CRUNCHING UP BEHIND ME UNTIL IT WAS TOO LATE.
-GASP-

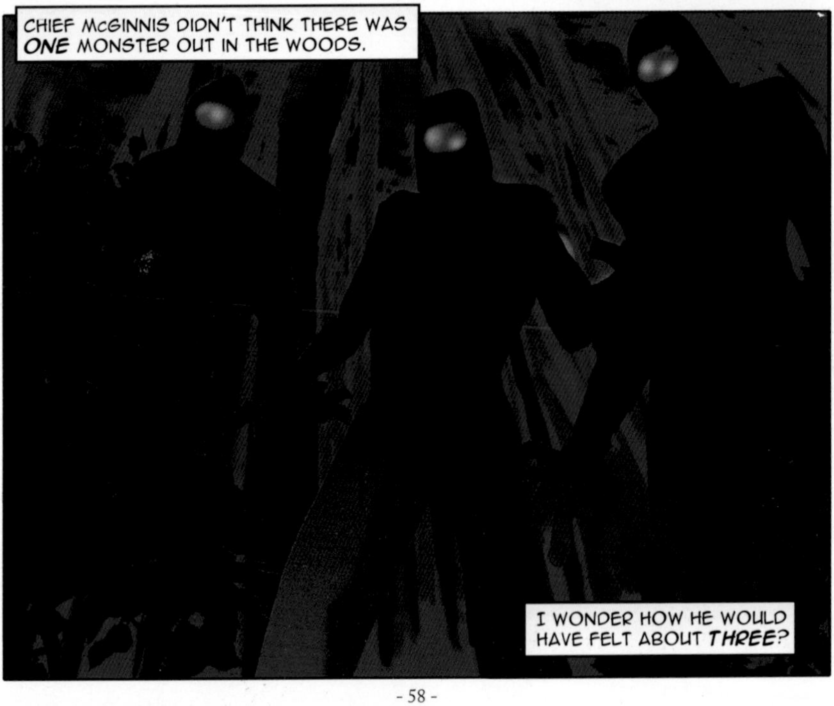
CHIEF McGINNIS DIDN'T THINK THERE WAS *ONE* MONSTER OUT IN THE WOODS.
I WONDER HOW HE WOULD HAVE FELT ABOUT *THREE*?

LAST TIME, THERE WAS ONE MONSTER TO THREE GIRLS, NOW THE ODDS WERE *REVERSED*.

I RAN, FAST AS I COULD, BRANCHES SCRATCHING MY ARMS AND LEGS, TERRIFIED I WOULD FALL.

AND THEN, WELL... EVER HAVE THAT TERRIFIC MOMENT OF *RELIEF*, LIKE AT THE END OF A RACE WHEN YOU REALIZE YOU'VE *WON*?

THAT WAS HOW I FELT WHEN I SAW MY CAR.

BUT ONLY FOR A SECOND.

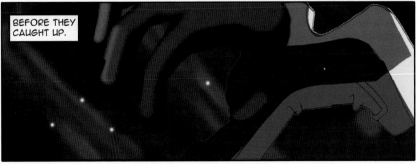

BEFORE THEY CAUGHT UP.

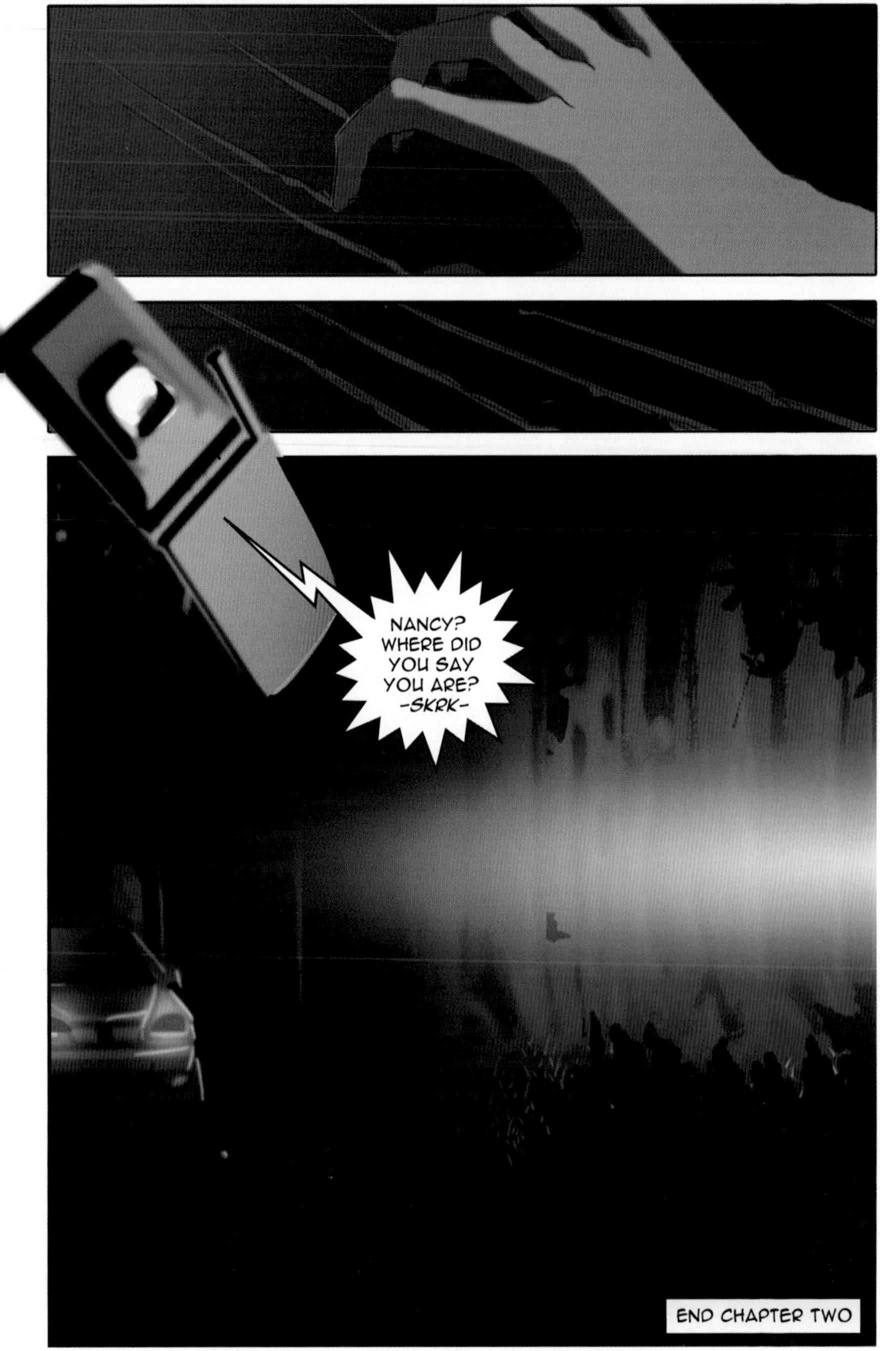
NANCY? WHERE DID YOU SAY YOU ARE? -SKRK-
END CHAPTER TWO

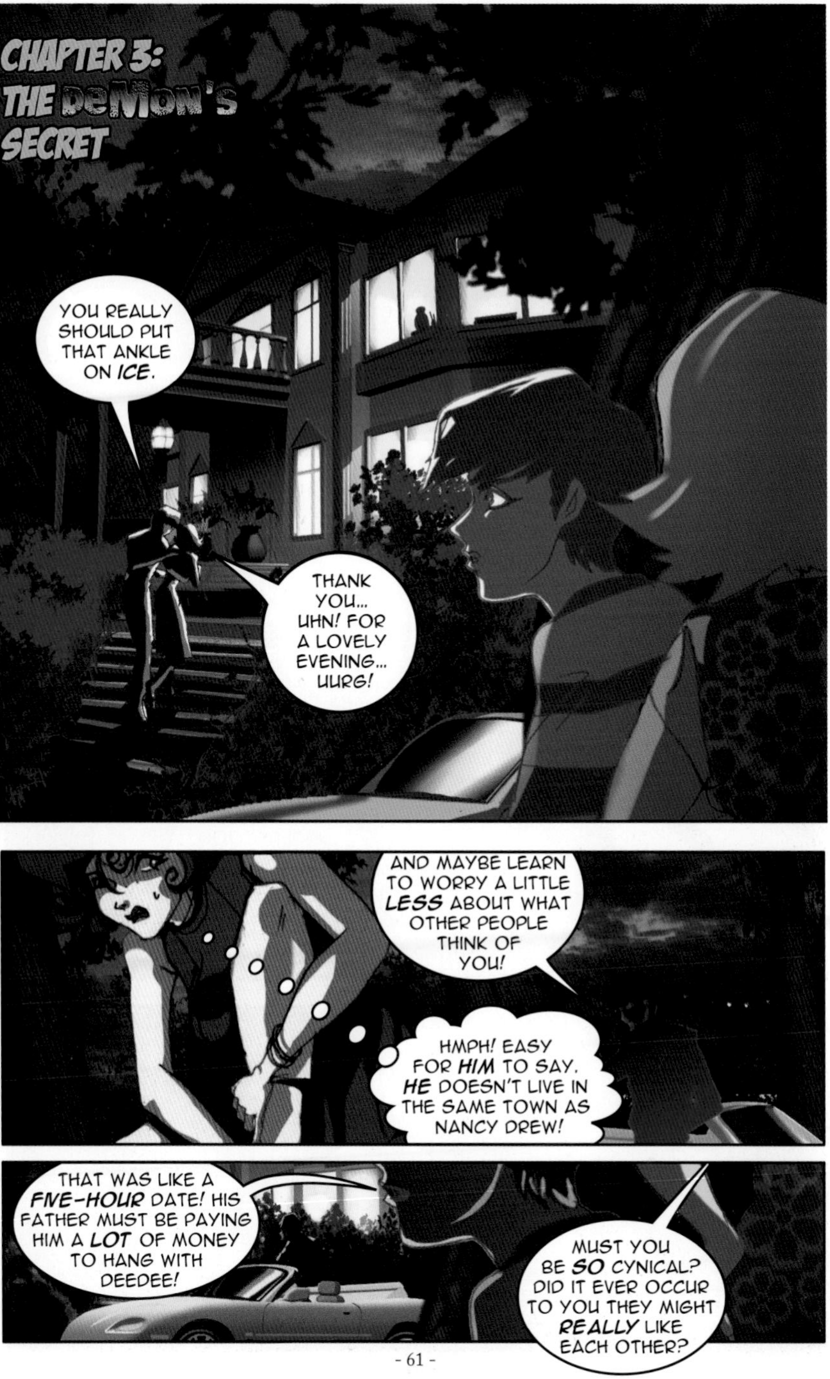
CHAPTER 3:
THE DEMON'S
SECRET
YOU REALLY SHOULD PUT THAT ANKLE ON ICE.
THANK YOU... UHN! FOR A LOVELY EVENING... UURG!
AND MAYBE LEARN TO WORRY A LITTLE LESS ABOUT WHAT OTHER PEOPLE THINK OF YOU!
HMPH! EASY FOR HIM TO SAY. HE DOESN'T LIVE IN THE SAME TOWN AS NANCY DREW!
THAT WAS LIKE A FIVE-HOUR DATE! HIS FATHER MUST BE PAYING HIM A LOT OF MONEY TO HANG WITH DEEDEE!
MUST YOU BE SO CYNICAL? DID IT EVER OCCUR TO YOU THEY MIGHT REALLY LIKE EACH OTHER?

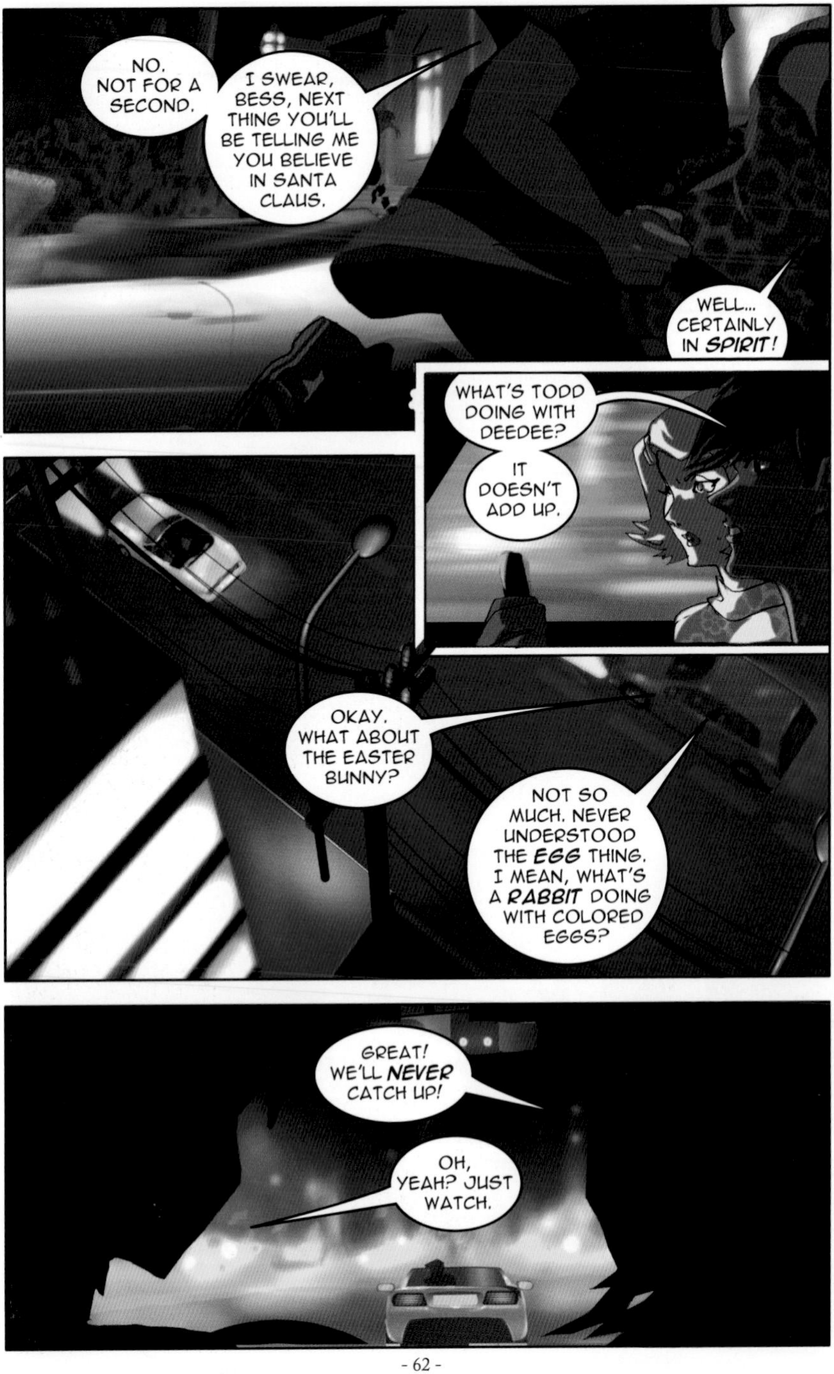
NO. NOT FOR A SECOND.
I SWEAR, BESS, NEXT THING YOU'LL BE TELLING ME YOU BELIEVE IN SANTA CLAUS.
WELL... CERTAINLY IN SPIRIT!
WHAT'S TODD DOING WITH DEEDEE?
IT DOESN'T ADD UP.
OKAY. WHAT ABOUT THE EASTER BUNNY?
NOT SO MUCH. NEVER UNDERSTOOD THE EGG THING. I MEAN, WHAT'S A RABBIT DOING WITH COLORED EGGS?
GREAT! WE'LL NEVER CATCH UP!
OH, YEAH? JUST WATCH.

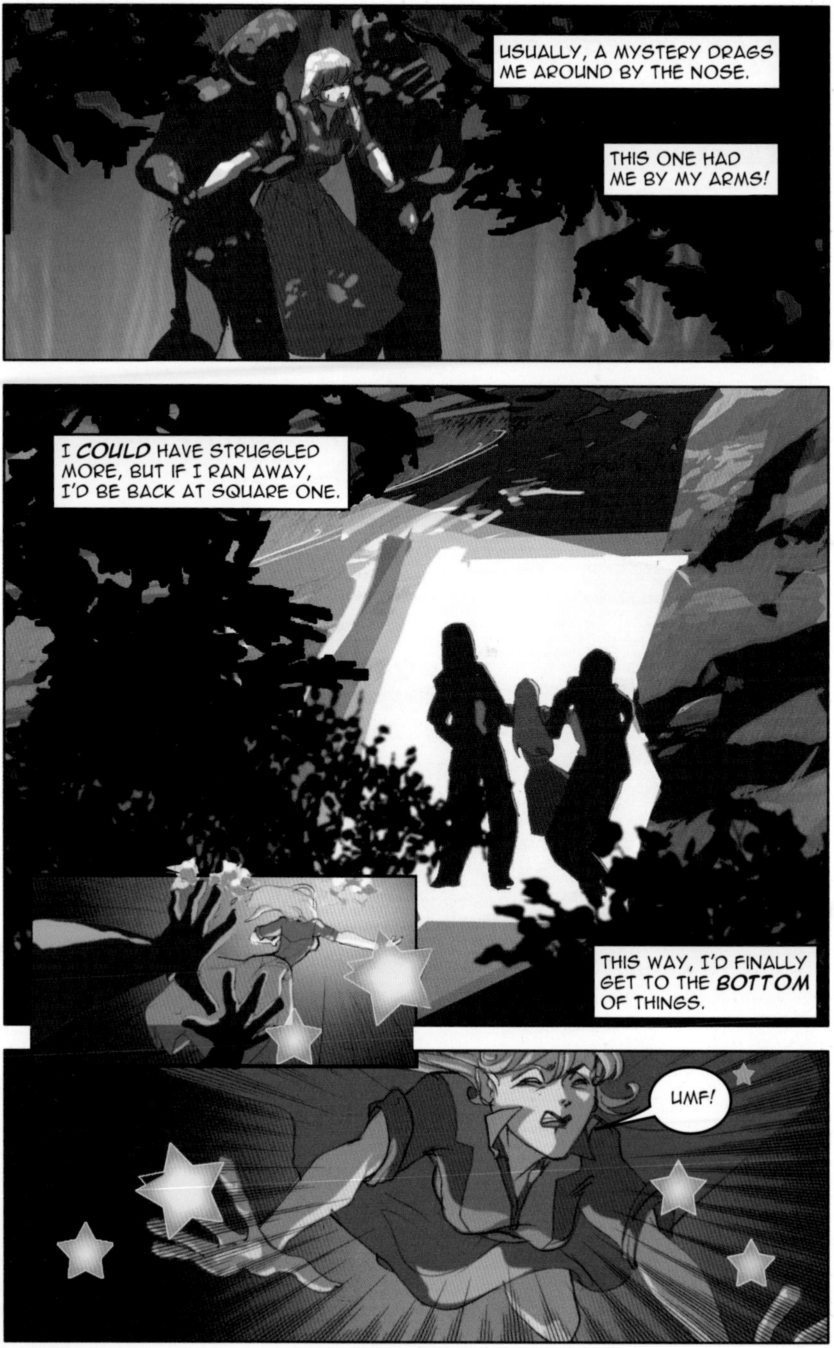
USUALLY, A MYSTERY DRAGS ME AROUND BY THE NOSE.
THIS ONE HAD ME BY MY ARMS!
I *COULD* HAVE STRUGGLED MORE, BUT IF I RAN AWAY, I'D BE BACK AT SQUARE ONE.
THIS WAY, I'D FINALLY GET TO THE *BOTTOM* OF THINGS.
UMF!

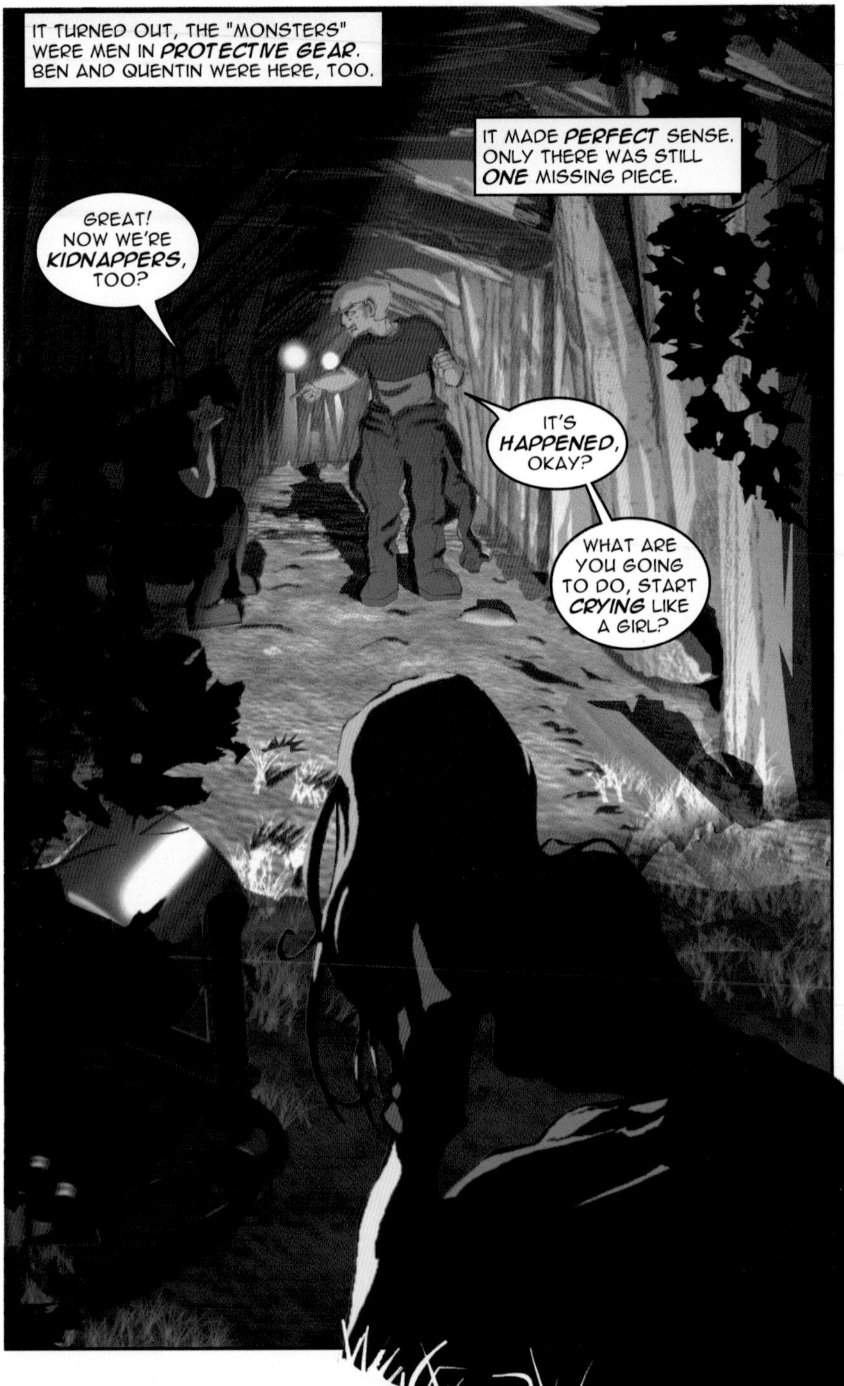
IT TURNED OUT, THE "MONSTERS" WERE MEN IN PROTECTIVE GEAR. BEN AND QUENTIN WERE HERE, TOO.
IT MADE PERFECT SENSE. ONLY THERE WAS STILL ONE MISSING PIECE.
GREAT! NOW WE'RE KIDNAPPERS, TOO?
IT'S HAPPENED, OKAY?
WHAT ARE YOU GOING TO DO, START CRYING LIKE A GIRL?

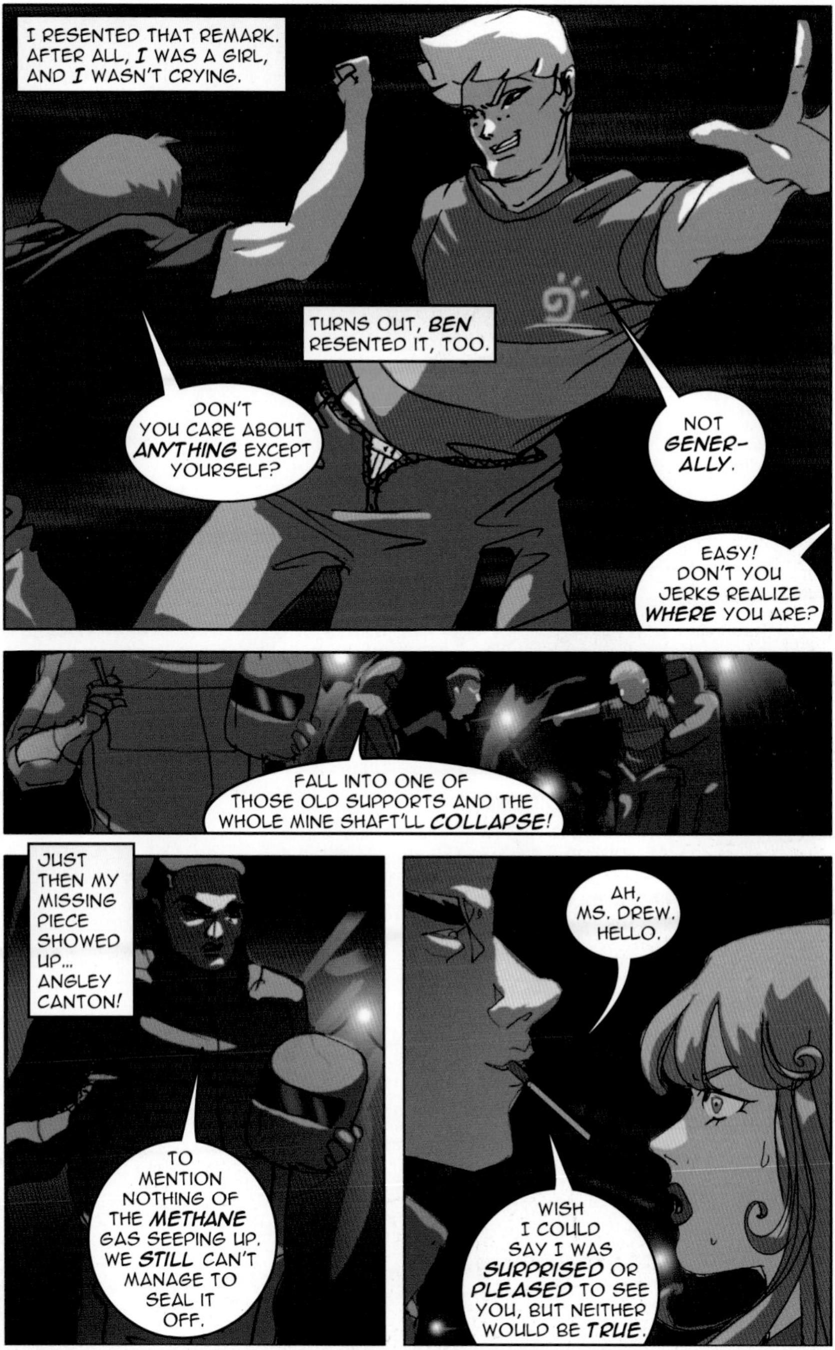
I RESENTED THAT REMARK. AFTER ALL, I WAS A GIRL, AND I WASN'T CRYING.
TURNS OUT, BEN RESENTED IT, TOO.
DON'T YOU CARE ABOUT ANYTHING EXCEPT YOURSELF?
NOT GENER-ALLY.
EASY! DON'T YOU JERKS REALIZE WHERE YOU ARE?
FALL INTO ONE OF THOSE OLD SUPPORTS AND THE WHOLE MINE SHAFT'LL COLLAPSE!
JUST THEN MY MISSING PIECE SHOWED UP... ANGLEY CANTON!
TO MENTION NOTHING OF THE METHANE GAS SEEPING UP. WE STILL CAN'T MANAGE TO SEAL IT OFF.
AH, MS. DREW. HELLO.
WISH I COULD SAY I WAS SURPRISED OR PLEASED TO SEE YOU, BUT NEITHER WOULD BE TRUE.

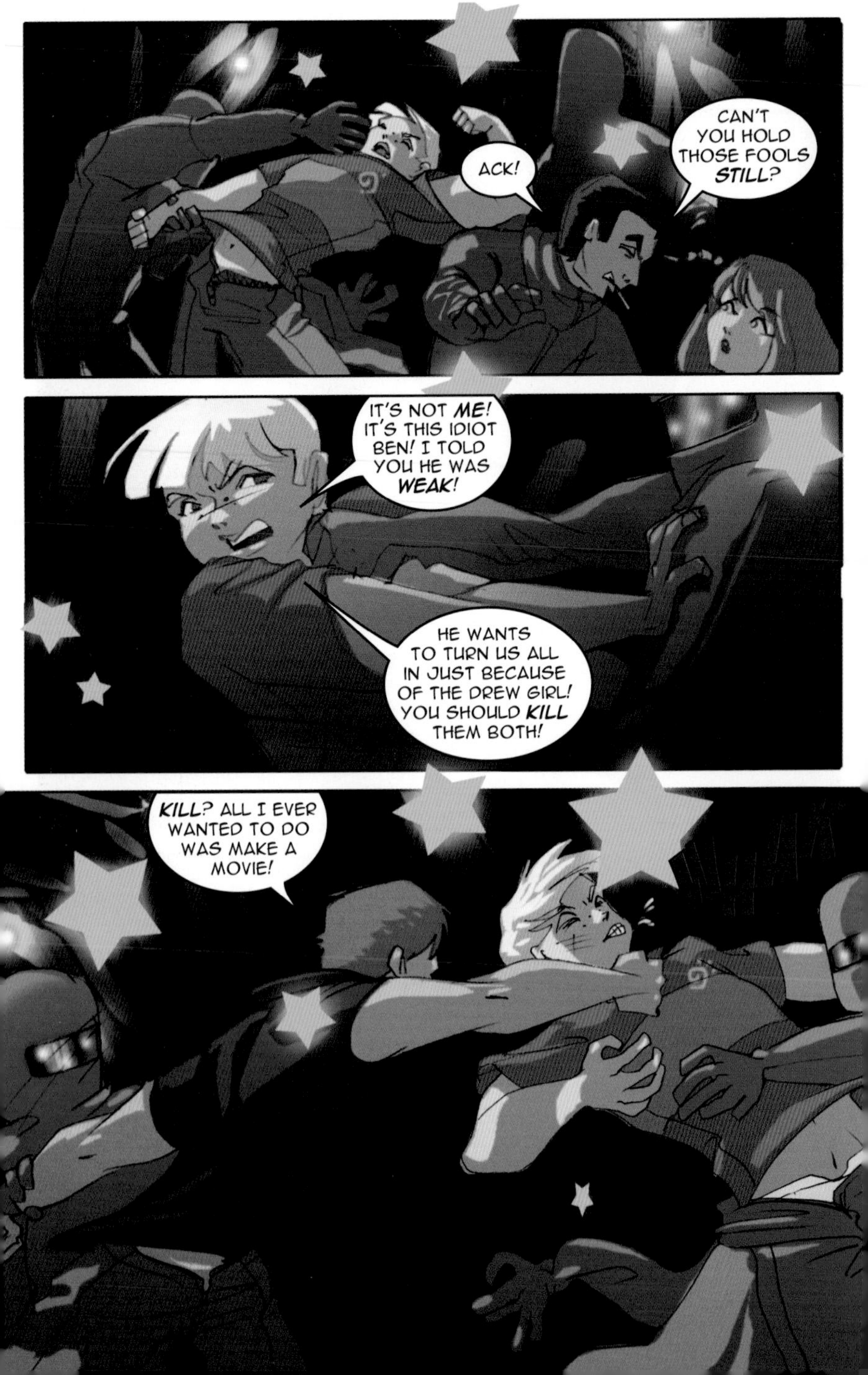
ACK!
CAN'T YOU HOLD THOSE FOOLS STILL?
IT'S NOT ME! IT'S THIS IDIOT BEN! I TOLD YOU HE WAS WEAK!
HE WANTS TO TURN US ALL IN JUST BECAUSE OF THE DREW GIRL! YOU SHOULD KILL THEM BOTH!
KILL? ALL I EVER WANTED TO DO WAS MAKE A MOVIE!

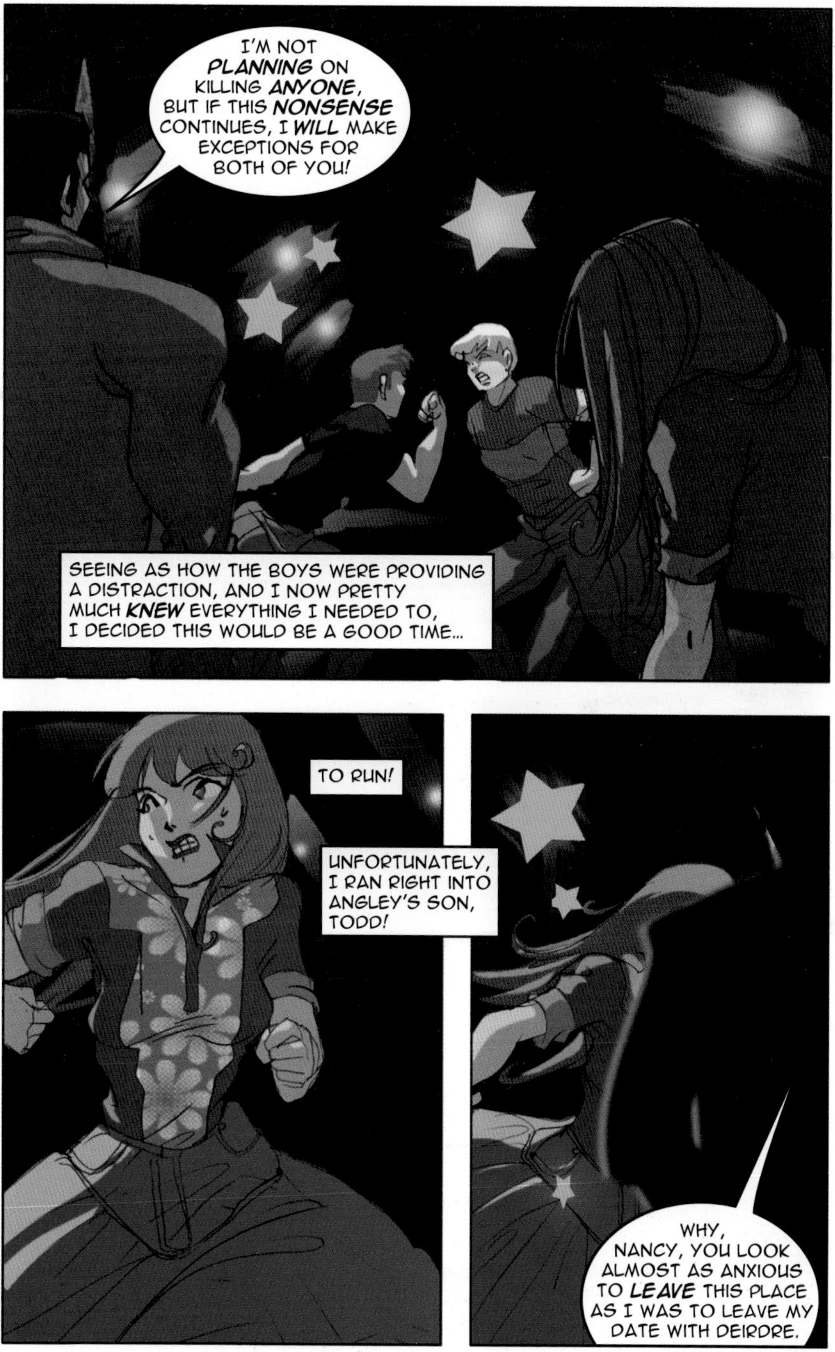
I'M NOT PLANNING ON KILLING ANYONE, BUT IF THIS NONSENSE CONTINUES, I WILL MAKE EXCEPTIONS FOR BOTH OF YOU!
SEEING AS HOW THE BOYS WERE PROVIDING A DISTRACTION, AND I NOW PRETTY MUCH KNEW EVERYTHING I NEEDED TO, I DECIDED THIS WOULD BE A GOOD TIME...
TO RUN!
UNFORTUNATELY, I RAN RIGHT INTO ANGLEY'S SON, TODD!
WHY, NANCY, YOU LOOK ALMOST AS ANXIOUS TO LEAVE THIS PLACE AS I WAS TO LEAVE MY DATE WITH DEIRDRE.

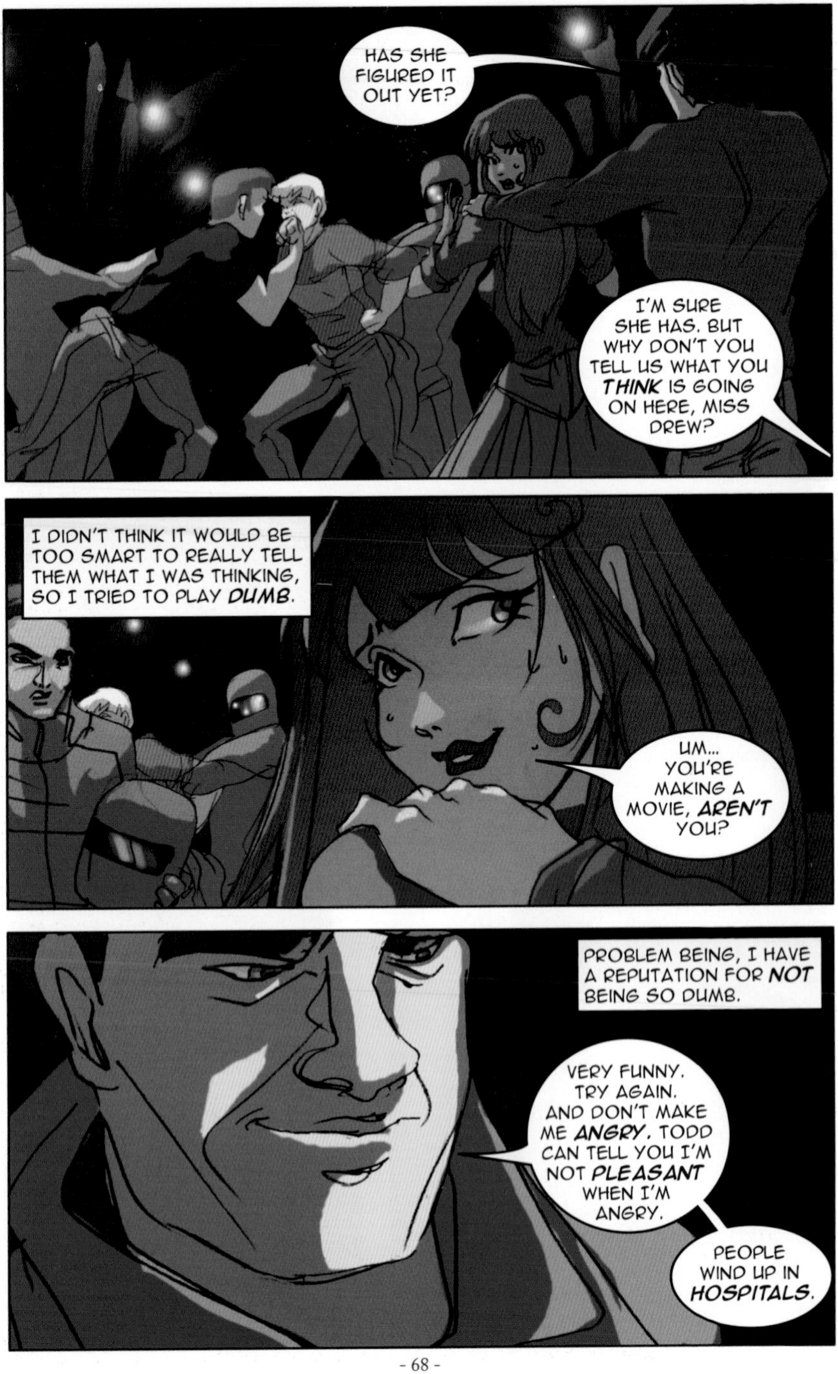
HAS SHE FIGURED IT OUT YET?
I'M SURE SHE HAS. BUT WHY DON'T YOU TELL US WHAT YOU *THINK* IS GOING ON HERE, MISS DREW?
I DIDN'T THINK IT WOULD BE TOO SMART TO REALLY TELL THEM WHAT I WAS THINKING, SO I TRIED TO PLAY *DUMB*.
UM... YOU'RE MAKING A MOVIE, *AREN'T* YOU?
PROBLEM BEING, I HAVE A REPUTATION FOR *NOT* BEING SO DUMB.
VERY FUNNY. TRY AGAIN. AND DON'T MAKE ME *ANGRY*. TODD CAN TELL YOU I'M NOT *PLEASANT* WHEN I'M ANGRY.
PEOPLE WIND UP IN *HOSPITALS*.

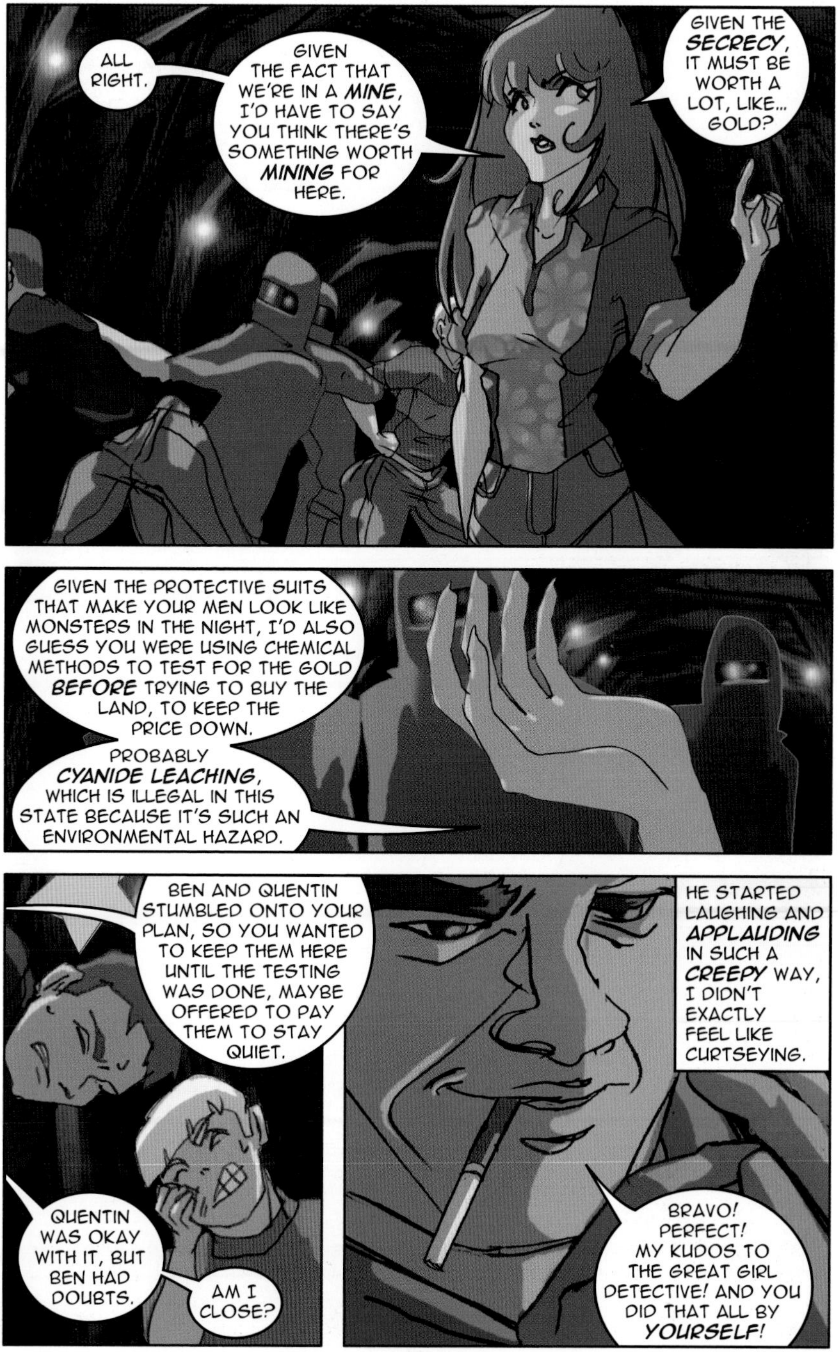
ALL RIGHT.
GIVEN THE FACT THAT WE'RE IN A MINE, I'D HAVE TO SAY YOU THINK THERE'S SOMETHING WORTH MINING FOR HERE.
GIVEN THE SECRECY, IT MUST BE WORTH A LOT, LIKE... GOLD?
GIVEN THE PROTECTIVE SUITS THAT MAKE YOUR MEN LOOK LIKE MONSTERS IN THE NIGHT, I'D ALSO GUESS YOU WERE USING CHEMICAL METHODS TO TEST FOR THE GOLD BEFORE TRYING TO BUY THE LAND, TO KEEP THE PRICE DOWN.
PROBABLY CYANIDE LEACHING, WHICH IS ILLEGAL IN THIS STATE BECAUSE IT'S SUCH AN ENVIRONMENTAL HAZARD.
BEN AND QUENTIN STUMBLED ONTO YOUR PLAN, SO YOU WANTED TO KEEP THEM HERE UNTIL THE TESTING WAS DONE, MAYBE OFFERED TO PAY THEM TO STAY QUIET.
QUENTIN WAS OKAY WITH IT, BUT BEN HAD DOUBTS.
AM I CLOSE?
HE STARTED LAUGHING AND APPLAUDING IN SUCH A CREEPY WAY, I DIDN'T EXACTLY FEEL LIKE CURTSEYING.
BRAVO! PERFECT! MY KUDOS TO THE GREAT GIRL DETECTIVE! AND YOU DID THAT ALL BY YOURSELF!

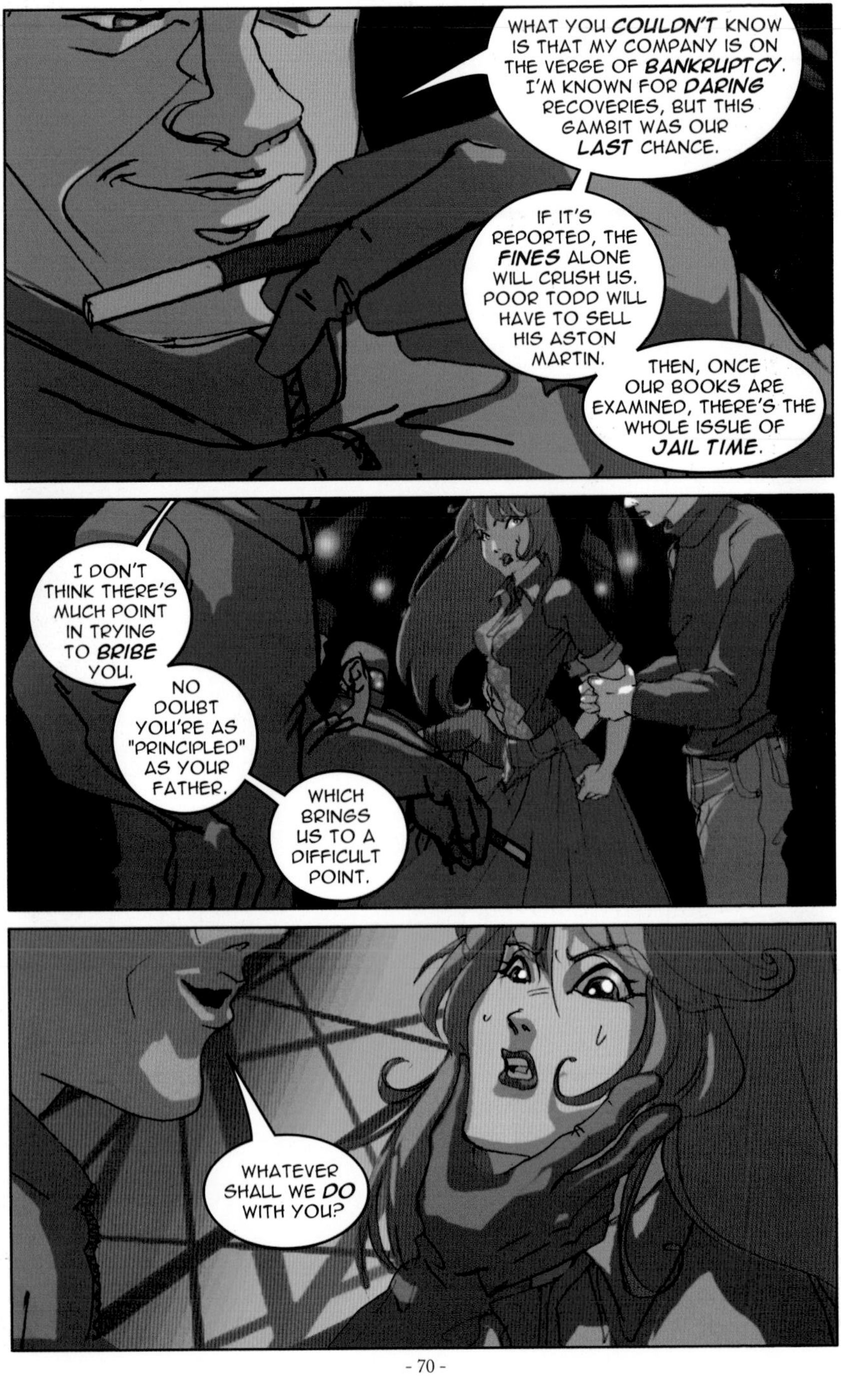
WHAT YOU COULDN'T KNOW IS THAT MY COMPANY IS ON THE VERGE OF BANKRUPTCY. I'M KNOWN FOR DARING RECOVERIES, BUT THIS GAMBIT WAS OUR LAST CHANCE.
IF IT'S REPORTED, THE FINES ALONE WILL CRUSH US. POOR TODD WILL HAVE TO SELL HIS ASTON MARTIN.
THEN, ONCE OUR BOOKS ARE EXAMINED, THERE'S THE WHOLE ISSUE OF JAIL TIME.
I DON'T THINK THERE'S MUCH POINT IN TRYING TO BRIBE YOU.
NO DOUBT YOU'RE AS "PRINCIPLED" AS YOUR FATHER.
WHICH BRINGS US TO A DIFFICULT POINT.
WHATEVER SHALL WE DO WITH YOU?

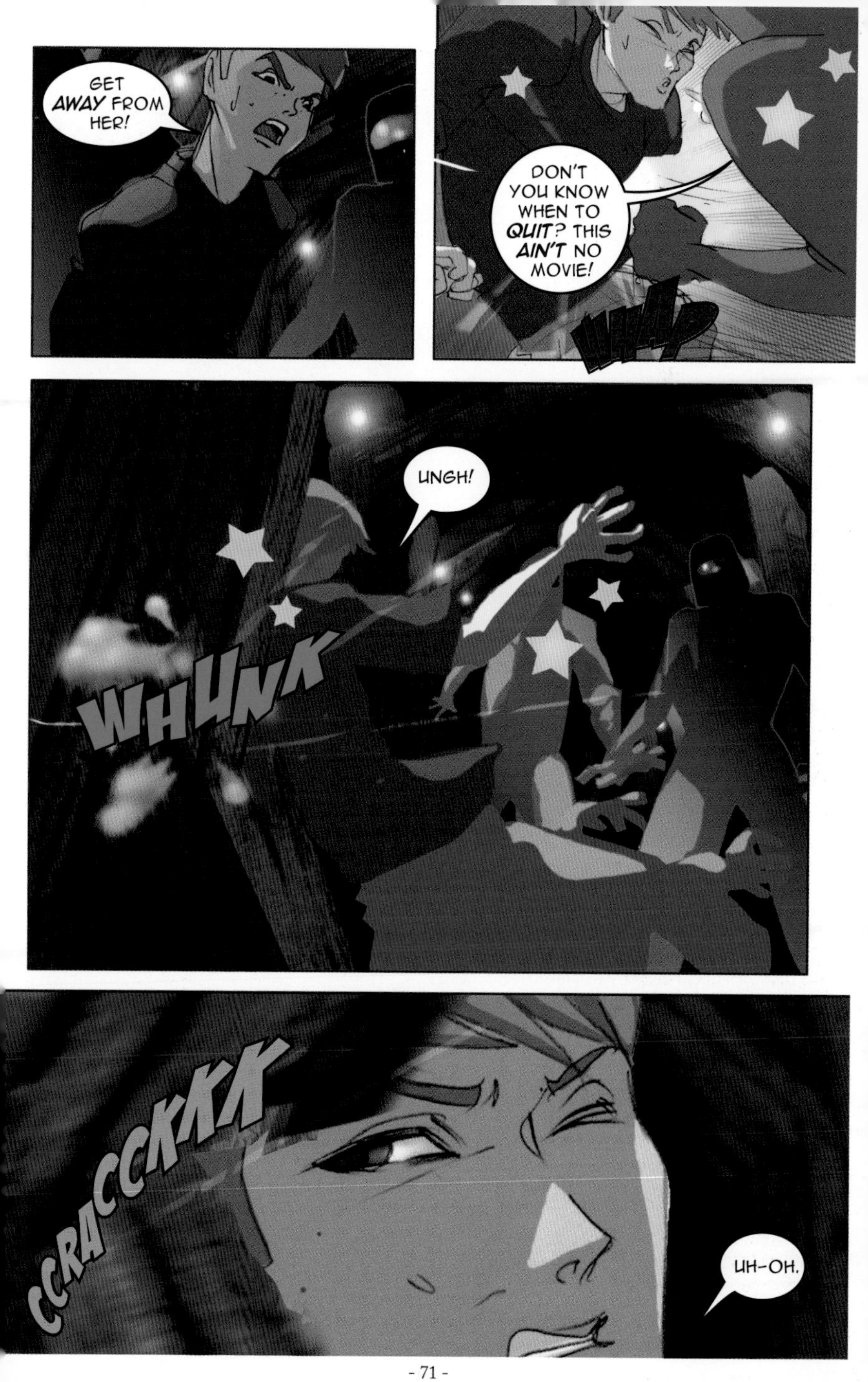
GET AWAY FROM HER!
DON'T YOU KNOW WHEN TO QUIT? THIS AIN'T NO MOVIE!
WHAP
UNGH!
WHUNK
CCRACCKKK
UH-OH.

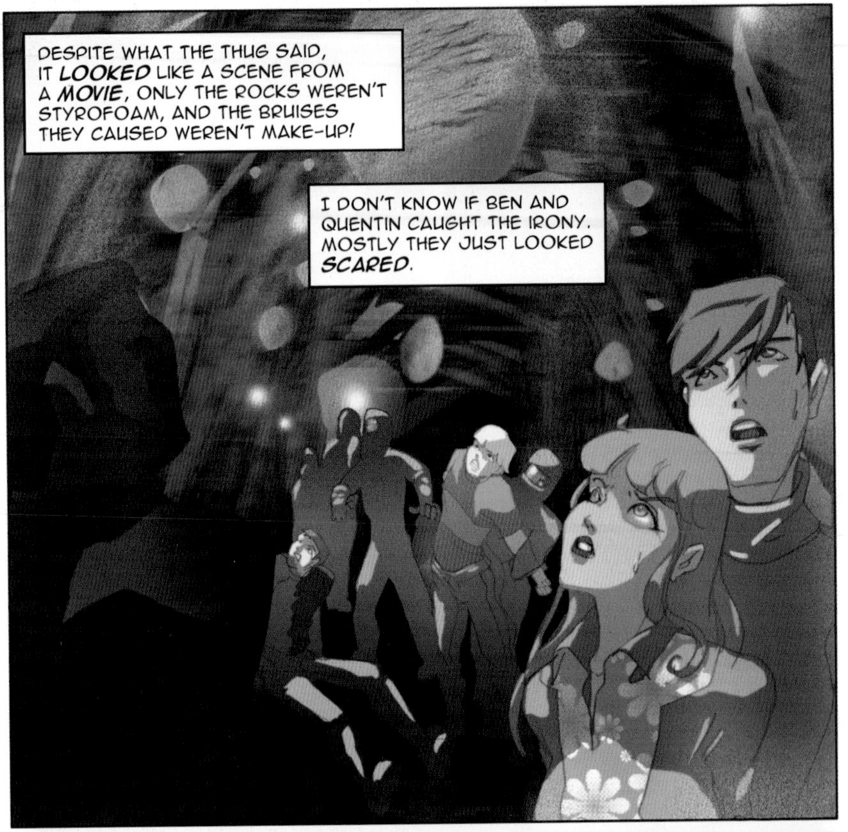
DESPITE WHAT THE THUG SAID, IT LOOKED LIKE A SCENE FROM A MOVIE, ONLY THE ROCKS WEREN'T STYROFOAM, AND THE BRUISES THEY CAUSED WEREN'T MAKE-UP!
I DON'T KNOW IF BEN AND QUENTIN CAUGHT THE IRONY. MOSTLY THEY JUST LOOKED SCARED.

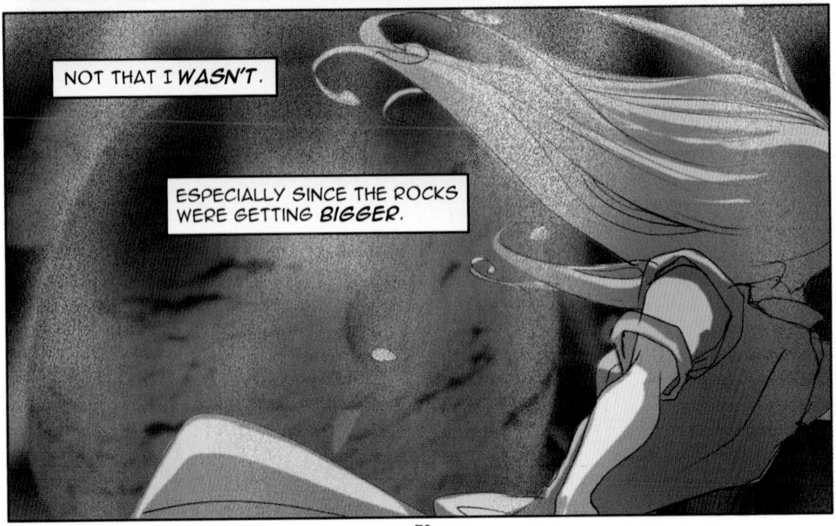
NOT THAT I WASN'T.
ESPECIALLY SINCE THE ROCKS WERE GETTING BIGGER.

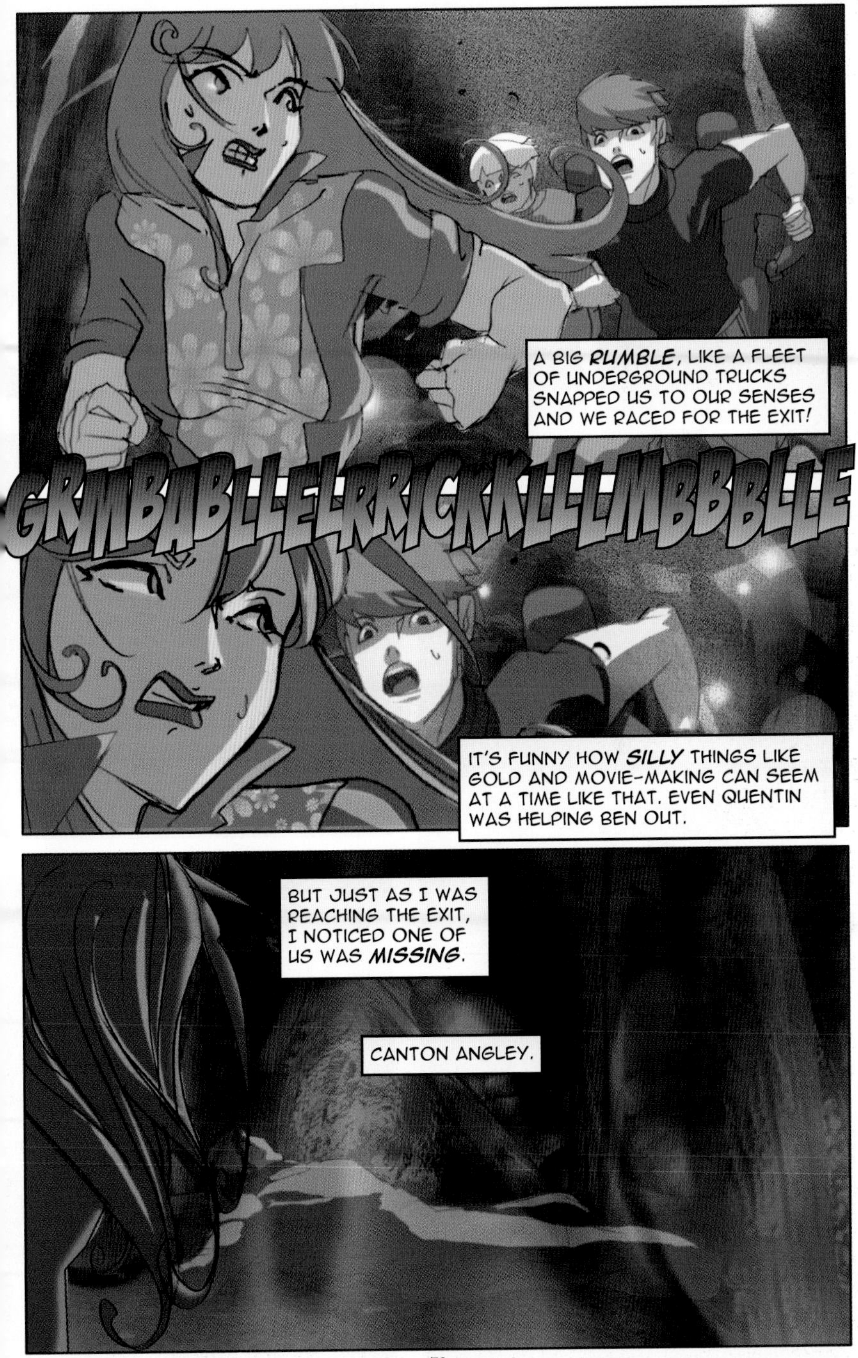
A BIG *RUMBLE*, LIKE A FLEET OF UNDERGROUND TRUCKS SNAPPED US TO OUR SENSES AND WE RACED FOR THE EXIT!
GRMBABLLELRRICKKLLLMBBBLLE
IT'S FUNNY HOW *SILLY* THINGS LIKE GOLD AND MOVIE-MAKING CAN SEEM AT A TIME LIKE THAT. EVEN QUENTIN WAS HELPING BEN OUT.
BUT JUST AS I WAS REACHING THE EXIT, I NOTICED ONE OF US WAS *MISSING*.
CANTON ANGLEY.

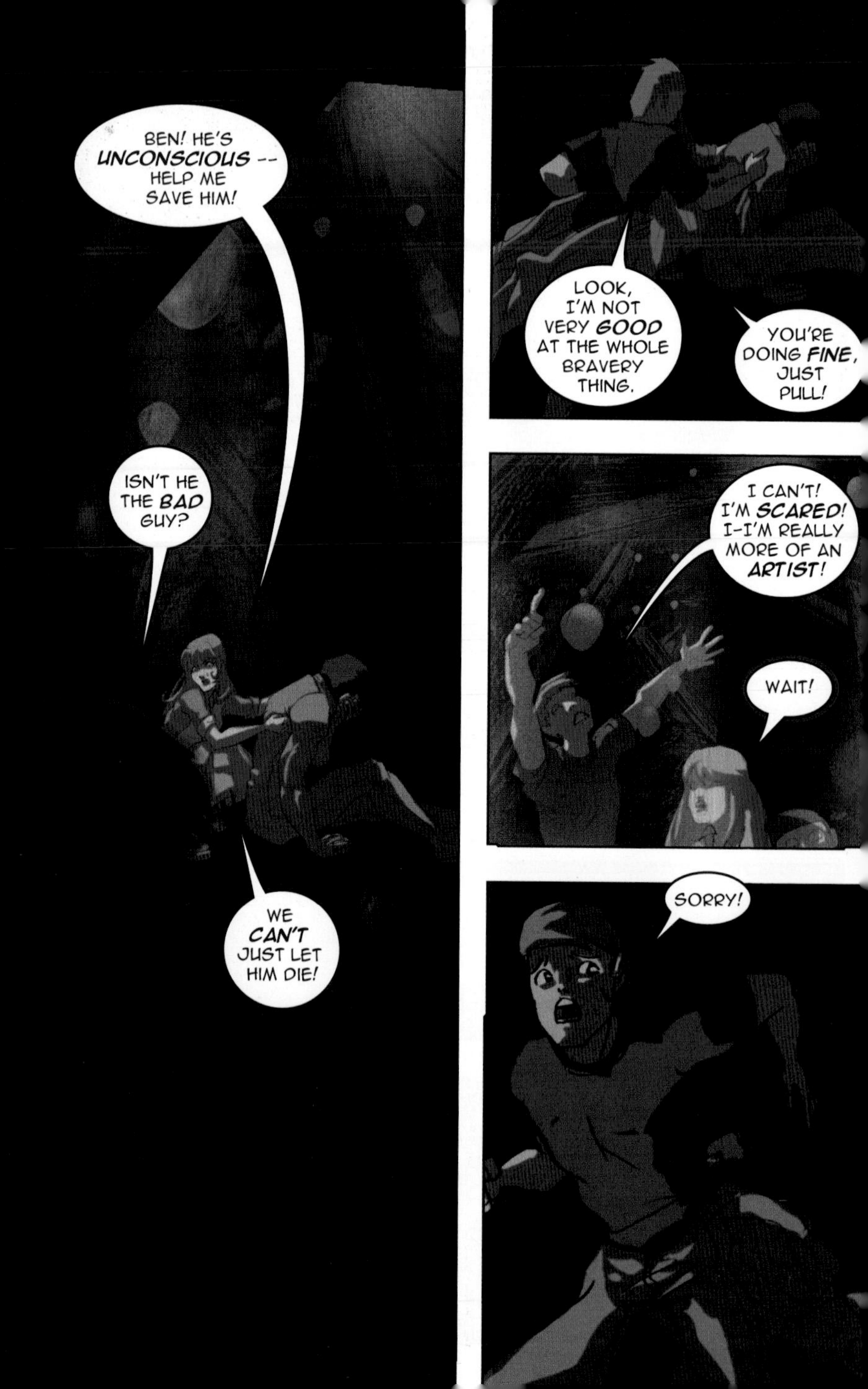
BEN! HE'S UNCONSCIOUS -- HELP ME SAVE HIM!
ISN'T HE THE BAD GUY?
WE CAN'T JUST LET HIM DIE!
LOOK, I'M NOT VERY GOOD AT THE WHOLE BRAVERY THING.
YOU'RE DOING FINE, JUST PULL!
I CAN'T! I'M SCARED! I-I'M REALLY MORE OF AN ARTIST!
WAIT!
SORRY!

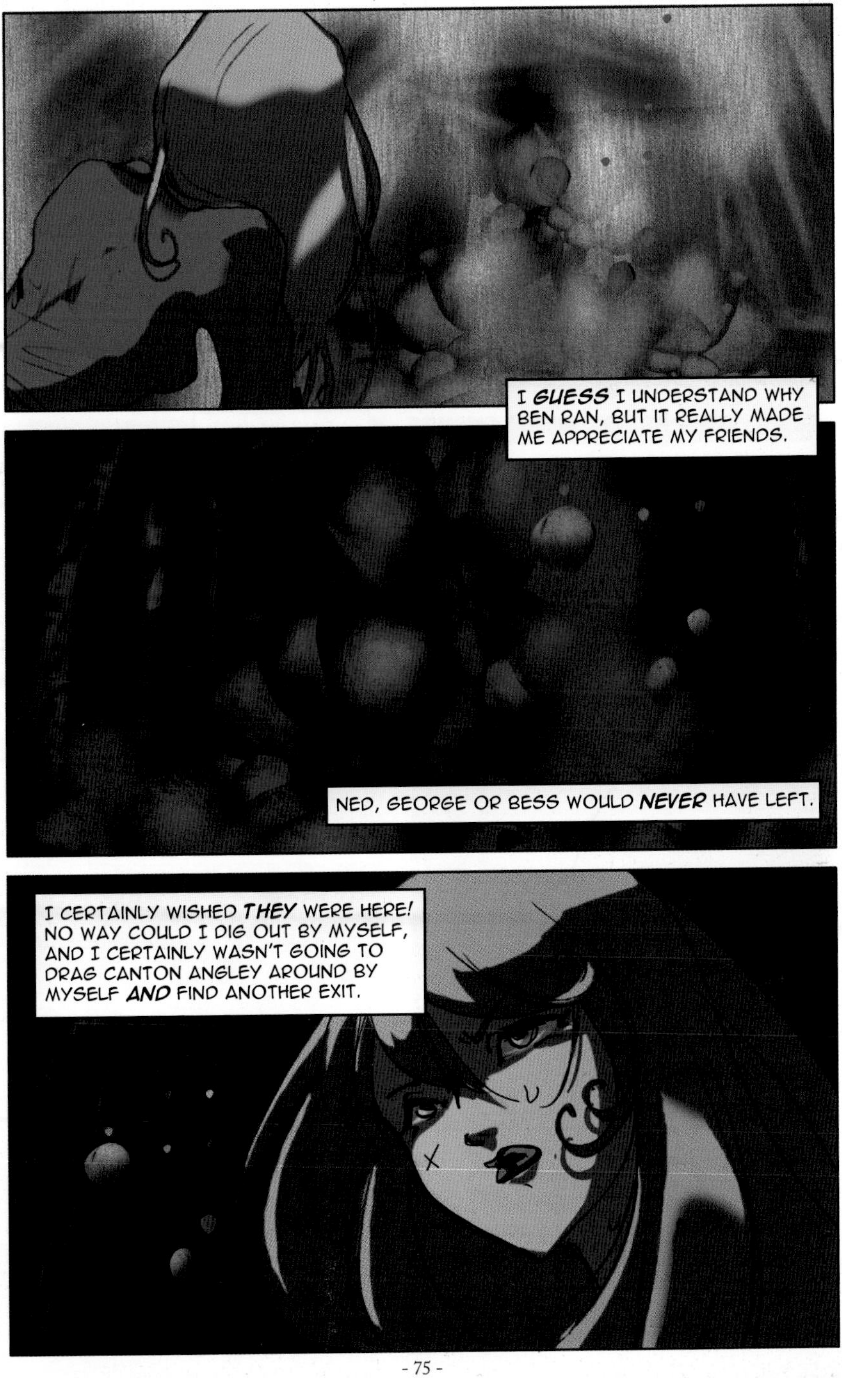
I GUESS I UNDERSTAND WHY BEN RAN, BUT IT REALLY MADE ME APPRECIATE MY FRIENDS.
NED, GEORGE OR BESS WOULD NEVER HAVE LEFT.
I CERTAINLY WISHED THEY WERE HERE! NO WAY COULD I DIG OUT BY MYSELF, AND I CERTAINLY WASN'T GOING TO DRAG CANTON ANGLEY AROUND BY MYSELF AND FIND ANOTHER EXIT.

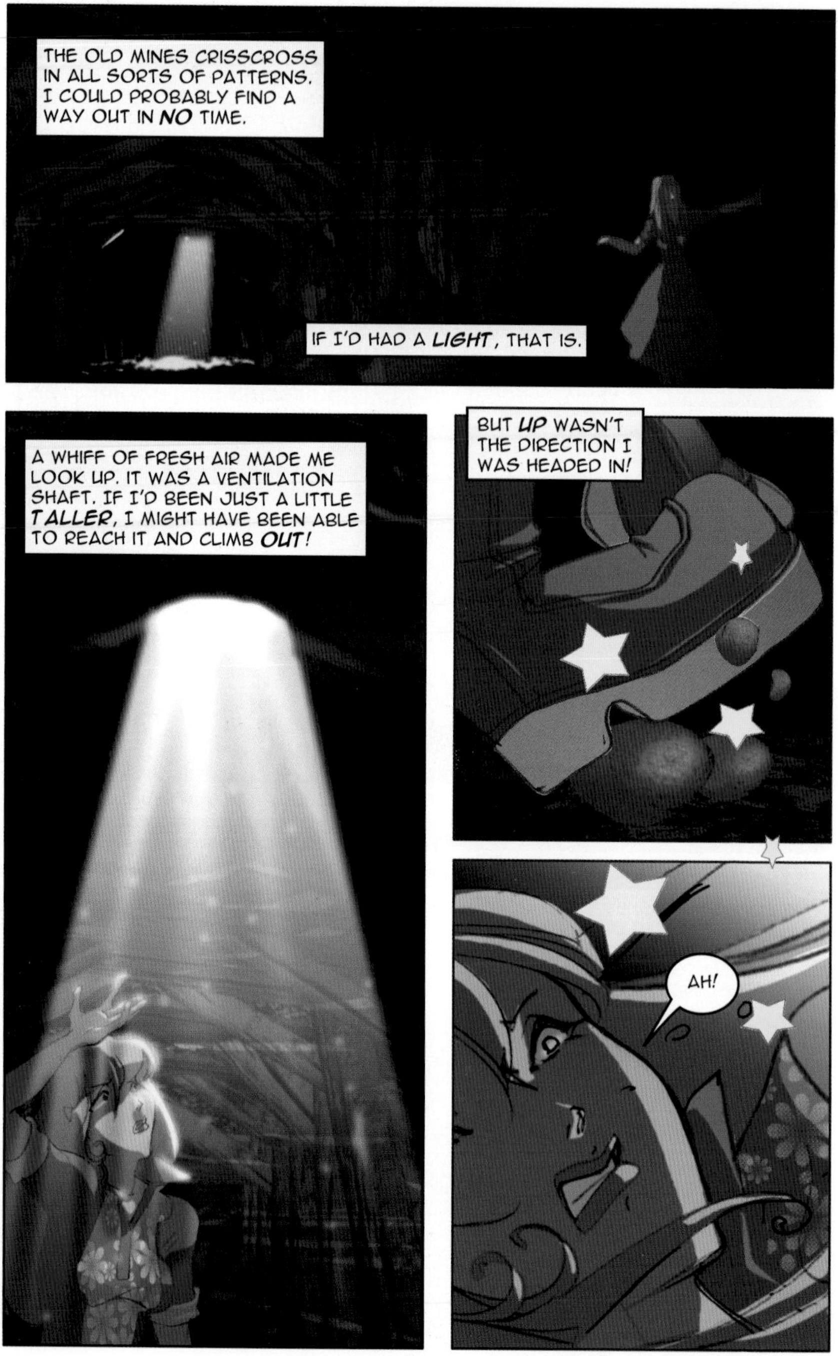
THE OLD MINES CRISSCROSS IN ALL SORTS OF PATTERNS. I COULD PROBABLY FIND A WAY OUT IN NO TIME.
IF I'D HAD A LIGHT, THAT IS.
A WHIFF OF FRESH AIR MADE ME LOOK UP. IT WAS A VENTILATION SHAFT. IF I'D BEEN JUST A LITTLE TALLER, I MIGHT HAVE BEEN ABLE TO REACH IT AND CLIMB OUT!
BUT UP WASN'T THE DIRECTION I WAS HEADED IN!
AH!

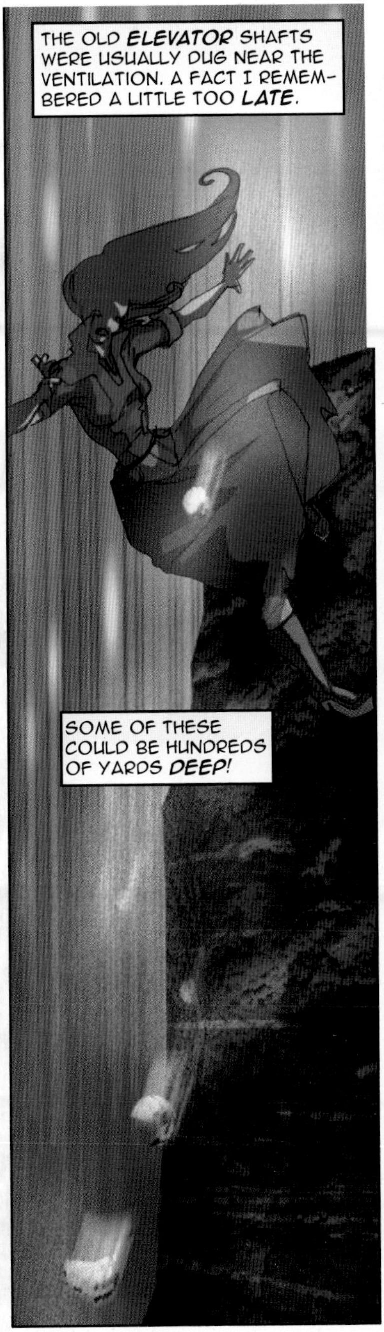
THE OLD ELEVATOR SHAFTS WERE USUALLY DUG NEAR THE VENTILATION. A FACT I REMEMBERED A LITTLE TOO LATE.
SOME OF THESE COULD BE HUNDREDS OF YARDS DEEP!

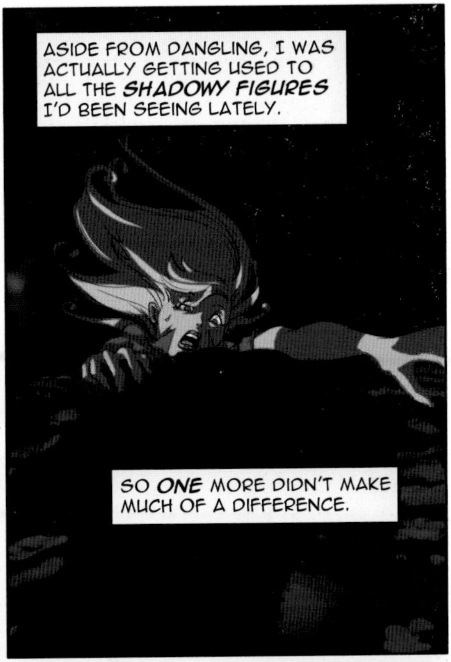
ASIDE FROM DANGLING, I WAS ACTUALLY GETTING USED TO ALL THE SHADOWY FIGURES I'D BEEN SEEING LATELY.
SO ONE MORE DIDN'T MAKE MUCH OF A DIFFERENCE.

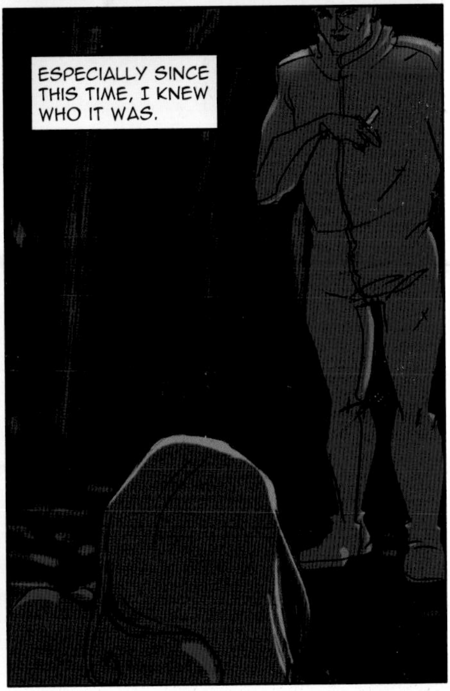
ESPECIALLY SINCE THIS TIME, I KNEW WHO IT WAS.

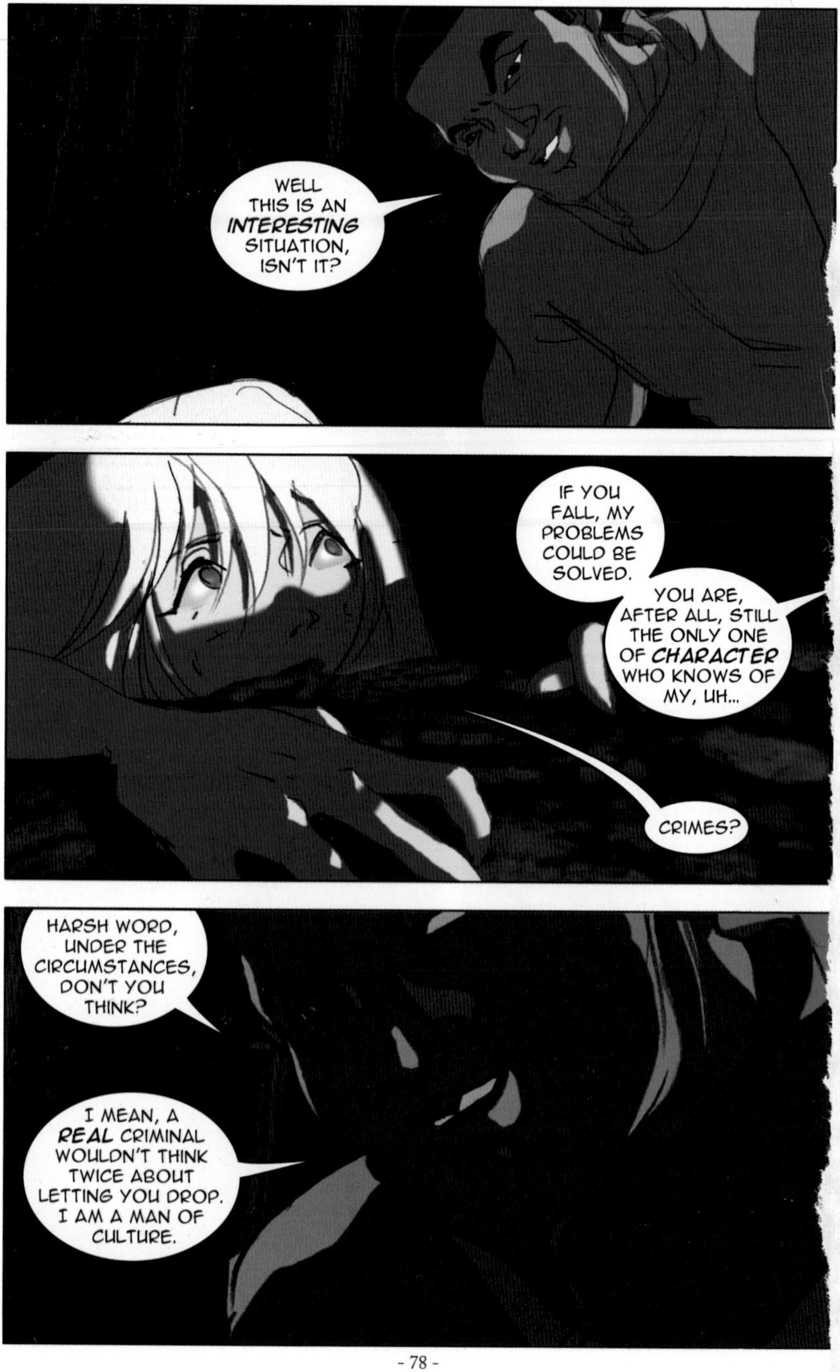
WELL THIS IS AN INTERESTING SITUATION, ISN'T IT?
IF YOU FALL, MY PROBLEMS COULD BE SOLVED.
YOU ARE, AFTER ALL, STILL THE ONLY ONE OF CHARACTER WHO KNOWS OF MY, UH...
CRIMES?
HARSH WORD, UNDER THE CIRCUMSTANCES, DON'T YOU THINK?
I MEAN, A REAL CRIMINAL WOULDN'T THINK TWICE ABOUT LETTING YOU DROP. I AM A MAN OF CULTURE.

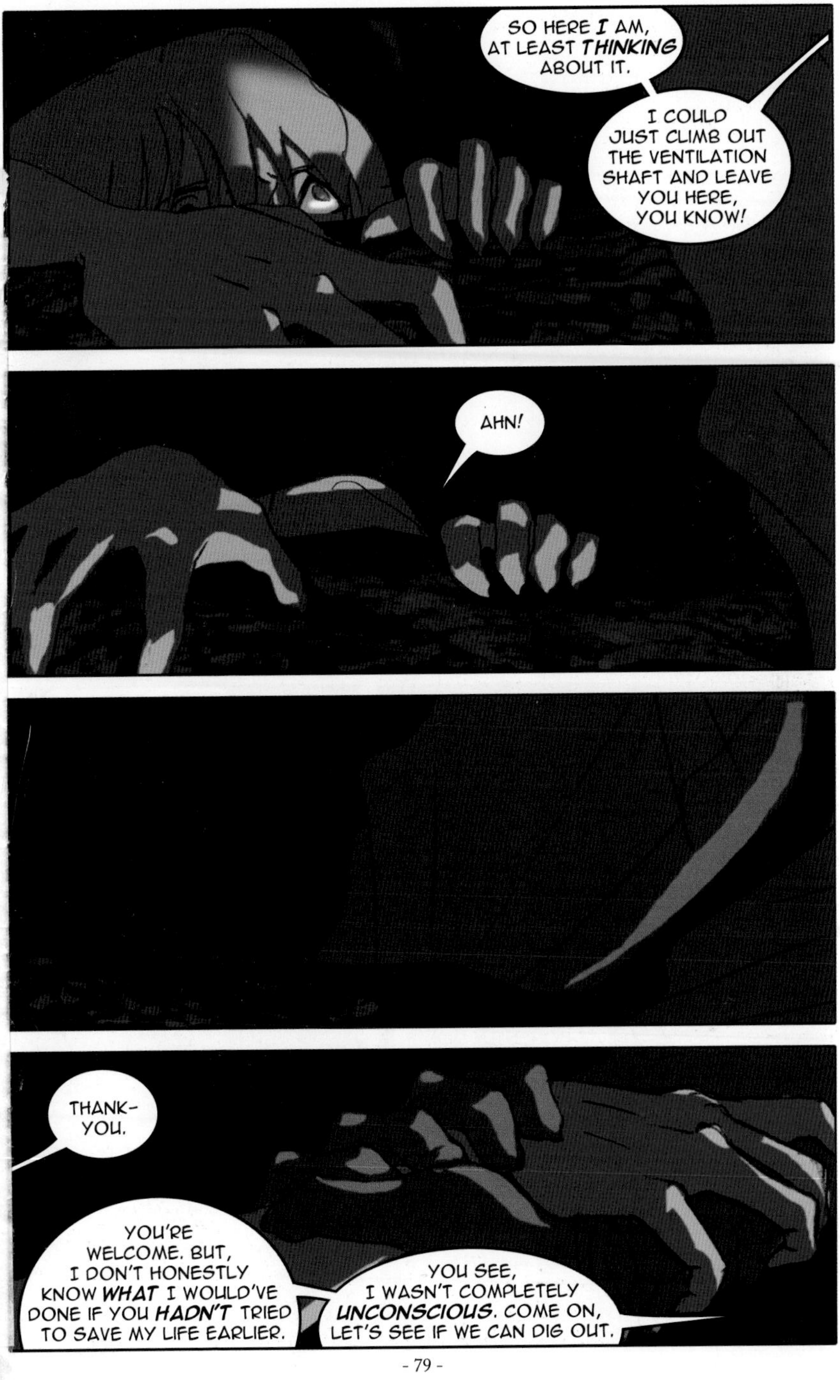
SO HERE *I* AM, AT LEAST *THINKING* ABOUT IT.
I COULD JUST CLIMB OUT THE VENTILATION SHAFT AND LEAVE YOU HERE, YOU KNOW!
AHN!
THANK-YOU.
YOU'RE WELCOME. BUT, I DON'T HONESTLY KNOW *WHAT* I WOULD'VE DONE IF YOU *HADN'T* TRIED TO SAVE MY LIFE EARLIER.
YOU SEE, I WASN'T COMPLETELY *UNCONSCIOUS*. COME ON, LET'S SEE IF WE CAN DIG OUT.

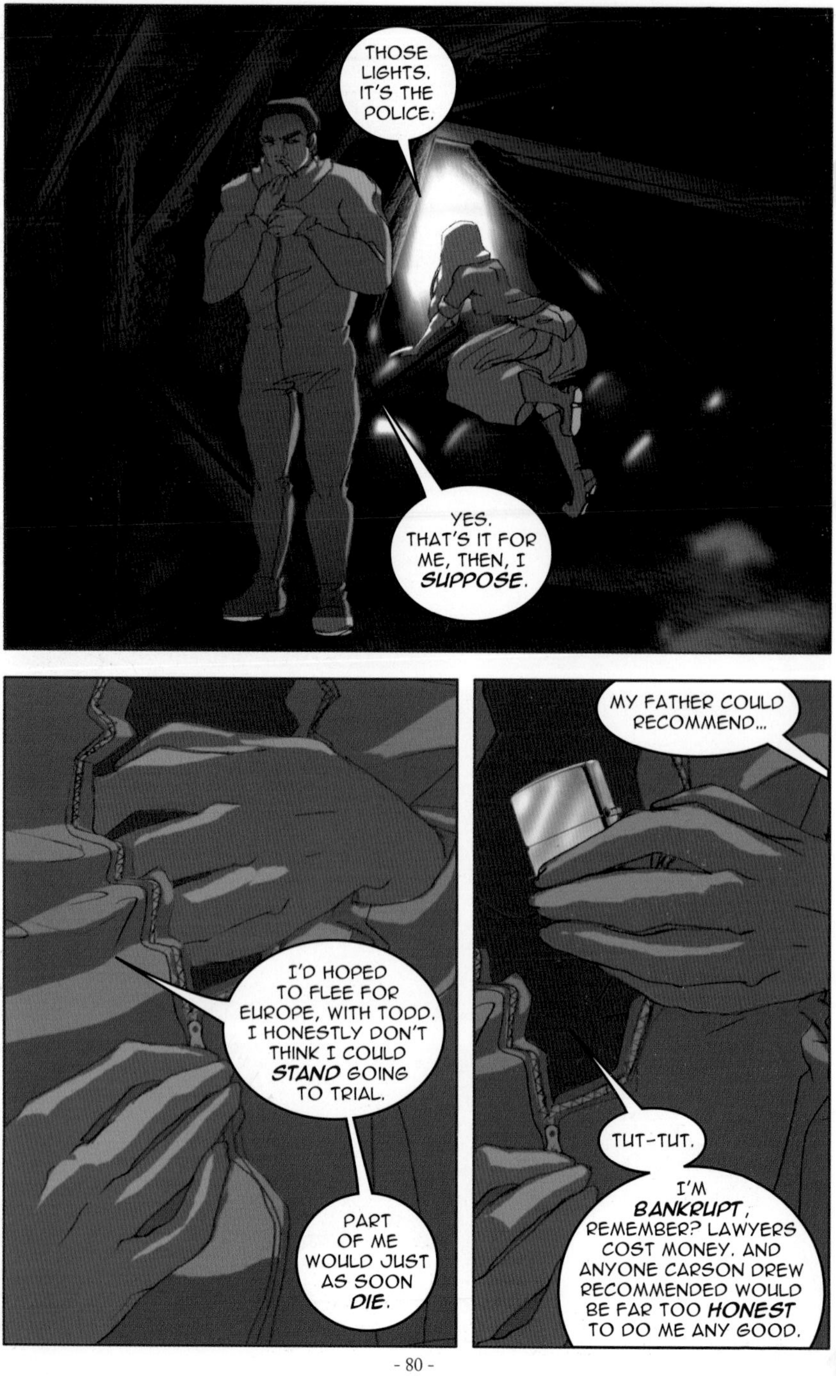
THOSE LIGHTS. IT'S THE POLICE.
YES. THAT'S IT FOR ME, THEN, I SUPPOSE.
I'D HOPED TO FLEE FOR EUROPE, WITH TODD. I HONESTLY DON'T THINK I COULD STAND GOING TO TRIAL.
PART OF ME WOULD JUST AS SOON DIE.
MY FATHER COULD RECOMMEND...
TUT-TUT.
I'M BANKRUPT, REMEMBER? LAWYERS COST MONEY. AND ANYONE CARSON DREW RECOMMENDED WOULD BE FAR TOO HONEST TO DO ME ANY GOOD.

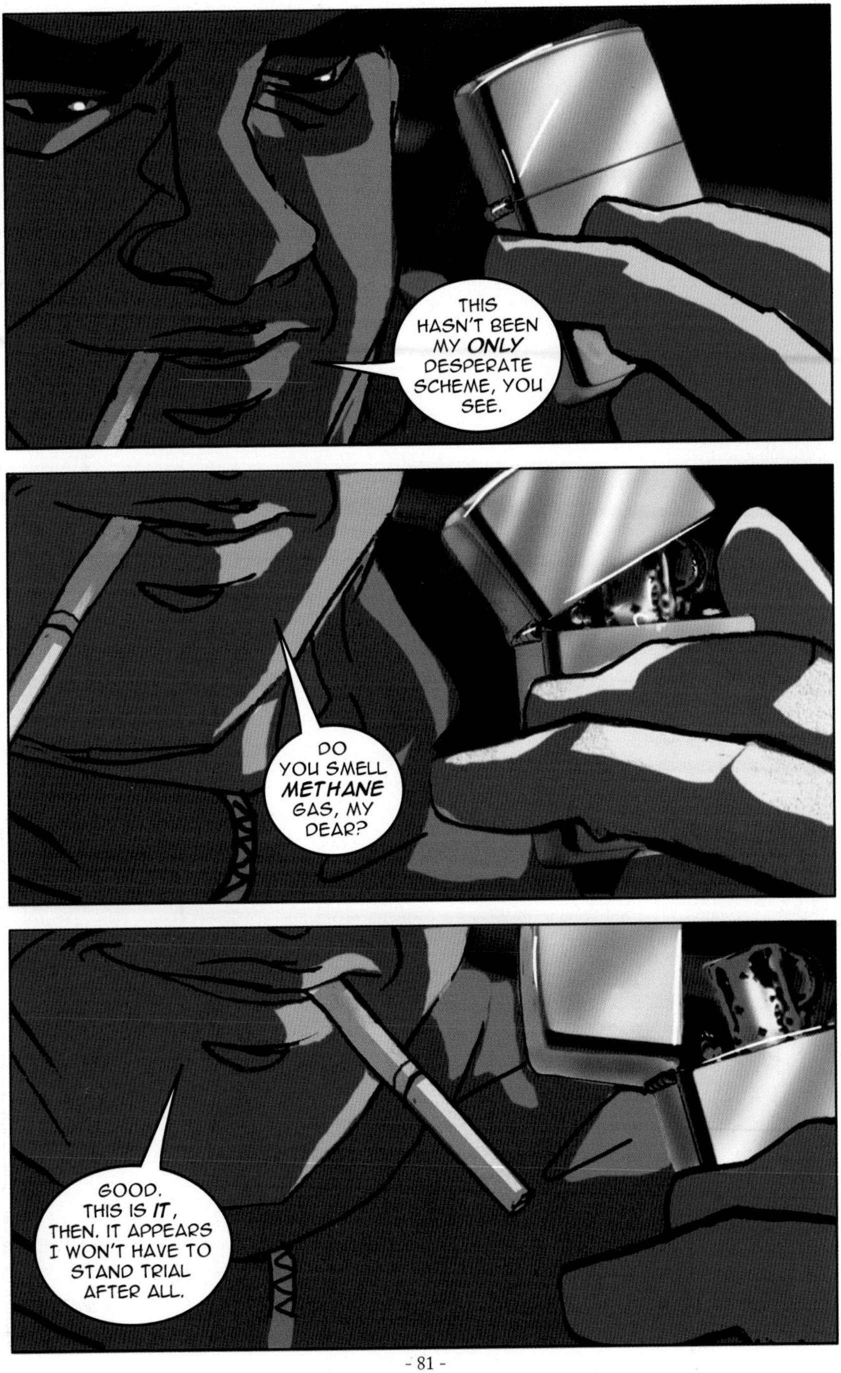
THIS HASN'T BEEN MY ONLY DESPERATE SCHEME, YOU SEE.
DO YOU SMELL METHANE GAS, MY DEAR?
GOOD. THIS IS IT, THEN. IT APPEARS I WON'T HAVE TO STAND TRIAL AFTER ALL.

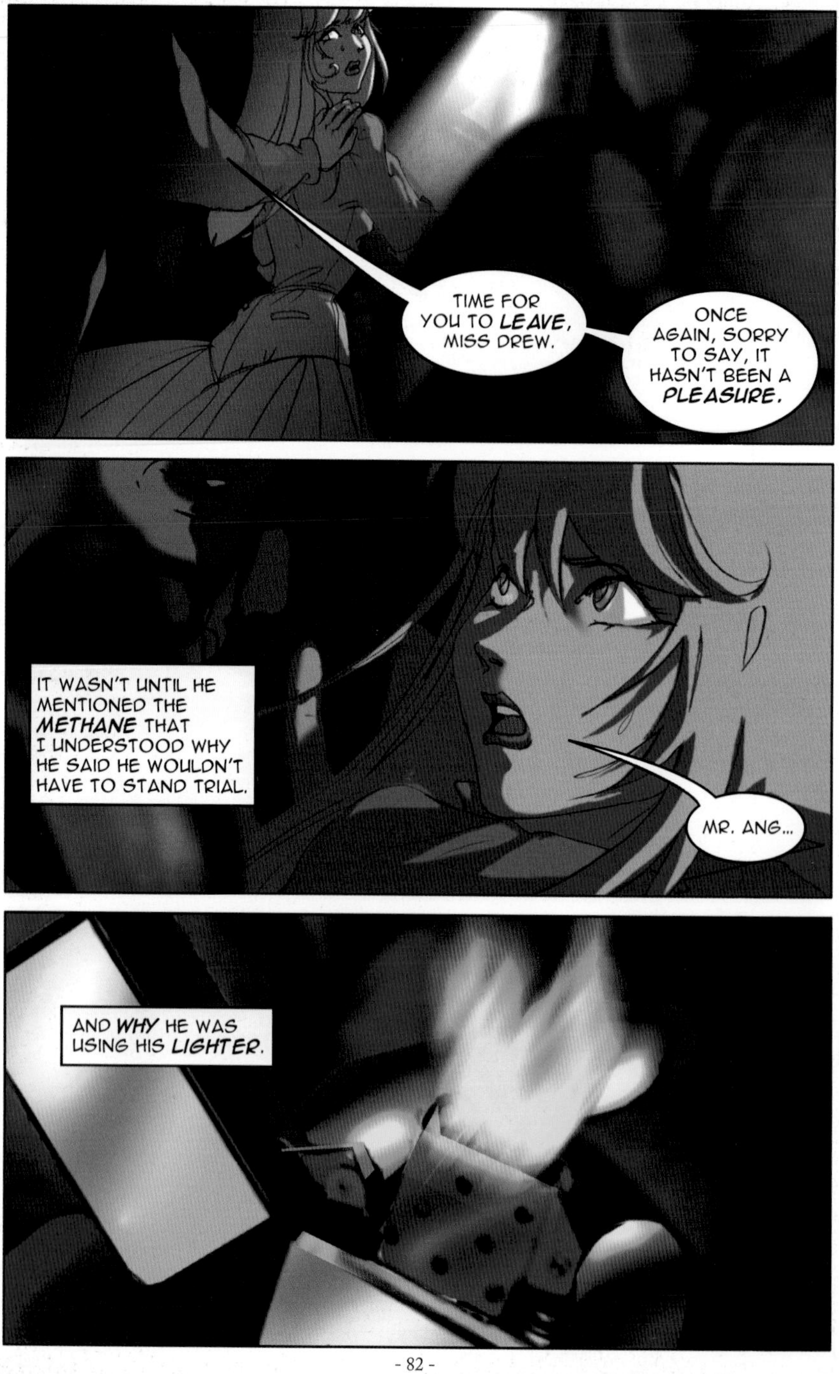
TIME FOR YOU TO LEAVE, MISS DREW.
ONCE AGAIN, SORRY TO SAY, IT HASN'T BEEN A PLEASURE.
IT WASN'T UNTIL HE MENTIONED THE METHANE THAT I UNDERSTOOD WHY HE SAID HE WOULDN'T HAVE TO STAND TRIAL.
MR. ANG...
AND WHY HE WAS USING HIS LIGHTER.

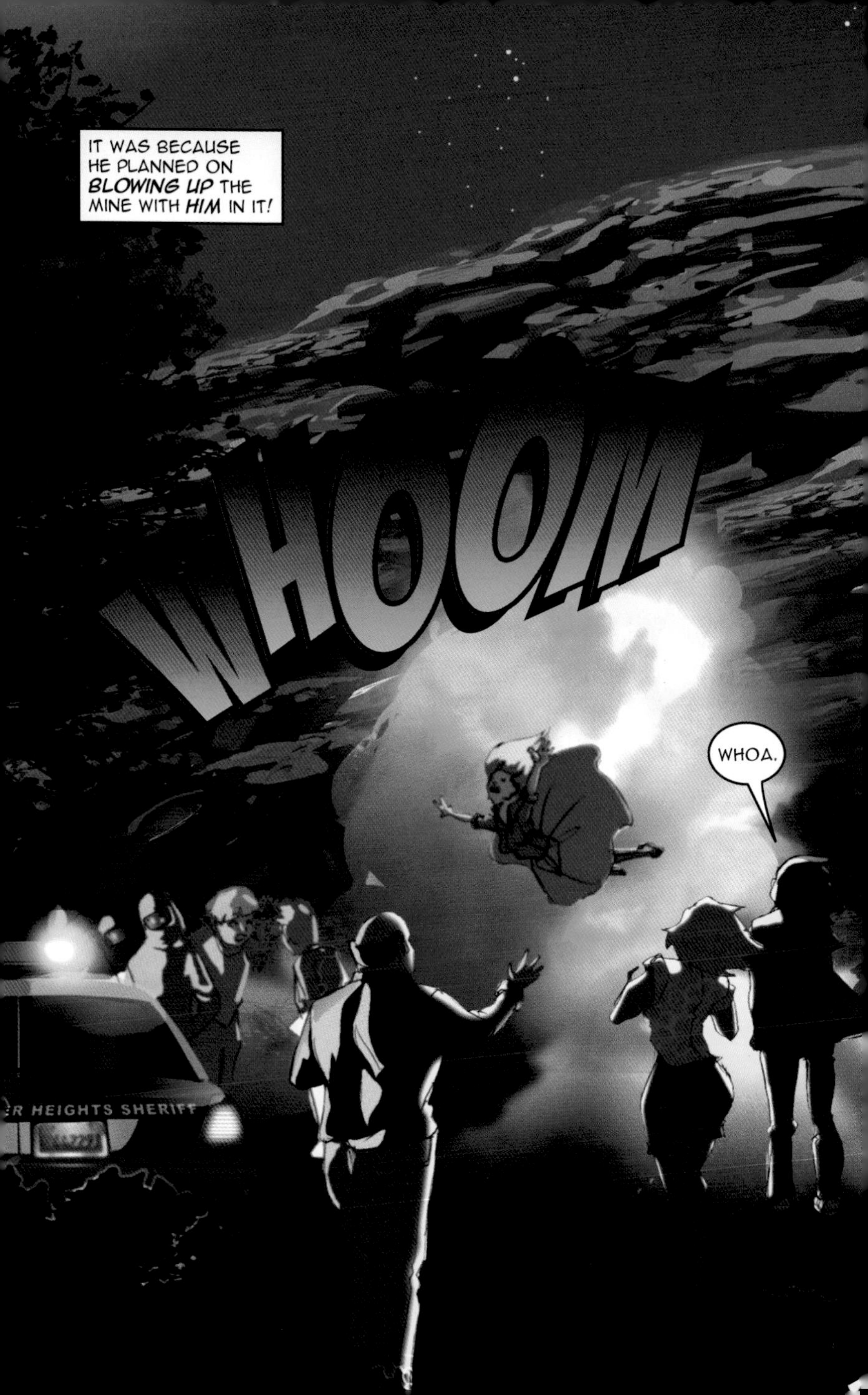
IT WAS BECAUSE HE PLANNED ON BLOWING UP THE MINE WITH HIM IN IT!
WHOOM
WHOA.
R HEIGHTS SHERIFF

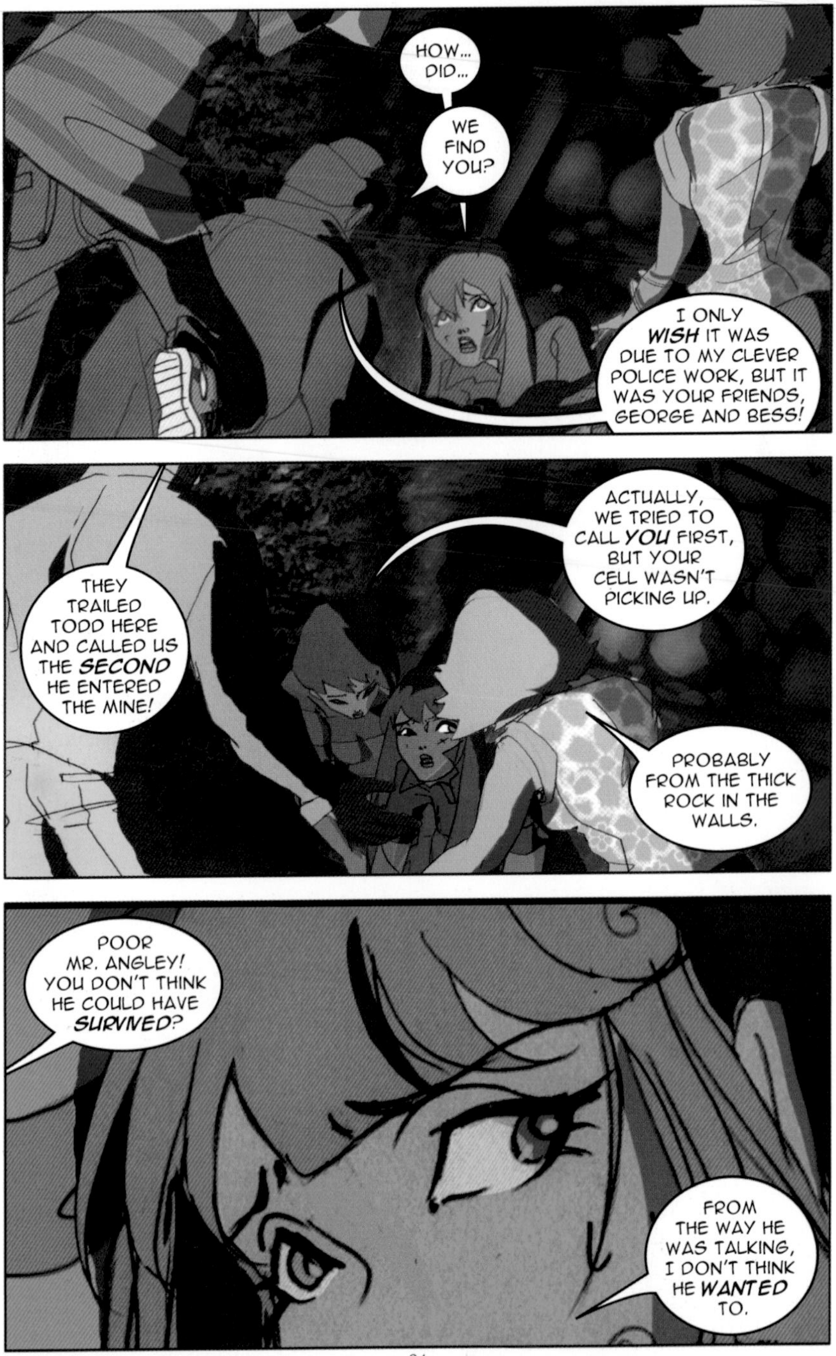
HOW... DID...
WE FIND YOU?
I ONLY WISH IT WAS DUE TO MY CLEVER POLICE WORK, BUT IT WAS YOUR FRIENDS, GEORGE AND BESS!
THEY TRAILED TODD HERE AND CALLED US THE SECOND HE ENTERED THE MINE!
ACTUALLY, WE TRIED TO CALL YOU FIRST, BUT YOUR CELL WASN'T PICKING UP.
PROBABLY FROM THE THICK ROCK IN THE WALLS.
POOR MR. ANGLEY! YOU DON'T THINK HE COULD HAVE SURVIVED?
FROM THE WAY HE WAS TALKING, I DON'T THINK HE WANTED TO.

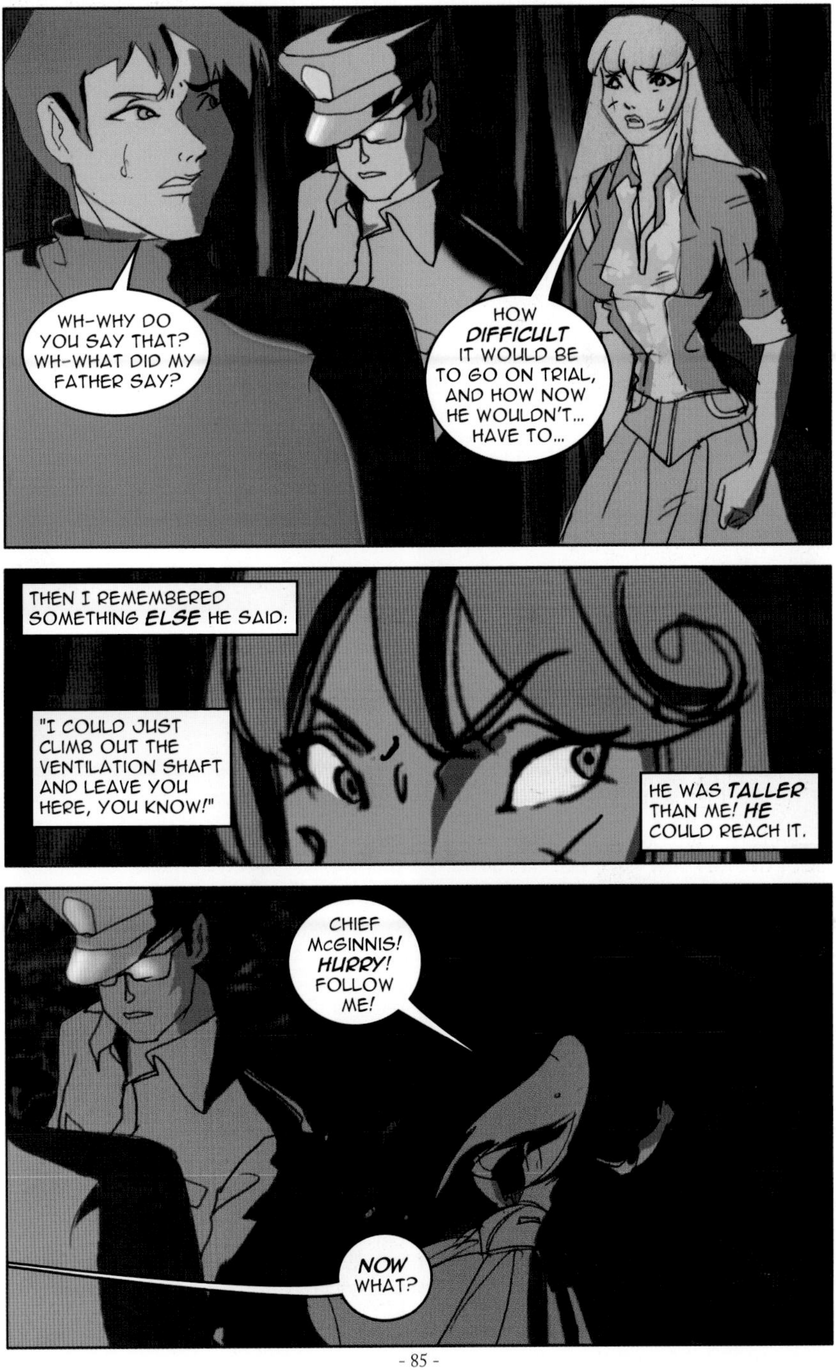
WH-WHY DO YOU SAY THAT? WH-WHAT DID MY FATHER SAY?
HOW *DIFFICULT* IT WOULD BE TO GO ON TRIAL, AND HOW NOW HE WOULDN'T... HAVE TO...
THEN I REMEMBERED SOMETHING *ELSE* HE SAID:
"I COULD JUST CLIMB OUT THE VENTILATION SHAFT AND LEAVE YOU HERE, YOU KNOW!"
HE WAS *TALLER* THAN ME! *HE* COULD REACH IT.
CHIEF McGINNIS! *HURRY*! FOLLOW ME!
NOW WHAT?

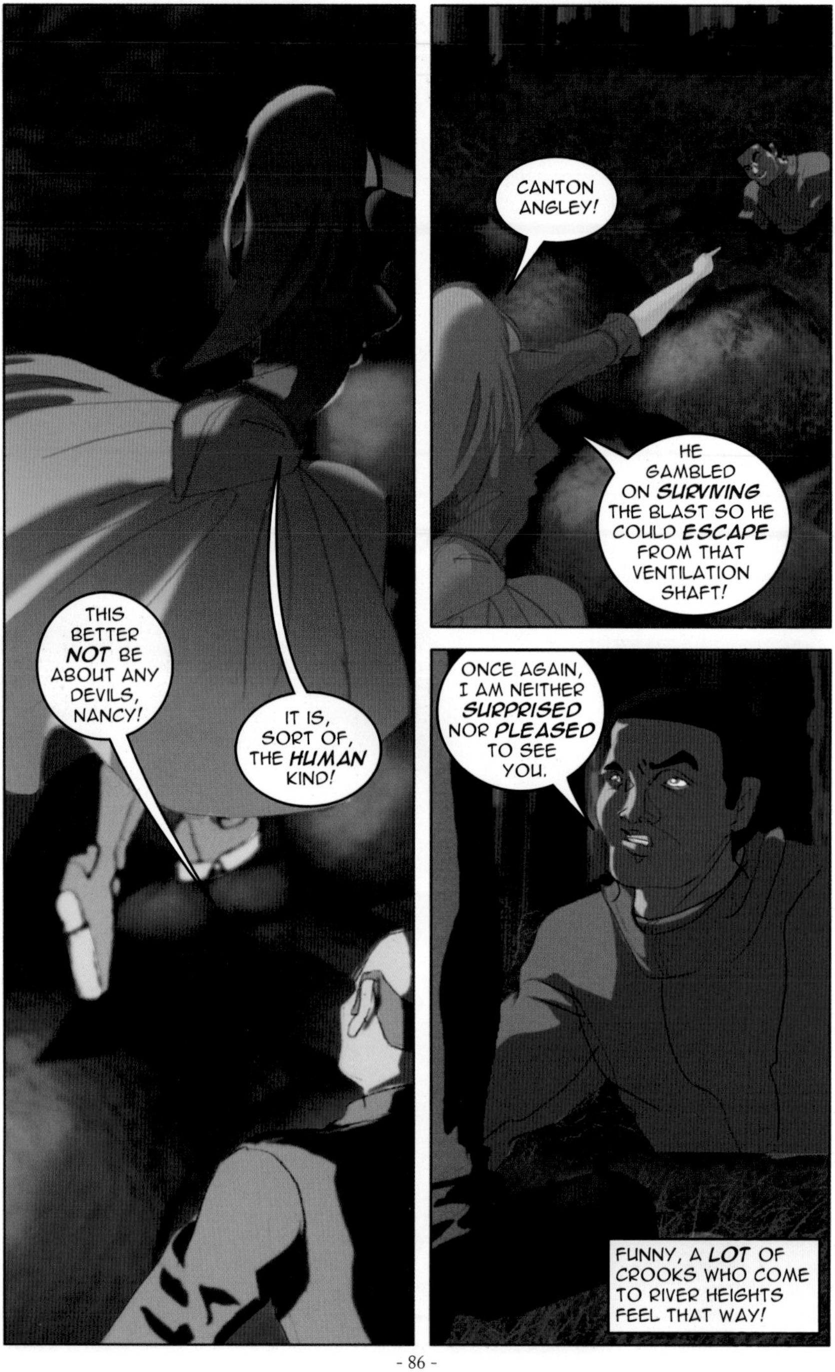
THIS BETTER NOT BE ABOUT ANY DEVILS, NANCY!
IT IS, SORT OF, THE HUMAN KIND!
CANTON ANGLEY!
HE GAMBLED ON SURVIVING THE BLAST SO HE COULD ESCAPE FROM THAT VENTILATION SHAFT!
ONCE AGAIN, I AM NEITHER SURPRISED NOR PLEASED TO SEE YOU.
FUNNY, A LOT OF CROOKS WHO COME TO RIVER HEIGHTS FEEL THAT WAY!

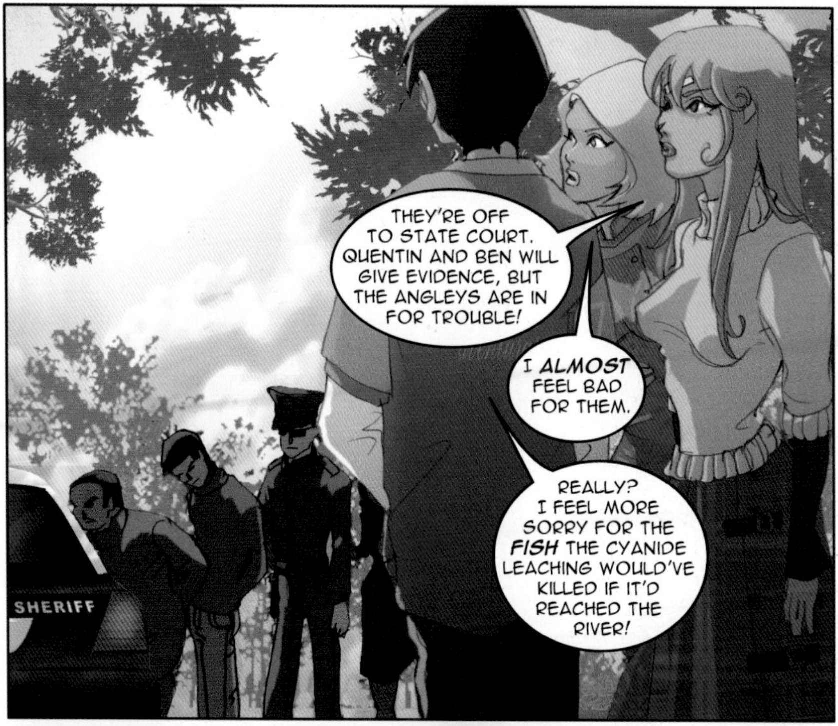
THEY'RE OFF TO STATE COURT. QUENTIN AND BEN WILL GIVE EVIDENCE, BUT THE ANGLEYS ARE IN FOR TROUBLE!
I ALMOST FEEL BAD FOR THEM.
REALLY? I FEEL MORE SORRY FOR THE FISH THE CYANIDE LEACHING WOULD'VE KILLED IF IT'D REACHED THE RIVER!
SHERIFF

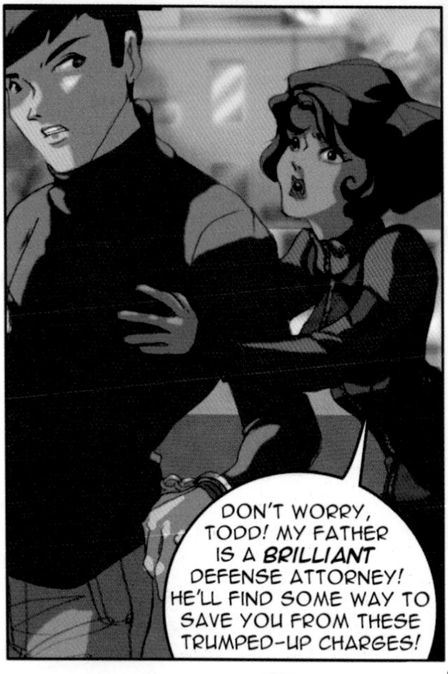
DON'T WORRY, TODD! MY FATHER IS A BRILLIANT DEFENSE ATTORNEY! HE'LL FIND SOME WAY TO SAVE YOU FROM THESE TRUMPED-UP CHARGES!

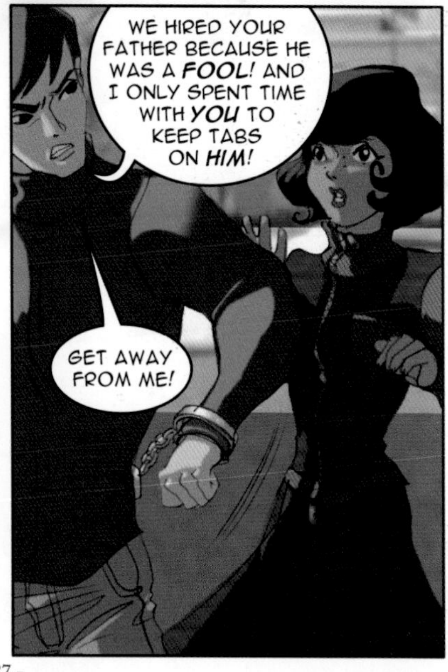
WE HIRED YOUR FATHER BECAUSE HE WAS A FOOL! AND I ONLY SPENT TIME WITH YOU TO KEEP TABS ON HIM!
GET AWAY FROM ME!

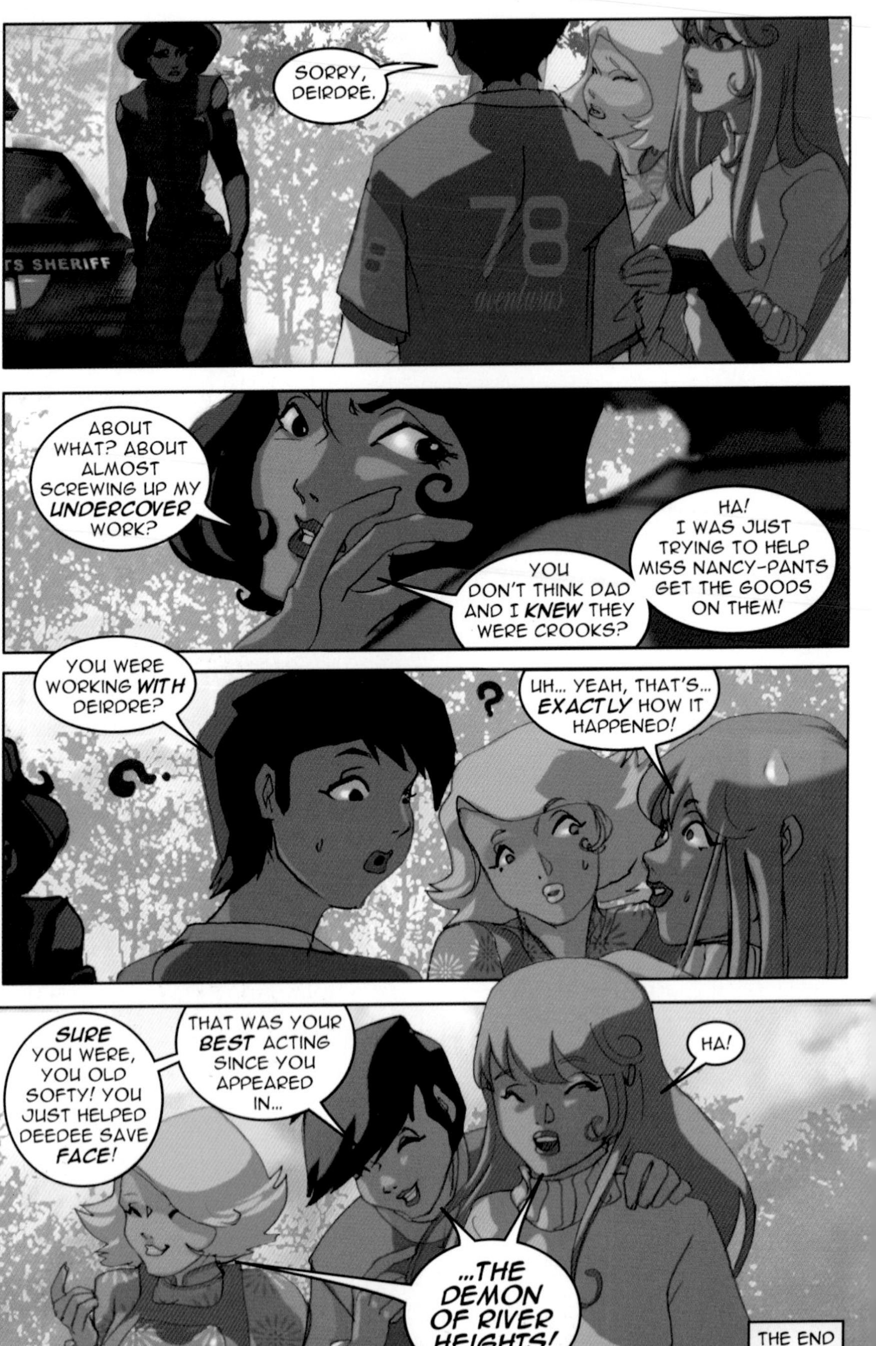
TS SHERIFF
SORRY, DEIRDRE.
ABOUT WHAT? ABOUT ALMOST SCREWING UP MY UNDERCOVER WORK?
YOU DON'T THINK DAD AND I KNEW THEY WERE CROOKS?
HA! I WAS JUST TRYING TO HELP MISS NANCY-PANTS GET THE GOODS ON THEM!
YOU WERE WORKING WITH DEIRDRE?
?
?
UH... YEAH, THAT'S... EXACTLY HOW IT HAPPENED!
SURE YOU WERE, YOU OLD SOFTY! YOU JUST HELPED DEEDEE SAVE FACE!
THAT WAS YOUR BEST ACTING SINCE YOU APPEARED IN...
HA!
...THE DEMON OF RIVER HEIGHTS!
THE END

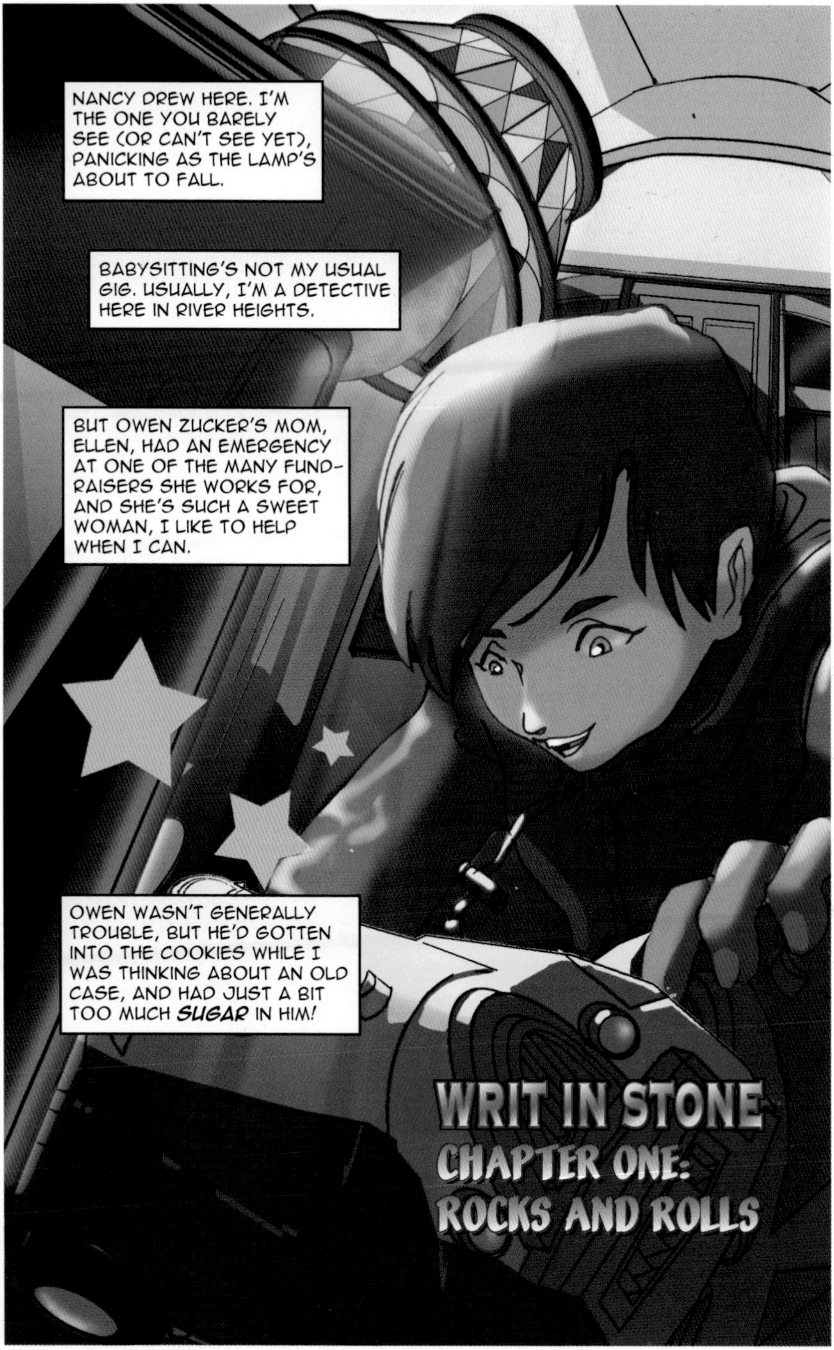
NANCY DREW HERE. I'M THE ONE YOU BARELY SEE (OR CAN'T SEE YET), PANICKING AS THE LAMP'S ABOUT TO FALL.
BABYSITTING'S NOT MY USUAL GIG. USUALLY, I'M A DETECTIVE HERE IN RIVER HEIGHTS.
BUT OWEN ZUCKER'S MOM, ELLEN, HAD AN EMERGENCY AT ONE OF THE MANY FUND-RAISERS SHE WORKS FOR, AND SHE'S SUCH A SWEET WOMAN, I LIKE TO HELP WHEN I CAN.
OWEN WASN'T GENERALLY TROUBLE, BUT HE'D GOTTEN INTO THE COOKIES WHILE I WAS THINKING ABOUT AN OLD CASE, AND HAD JUST A BIT TOO MUCH SUGAR IN HIM!
WRIT IN STONE
CHAPTER ONE:
ROCKS AND ROLLS

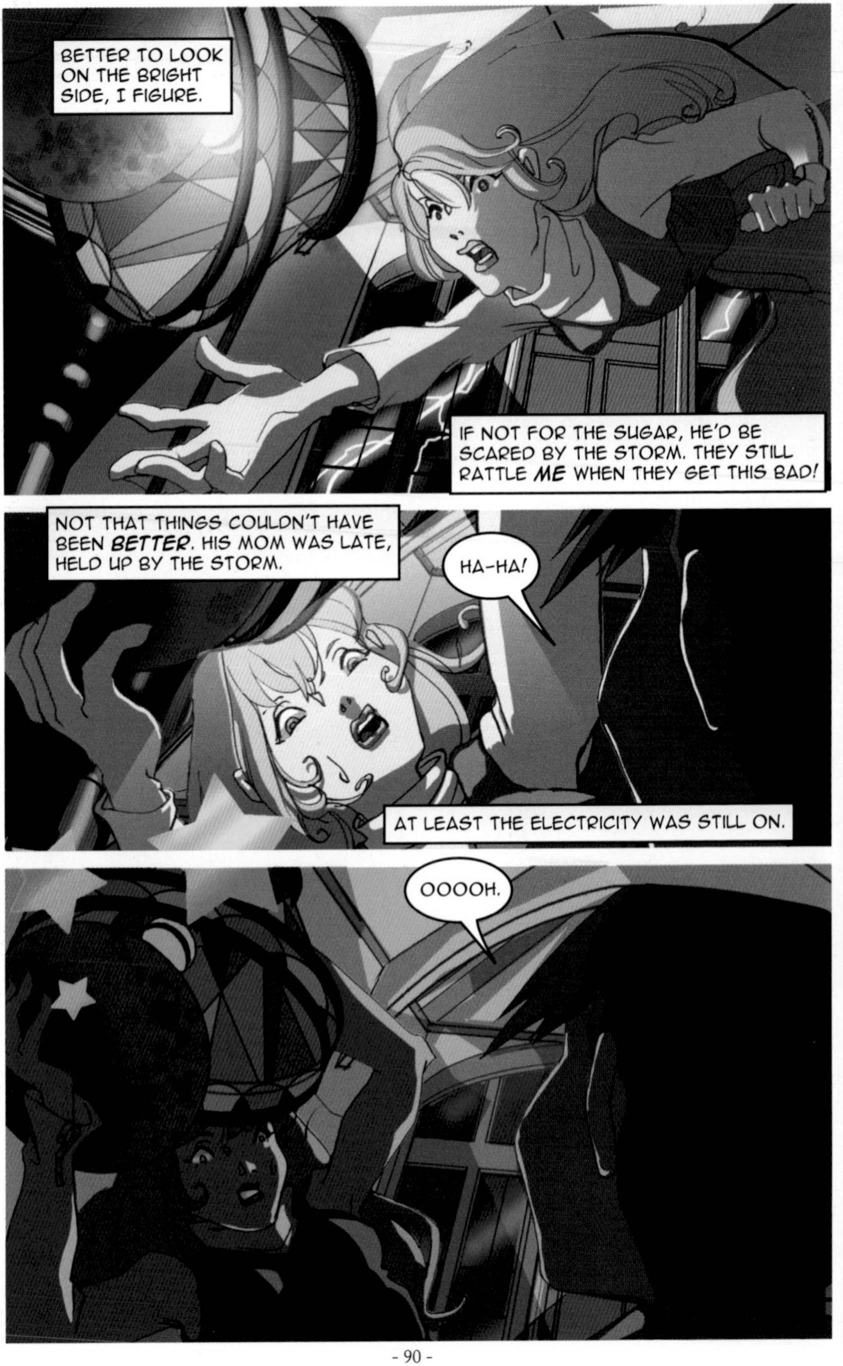
BETTER TO LOOK ON THE BRIGHT SIDE, I FIGURE.
IF NOT FOR THE SUGAR, HE'D BE SCARED BY THE STORM. THEY STILL RATTLE *ME* WHEN THEY GET THIS BAD!
NOT THAT THINGS COULDN'T HAVE BEEN *BETTER*. HIS MOM WAS LATE, HELD UP BY THE STORM.
HA-HA!
AT LEAST THE ELECTRICITY WAS STILL ON.
OOOOH.

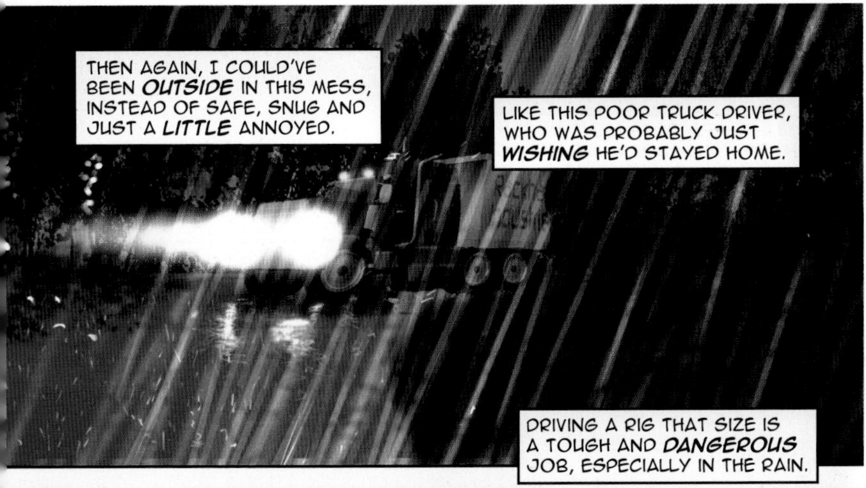
THEN AGAIN, I COULD'VE BEEN OUTSIDE IN THIS MESS, INSTEAD OF SAFE, SNUG AND JUST A LITTLE ANNOYED.
LIKE THIS POOR TRUCK DRIVER, WHO WAS PROBABLY JUST WISHING HE'D STAYED HOME.
DRIVING A RIG THAT SIZE IS A TOUGH AND DANGEROUS JOB, ESPECIALLY IN THE RAIN.

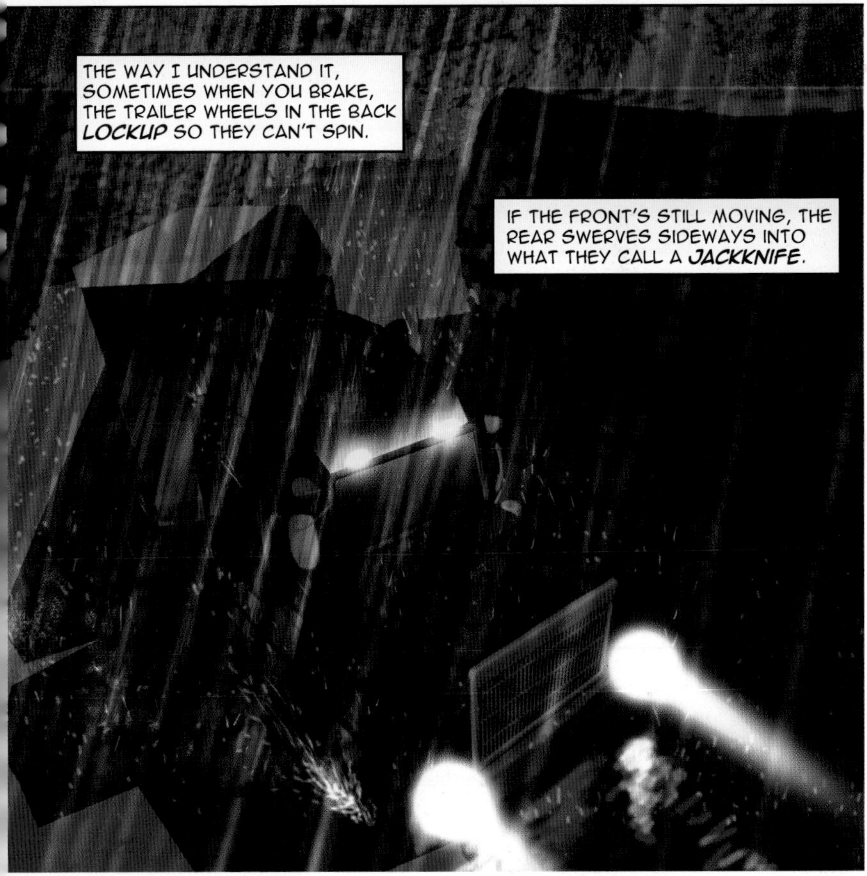
THE WAY I UNDERSTAND IT, SOMETIMES WHEN YOU BRAKE, THE TRAILER WHEELS IN THE BACK LOCKUP SO THEY CAN'T SPIN.
IF THE FRONT'S STILL MOVING, THE REAR SWERVES SIDEWAYS INTO WHAT THEY CALL A JACKKNIFE.

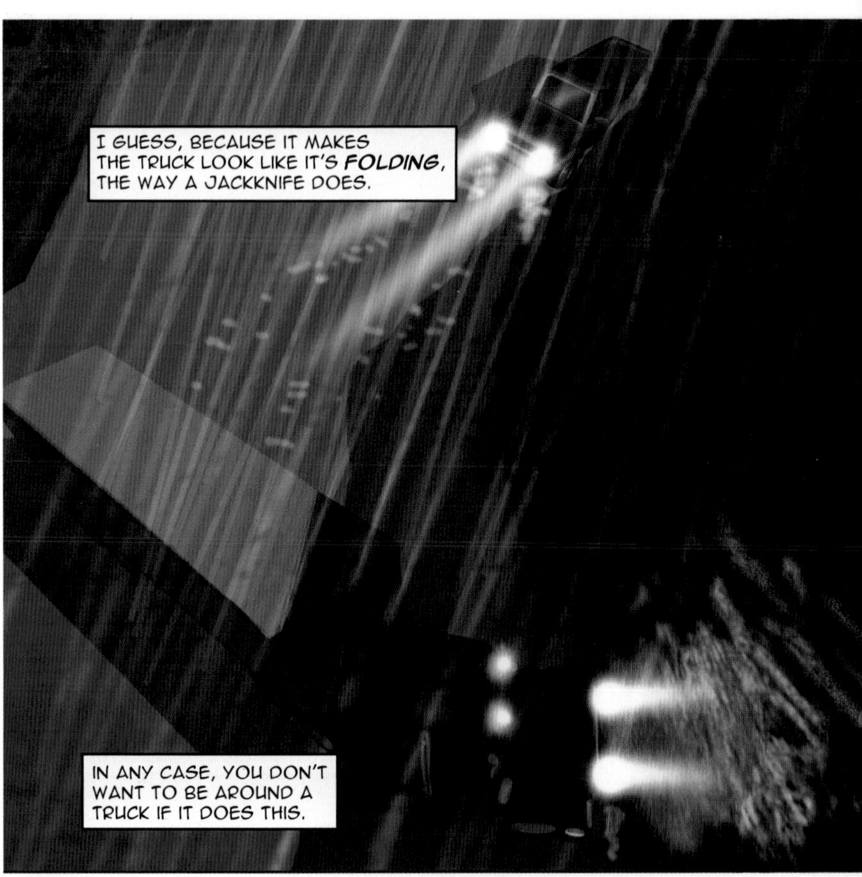
I GUESS, BECAUSE IT MAKES THE TRUCK LOOK LIKE IT'S *FOLDING*, THE WAY A JACKKNIFE DOES.
IN ANY CASE, YOU DON'T WANT TO BE AROUND A TRUCK IF IT DOES THIS.

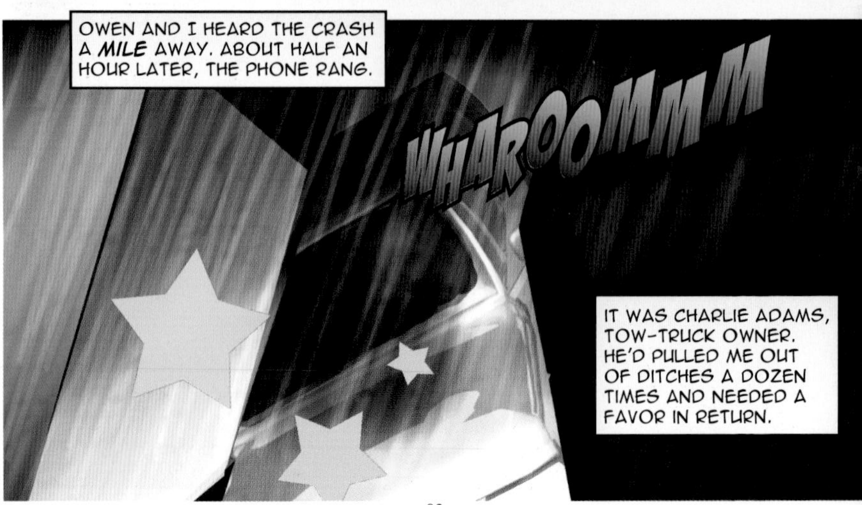
OWEN AND I HEARD THE CRASH A *MILE* AWAY. ABOUT HALF AN HOUR LATER, THE PHONE RANG.
WHAROOMMM
IT WAS CHARLIE ADAMS, TOW-TRUCK OWNER. HE'D PULLED ME OUT OF DITCHES A DOZEN TIMES AND NEEDED A FAVOR IN RETURN.

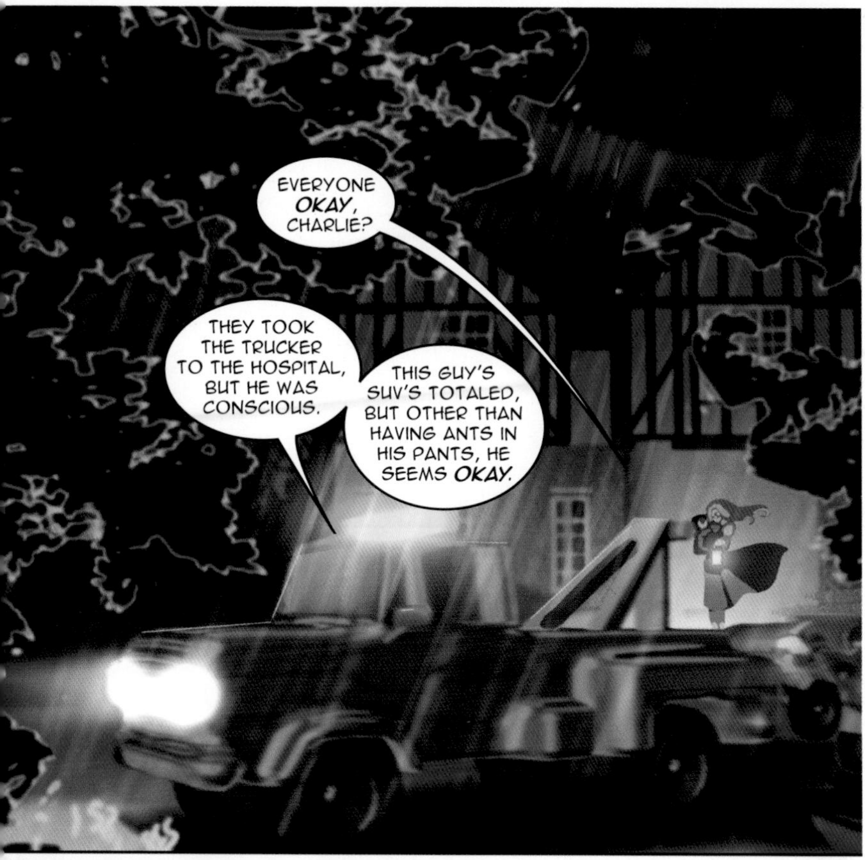
EVERYONE OKAY, CHARLIE?
THEY TOOK THE TRUCKER TO THE HOSPITAL, BUT HE WAS CONSCIOUS.
THIS GUY'S SUV'S TOTALED, BUT OTHER THAN HAVING ANTS IN HIS PANTS, HE SEEMS OKAY.

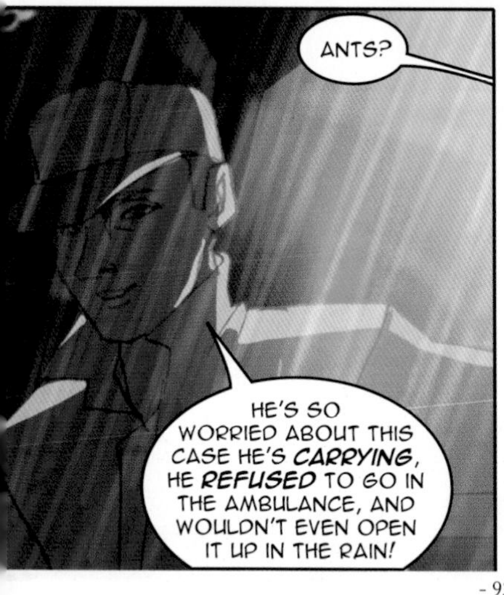
ANTS?
HE'S SO WORRIED ABOUT THIS CASE HE'S CARRYING, HE REFUSED TO GO IN THE AMBULANCE, AND WOULDN'T EVEN OPEN IT UP IN THE RAIN!

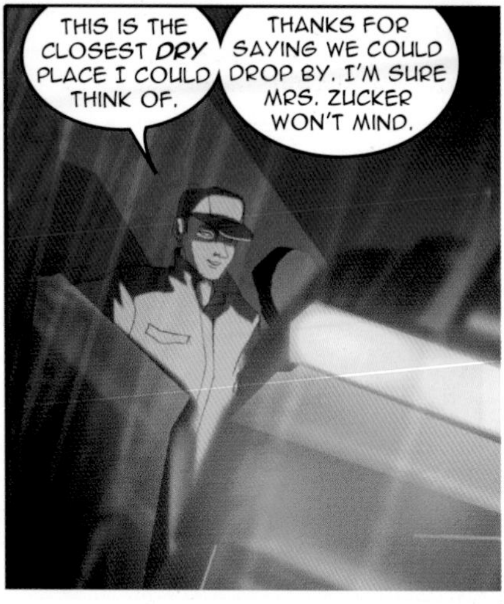
THIS IS THE CLOSEST DRY PLACE I COULD THINK OF.
THANKS FOR SAYING WE COULD DROP BY. I'M SURE MRS. ZUCKER WON'T MIND.

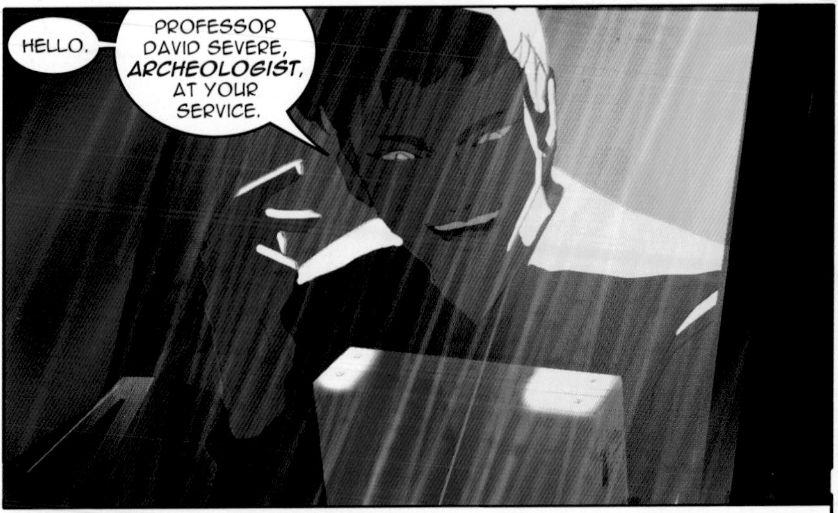
HELLO.
PROFESSOR DAVID SEVERE, ARCHEOLOGIST, AT YOUR SERVICE.

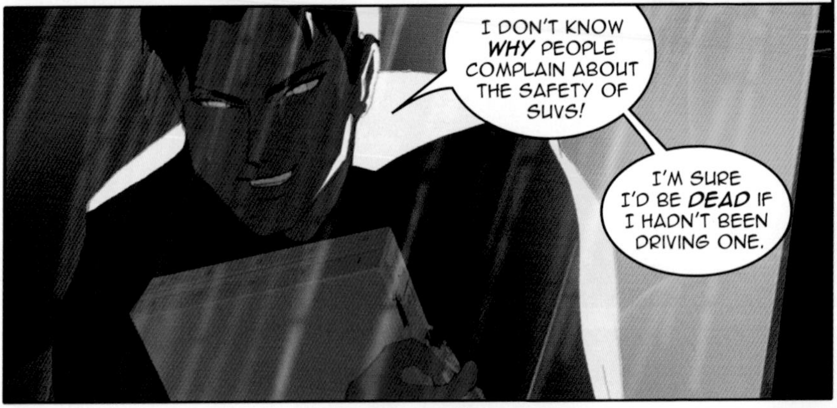
I DON'T KNOW WHY PEOPLE COMPLAIN ABOUT THE SAFETY OF SUVS!
I'M SURE I'D BE DEAD IF I HADN'T BEEN DRIVING ONE.

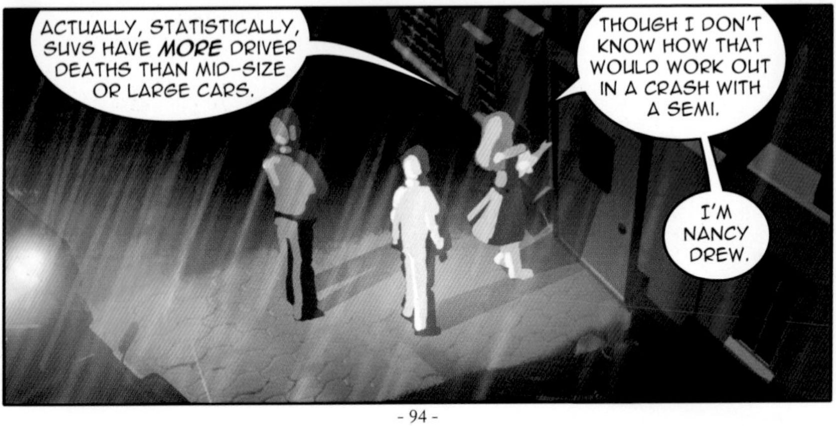
ACTUALLY, STATISTICALLY, SUVS HAVE MORE DRIVER DEATHS THAN MID-SIZE OR LARGE CARS.
THOUGH I DON'T KNOW HOW THAT WOULD WORK OUT IN A CRASH WITH A SEMI.
I'M NANCY DREW.

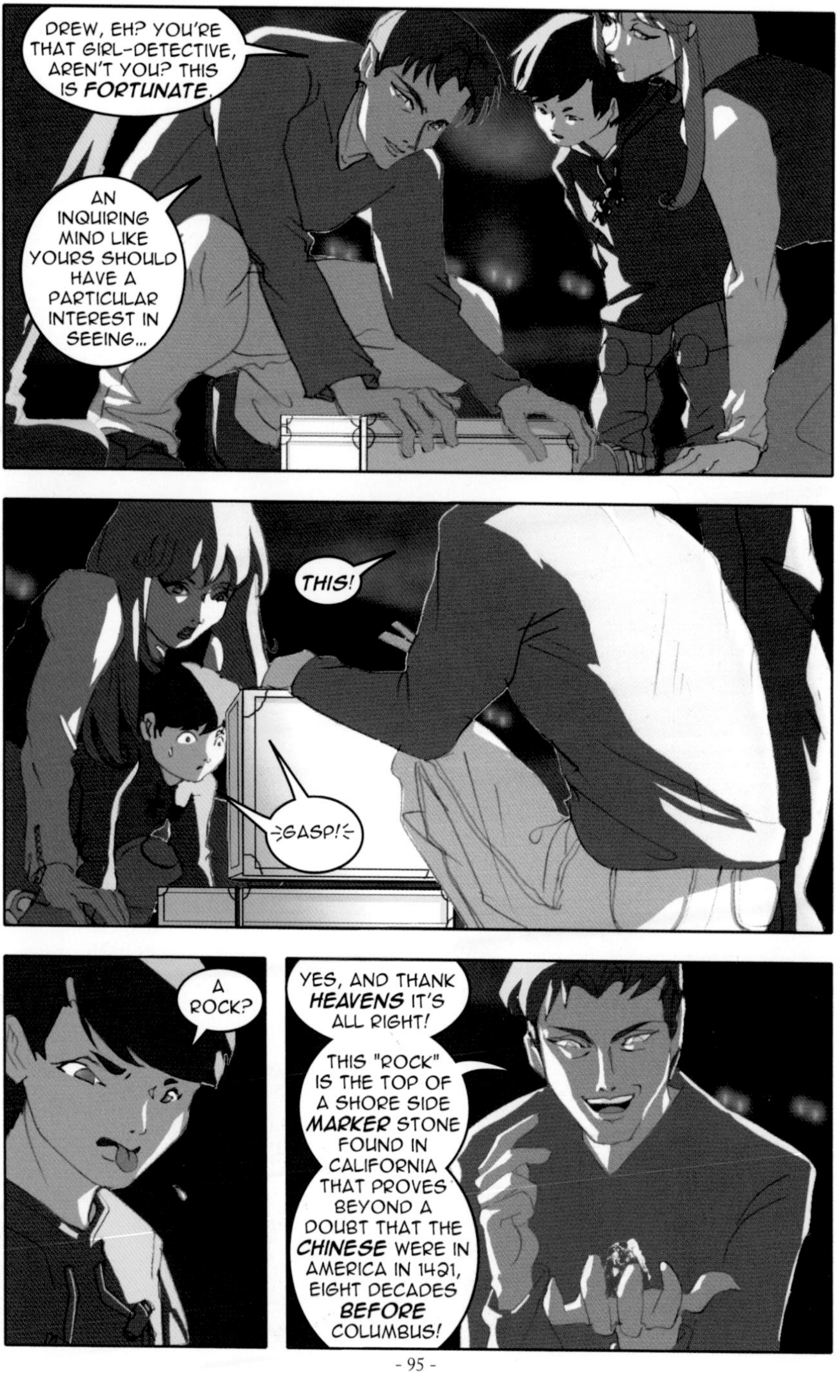
DREW, EH? YOU'RE THAT GIRL-DETECTIVE, AREN'T YOU? THIS IS FORTUNATE.
AN INQUIRING MIND LIKE YOURS SHOULD HAVE A PARTICULAR INTEREST IN SEEING...
THIS!
GASP!
A ROCK?
YES, AND THANK HEAVENS IT'S ALL RIGHT!
THIS "ROCK" IS THE TOP OF A SHORE SIDE MARKER STONE FOUND IN CALIFORNIA THAT PROVES BEYOND A DOUBT THAT THE CHINESE WERE IN AMERICA IN 1421, EIGHT DECADES BEFORE COLUMBUS!

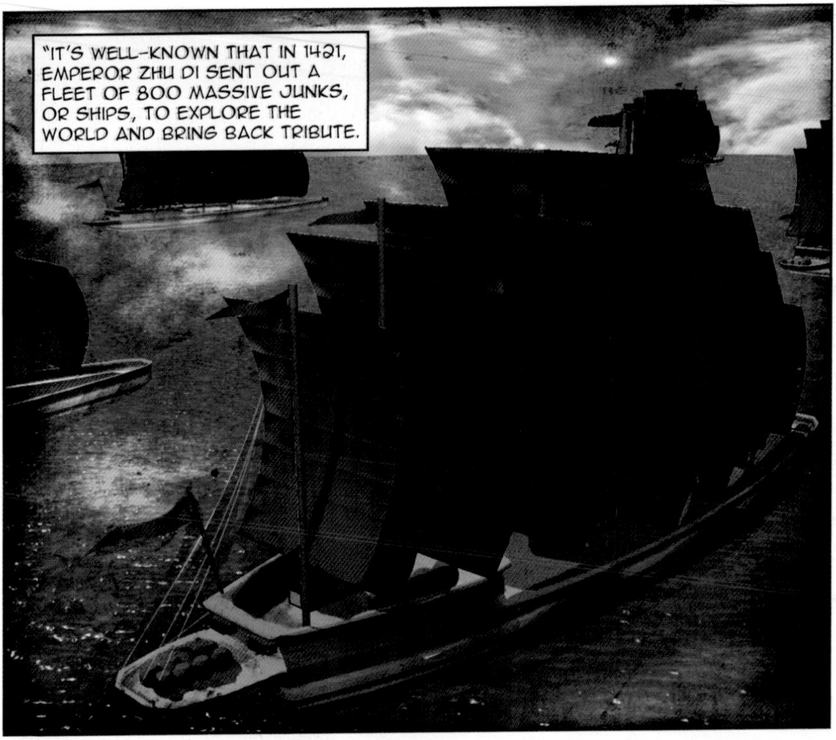
"IT'S WELL-KNOWN THAT IN 1421, EMPEROR ZHU DI SENT OUT A FLEET OF 800 MASSIVE JUNKS, OR SHIPS, TO EXPLORE THE WORLD AND BRING BACK TRIBUTE.

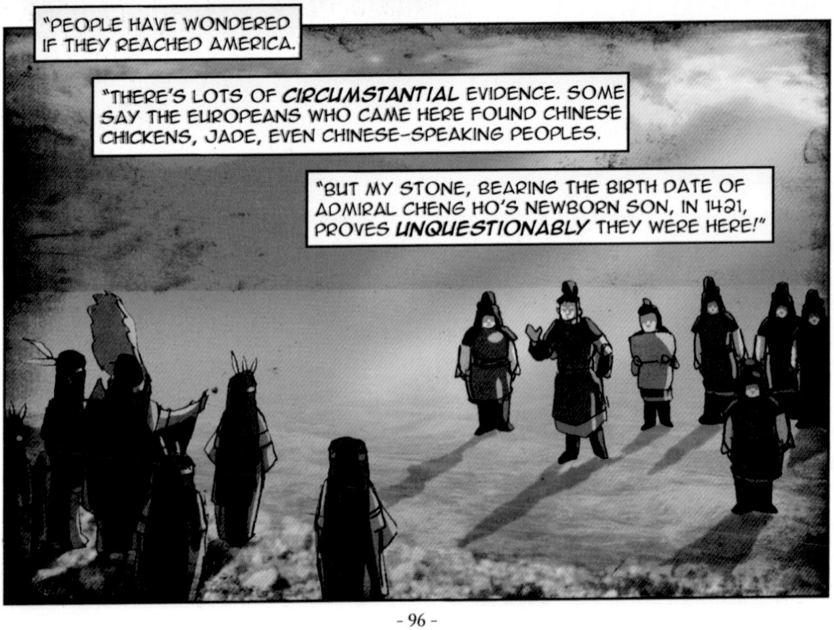
"PEOPLE HAVE WONDERED IF THEY REACHED AMERICA.
"THERE'S LOTS OF *CIRCUMSTANTIAL* EVIDENCE. SOME SAY THE EUROPEANS WHO CAME HERE FOUND CHINESE CHICKENS, JADE, EVEN CHINESE-SPEAKING PEOPLES.
"BUT MY STONE, BEARING THE BIRTH DATE OF ADMIRAL CHENG HO'S NEWBORN SON, IN 1421, PROVES *UNQUESTIONABLY* THEY WERE HERE!"

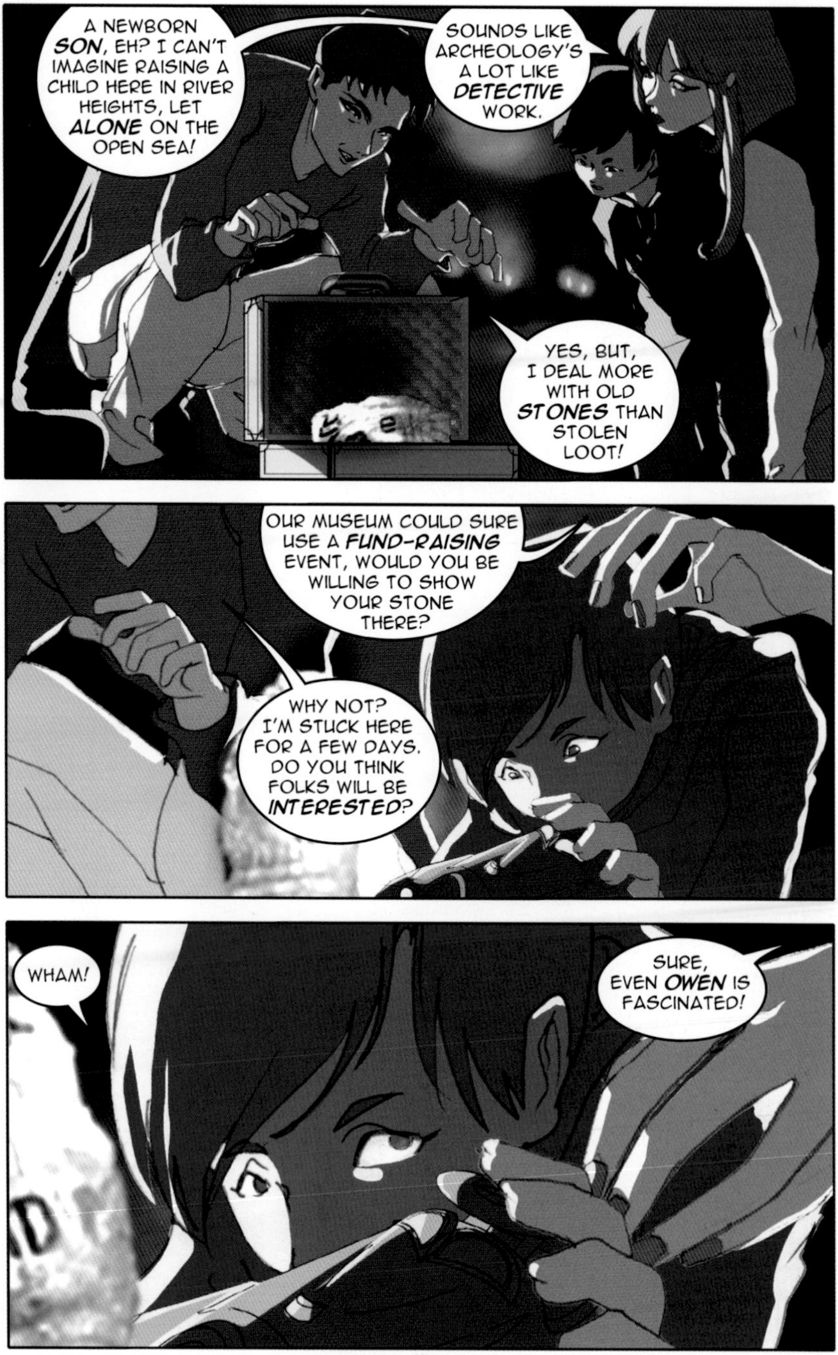
A NEWBORN SON, EH? I CAN'T IMAGINE RAISING A CHILD HERE IN RIVER HEIGHTS, LET ALONE ON THE OPEN SEA!
SOUNDS LIKE ARCHEOLOGY'S A LOT LIKE DETECTIVE WORK.
YES, BUT, I DEAL MORE WITH OLD STONES THAN STOLEN LOOT!
OUR MUSEUM COULD SURE USE A FUND-RAISING EVENT, WOULD YOU BE WILLING TO SHOW YOUR STONE THERE?
WHY NOT? I'M STUCK HERE FOR A FEW DAYS. DO YOU THINK FOLKS WILL BE INTERESTED?
WHAM!
SURE, EVEN OWEN IS FASCINATED!

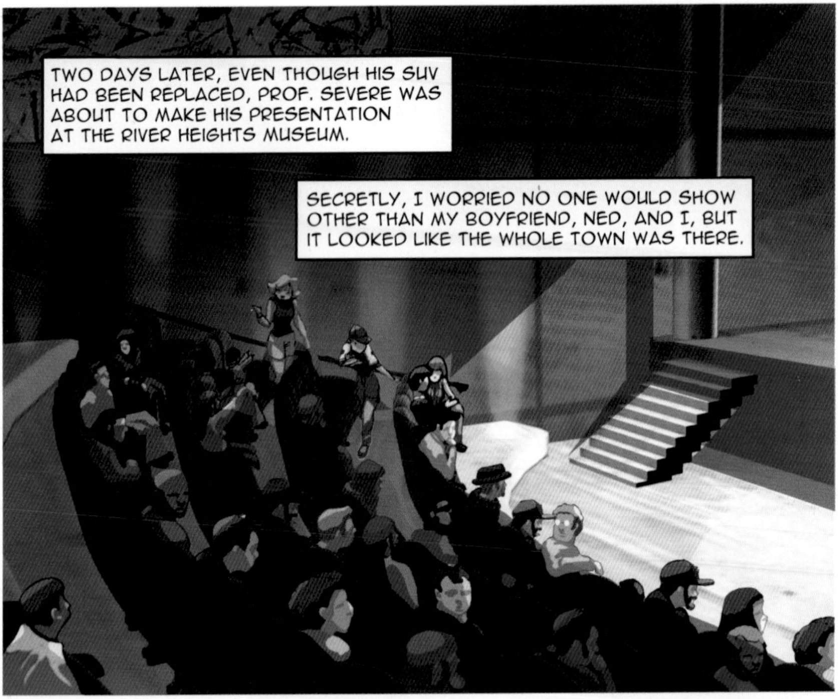
TWO DAYS LATER, EVEN THOUGH HIS SUV HAD BEEN REPLACED, PROF. SEVERE WAS ABOUT TO MAKE HIS PRESENTATION AT THE RIVER HEIGHTS MUSEUM.
SECRETLY, I WORRIED NO ONE WOULD SHOW OTHER THAN MY BOYFRIEND, NED, AND I, BUT IT LOOKED LIKE THE WHOLE TOWN WAS THERE.

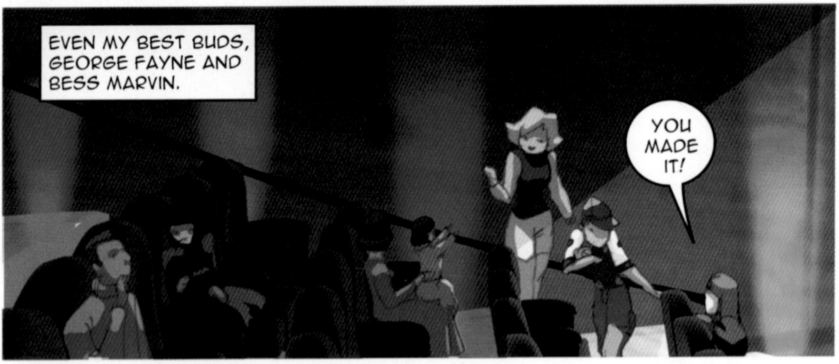
EVEN MY BEST BUDS, GEORGE FAYNE AND BESS MARVIN.
YOU MADE IT!

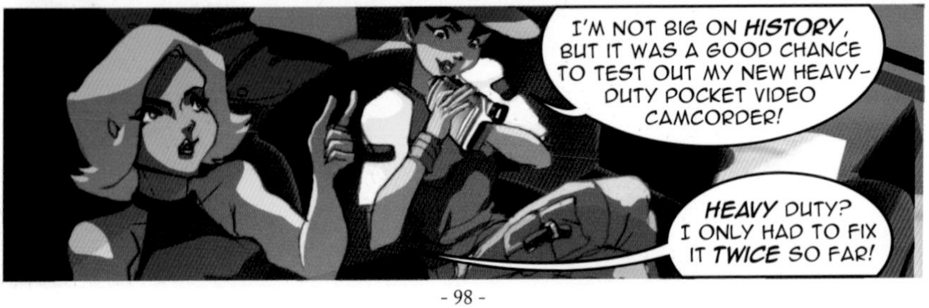
I'M NOT BIG ON ***HISTORY***, BUT IT WAS A GOOD CHANCE TO TEST OUT MY NEW HEAVY-DUTY POCKET VIDEO CAMCORDER!
HEAVY DUTY? I ONLY HAD TO FIX IT ***TWICE*** SO FAR!

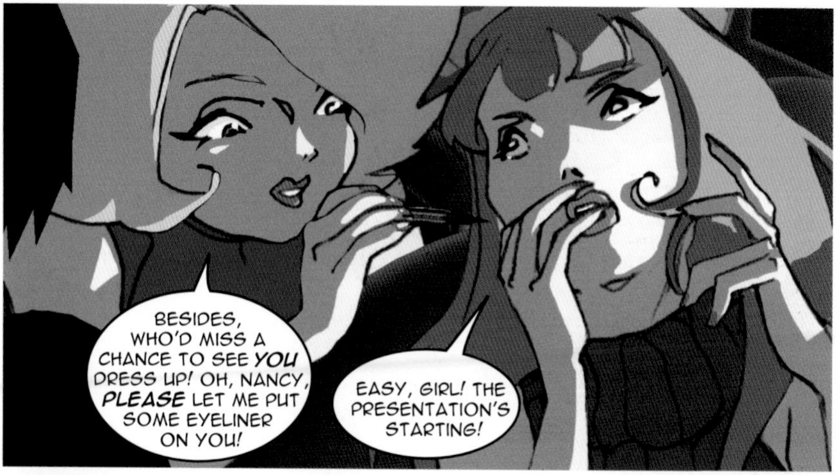
BESIDES, WHO'D MISS A CHANCE TO SEE *YOU* DRESS UP! OH, NANCY, ***PLEASE*** LET ME PUT SOME EYELINER ON YOU!
EASY, GIRL! THE PRESENTATION'S STARTING!

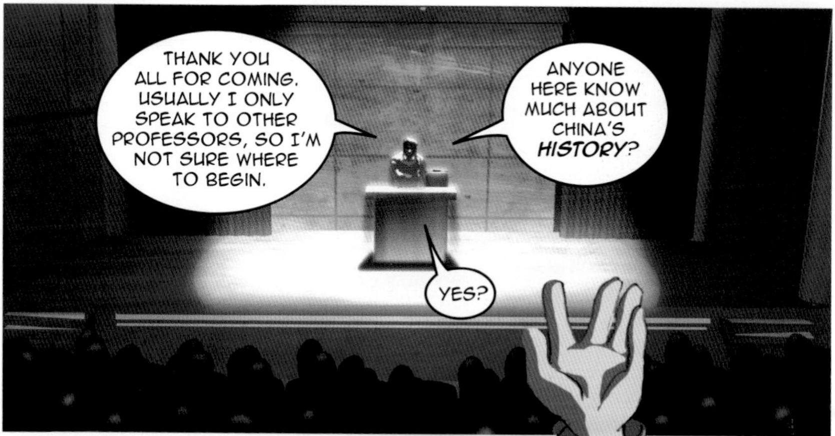
THANK YOU ALL FOR COMING. USUALLY I ONLY SPEAK TO OTHER PROFESSORS, SO I'M NOT SURE WHERE TO BEGIN.
ANYONE HERE KNOW MUCH ABOUT CHINA'S ***HISTORY***?
YES?

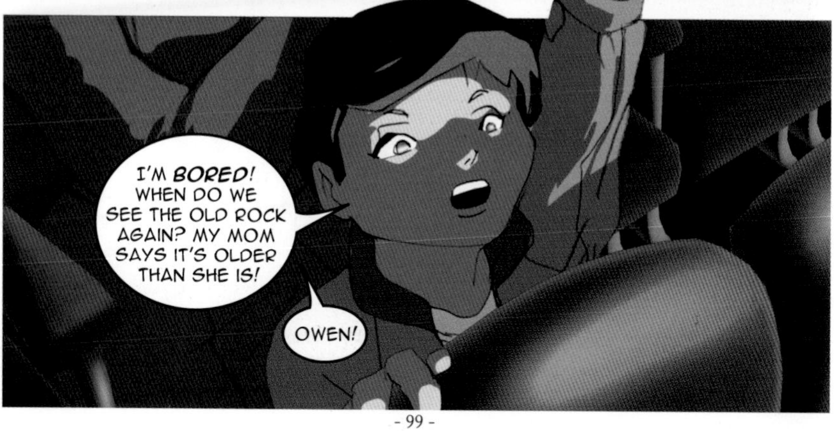
I'M ***BORED***! WHEN DO WE SEE THE OLD ROCK AGAIN? MY MOM SAYS IT'S OLDER THAN SHE IS!
OWEN!

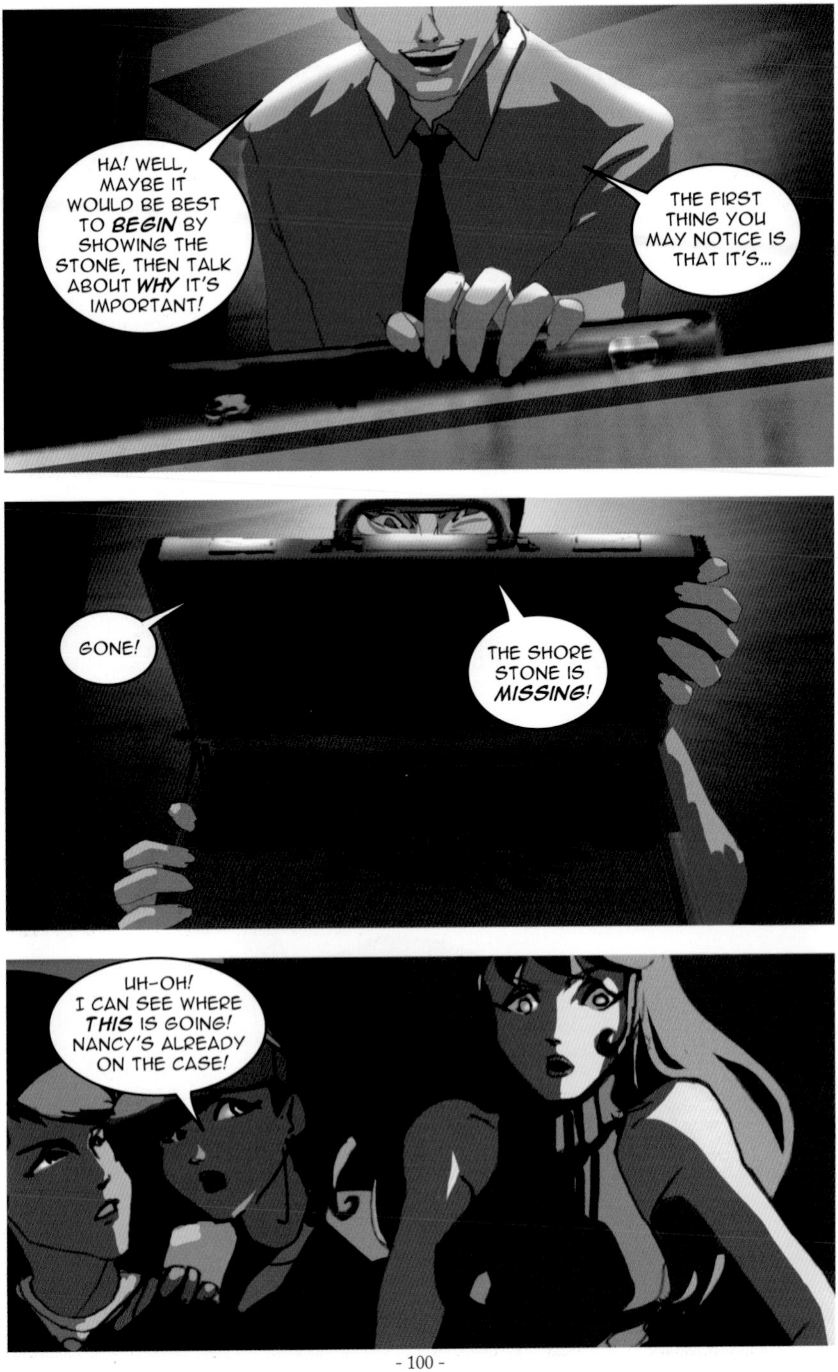
HA! WELL, MAYBE IT WOULD BE BEST TO BEGIN BY SHOWING THE STONE, THEN TALK ABOUT WHY IT'S IMPORTANT!
THE FIRST THING YOU MAY NOTICE IS THAT IT'S...
GONE!
THE SHORE STONE IS MISSING!
UH-OH! I CAN SEE WHERE THIS IS GOING! NANCY'S ALREADY ON THE CASE!

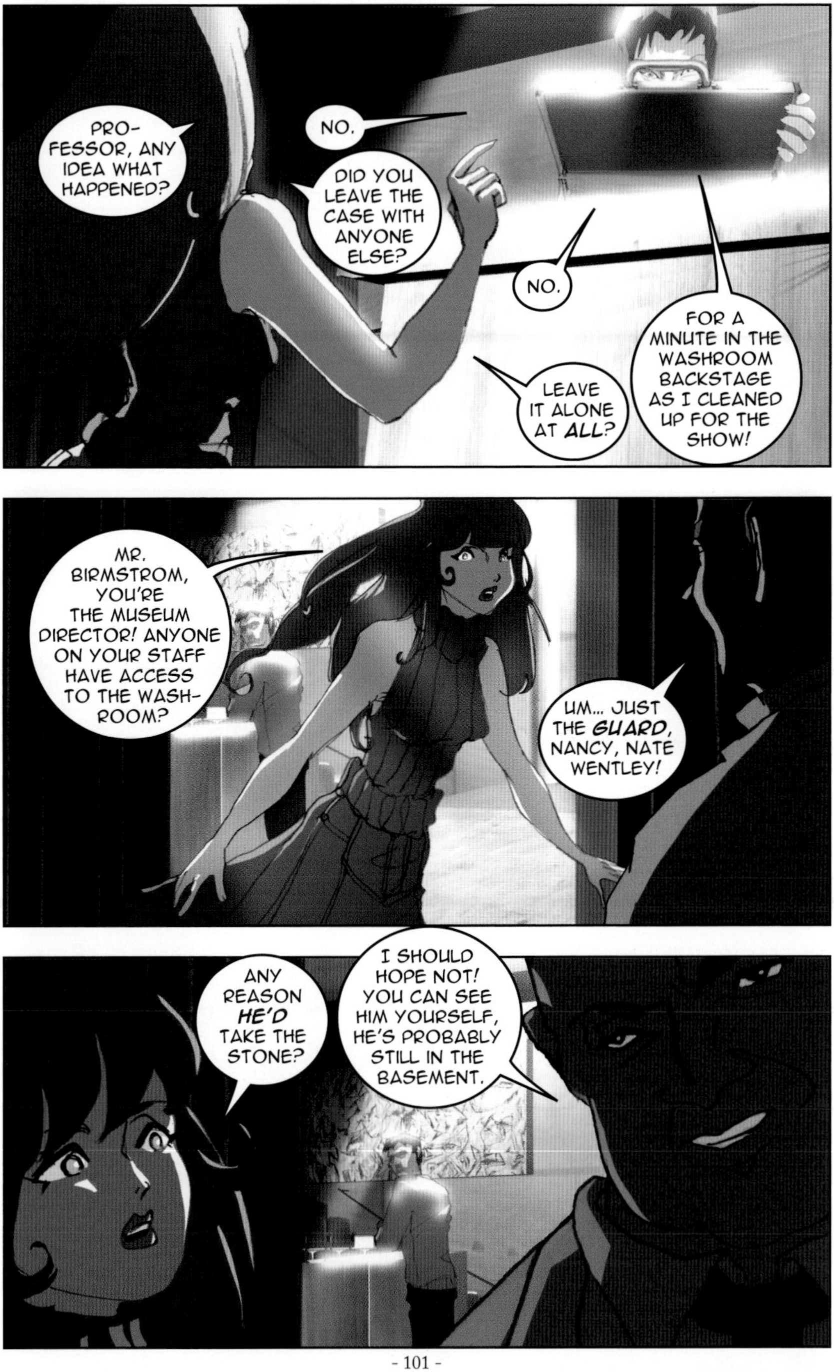
PRO-FESSOR, ANY IDEA WHAT HAPPENED?
NO.
DID YOU LEAVE THE CASE WITH ANYONE ELSE?
NO.
LEAVE IT ALONE AT ALL?
FOR A MINUTE IN THE WASHROOM BACKSTAGE AS I CLEANED UP FOR THE SHOW!
MR. BIRMSTROM, YOU'RE THE MUSEUM DIRECTOR! ANYONE ON YOUR STAFF HAVE ACCESS TO THE WASH-ROOM?
UM... JUST THE GUARD, NANCY, NATE WENTLEY!
ANY REASON HE'D TAKE THE STONE?
I SHOULD HOPE NOT! YOU CAN SEE HIM YOURSELF, HE'S PROBABLY STILL IN THE BASEMENT.

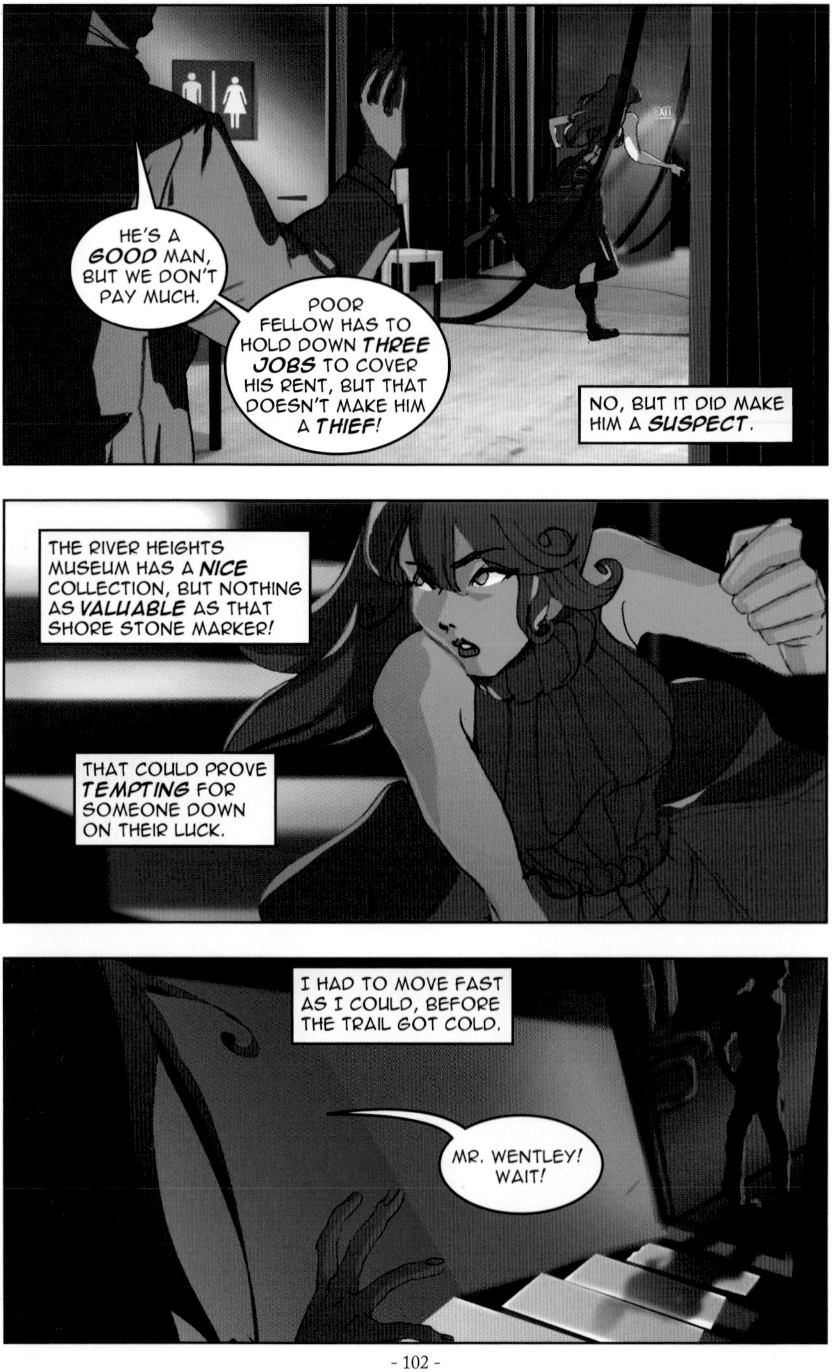
HE'S A GOOD MAN, BUT WE DON'T PAY MUCH.
POOR FELLOW HAS TO HOLD DOWN THREE JOBS TO COVER HIS RENT, BUT THAT DOESN'T MAKE HIM A THIEF!
NO, BUT IT DID MAKE HIM A SUSPECT.
THE RIVER HEIGHTS MUSEUM HAS A NICE COLLECTION, BUT NOTHING AS VALUABLE AS THAT SHORE STONE MARKER!
THAT COULD PROVE TEMPTING FOR SOMEONE DOWN ON THEIR LUCK.
I HAD TO MOVE FAST AS I COULD, BEFORE THE TRAIL GOT COLD.
MR. WENTLEY! WAIT!

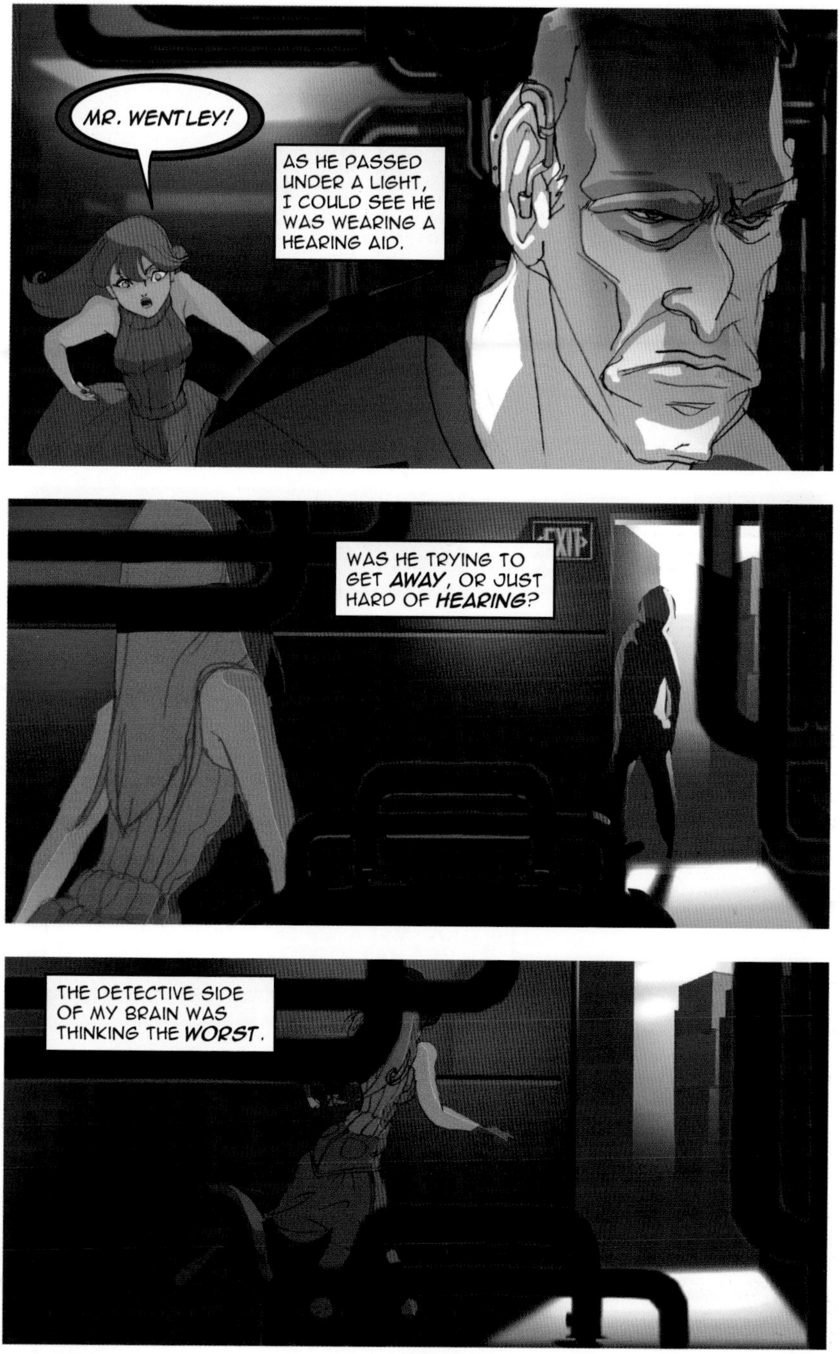
MR. WENTLEY!
AS HE PASSED UNDER A LIGHT, I COULD SEE HE WAS WEARING A HEARING AID.
EXIT
WAS HE TRYING TO GET **AWAY**, OR JUST HARD OF **HEARING**?
THE DETECTIVE SIDE OF MY BRAIN WAS THINKING THE **WORST**.

THE PROBLEM WITH THAT DETECTIVE BRAIN IS THAT WHILE IT'S *GREAT* ON *CRIME* DETAILS...

MR. WENTLEY! PLEASE OPEN THE DOOR! I JUST WANT TO *TALK* TO YOU!

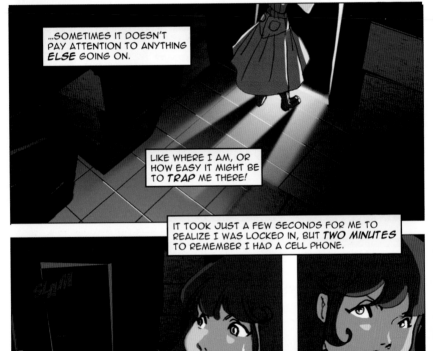

...SOMETIMES IT DOESN'T PAY ATTENTION TO ANYTHING *ELSE* GOING ON.

LIKE WHERE I AM, OR HOW EASY IT MIGHT BE TO *TRAP* ME THERE!

IT TOOK JUST A FEW SECONDS FOR ME TO REALIZE I WAS LOCKED IN, BUT *TWO MINUTES* TO REMEMBER I HAD A CELL PHONE.

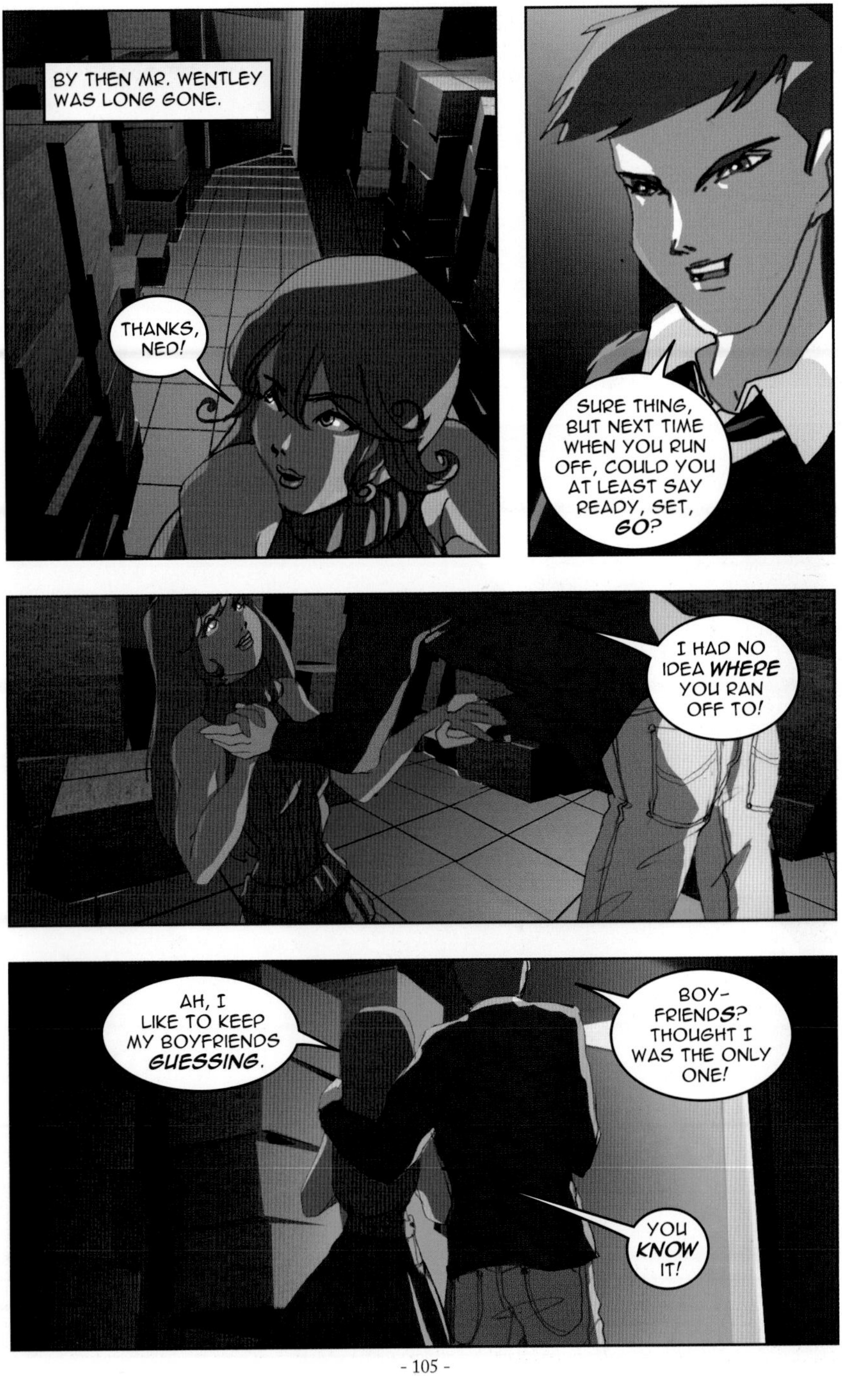
BY THEN MR. WENTLEY WAS LONG GONE.
THANKS, NED!
SURE THING, BUT NEXT TIME WHEN YOU RUN OFF, COULD YOU AT LEAST SAY READY, SET, GO?
I HAD NO IDEA WHERE YOU RAN OFF TO!
AH, I LIKE TO KEEP MY BOYFRIENDS GUESSING.
BOY-FRIENDS? THOUGHT I WAS THE ONLY ONE!
YOU KNOW IT!

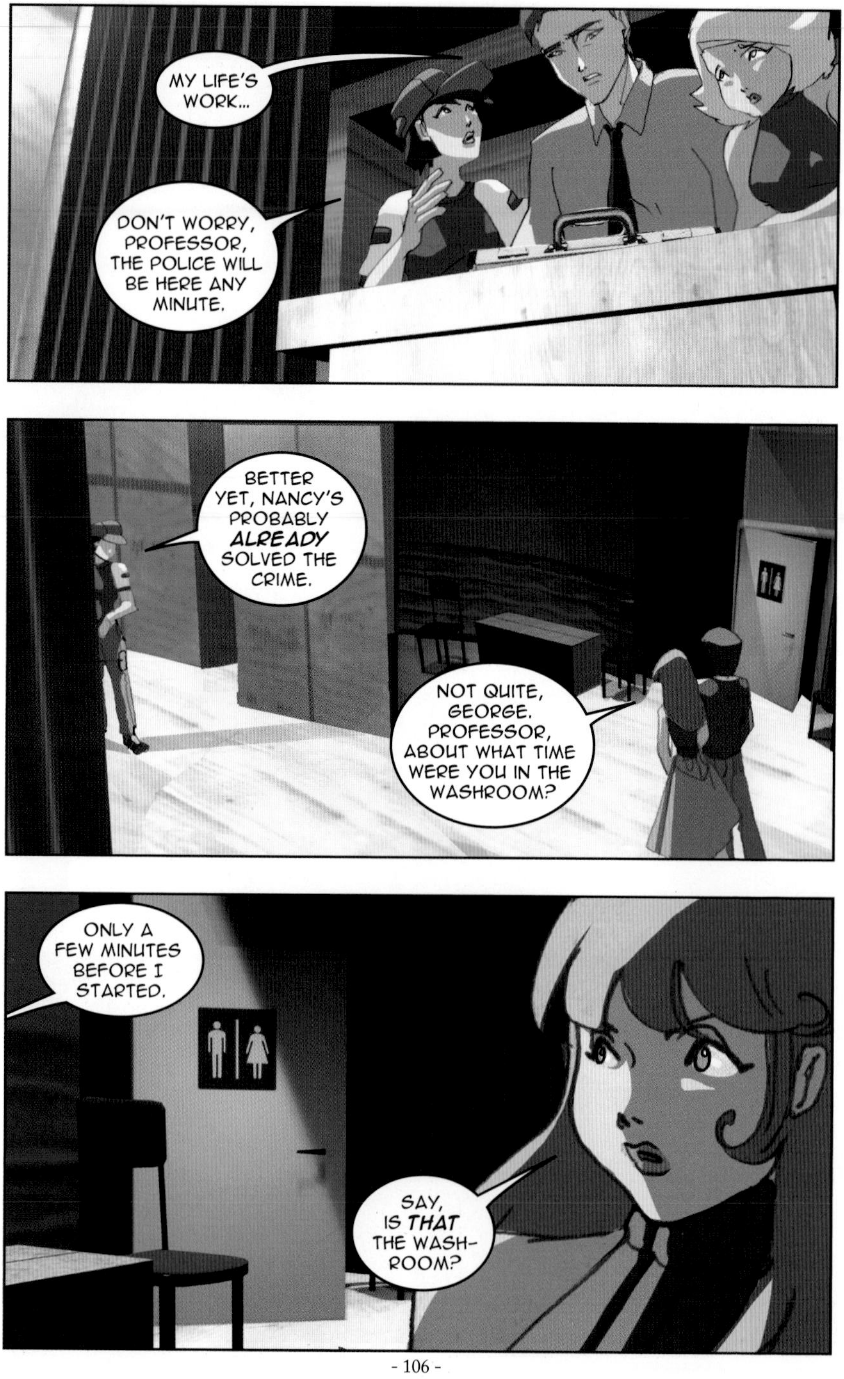
MY LIFE'S WORK...
DON'T WORRY, PROFESSOR, THE POLICE WILL BE HERE ANY MINUTE.
BETTER YET, NANCY'S PROBABLY ***ALREADY*** SOLVED THE CRIME.
NOT QUITE, GEORGE. PROFESSOR, ABOUT WHAT TIME WERE YOU IN THE WASHROOM?
ONLY A FEW MINUTES BEFORE I STARTED.
SAY, IS ***THAT*** THE WASH-ROOM?

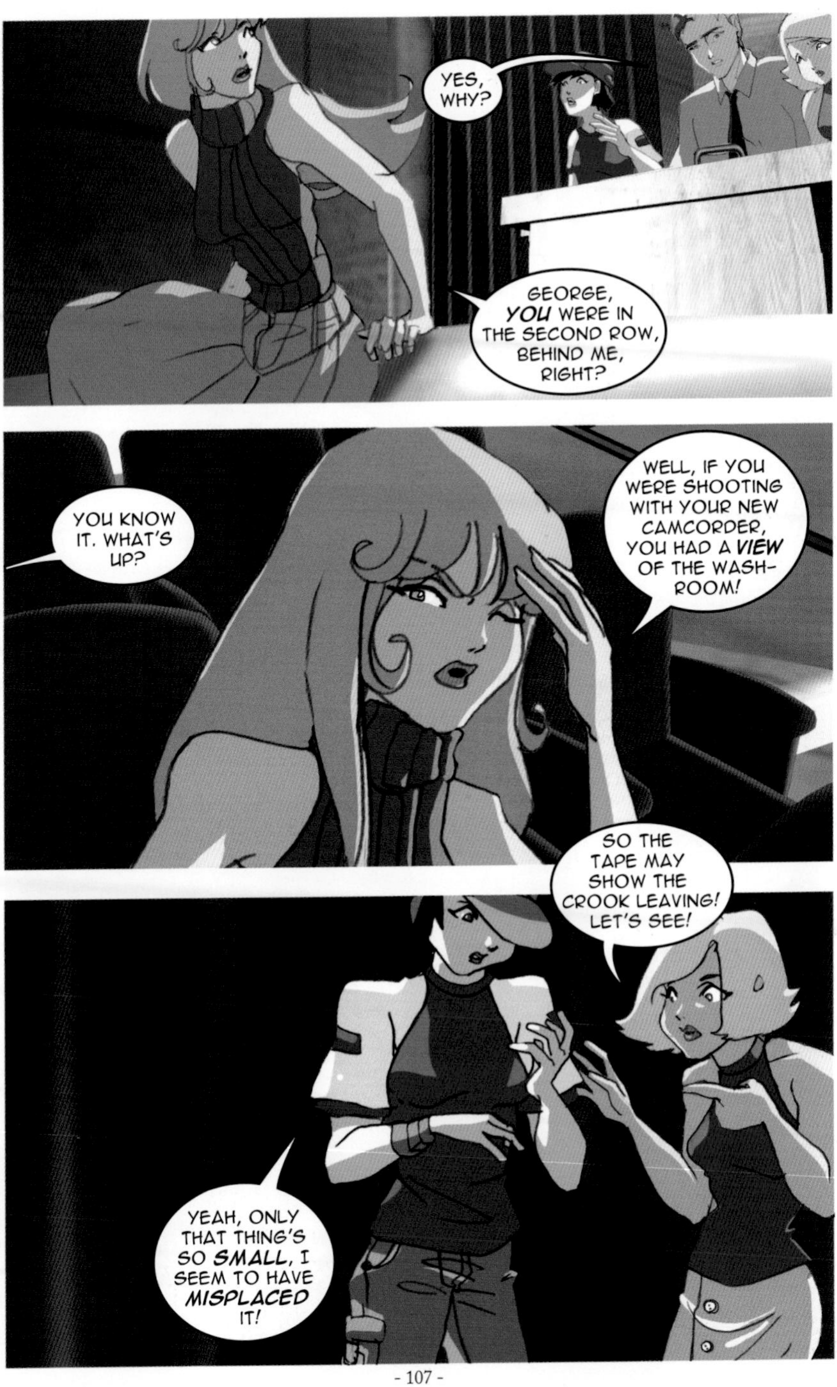
YES, WHY?
GEORGE, YOU WERE IN THE SECOND ROW, BEHIND ME, RIGHT?
YOU KNOW IT. WHAT'S UP?
WELL, IF YOU WERE SHOOTING WITH YOUR NEW CAMCORDER, YOU HAD A VIEW OF THE WASH-ROOM!
SO THE TAPE MAY SHOW THE CROOK LEAVING! LET'S SEE!
YEAH, ONLY THAT THING'S SO SMALL, I SEEM TO HAVE MISPLACED IT!

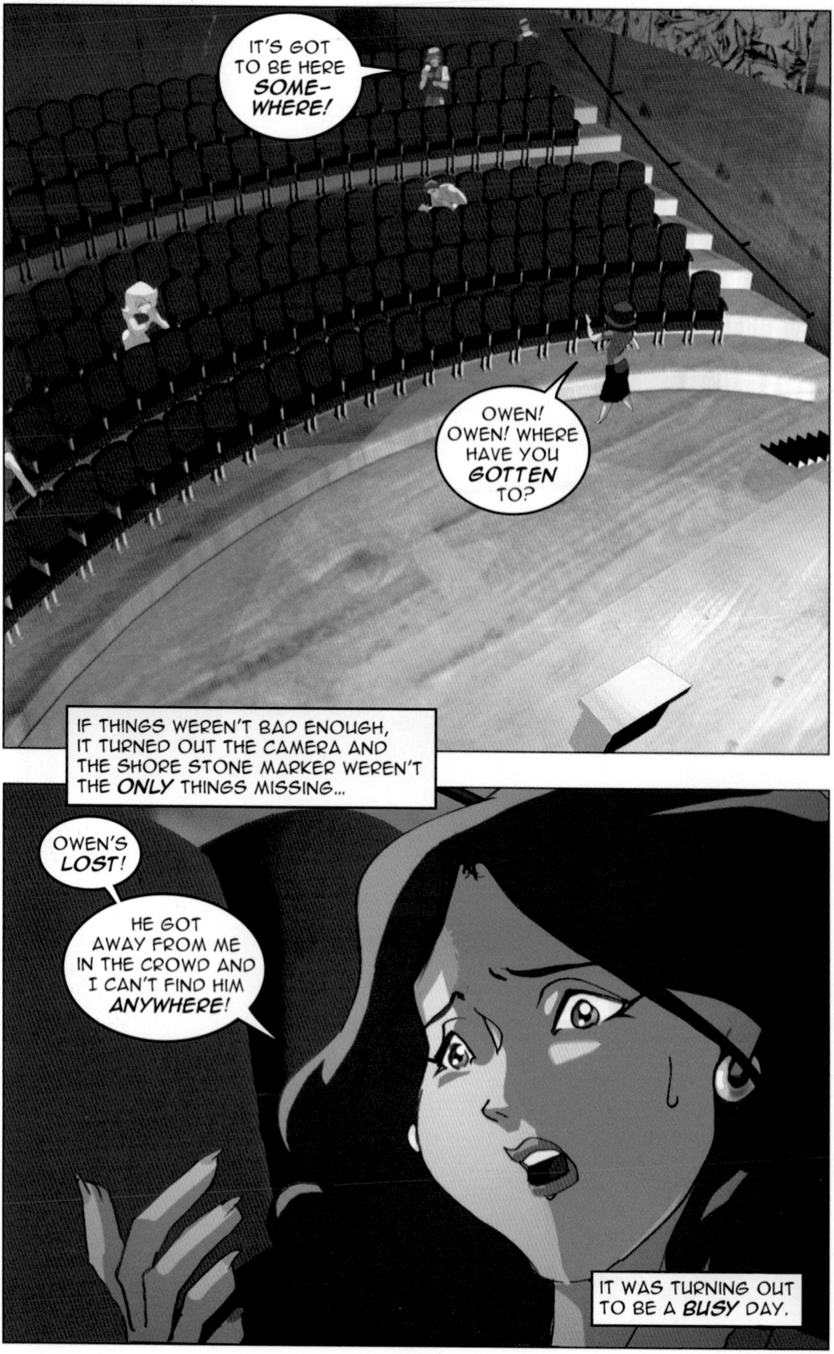
IT'S GOT TO BE HERE SOME-WHERE!
OWEN! OWEN! WHERE HAVE YOU GOTTEN TO?
IF THINGS WEREN'T BAD ENOUGH, IT TURNED OUT THE CAMERA AND THE SHORE STONE MARKER WEREN'T THE ONLY THINGS MISSING...
OWEN'S LOST!
HE GOT AWAY FROM ME IN THE CROWD AND I CAN'T FIND HIM ANYWHERE!
IT WAS TURNING OUT TO BE A BUSY DAY.

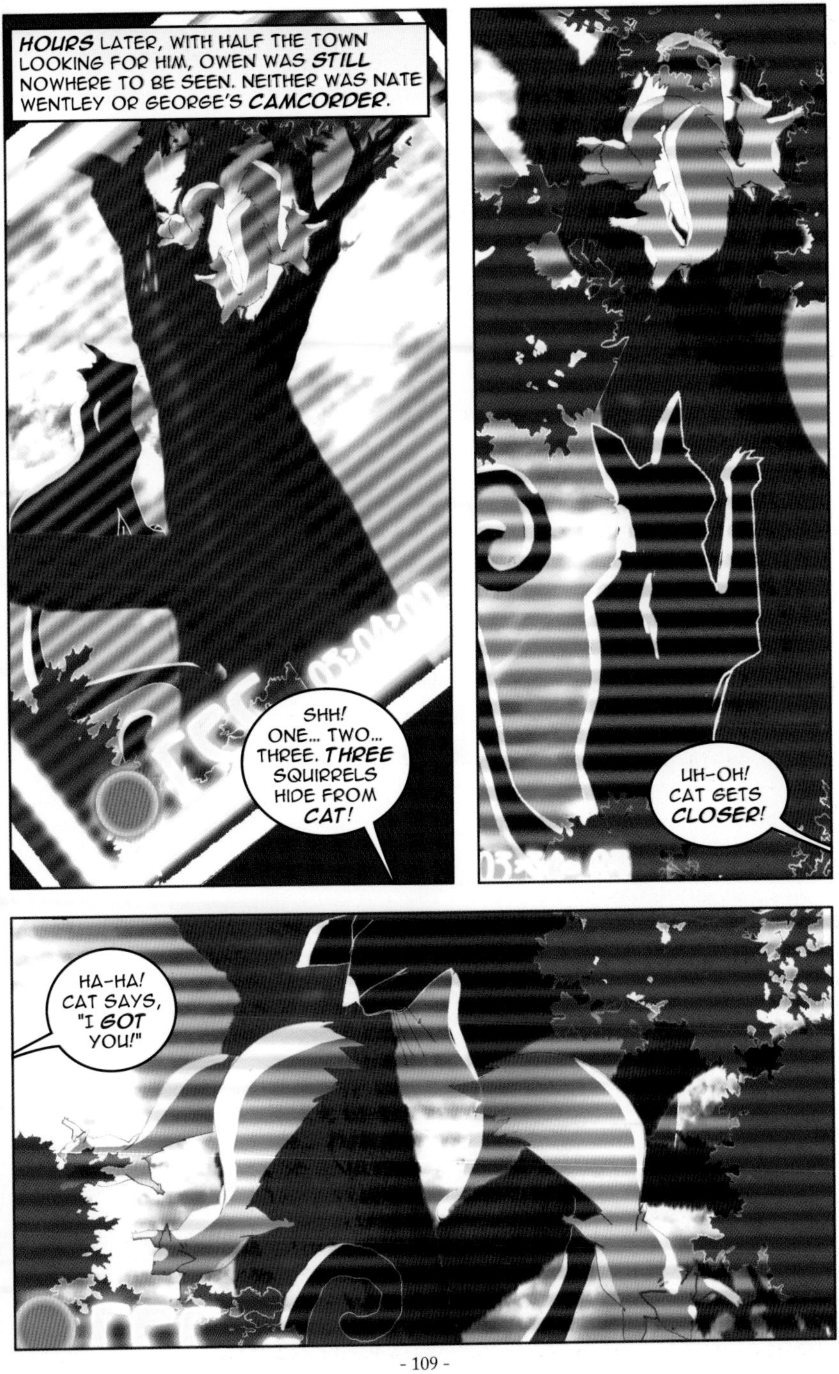
HOURS LATER, WITH HALF THE TOWN LOOKING FOR HIM, OWEN WAS STILL NOWHERE TO BE SEEN. NEITHER WAS NATE WENTLEY OR GEORGE'S CAMCORDER.
SHH! ONE... TWO... THREE. THREE SQUIRRELS HIDE FROM CAT!
UH-OH! CAT GETS CLOSER!
HA-HA! CAT SAYS, "I GOT YOU!"

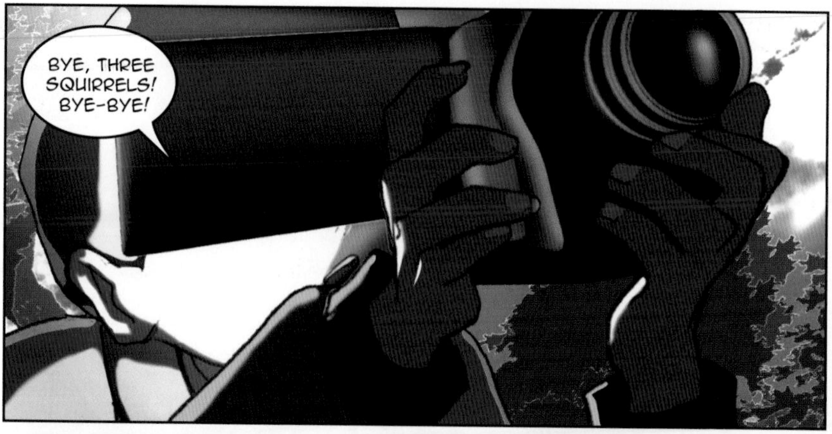
BYE, THREE SQUIRRELS! BYE-BYE!

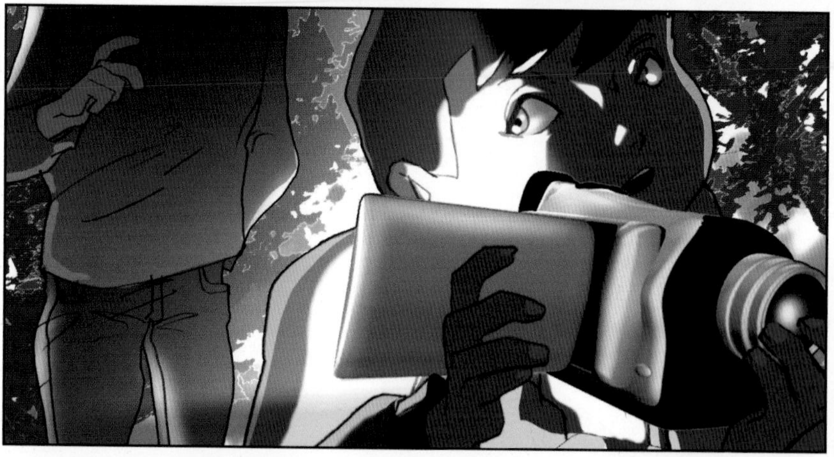

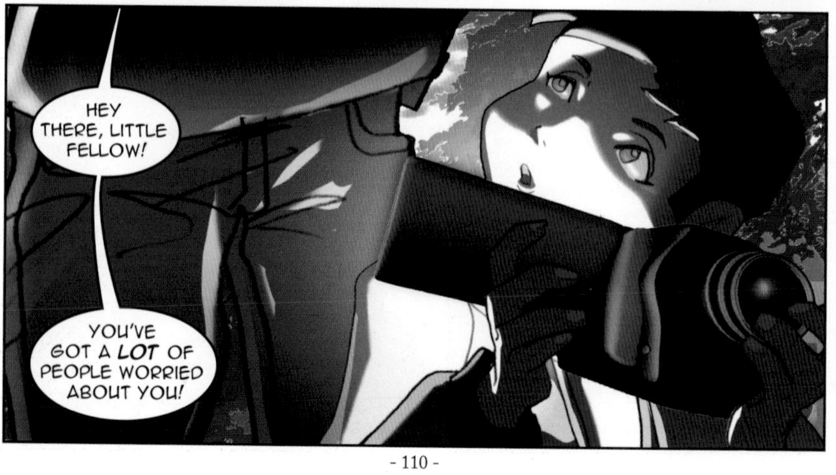
HEY THERE, LITTLE FELLOW!
YOU'VE GOT A **LOT** OF PEOPLE WORRIED ABOUT YOU!

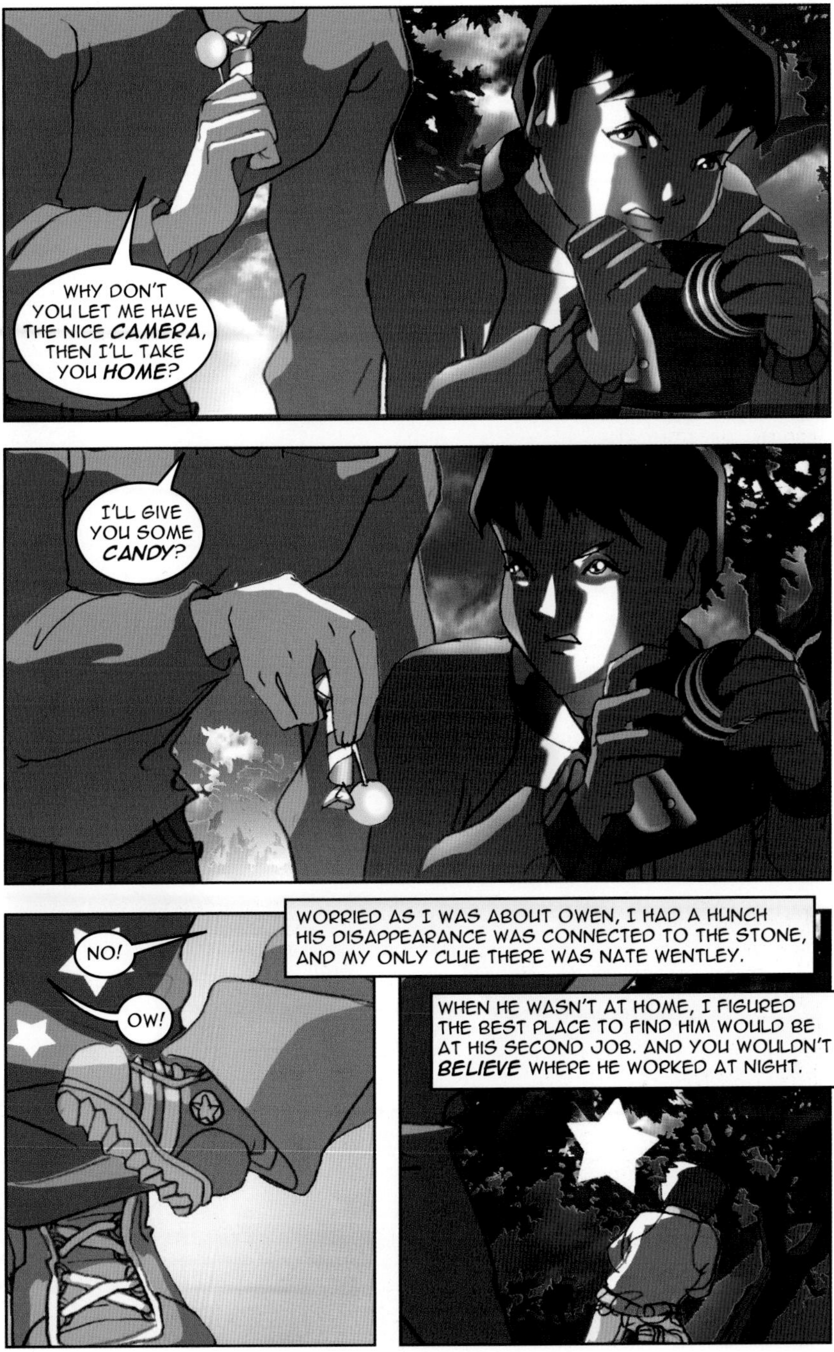
WHY DON'T YOU LET ME HAVE THE NICE CAMERA, THEN I'LL TAKE YOU HOME?
I'LL GIVE YOU SOME CANDY?
WORRIED AS I WAS ABOUT OWEN, I HAD A HUNCH HIS DISAPPEARANCE WAS CONNECTED TO THE STONE, AND MY ONLY CLUE THERE WAS NATE WENTLEY.
NO!
OW!
WHEN HE WASN'T AT HOME, I FIGURED THE BEST PLACE TO FIND HIM WOULD BE AT HIS SECOND JOB. AND YOU WOULDN'T BELIEVE WHERE HE WORKED AT NIGHT.

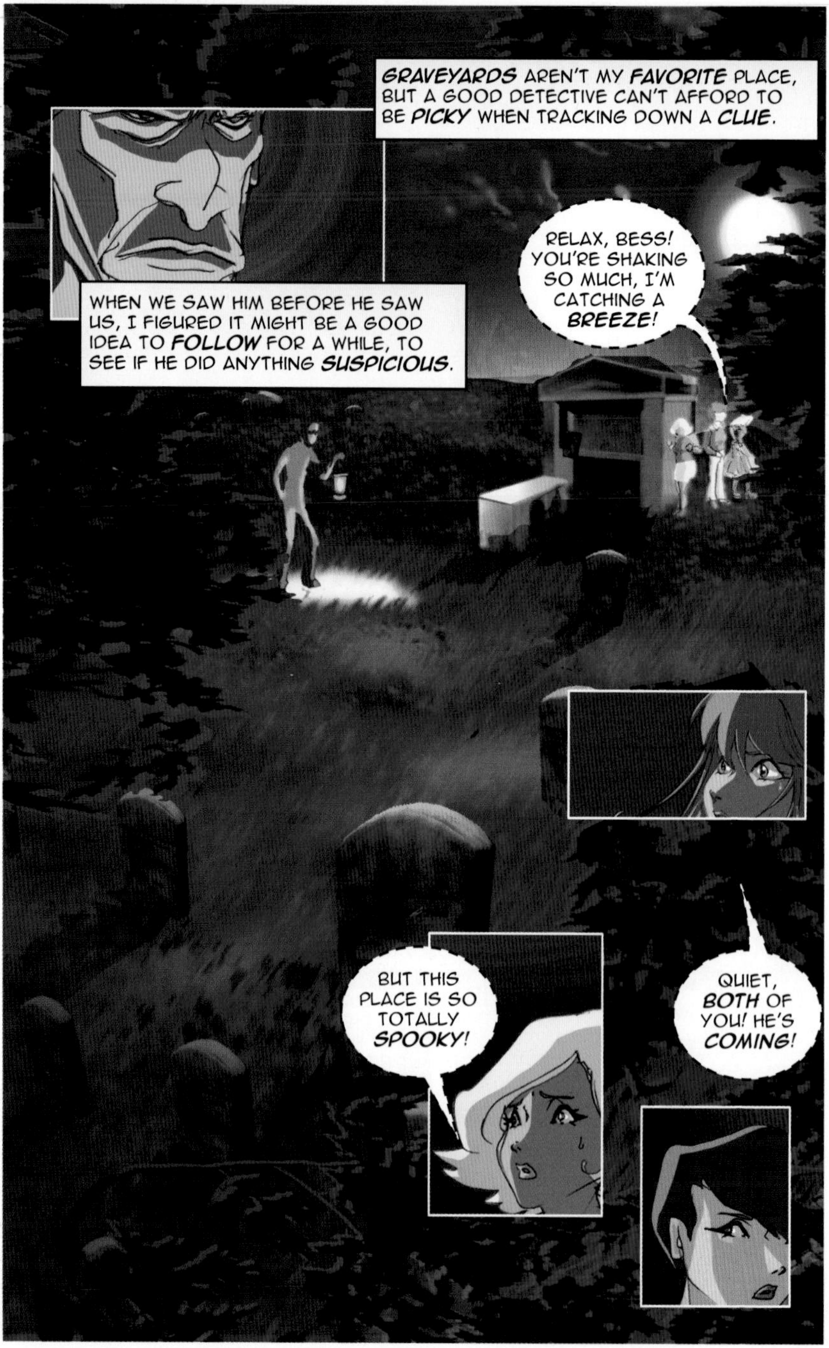
GRAVEYARDS AREN'T MY FAVORITE PLACE, BUT A GOOD DETECTIVE CAN'T AFFORD TO BE PICKY WHEN TRACKING DOWN A CLUE.
WHEN WE SAW HIM BEFORE HE SAW US, I FIGURED IT MIGHT BE A GOOD IDEA TO FOLLOW FOR A WHILE, TO SEE IF HE DID ANYTHING SUSPICIOUS.
RELAX, BESS! YOU'RE SHAKING SO MUCH, I'M CATCHING A BREEZE!
BUT THIS PLACE IS SO TOTALLY SPOOKY!
QUIET, BOTH OF YOU! HE'S COMING!

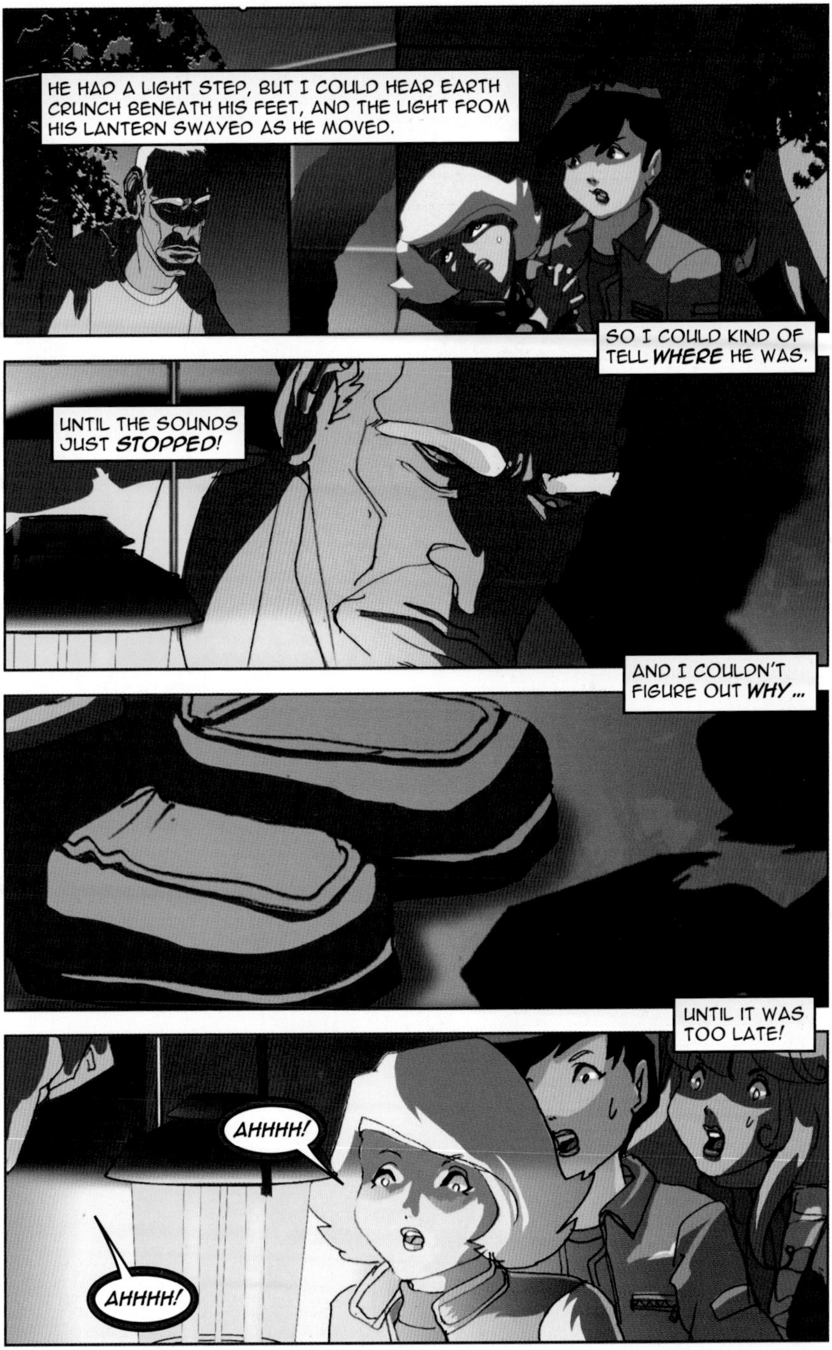
HE HAD A LIGHT STEP, BUT I COULD HEAR EARTH CRUNCH BENEATH HIS FEET, AND THE LIGHT FROM HIS LANTERN SWAYED AS HE MOVED.
SO I COULD KIND OF TELL WHERE HE WAS.
UNTIL THE SOUNDS JUST STOPPED!
AND I COULDN'T FIGURE OUT WHY...
UNTIL IT WAS TOO LATE!
AHHHH!
AHHHH!

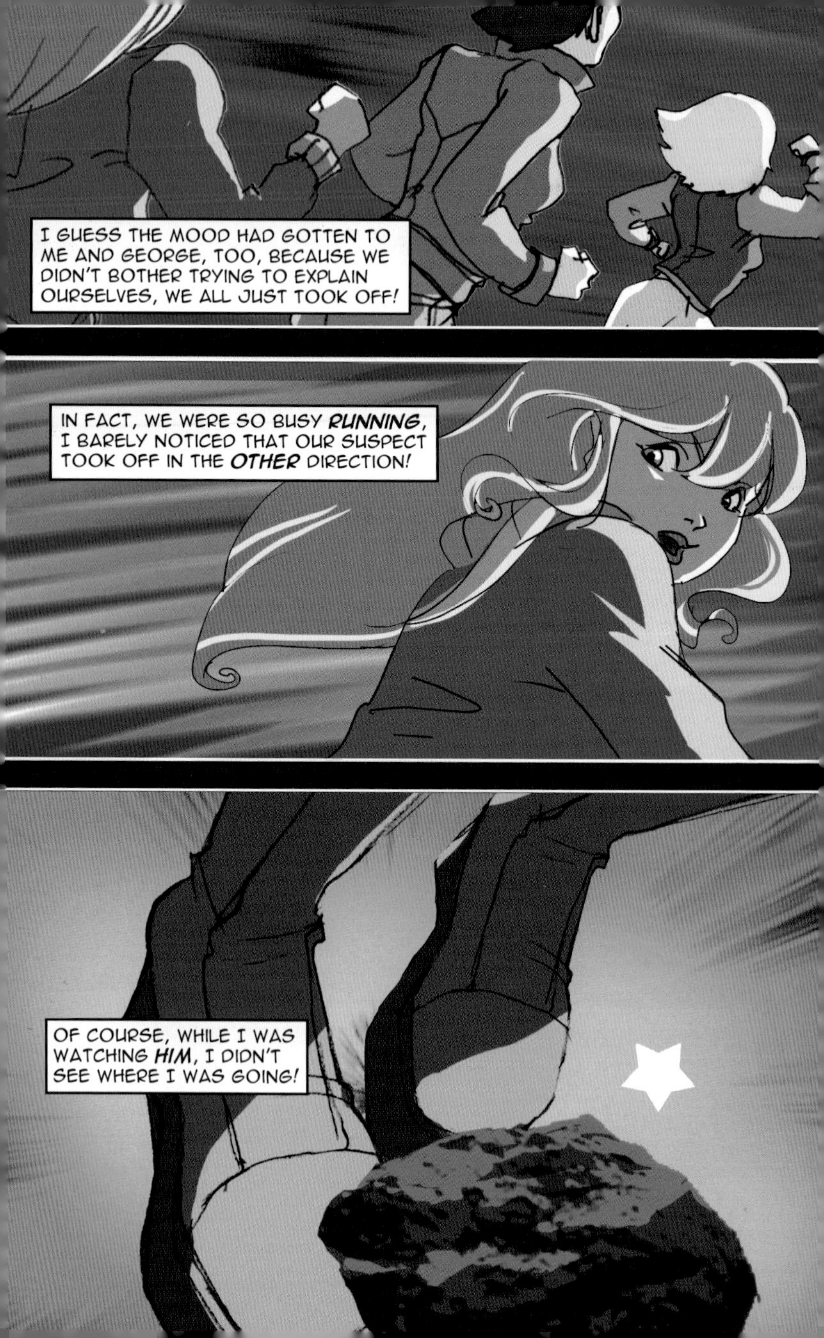
I GUESS THE MOOD HAD GOTTEN TO ME AND GEORGE, TOO, BECAUSE WE DIDN'T BOTHER TRYING TO EXPLAIN OURSELVES, WE ALL JUST TOOK OFF!
IN FACT, WE WERE SO BUSY RUNNING, I BARELY NOTICED THAT OUR SUSPECT TOOK OFF IN THE OTHER DIRECTION!
OF COURSE, WHILE I WAS WATCHING HIM, I DIDN'T SEE WHERE I WAS GOING!

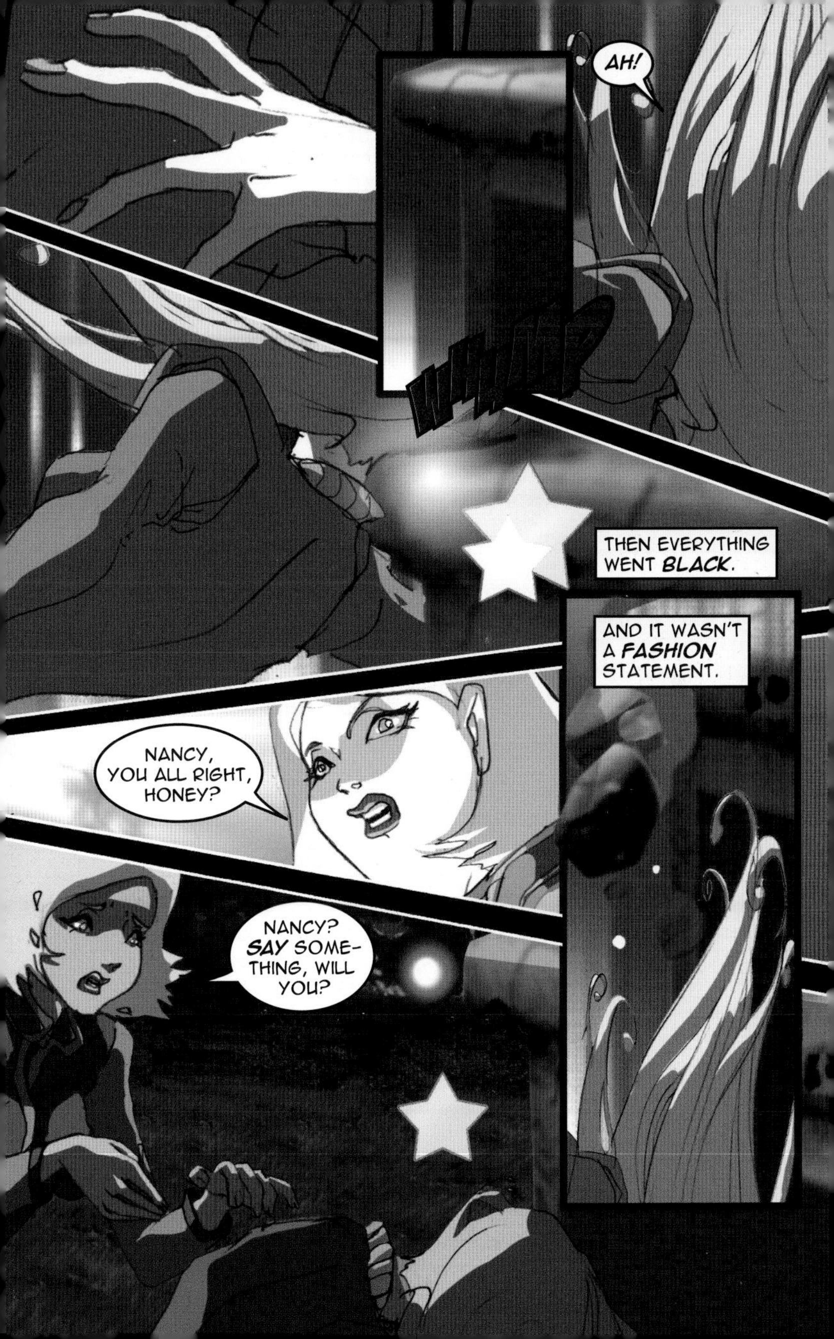
AH!
THEN EVERYTHING WENT BLACK.
AND IT WASN'T A FASHION STATEMENT.
NANCY, YOU ALL RIGHT, HONEY?
NANCY? SAY SOME-THING, WILL YOU?

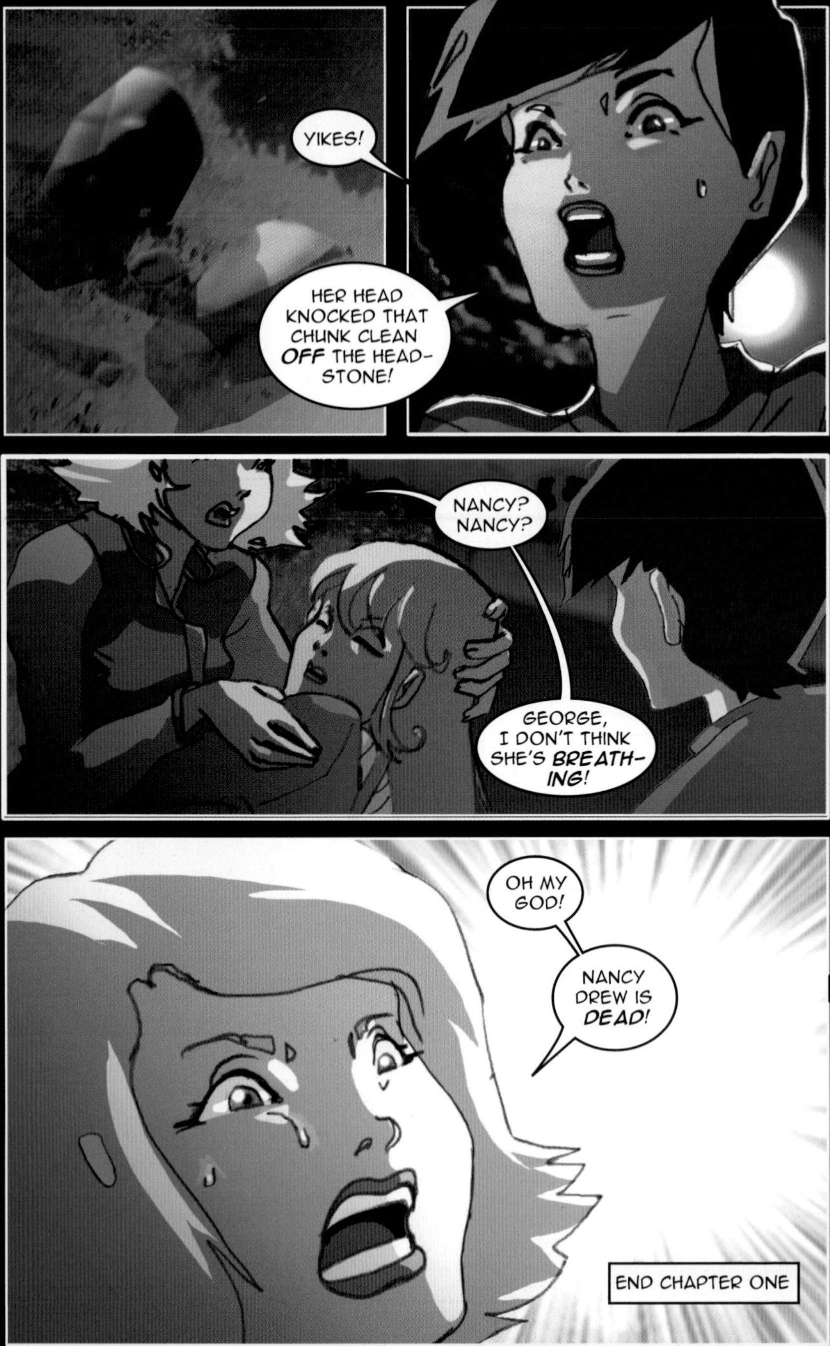
YIKES!
HER HEAD KNOCKED THAT CHUNK CLEAN OFF THE HEAD-STONE!
NANCY? NANCY?
GEORGE, I DON'T THINK SHE'S BREATH-ING!
OH MY GOD!
NANCY DREW IS DEAD!
END CHAPTER ONE

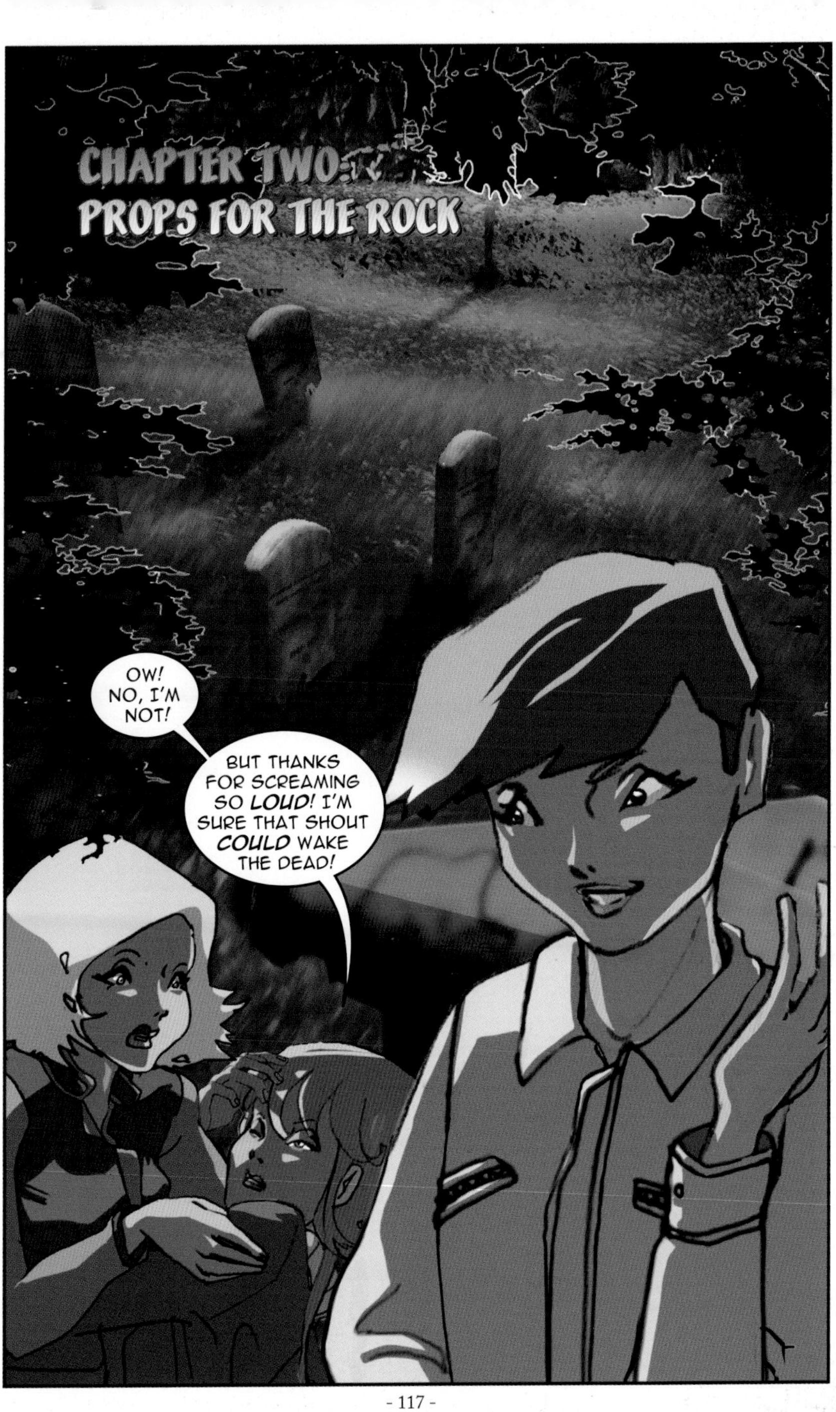
CHAPTER TWO:
PROPS FOR THE ROCK
OW! NO, I'M NOT!
BUT THANKS FOR SCREAMING SO LOUD! I'M SURE THAT SHOUT COULD WAKE THE DEAD!

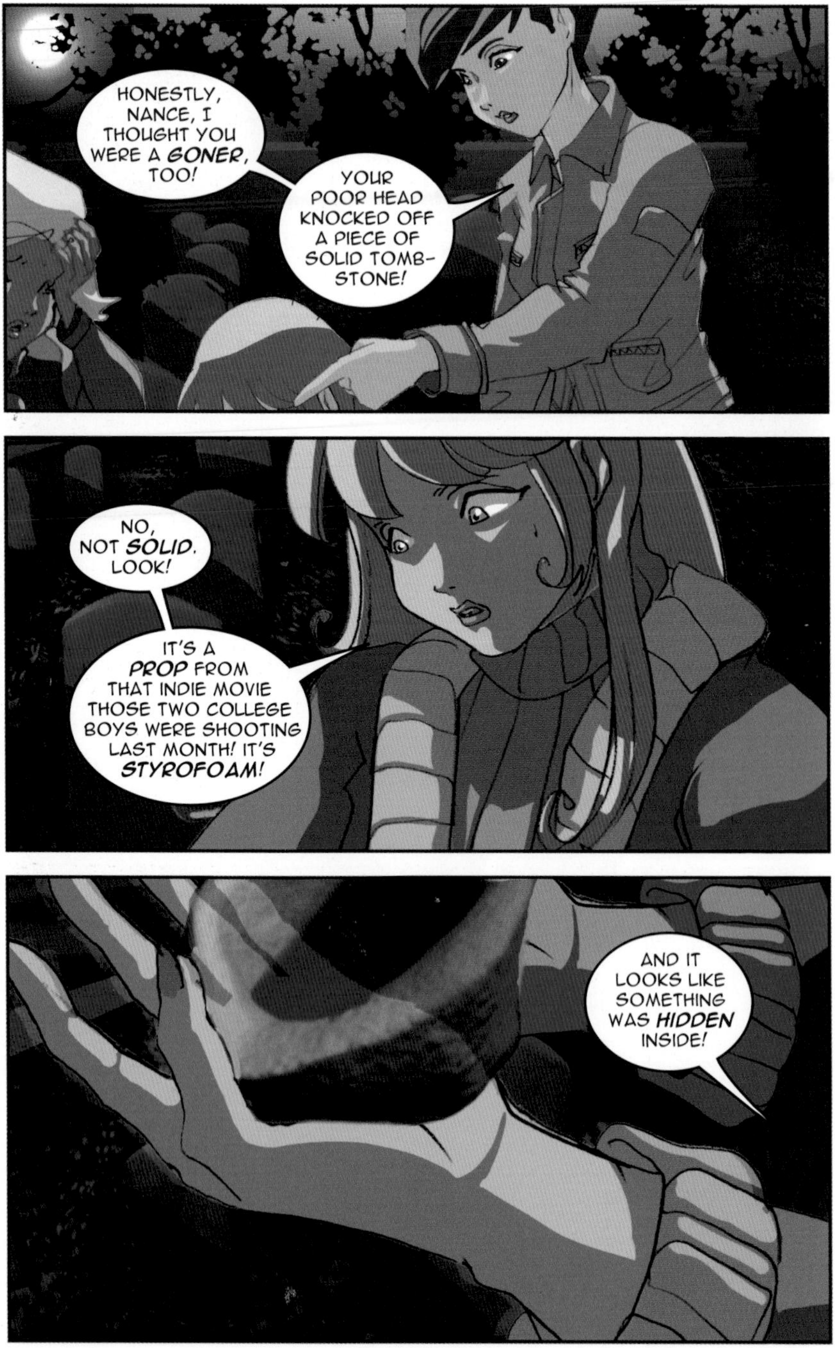
HONESTLY, NANCE, I THOUGHT YOU WERE A GONER, TOO!
YOUR POOR HEAD KNOCKED OFF A PIECE OF SOLID TOMB-STONE!
NO, NOT SOLID. LOOK!
IT'S A PROP FROM THAT INDIE MOVIE THOSE TWO COLLEGE BOYS WERE SHOOTING LAST MONTH! IT'S STYROFOAM!
AND IT LOOKS LIKE SOMETHING WAS HIDDEN INSIDE!

THIS DOESN'T TELL US **WHERE** THE MARKER OR OWEN ARE, BUT CHIEF McGINNIS CAN SURE USE THIS EVIDENCE TO CALL NATE WENTLEY IN FOR QUESTIONING!

Y'KNOW, YOU BORROW MY CELL PHONE CAMERA SO **OFTEN**, I THINK I KNOW WHAT YOUR DAD SHOULD GET FOR YOUR BIRTHDAY!

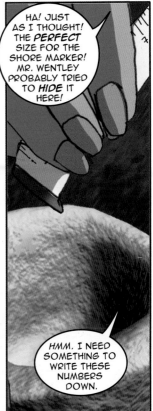

HA! JUST AS I THOUGHT! THE **PERFECT** SIZE FOR THE SHORE MARKER! MR. WENTLEY PROBABLY TRIED TO **HIDE** IT HERE!

HMM. I NEED SOMETHING TO WRITE THESE NUMBERS DOWN.

THANKS FOR THE **EYELINER**, BESS! IT'S PRETTY HANDY!

DID YOU KNOW THEY USED EYELINER 6,000 YEARS AGO, IN EGYPT?

I BET THEY DIDN'T USE IT TO WRITE DOWN MEASUREMENTS FOR THE PYRAMIDS!

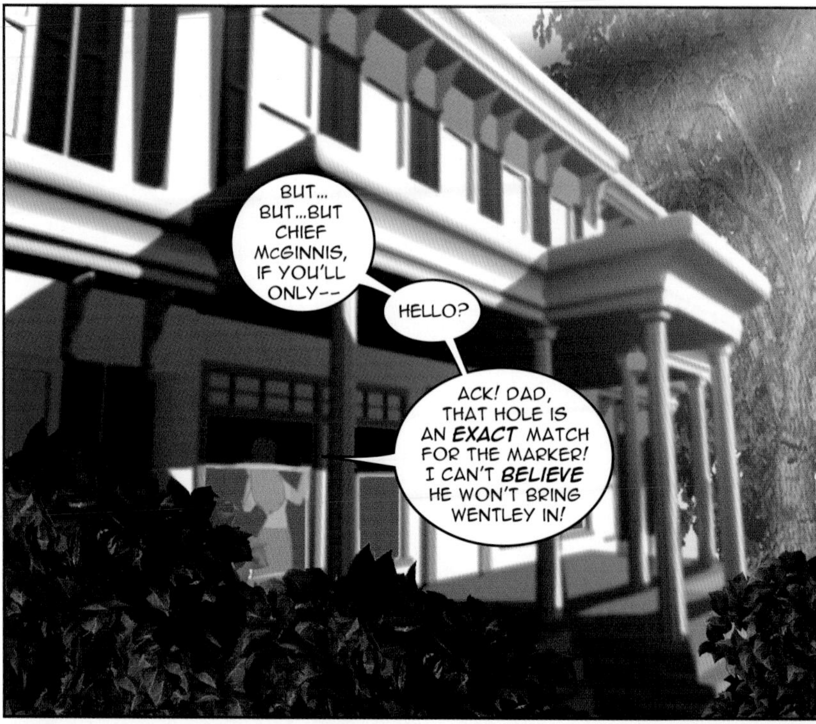
BUT... BUT...BUT CHIEF McGINNIS, IF YOU'LL ONLY--
HELLO?
ACK! DAD, THAT HOLE IS AN *EXACT* MATCH FOR THE MARKER! I CAN'T *BELIEVE* HE WON'T BRING WENTLEY IN!

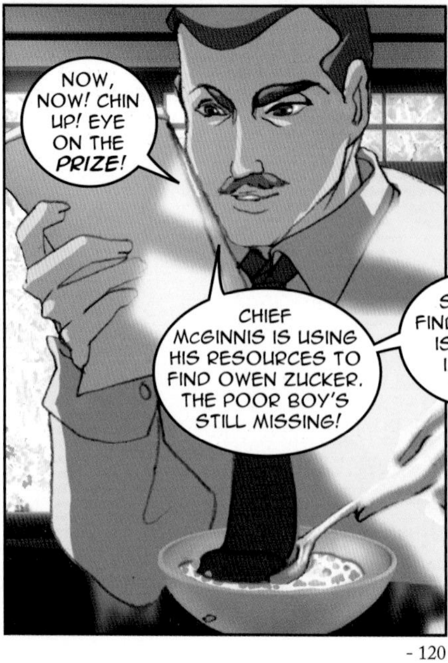
NOW, NOW! CHIN UP! EYE ON THE *PRIZE*!
CHIEF McGINNIS IS USING HIS RESOURCES TO FIND OWEN ZUCKER. THE POOR BOY'S STILL MISSING!
SURELY FINDING *HIM* IS MORE IMPOR-TANT!

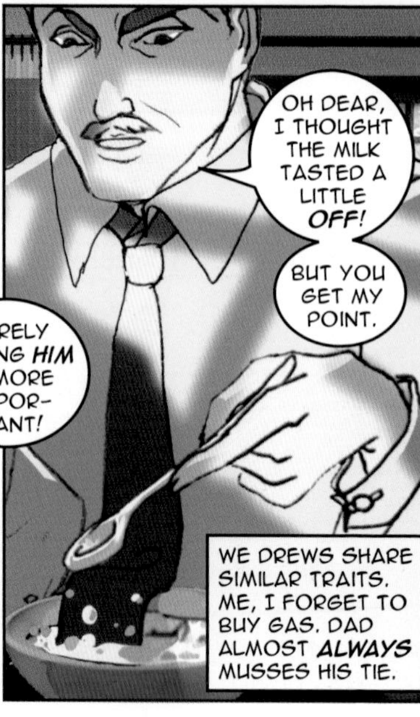
OH DEAR, I THOUGHT THE MILK TASTED A LITTLE *OFF*!
BUT YOU GET MY POINT.
WE DREWS SHARE SIMILAR TRAITS. ME, I FORGET TO BUY GAS. DAD ALMOST *ALWAYS* MUSSES HIS TIE.

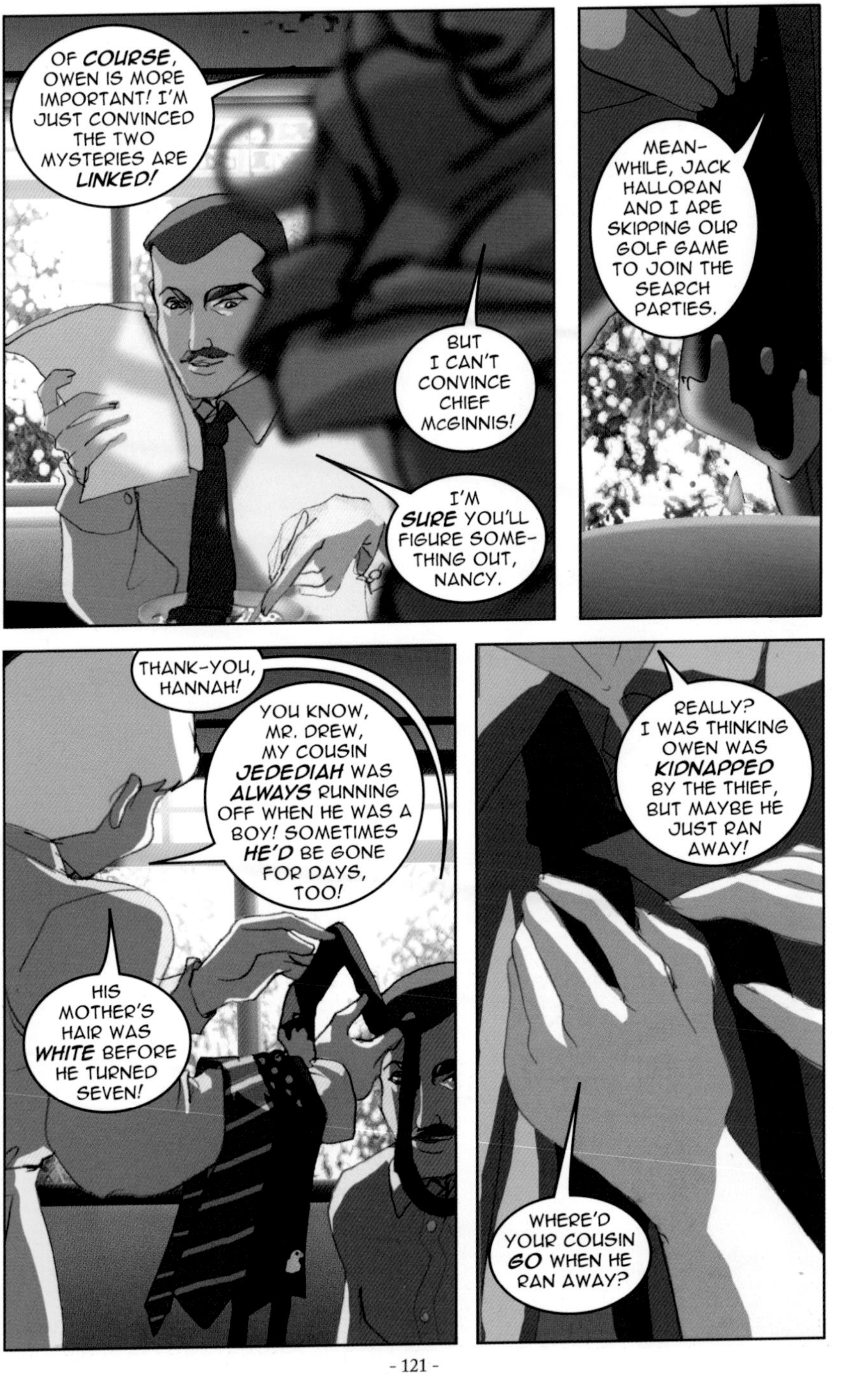
OF COURSE, OWEN IS MORE IMPORTANT! I'M JUST CONVINCED THE TWO MYSTERIES ARE LINKED!
BUT I CAN'T CONVINCE CHIEF McGINNIS!
I'M SURE YOU'LL FIGURE SOMETHING OUT, NANCY.
MEANWHILE, JACK HALLORAN AND I ARE SKIPPING OUR GOLF GAME TO JOIN THE SEARCH PARTIES.
THANK-YOU, HANNAH!
YOU KNOW, MR. DREW, MY COUSIN JEDEDIAH WAS ALWAYS RUNNING OFF WHEN HE WAS A BOY! SOMETIMES HE'D BE GONE FOR DAYS, TOO!
HIS MOTHER'S HAIR WAS WHITE BEFORE HE TURNED SEVEN!
REALLY? I WAS THINKING OWEN WAS KIDNAPPED BY THE THIEF, BUT MAYBE HE JUST RAN AWAY!
WHERE'D YOUR COUSIN GO WHEN HE RAN AWAY?

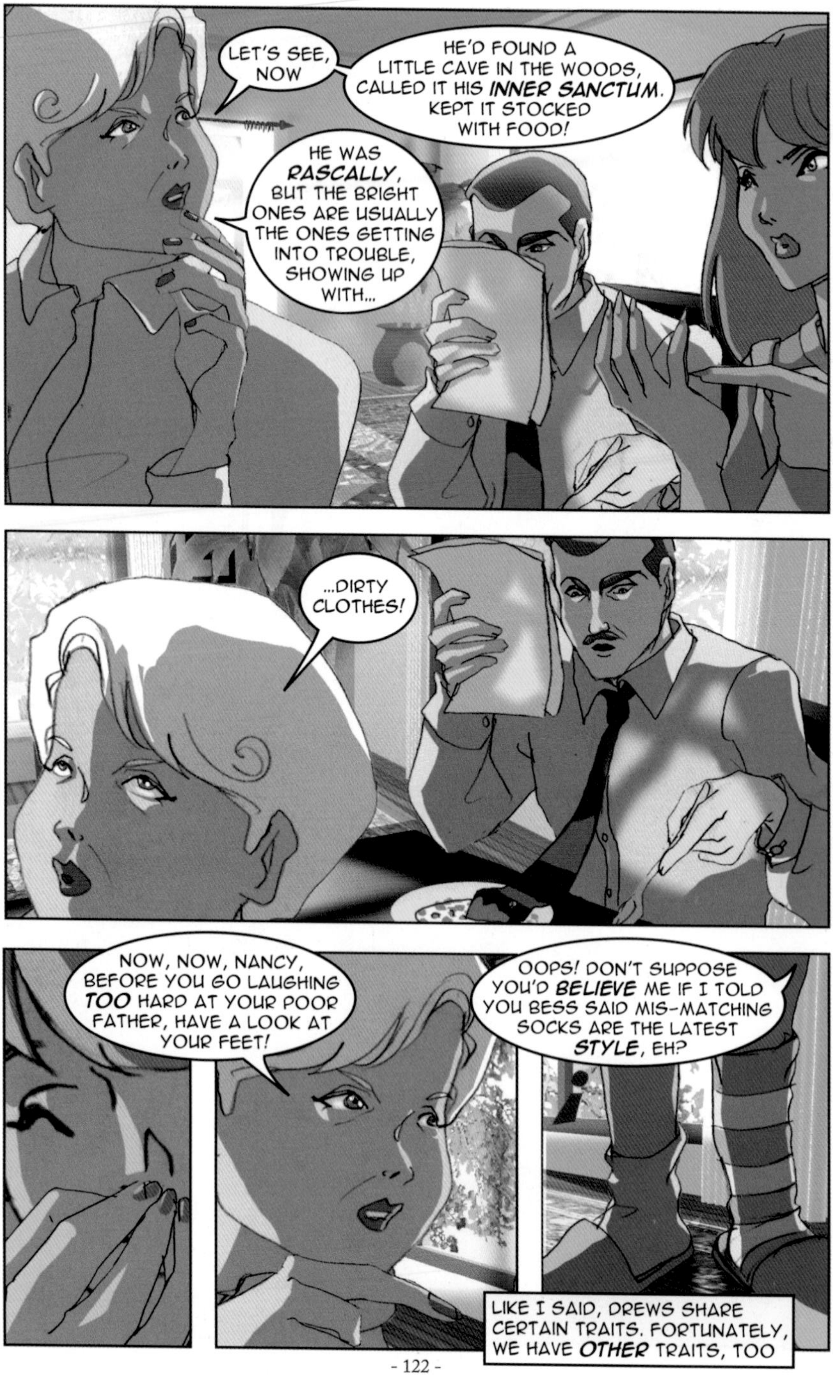
LET'S SEE, NOW
HE'D FOUND A LITTLE CAVE IN THE WOODS, CALLED IT HIS INNER SANCTUM. KEPT IT STOCKED WITH FOOD!
HE WAS RASCALLY, BUT THE BRIGHT ONES ARE USUALLY THE ONES GETTING INTO TROUBLE, SHOWING UP WITH...
...DIRTY CLOTHES!
NOW, NOW, NANCY, BEFORE YOU GO LAUGHING TOO HARD AT YOUR POOR FATHER, HAVE A LOOK AT YOUR FEET!
OOPS! DON'T SUPPOSE YOU'D BELIEVE ME IF I TOLD YOU BESS SAID MIS-MATCHING SOCKS ARE THE LATEST STYLE, EH?
LIKE I SAID, DREWS SHARE CERTAIN TRAITS. FORTUNATELY, WE HAVE OTHER TRAITS, TOO

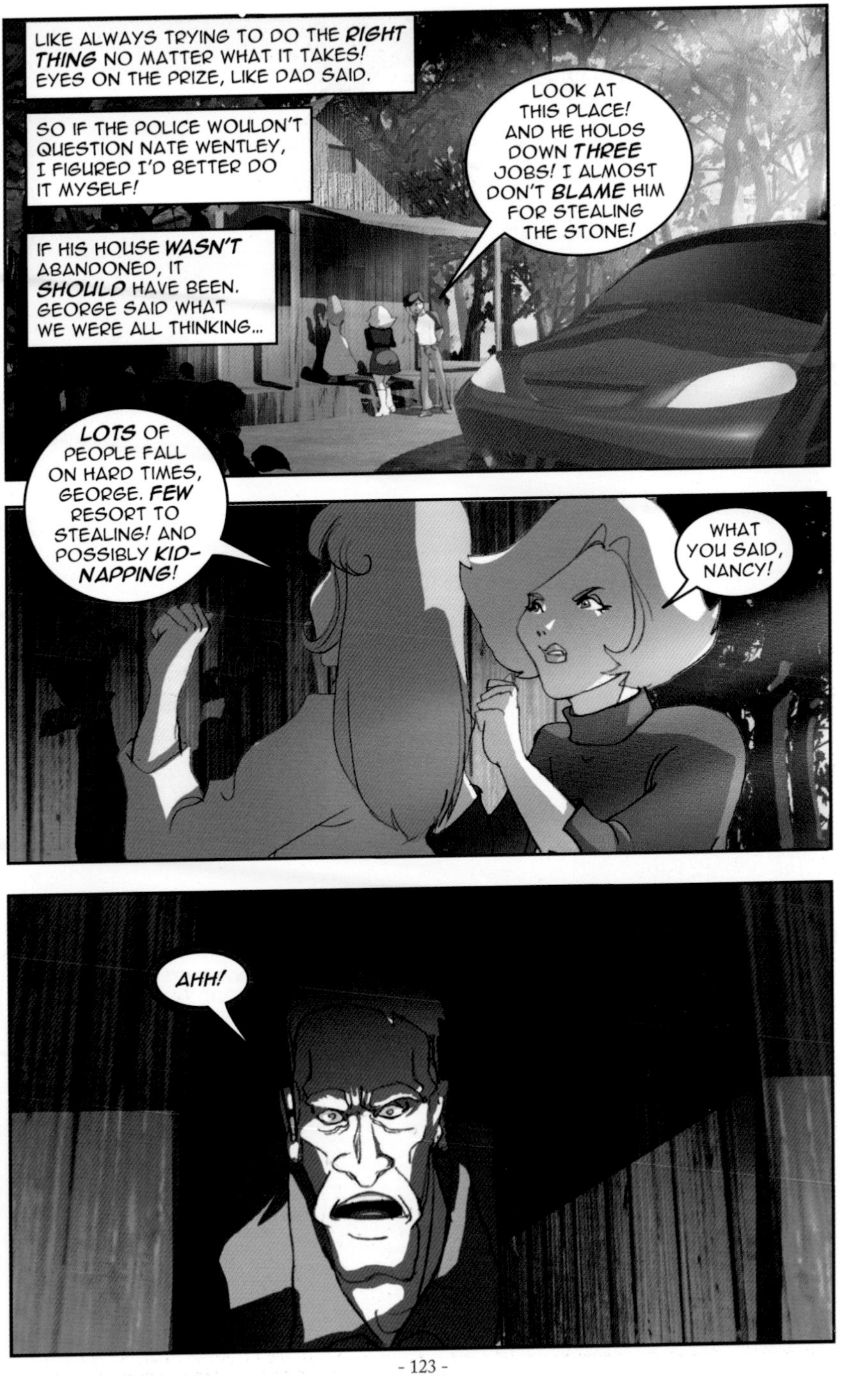
LIKE ALWAYS TRYING TO DO THE RIGHT THING NO MATTER WHAT IT TAKES! EYES ON THE PRIZE, LIKE DAD SAID.
SO IF THE POLICE WOULDN'T QUESTION NATE WENTLEY, I FIGURED I'D BETTER DO IT MYSELF!
IF HIS HOUSE WASN'T ABANDONED, IT SHOULD HAVE BEEN. GEORGE SAID WHAT WE WERE ALL THINKING...
LOOK AT THIS PLACE! AND HE HOLDS DOWN THREE JOBS! I ALMOST DON'T BLAME HIM FOR STEALING THE STONE!
LOTS OF PEOPLE FALL ON HARD TIMES, GEORGE. FEW RESORT TO STEALING! AND POSSIBLY KID-NAPPING!
WHAT YOU SAID, NANCY!
AHH!

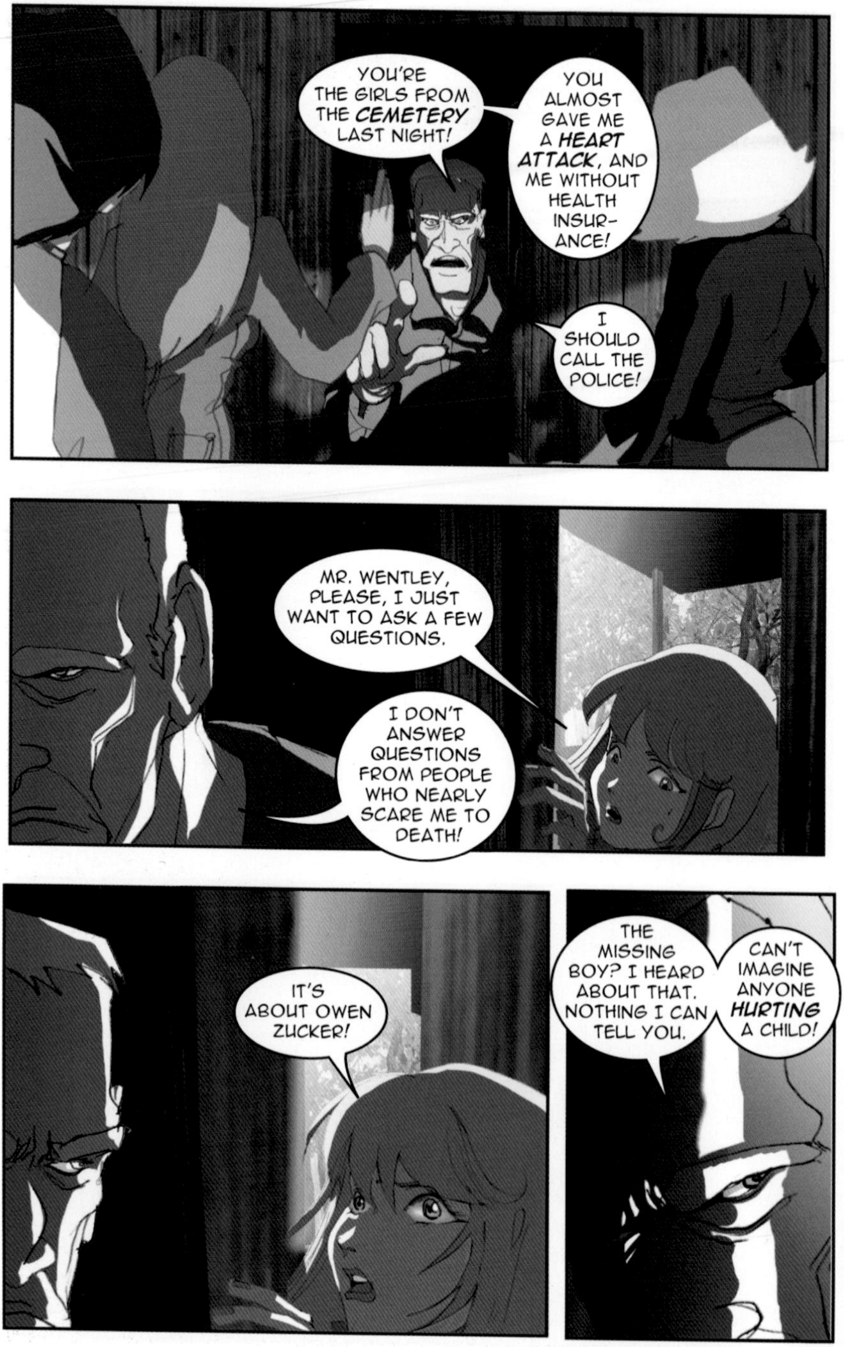
YOU'RE THE GIRLS FROM THE CEMETERY LAST NIGHT!
YOU ALMOST GAVE ME A HEART ATTACK, AND ME WITHOUT HEALTH INSUR-ANCE!
I SHOULD CALL THE POLICE!
MR. WENTLEY, PLEASE, I JUST WANT TO ASK A FEW QUESTIONS.
I DON'T ANSWER QUESTIONS FROM PEOPLE WHO NEARLY SCARE ME TO DEATH!
IT'S ABOUT OWEN ZUCKER!
THE MISSING BOY? I HEARD ABOUT THAT. NOTHING I CAN TELL YOU.
CAN'T IMAGINE ANYONE HURTING A CHILD!

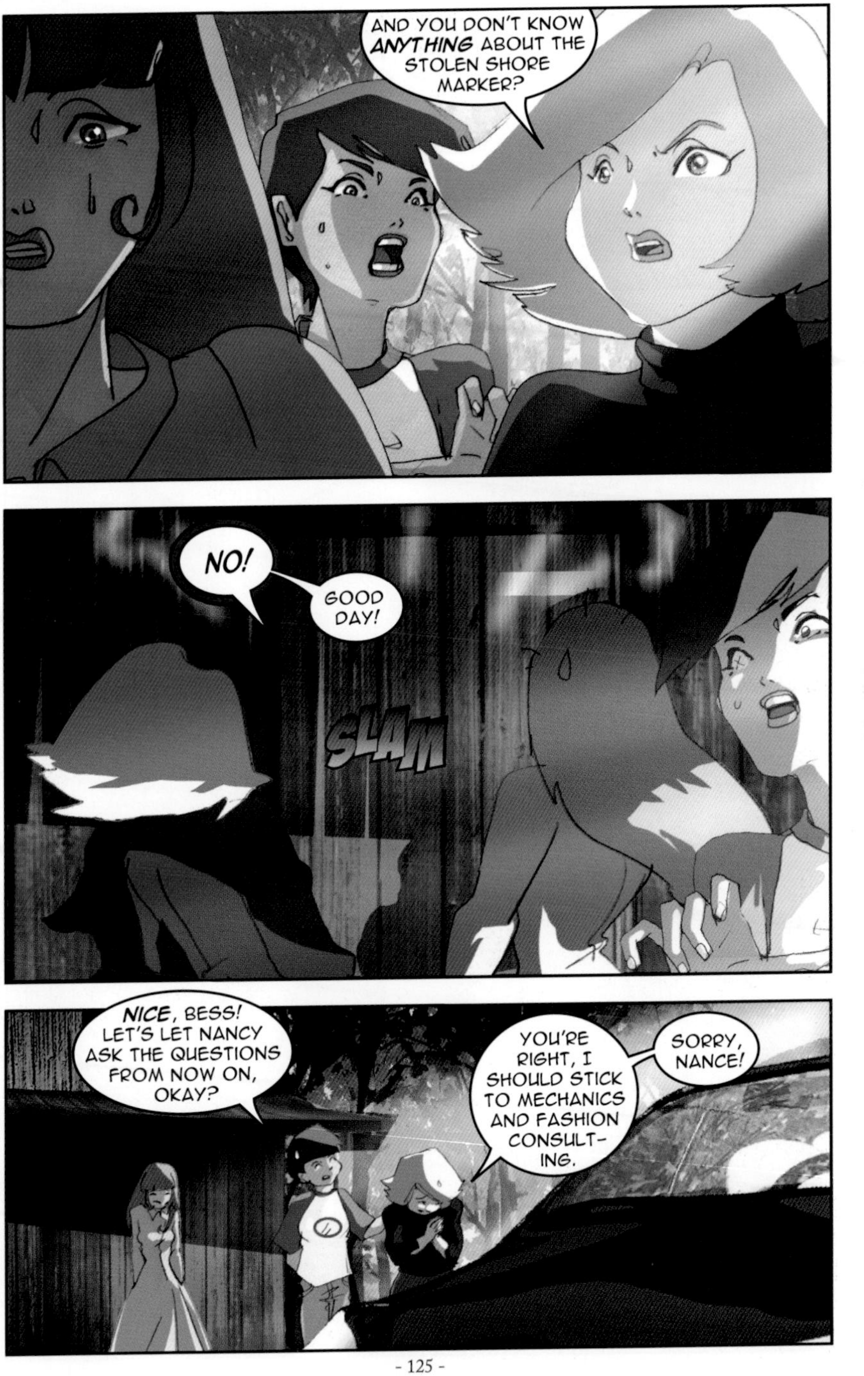
AND YOU DON'T KNOW *ANYTHING* ABOUT THE STOLEN SHORE MARKER?
NO!
GOOD DAY!
SLAM
NICE, BESS! LET'S LET NANCY ASK THE QUESTIONS FROM NOW ON, OKAY?
SORRY, NANCE!
YOU'RE RIGHT, I SHOULD STICK TO MECHANICS AND FASHION CONSULT-ING.

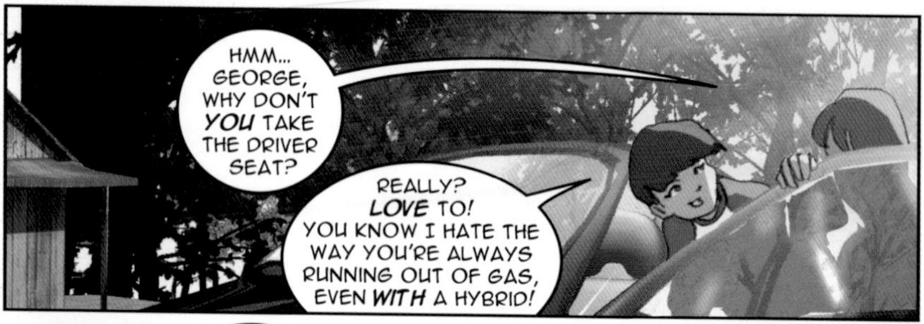
HMM... GEORGE, WHY DON'T *YOU* TAKE THE DRIVER SEAT?
REALLY? *LOVE* TO! YOU KNOW I HATE THE WAY YOU'RE ALWAYS RUNNING OUT OF GAS, EVEN *WITH* A HYBRID!

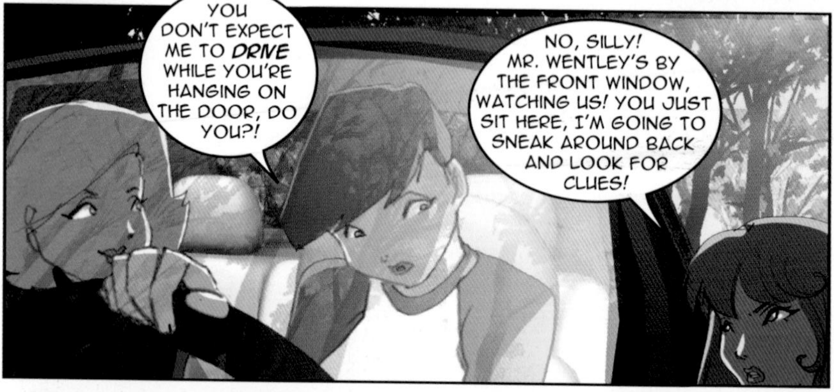
YOU DON'T EXPECT ME TO *DRIVE* WHILE YOU'RE HANGING ON THE DOOR, DO YOU?!
NO, SILLY! MR. WENTLEY'S BY THE FRONT WINDOW, WATCHING US! YOU JUST SIT HERE, I'M GOING TO SNEAK AROUND BACK AND LOOK FOR CLUES!

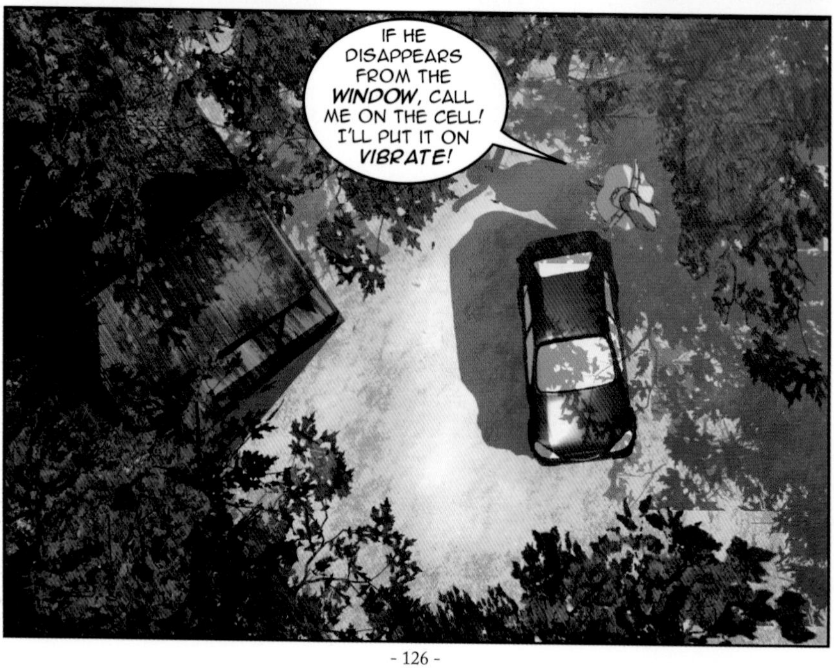
IF HE DISAPPEARS FROM THE *WINDOW*, CALL ME ON THE CELL! I'LL PUT IT ON *VIBRATE*!

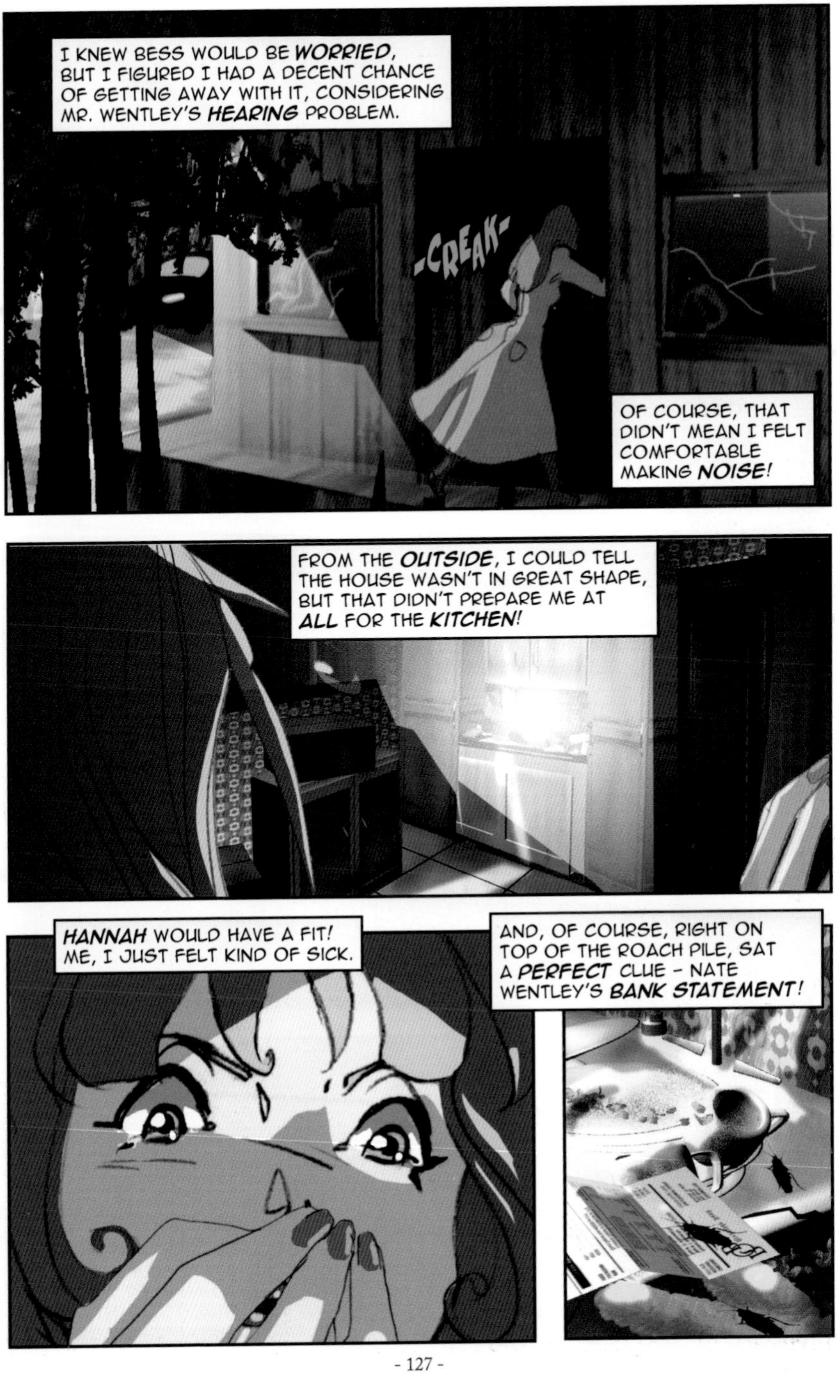
I KNEW BESS WOULD BE WORRIED, BUT I FIGURED I HAD A DECENT CHANCE OF GETTING AWAY WITH IT, CONSIDERING MR. WENTLEY'S HEARING PROBLEM.
-CREAK-
OF COURSE, THAT DIDN'T MEAN I FELT COMFORTABLE MAKING NOISE!
FROM THE OUTSIDE, I COULD TELL THE HOUSE WASN'T IN GREAT SHAPE, BUT THAT DIDN'T PREPARE ME AT ALL FOR THE KITCHEN!
HANNAH WOULD HAVE A FIT! ME, I JUST FELT KIND OF SICK.
AND, OF COURSE, RIGHT ON TOP OF THE ROACH PILE, SAT A PERFECT CLUE - NATE WENTLEY'S BANK STATEMENT!

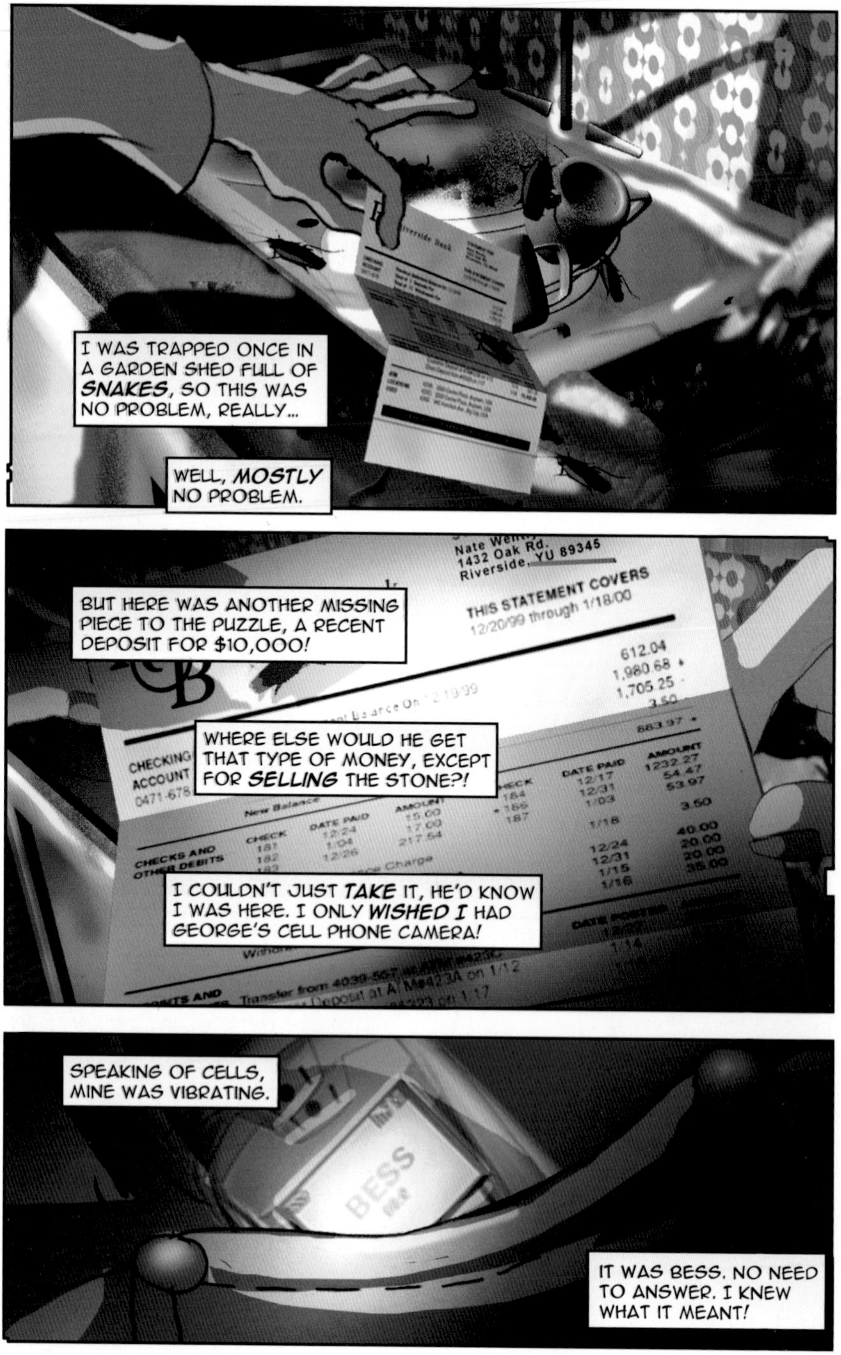
I WAS TRAPPED ONCE IN A GARDEN SHED FULL OF *SNAKES*, SO THIS WAS NO PROBLEM, REALLY...
WELL, *MOSTLY* NO PROBLEM.
1432 Oak Rd.
Riverside, YU 89345
THIS STATEMENT COVERS
12/20/99 through 1/18/00
BUT HERE WAS ANOTHER MISSING PIECE TO THE PUZZLE, A RECENT DEPOSIT FOR $10,000!
WHERE ELSE WOULD HE GET THAT TYPE OF MONEY, EXCEPT FOR *SELLING* THE STONE?!
I COULDN'T JUST *TAKE* IT, HE'D KNOW I WAS HERE. I ONLY *WISHED I* HAD GEORGE'S CELL PHONE CAMERA!
SPEAKING OF CELLS, MINE WAS VIBRATING.
BESS
IT WAS BESS. NO NEED TO ANSWER. I KNEW WHAT IT MEANT!

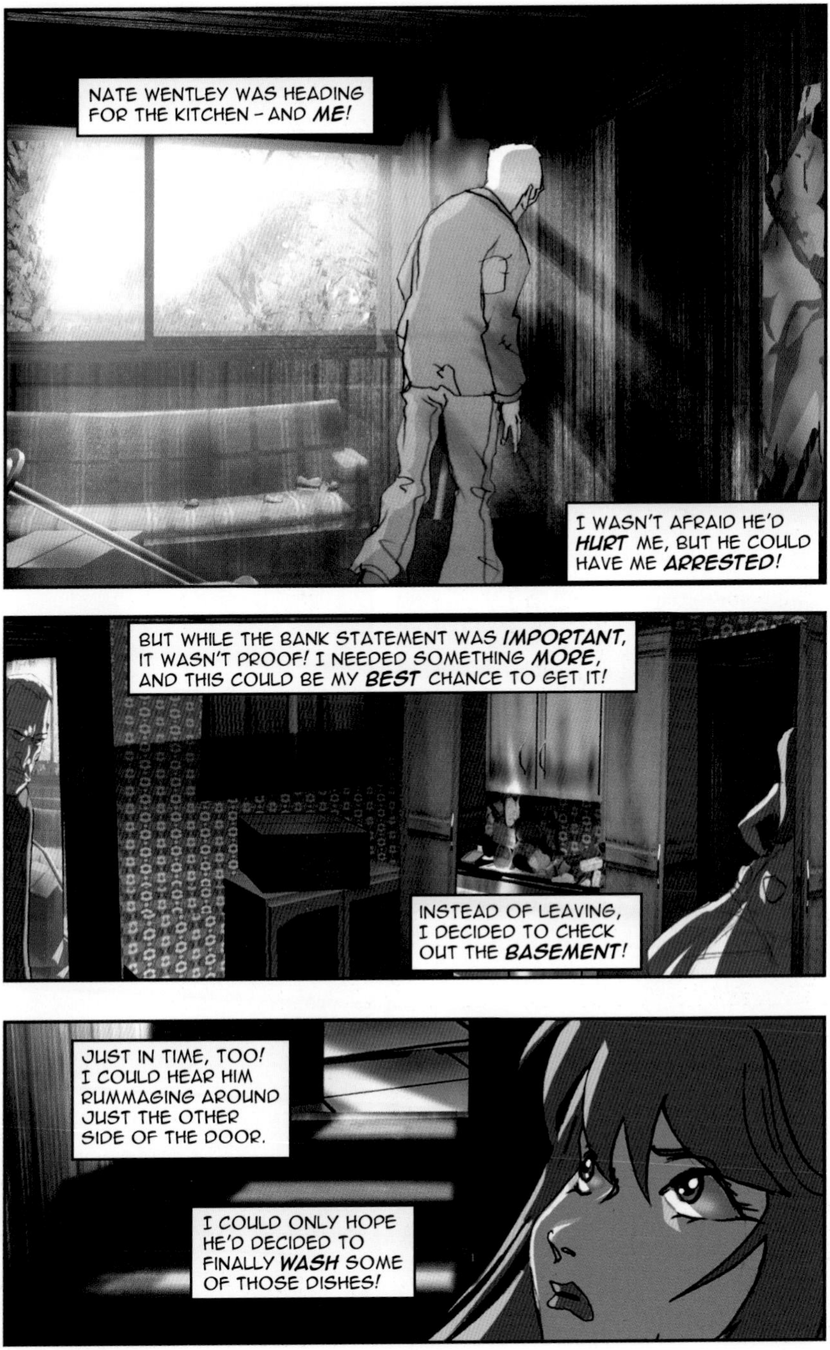
NATE WENTLEY WAS HEADING FOR THE KITCHEN – AND *ME!*
I WASN'T AFRAID HE'D *HURT* ME, BUT HE COULD HAVE ME *ARRESTED!*
BUT WHILE THE BANK STATEMENT WAS *IMPORTANT*, IT WASN'T PROOF! I NEEDED SOMETHING *MORE*, AND THIS COULD BE MY *BEST* CHANCE TO GET IT!
INSTEAD OF LEAVING, I DECIDED TO CHECK OUT THE *BASEMENT!*
JUST IN TIME, TOO! I COULD HEAR HIM RUMMAGING AROUND JUST THE OTHER SIDE OF THE DOOR.
I COULD ONLY HOPE HE'D DECIDED TO FINALLY *WASH* SOME OF THOSE DISHES!

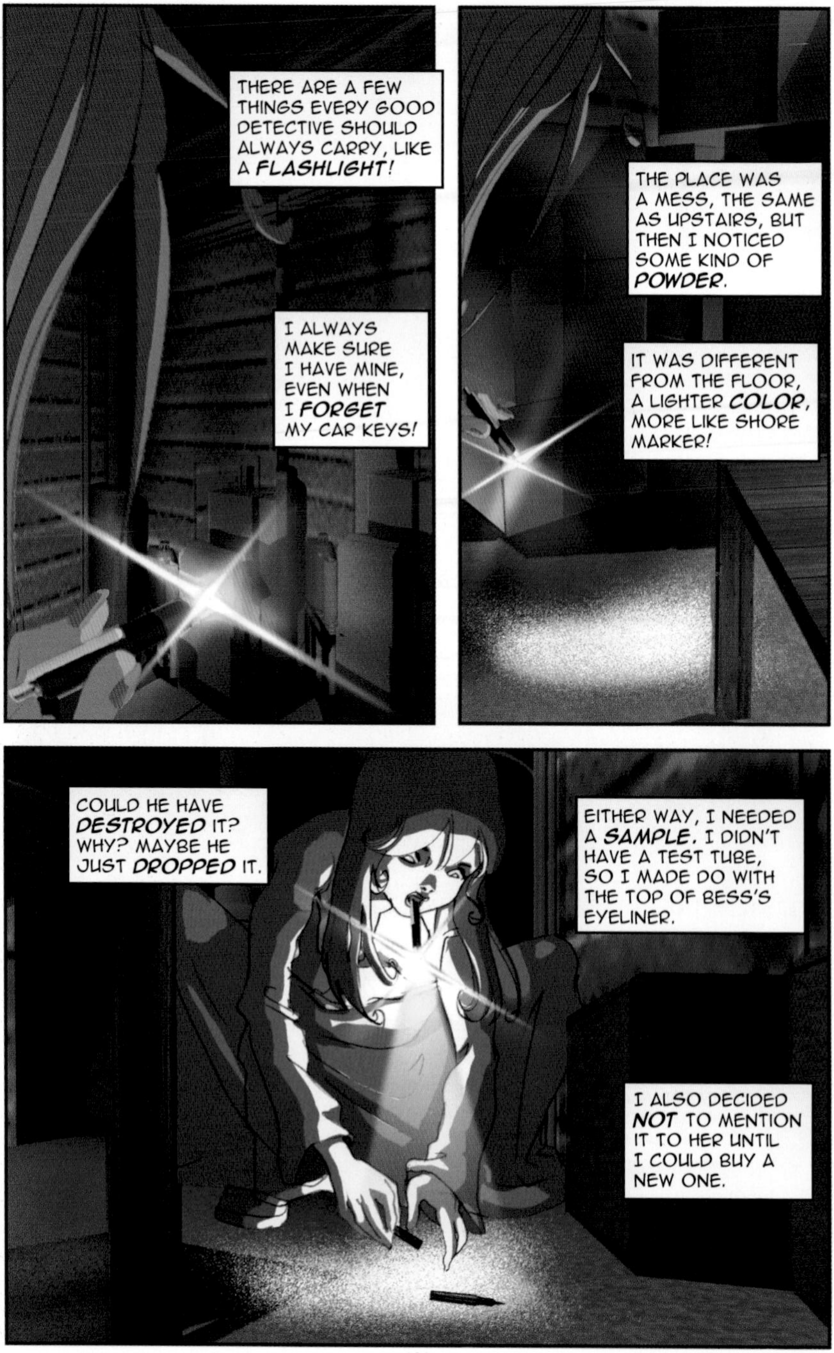
THERE ARE A FEW THINGS EVERY GOOD DETECTIVE SHOULD ALWAYS CARRY, LIKE A FLASHLIGHT!
I ALWAYS MAKE SURE I HAVE MINE, EVEN WHEN I FORGET MY CAR KEYS!
THE PLACE WAS A MESS, THE SAME AS UPSTAIRS, BUT THEN I NOTICED SOME KIND OF POWDER.
IT WAS DIFFERENT FROM THE FLOOR, A LIGHTER COLOR, MORE LIKE SHORE MARKER!
COULD HE HAVE DESTROYED IT? WHY? MAYBE HE JUST DROPPED IT.
EITHER WAY, I NEEDED A SAMPLE. I DIDN'T HAVE A TEST TUBE, SO I MADE DO WITH THE TOP OF BESS'S EYELINER.
I ALSO DECIDED NOT TO MENTION IT TO HER UNTIL I COULD BUY A NEW ONE.

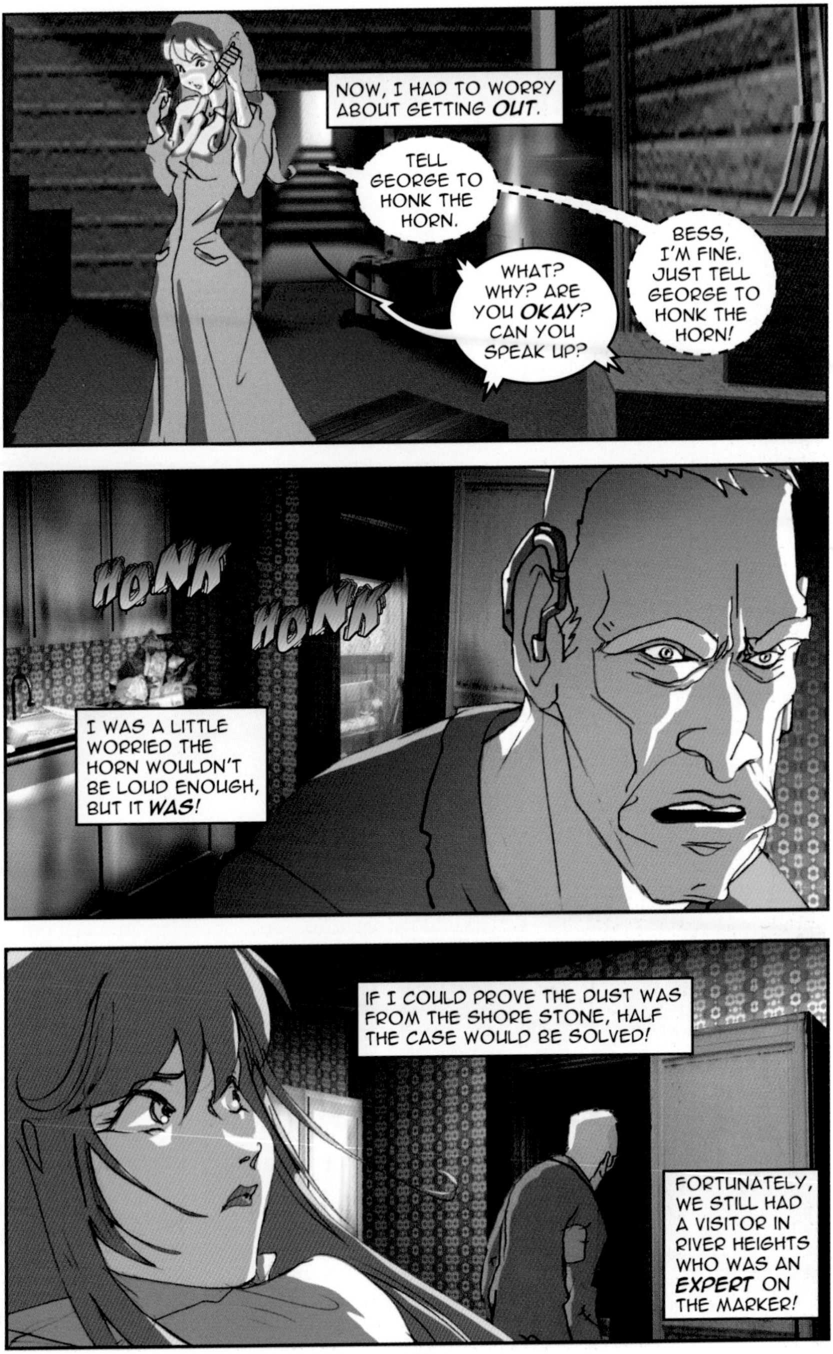
NOW, I HAD TO WORRY ABOUT GETTING *OUT*.
TELL GEORGE TO HONK THE HORN.
WHAT? WHY? ARE YOU *OKAY*? CAN YOU SPEAK UP?
BESS, I'M FINE. JUST TELL GEORGE TO HONK THE HORN!
HONK
HONK
I WAS A LITTLE WORRIED THE HORN WOULDN'T BE LOUD ENOUGH, BUT IT *WAS*!
IF I COULD PROVE THE DUST WAS FROM THE SHORE STONE, HALF THE CASE WOULD BE SOLVED!
FORTUNATELY, WE STILL HAD A VISITOR IN RIVER HEIGHTS WHO WAS AN *EXPERT* ON THE MARKER!

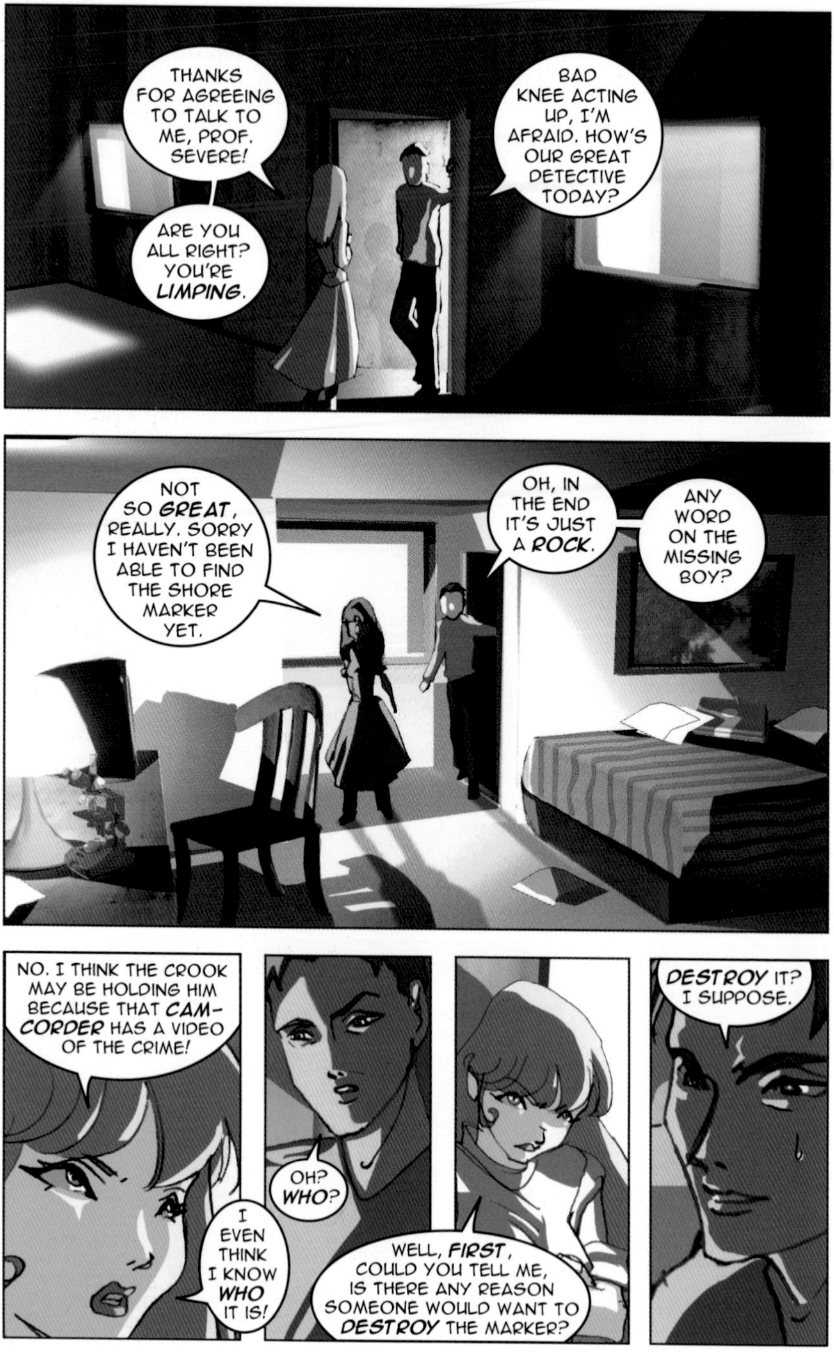
THANKS FOR AGREEING TO TALK TO ME, PROF. SEVERE!
ARE YOU ALL RIGHT? YOU'RE *LIMPING*.
BAD KNEE ACTING UP, I'M AFRAID. HOW'S OUR GREAT DETECTIVE TODAY?
NOT SO *GREAT*, REALLY. SORRY I HAVEN'T BEEN ABLE TO FIND THE SHORE MARKER YET.
OH, IN THE END IT'S JUST A *ROCK*.
ANY WORD ON THE MISSING BOY?
NO. I THINK THE CROOK MAY BE HOLDING HIM BECAUSE THAT *CAM-CORDER* HAS A VIDEO OF THE CRIME!
I EVEN THINK I KNOW *WHO* IT IS!
OH? *WHO*?
WELL, *FIRST*, COULD YOU TELL ME, IS THERE ANY REASON SOMEONE WOULD WANT TO *DESTROY* THE MARKER?
DESTROY IT? I SUPPOSE.

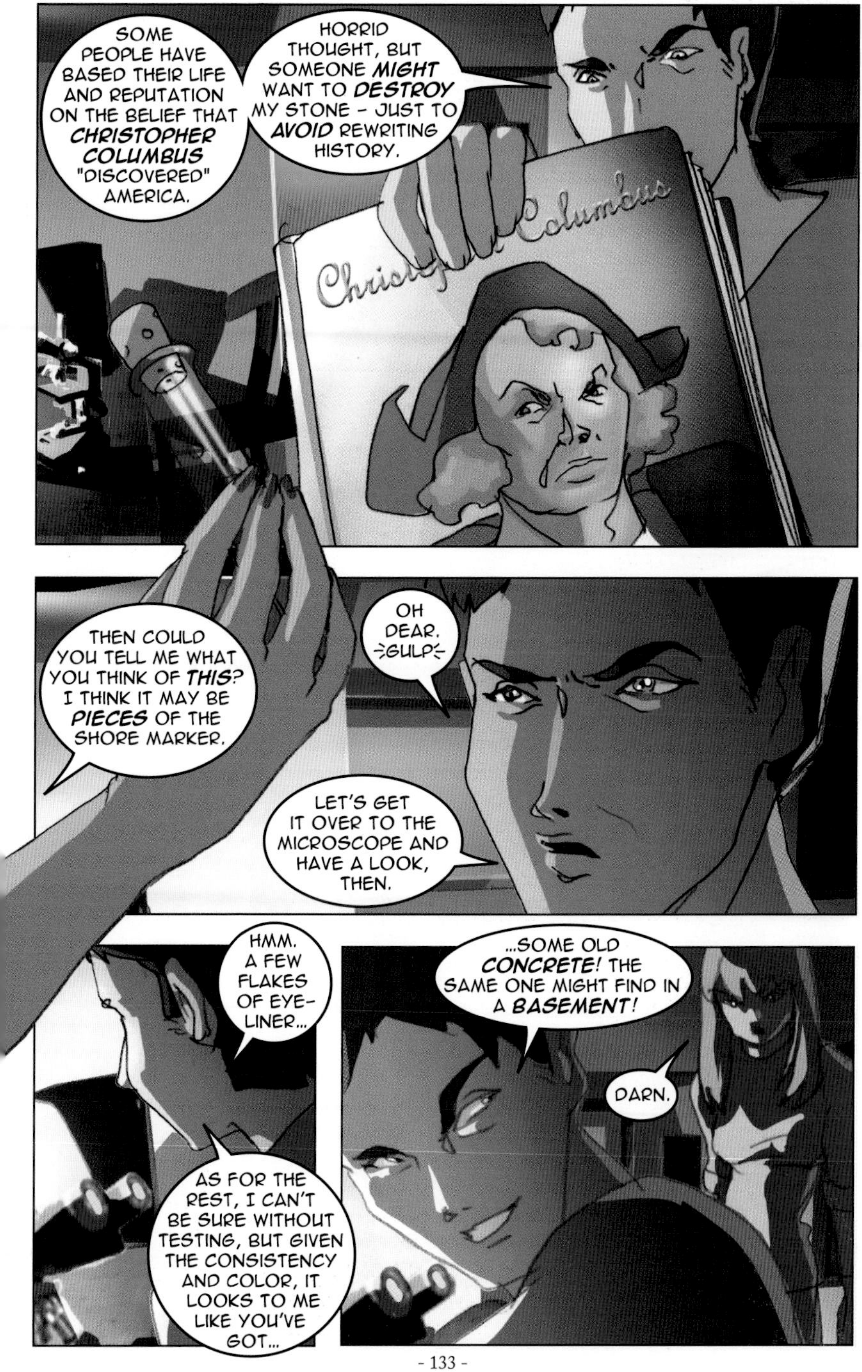
SOME PEOPLE HAVE BASED THEIR LIFE AND REPUTATION ON THE BELIEF THAT CHRISTOPHER COLUMBUS "DISCOVERED" AMERICA.
HORRID THOUGHT, BUT SOMEONE MIGHT WANT TO DESTROY MY STONE - JUST TO AVOID REWRITING HISTORY.
Christopher Columbus
THEN COULD YOU TELL ME WHAT YOU THINK OF THIS? I THINK IT MAY BE PIECES OF THE SHORE MARKER.
OH DEAR. GULP
LET'S GET IT OVER TO THE MICROSCOPE AND HAVE A LOOK, THEN.
HMM. A FEW FLAKES OF EYE-LINER...
AS FOR THE REST, I CAN'T BE SURE WITHOUT TESTING, BUT GIVEN THE CONSISTENCY AND COLOR, IT LOOKS TO ME LIKE YOU'VE GOT...
...SOME OLD CONCRETE! THE SAME ONE MIGHT FIND IN A BASEMENT!
DARN.

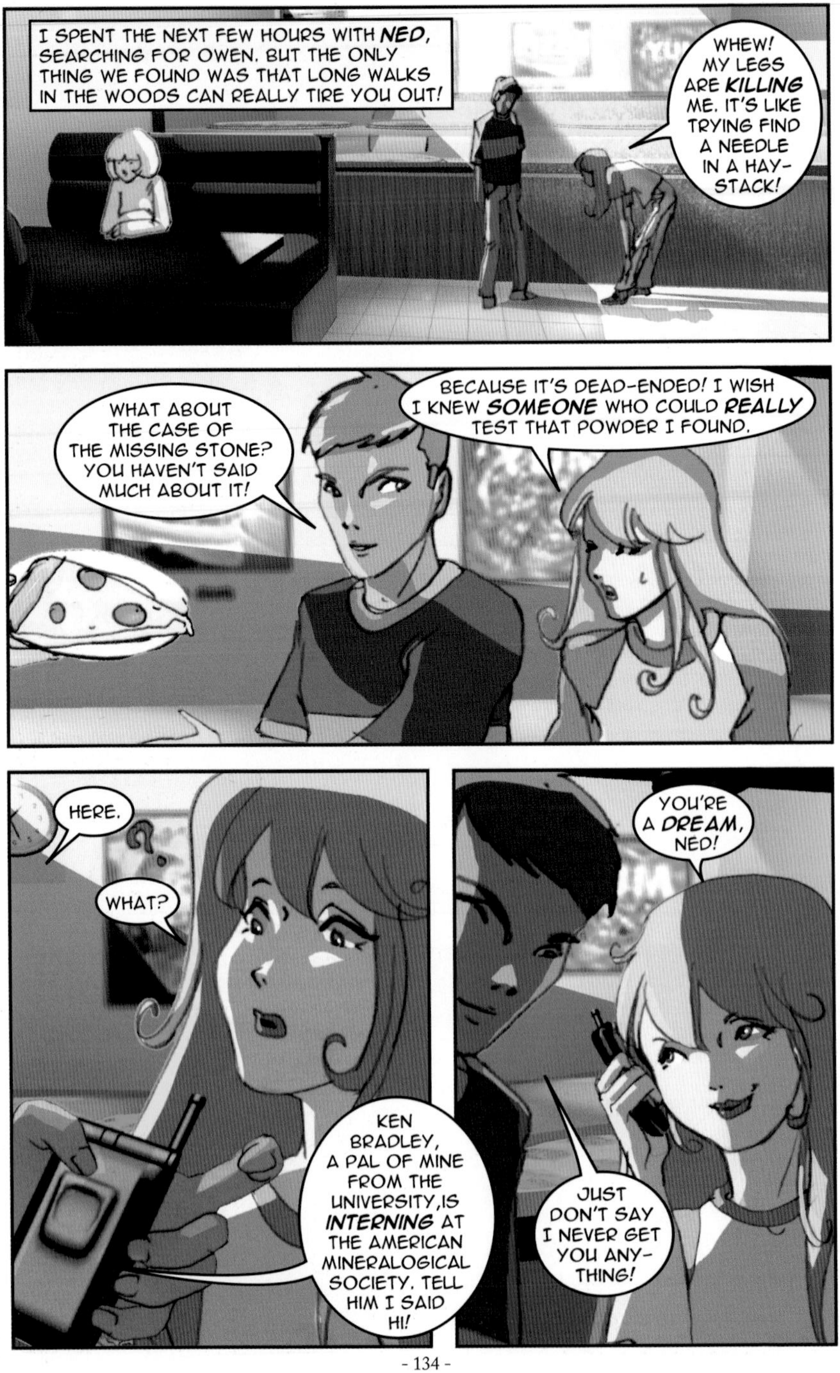
I SPENT THE NEXT FEW HOURS WITH NED, SEARCHING FOR OWEN. BUT THE ONLY THING WE FOUND WAS THAT LONG WALKS IN THE WOODS CAN REALLY TIRE YOU OUT!
WHEW! MY LEGS ARE KILLING ME. IT'S LIKE TRYING FIND A NEEDLE IN A HAY-STACK!
WHAT ABOUT THE CASE OF THE MISSING STONE? YOU HAVEN'T SAID MUCH ABOUT IT!
BECAUSE IT'S DEAD-ENDED! I WISH I KNEW SOMEONE WHO COULD REALLY TEST THAT POWDER I FOUND.
HERE.
WHAT?
KEN BRADLEY, A PAL OF MINE FROM THE UNIVERSITY,IS INTERNING AT THE AMERICAN MINERALOGICAL SOCIETY. TELL HIM I SAID HI!
YOU'RE A DREAM, NED!
JUST DON'T SAY I NEVER GET YOU ANY-THING!

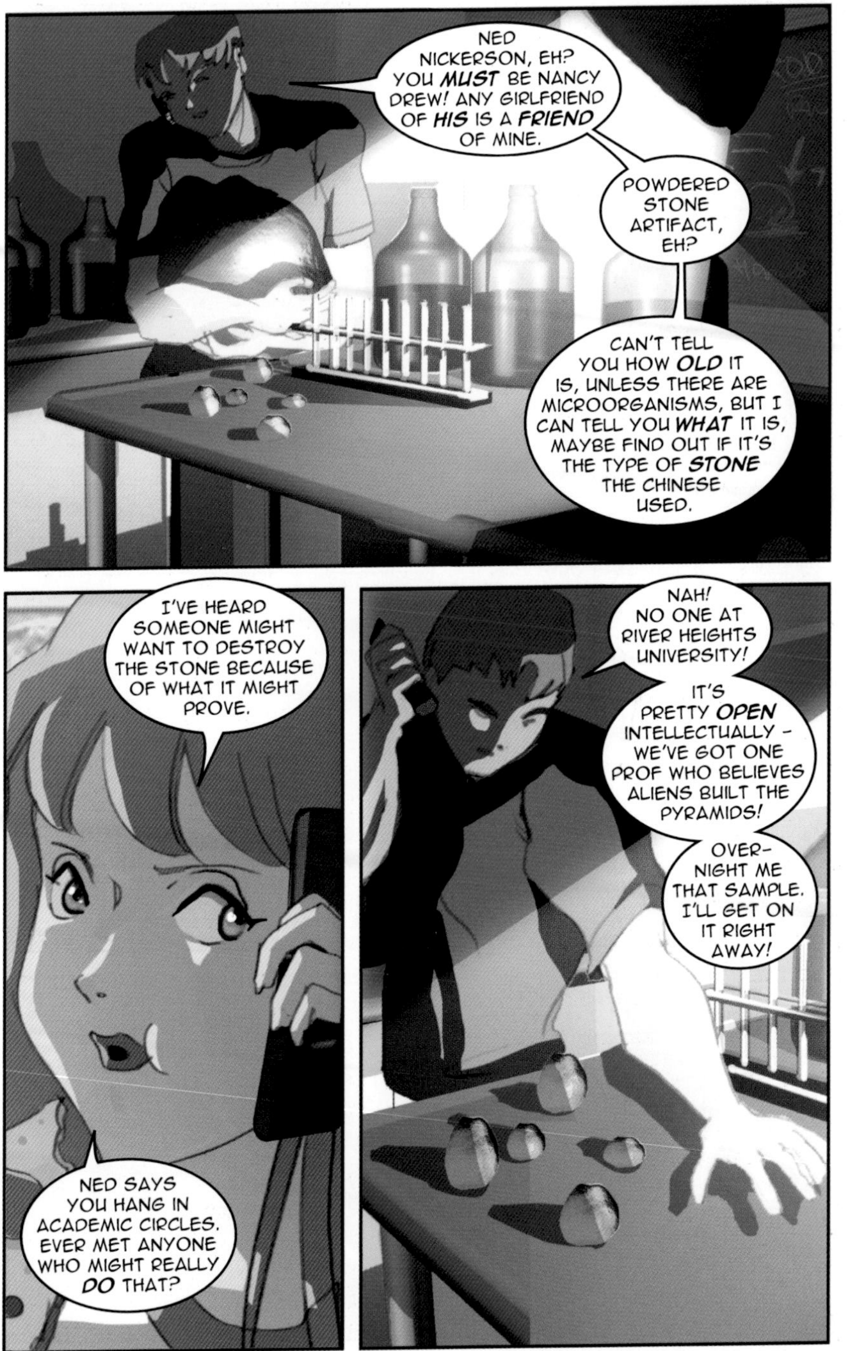

NED NICKERSON, EH? YOU MUST BE NANCY DREW! ANY GIRLFRIEND OF HIS IS A FRIEND OF MINE.
POWDERED STONE ARTIFACT, EH?
CAN'T TELL YOU HOW OLD IT IS, UNLESS THERE ARE MICROORGANISMS, BUT I CAN TELL YOU WHAT IT IS, MAYBE FIND OUT IF IT'S THE TYPE OF STONE THE CHINESE USED.
I'VE HEARD SOMEONE MIGHT WANT TO DESTROY THE STONE BECAUSE OF WHAT IT MIGHT PROVE.
NED SAYS YOU HANG IN ACADEMIC CIRCLES. EVER MET ANYONE WHO MIGHT REALLY DO THAT?
NAH! NO ONE AT RIVER HEIGHTS UNIVERSITY!
IT'S PRETTY OPEN INTELLECTUALLY - WE'VE GOT ONE PROF WHO BELIEVES ALIENS BUILT THE PYRAMIDS!
OVER-NIGHT ME THAT SAMPLE. I'LL GET ON IT RIGHT AWAY!

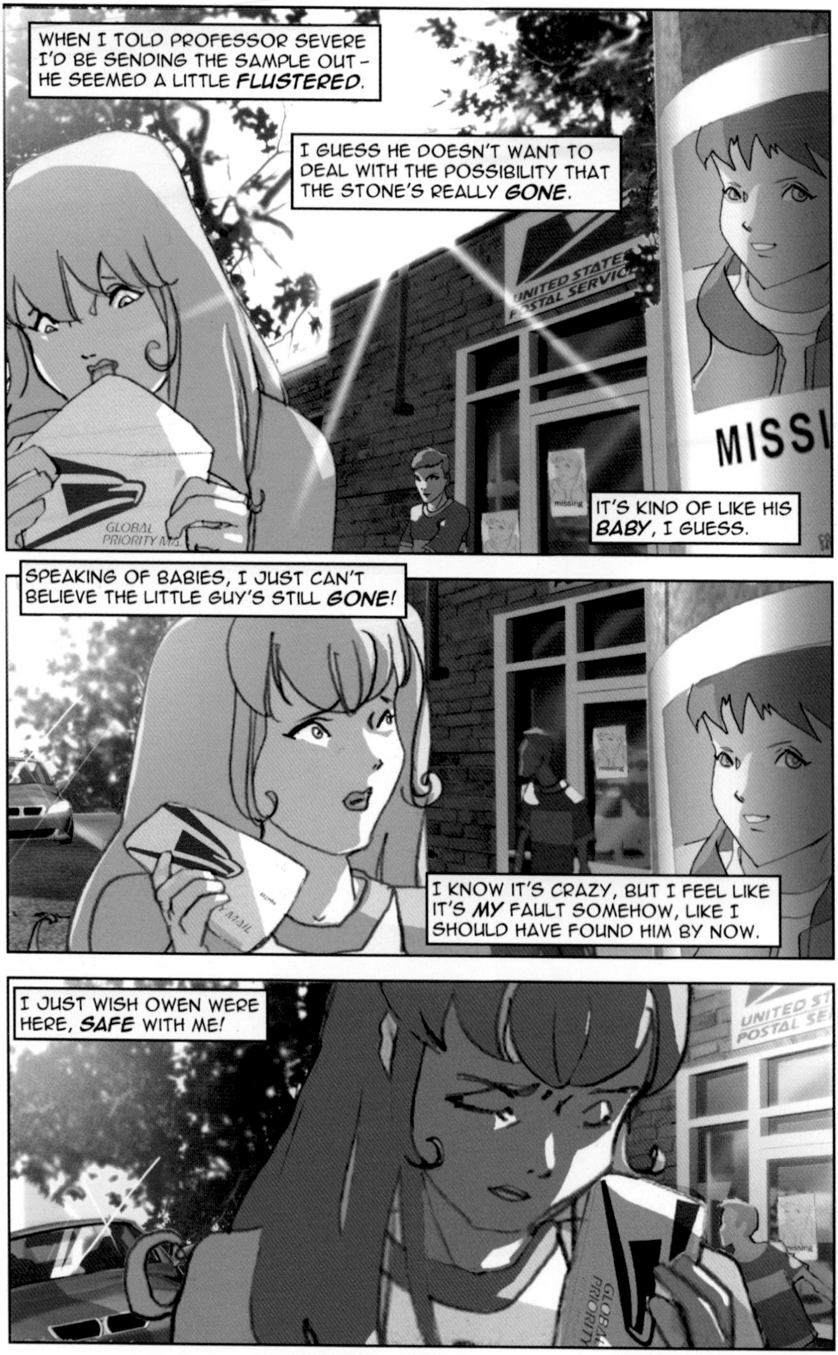
WHEN I TOLD PROFESSOR SEVERE I'D BE SENDING THE SAMPLE OUT - HE SEEMED A LITTLE FLUSTERED.
I GUESS HE DOESN'T WANT TO DEAL WITH THE POSSIBILITY THAT THE STONE'S REALLY GONE.
UNITED STATES POSTAL SERVICE
MISSI
missing
IT'S KIND OF LIKE HIS BABY, I GUESS.
GLOBAL PRIORITY MA
SPEAKING OF BABIES, I JUST CAN'T BELIEVE THE LITTLE GUY'S STILL GONE!
missing
I KNOW IT'S CRAZY, BUT I FEEL LIKE IT'S MY FAULT SOMEHOW, LIKE I SHOULD HAVE FOUND HIM BY NOW.
I JUST WISH OWEN WERE HERE, SAFE WITH ME!
UNITED ST POSTAL SE
missing
GLOBAL PRIORITY

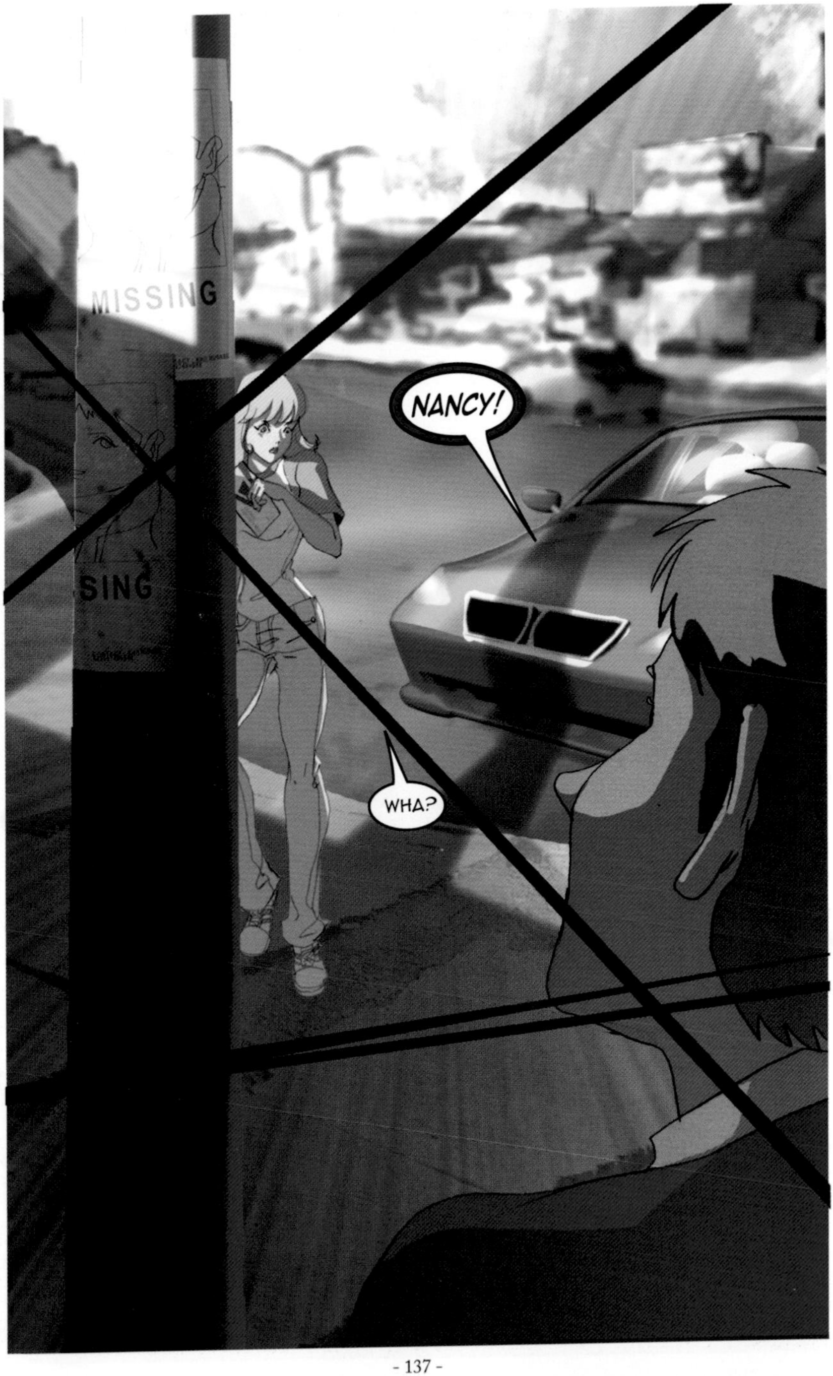
MISSING
SING
NANCY!
WHA?

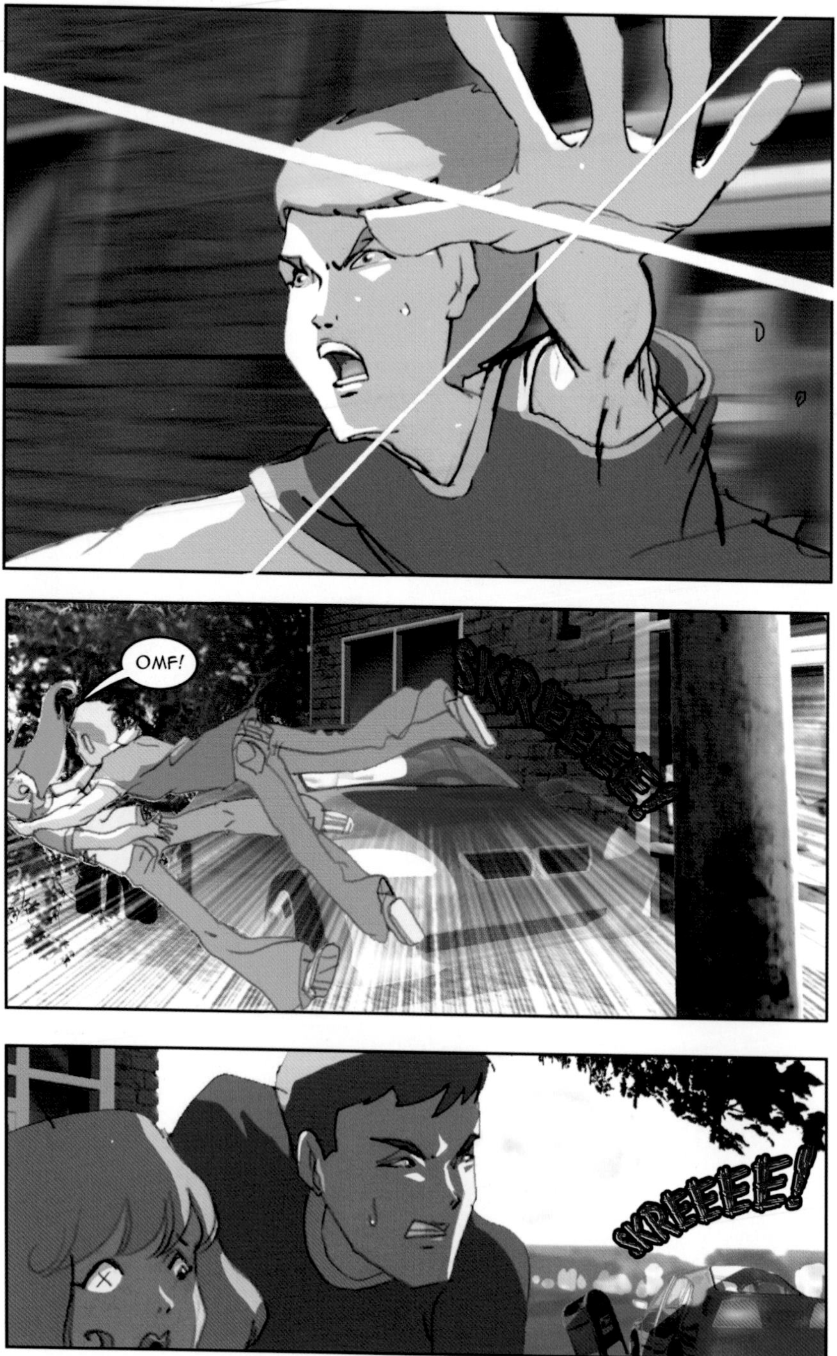
OMF!
SKREEEEE!
SKREEEE!

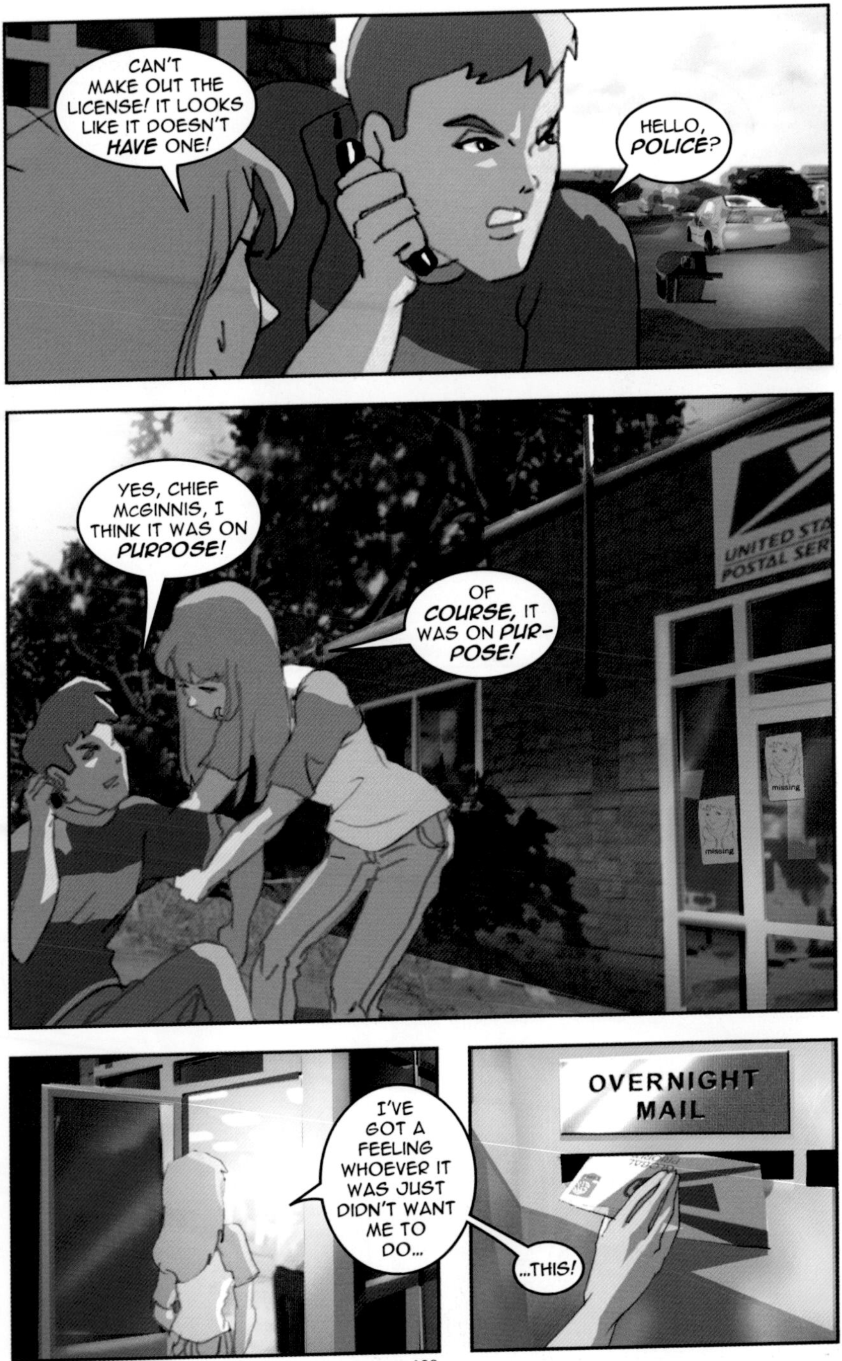

CAN'T MAKE OUT THE LICENSE! IT LOOKS LIKE IT DOESN'T HAVE ONE!
HELLO, POLICE?
YES, CHIEF McGINNIS, I THINK IT WAS ON PURPOSE!
OF COURSE, IT WAS ON PUR-POSE!
UNITED STA
POSTAL SER
missing
missing
I'VE GOT A FEELING WHOEVER IT WAS JUST DIDN'T WANT ME TO DO...
OVERNIGHT MAIL
...THIS!

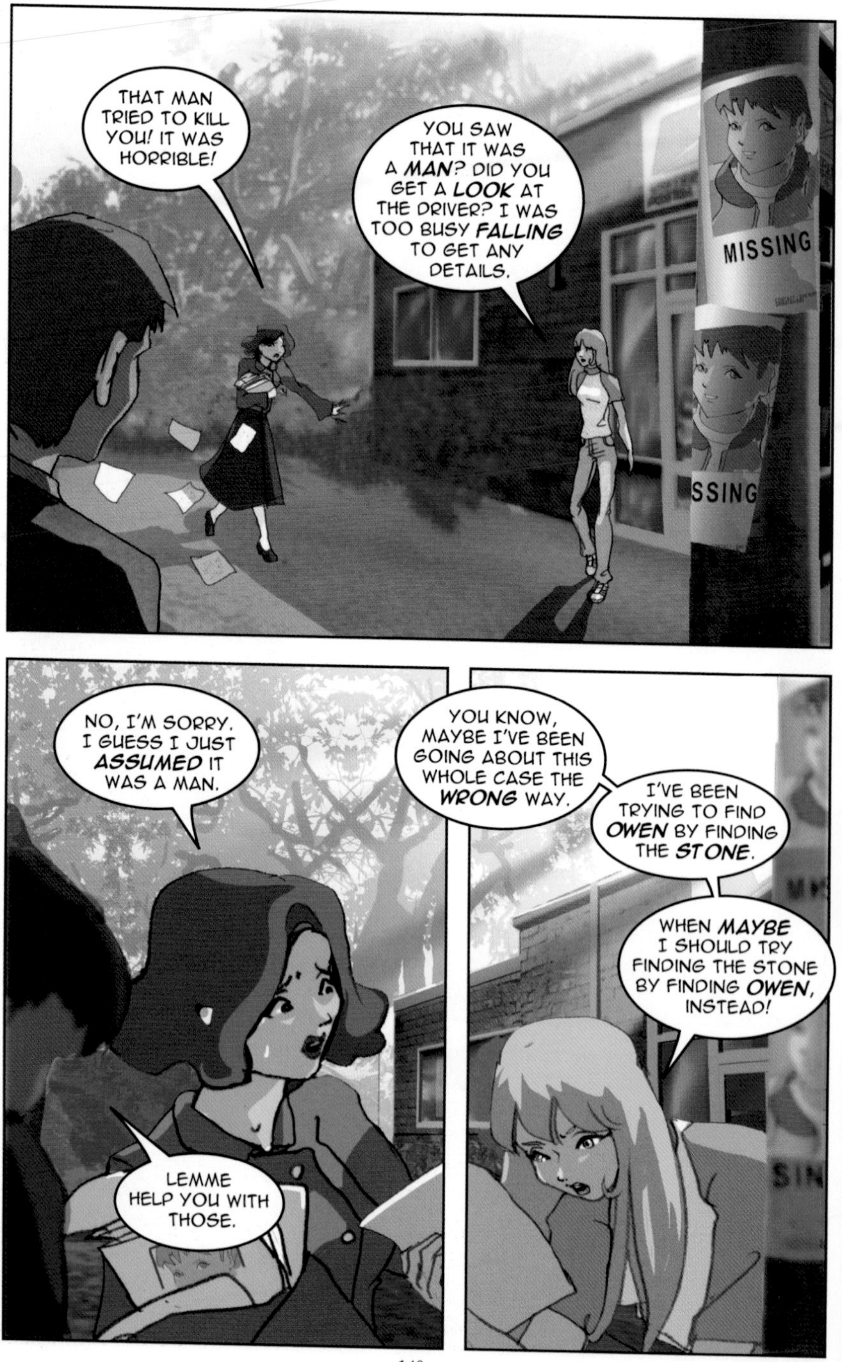
THAT MAN TRIED TO KILL YOU! IT WAS HORRIBLE!
YOU SAW THAT IT WAS A MAN? DID YOU GET A LOOK AT THE DRIVER? I WAS TOO BUSY FALLING TO GET ANY DETAILS.
MISSING
SSING
NO, I'M SORRY. I GUESS I JUST ASSUMED IT WAS A MAN.
LEMME HELP YOU WITH THOSE.
YOU KNOW, MAYBE I'VE BEEN GOING ABOUT THIS WHOLE CASE THE WRONG WAY.
I'VE BEEN TRYING TO FIND OWEN BY FINDING THE STONE.
WHEN MAYBE I SHOULD TRY FINDING THE STONE BY FINDING OWEN, INSTEAD!

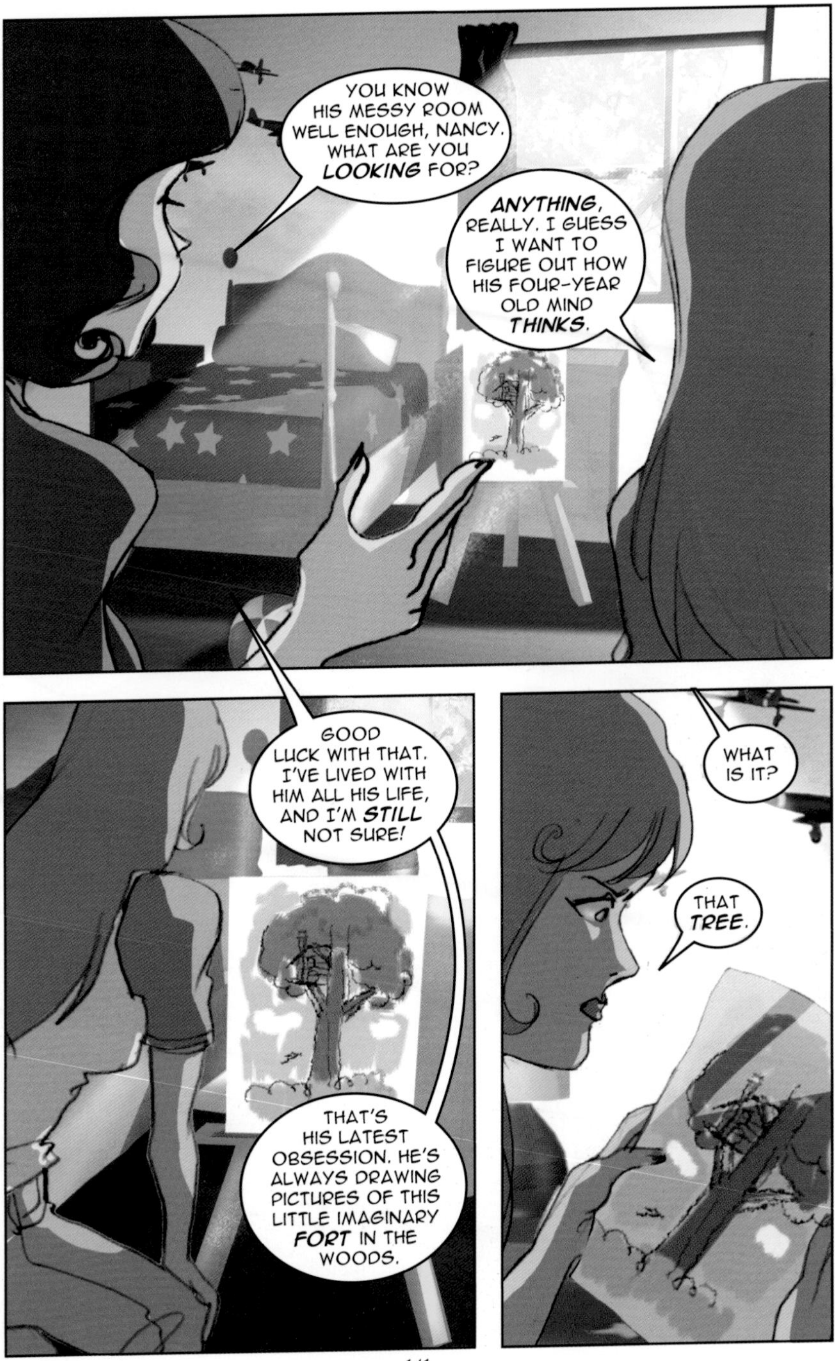
YOU KNOW HIS MESSY ROOM WELL ENOUGH, NANCY. WHAT ARE YOU *LOOKING* FOR?
ANYTHING, REALLY. I GUESS I WANT TO FIGURE OUT HOW HIS FOUR-YEAR OLD MIND *THINKS*.
GOOD LUCK WITH THAT. I'VE LIVED WITH HIM ALL HIS LIFE, AND I'M *STILL* NOT SURE!
THAT'S HIS LATEST OBSESSION. HE'S ALWAYS DRAWING PICTURES OF THIS LITTLE IMAGINARY *FORT* IN THE WOODS.
WHAT IS IT?
THAT *TREE*.

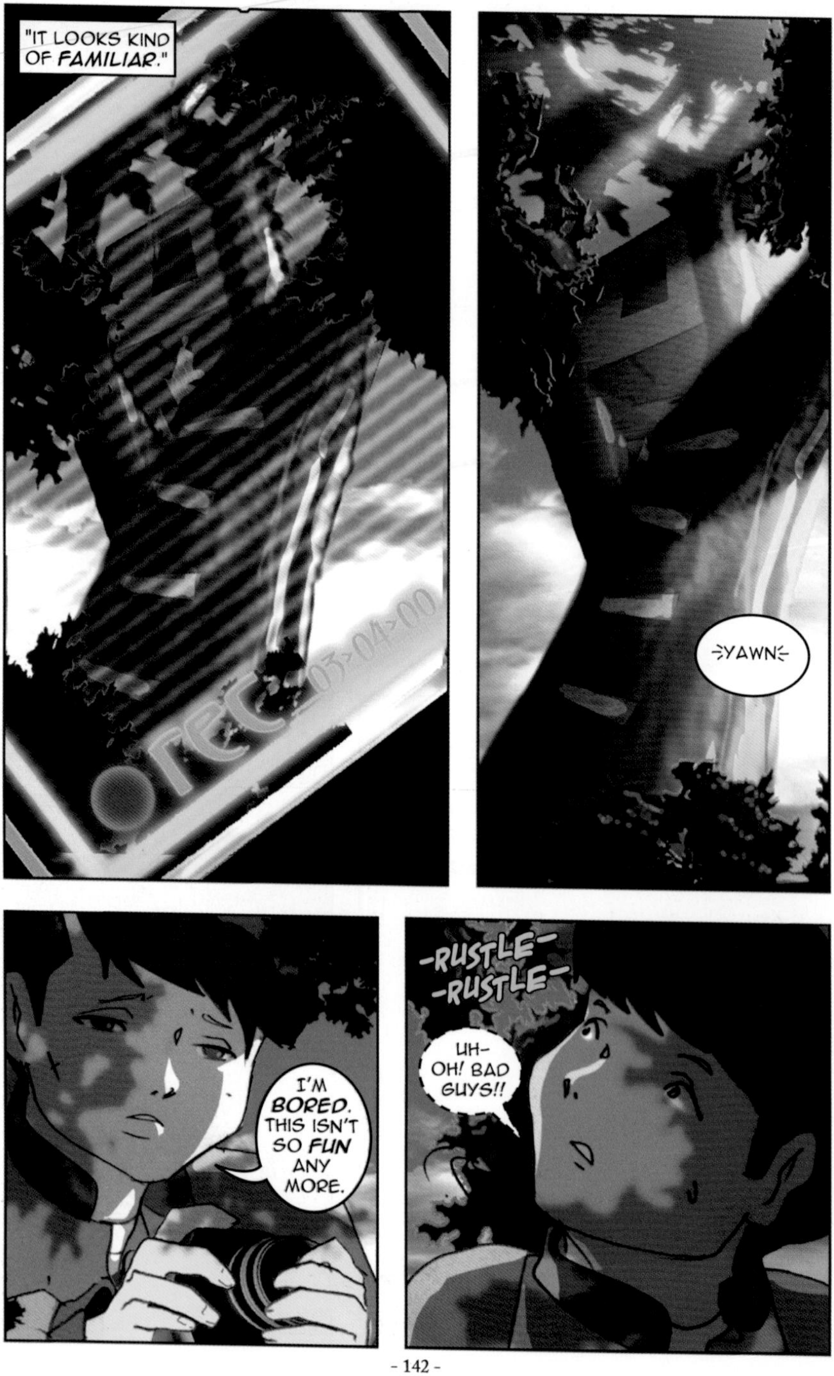
"IT LOOKS KIND OF FAMILIAR."
rec 03>04>00
YAWN
I'M BORED. THIS ISN'T SO FUN ANY MORE.
-RUSTLE-
-RUSTLE-
UH-OH! BAD GUYS!!

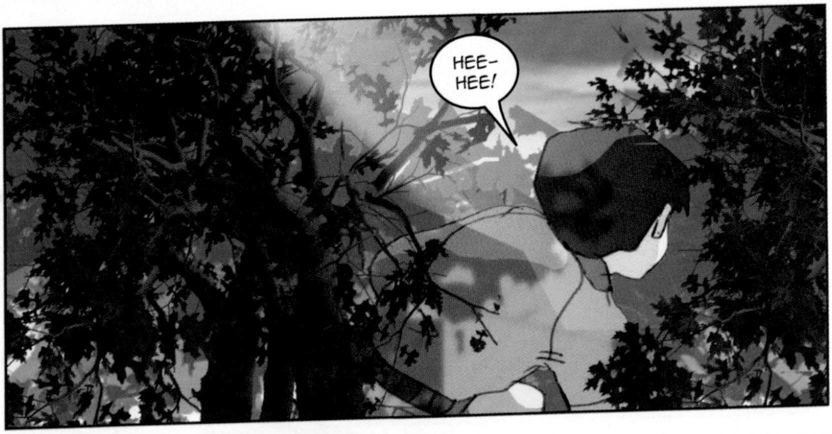
HEE-HEE!

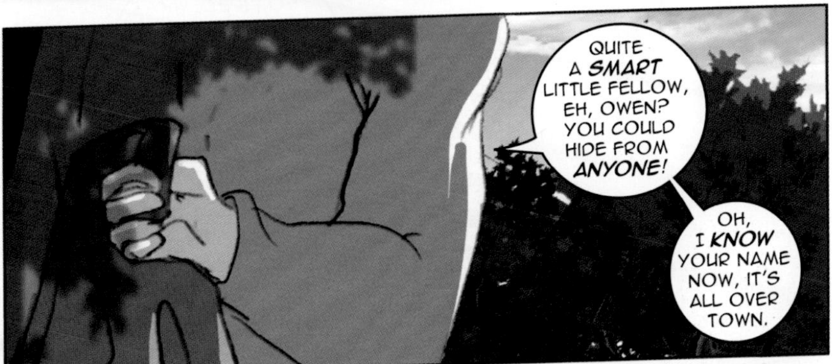
QUITE A SMART LITTLE FELLOW, EH, OWEN? YOU COULD HIDE FROM ANYONE!
OH, I KNOW YOUR NAME NOW, IT'S ALL OVER TOWN.

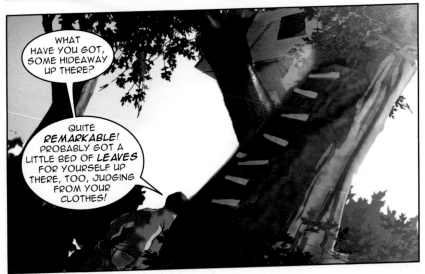

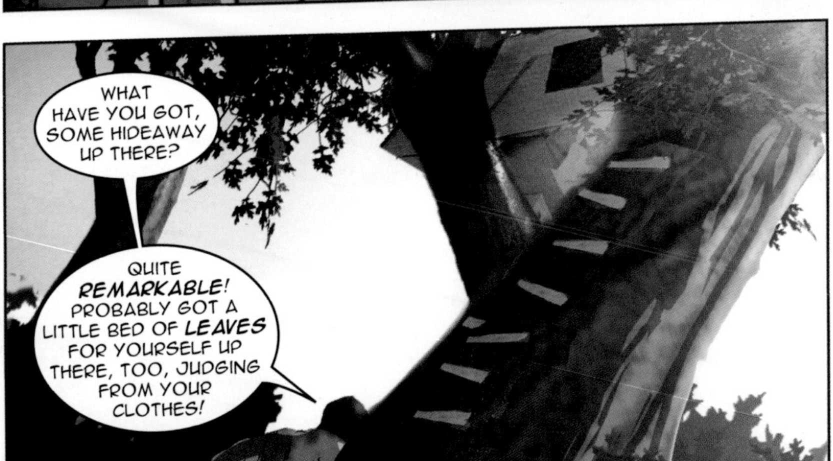
WHAT HAVE YOU GOT, SOME HIDEAWAY UP THERE?
QUITE REMARKABLE! PROBABLY GOT A LITTLE BED OF LEAVES FOR YOURSELF UP THERE, TOO, JUDGING FROM YOUR CLOTHES!

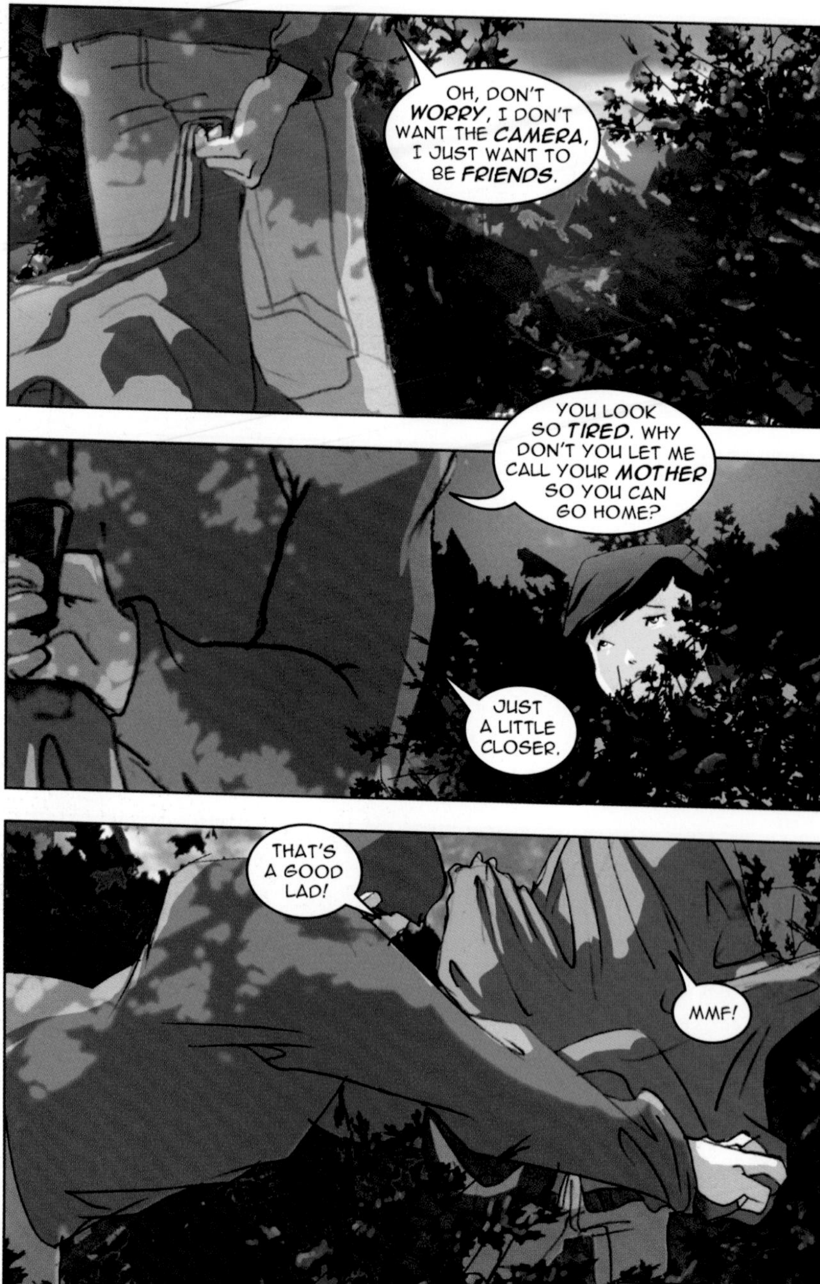

OH, DON'T WORRY, I DON'T WANT THE CAMERA, I JUST WANT TO BE FRIENDS.
YOU LOOK SO TIRED. WHY DON'T YOU LET ME CALL YOUR MOTHER SO YOU CAN GO HOME?
JUST A LITTLE CLOSER.
THAT'S A GOOD LAD!
MMF!
END CHAPTER TWO

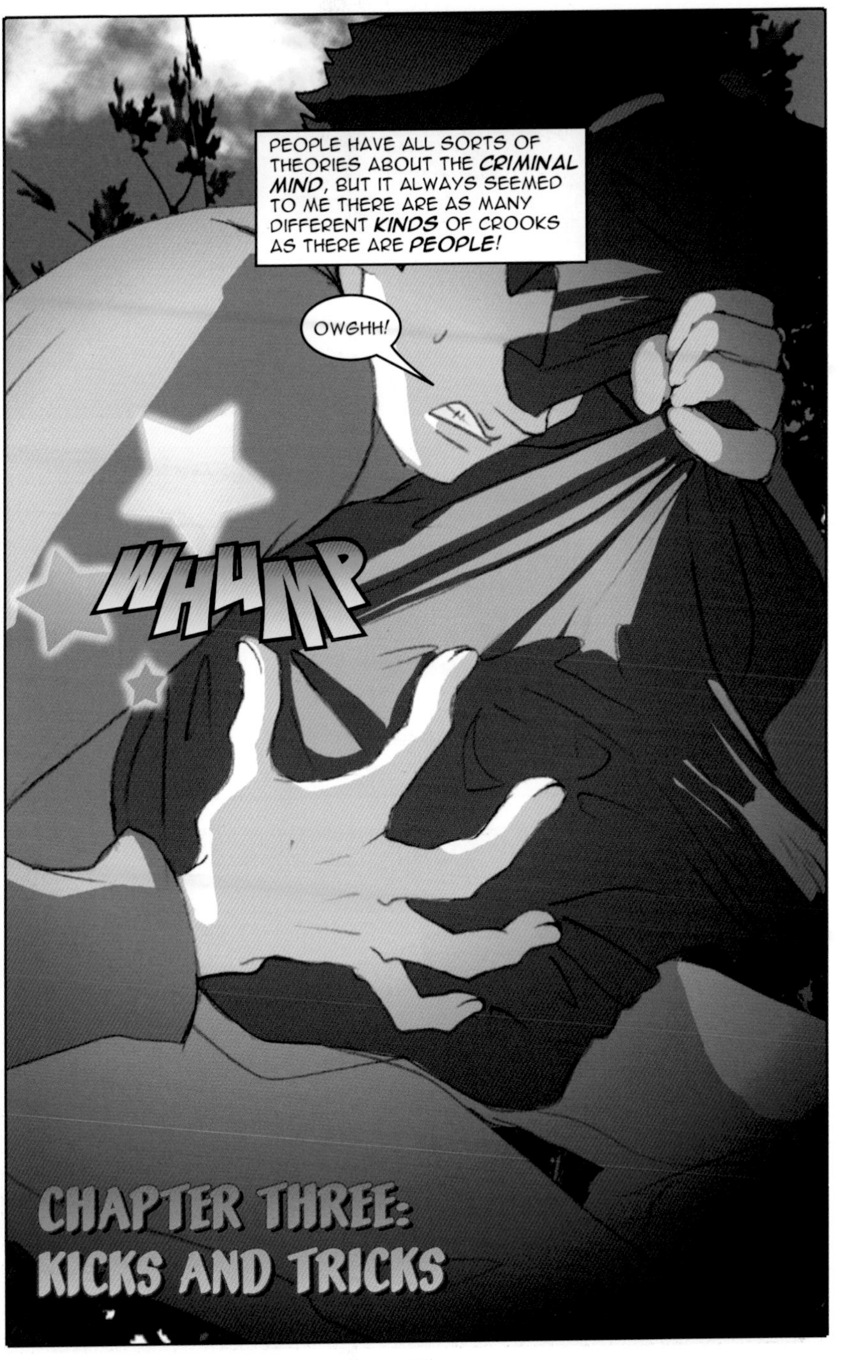
PEOPLE HAVE ALL SORTS OF THEORIES ABOUT THE CRIMINAL MIND, BUT IT ALWAYS SEEMED TO ME THERE ARE AS MANY DIFFERENT KINDS OF CROOKS AS THERE ARE PEOPLE!
OWGHH!
WHUMP
CHAPTER THREE:
KICKS AND TRICKS

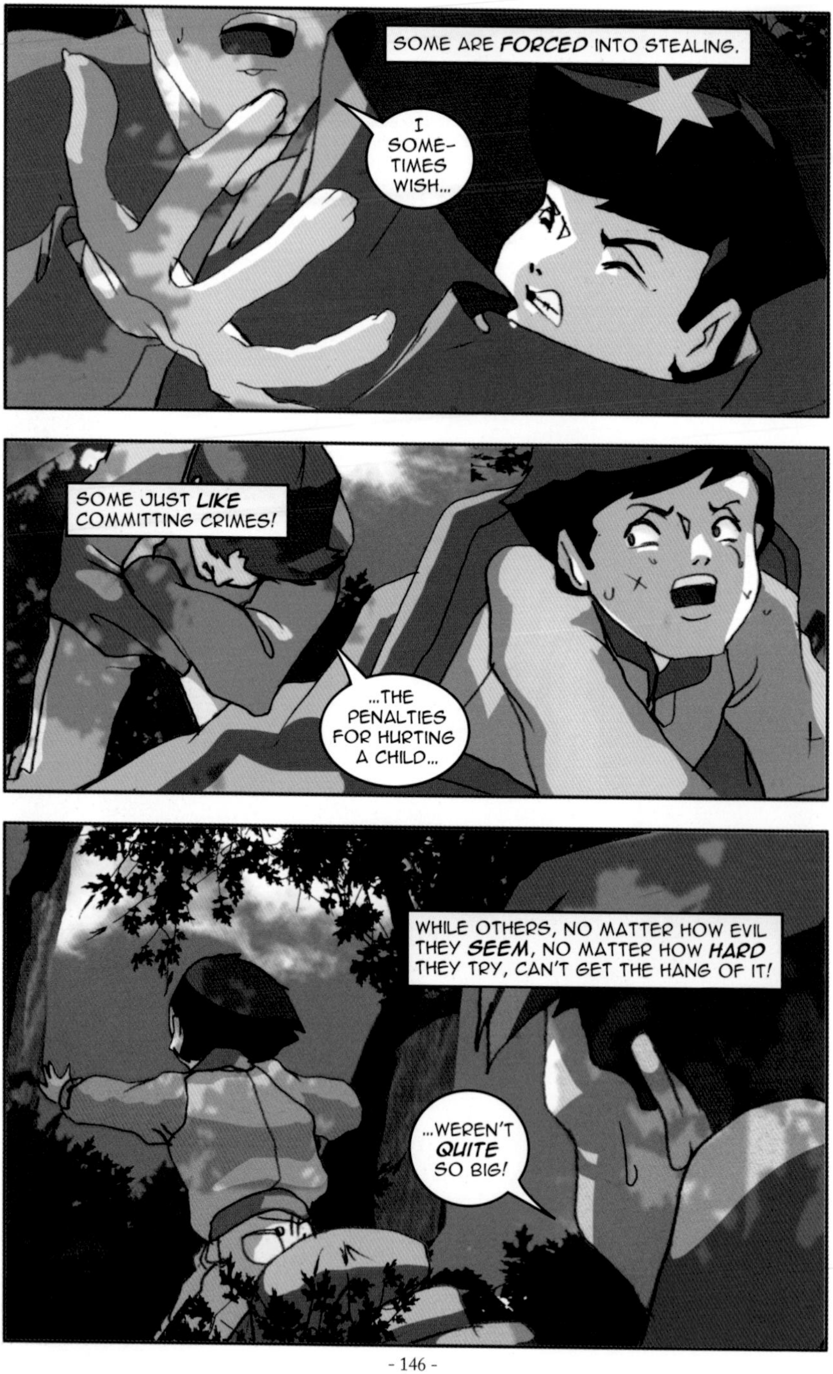
SOME ARE FORCED INTO STEALING.
I SOMETIMES WISH...
SOME JUST LIKE COMMITTING CRIMES!
...THE PENALTIES FOR HURTING A CHILD...
WHILE OTHERS, NO MATTER HOW EVIL THEY SEEM, NO MATTER HOW HARD THEY TRY, CAN'T GET THE HANG OF IT!
...WEREN'T QUITE SO BIG!

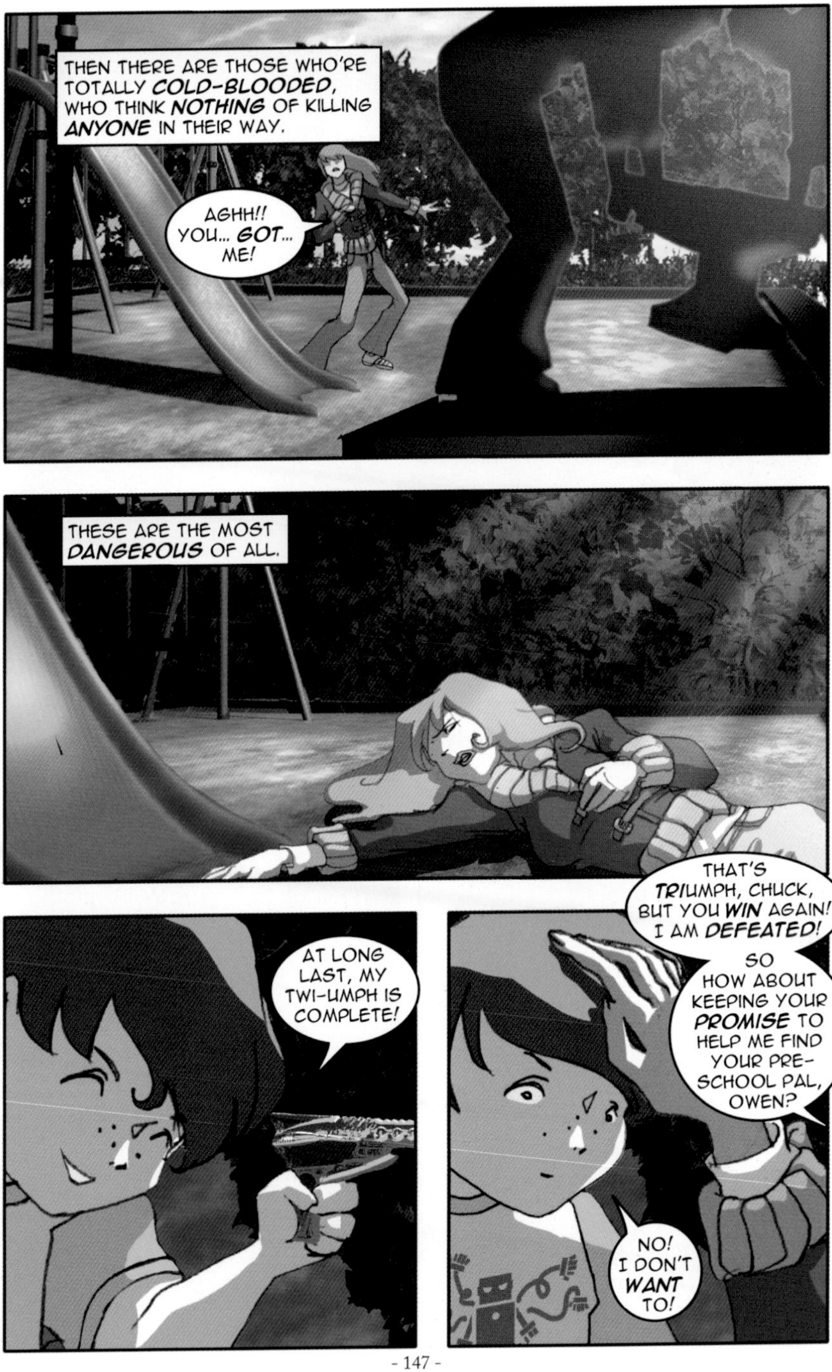
THEN THERE ARE THOSE WHO'RE TOTALLY COLD-BLOODED, WHO THINK NOTHING OF KILLING ANYONE IN THEIR WAY.
AGHH!! YOU... GOT... ME!
THESE ARE THE MOST DANGEROUS OF ALL.
AT LONG LAST, MY TWI-UMPH IS COMPLETE!
THAT'S TRIUMPH, CHUCK, BUT YOU WIN AGAIN! I AM DEFEATED!
SO HOW ABOUT KEEPING YOUR PROMISE TO HELP ME FIND YOUR PRE-SCHOOL PAL, OWEN?
NO! I DON'T WANT TO!

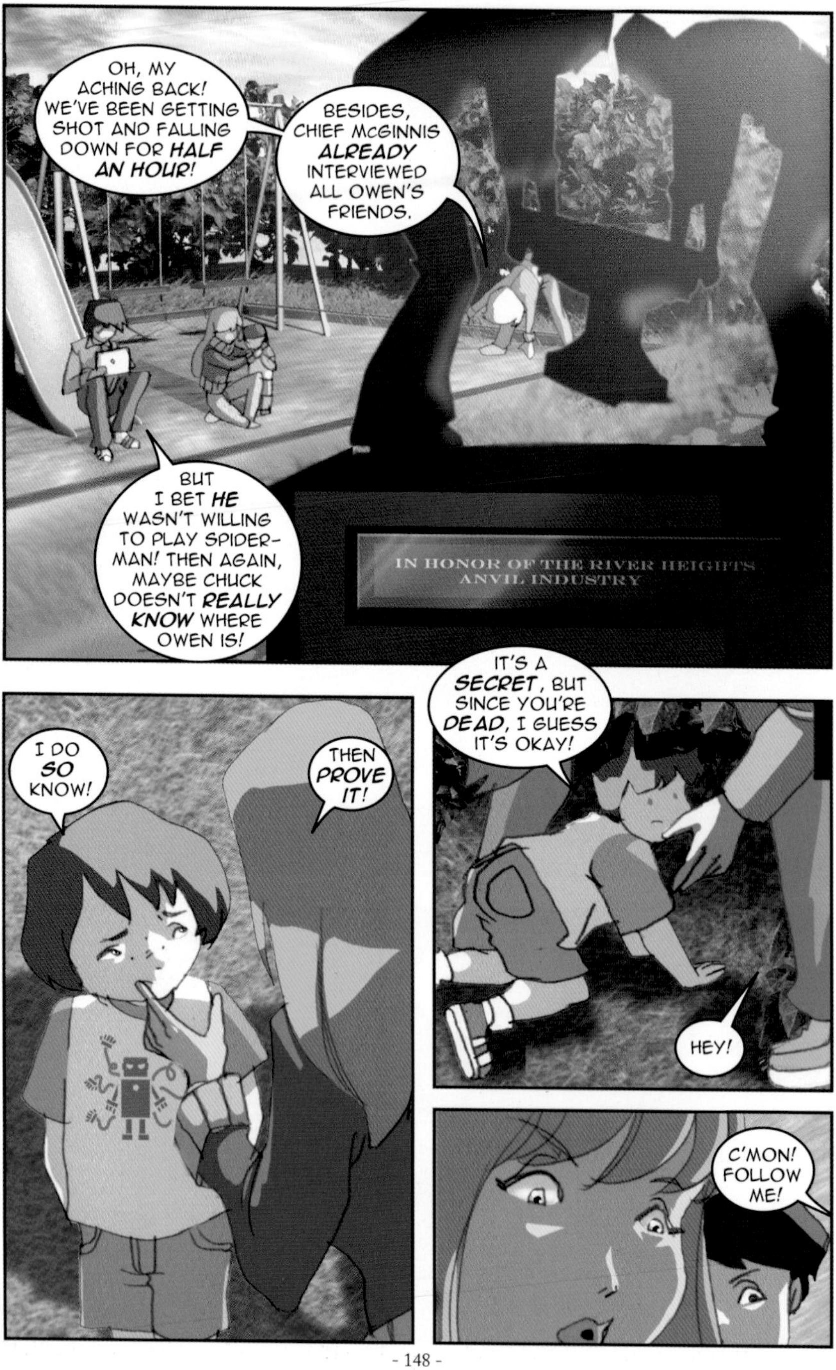
OH, MY ACHING BACK! WE'VE BEEN GETTING SHOT AND FALLING DOWN FOR HALF AN HOUR!
BESIDES, CHIEF McGINNIS ALREADY INTERVIEWED ALL OWEN'S FRIENDS.
BUT I BET HE WASN'T WILLING TO PLAY SPIDER-MAN! THEN AGAIN, MAYBE CHUCK DOESN'T REALLY KNOW WHERE OWEN IS!
IN HONOR OF THE RIVER HEIGHTS ANVIL INDUSTRY
I DO SO KNOW!
THEN PROVE IT!
IT'S A SECRET, BUT SINCE YOU'RE DEAD, I GUESS IT'S OKAY!
HEY!
C'MON! FOLLOW ME!

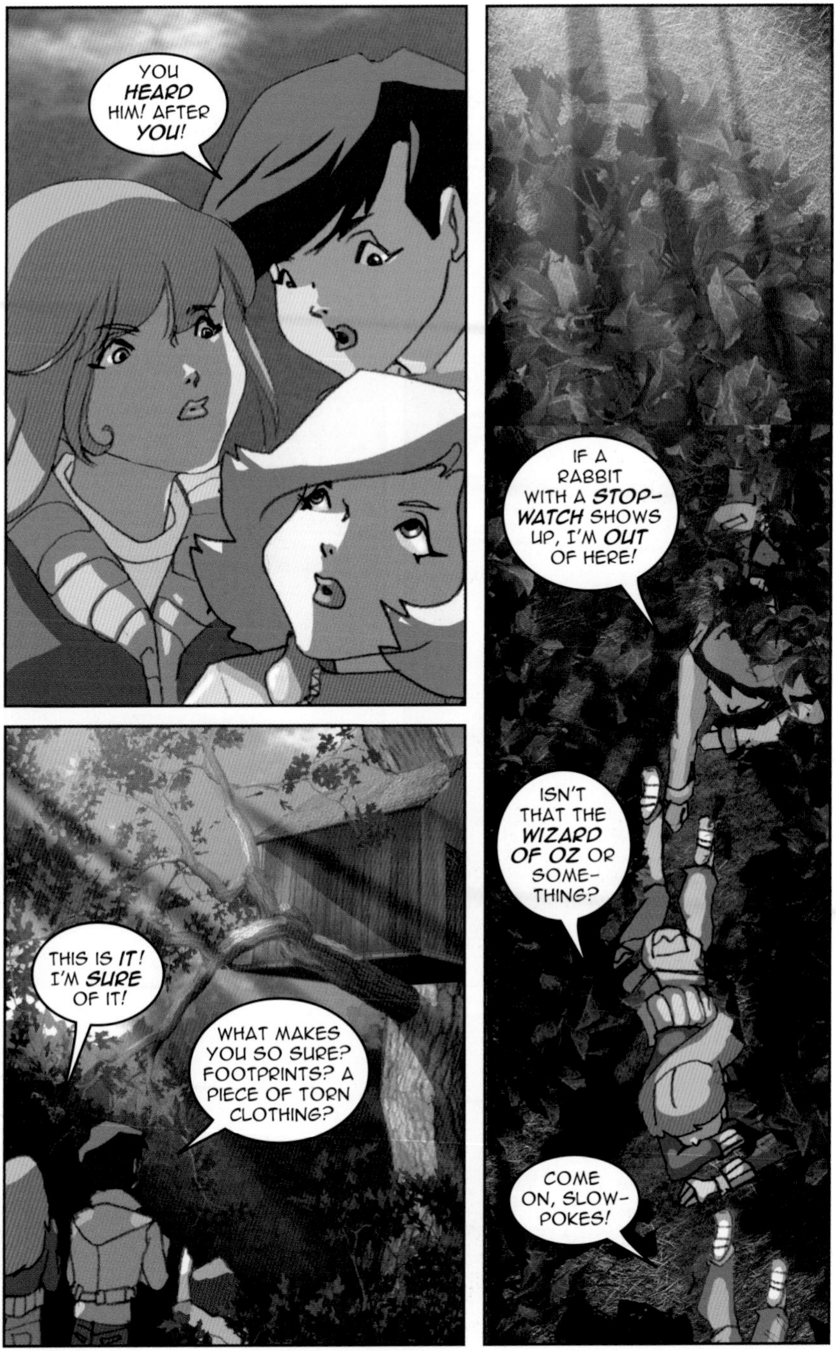
YOU HEARD HIM! AFTER YOU!
THIS IS IT! I'M SURE OF IT!
WHAT MAKES YOU SO SURE? FOOTPRINTS? A PIECE OF TORN CLOTHING?
IF A RABBIT WITH A STOP-WATCH SHOWS UP, I'M OUT OF HERE!
ISN'T THAT THE WIZARD OF OZ OR SOME-THING?
COME ON, SLOW-POKES!

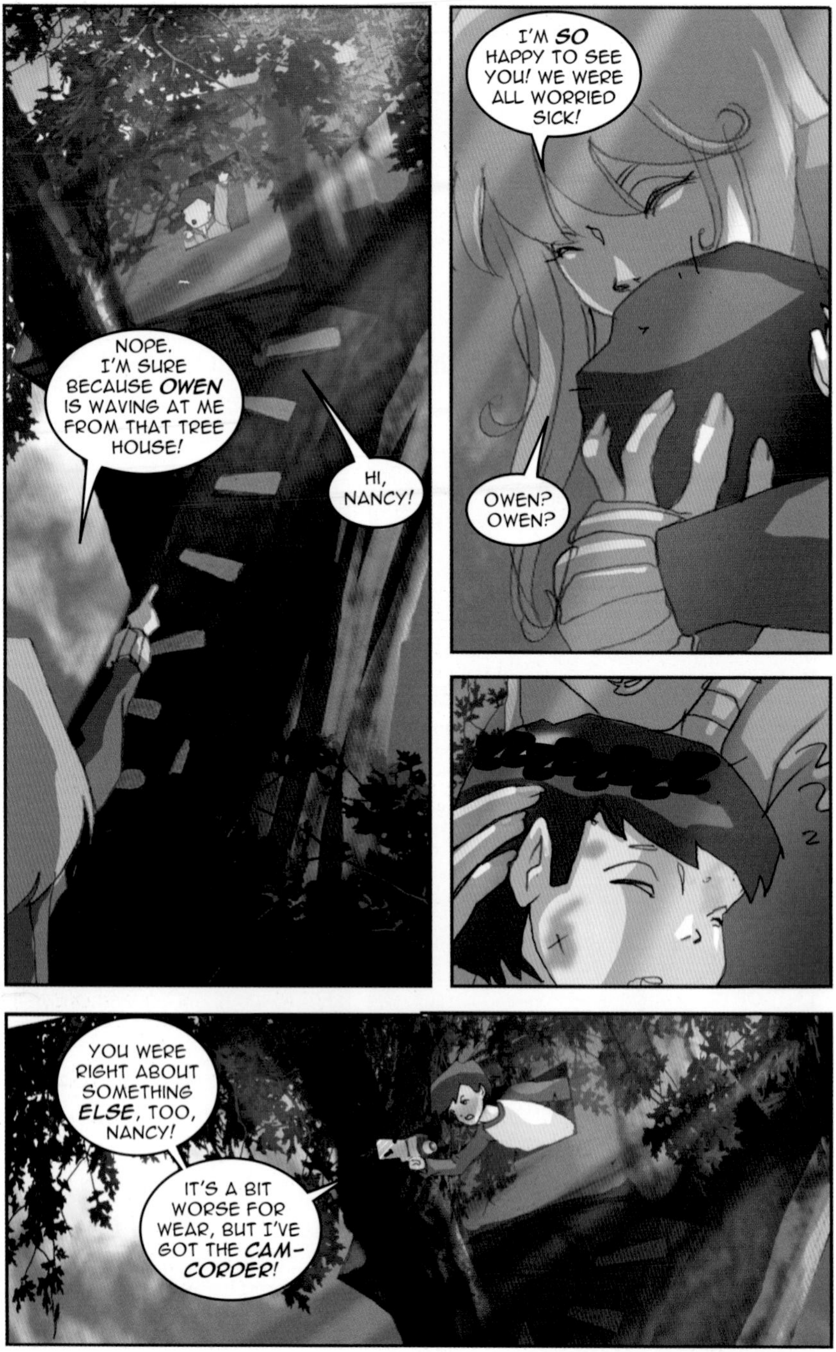
NOPE. I'M SURE BECAUSE OWEN IS WAVING AT ME FROM THAT TREE HOUSE!
HI, NANCY!
I'M SO HAPPY TO SEE YOU! WE WERE ALL WORRIED SICK!
OWEN? OWEN?
YOU WERE RIGHT ABOUT SOMETHING ELSE, TOO, NANCY!
IT'S A BIT WORSE FOR WEAR, BUT I'VE GOT THE CAM-CORDER!

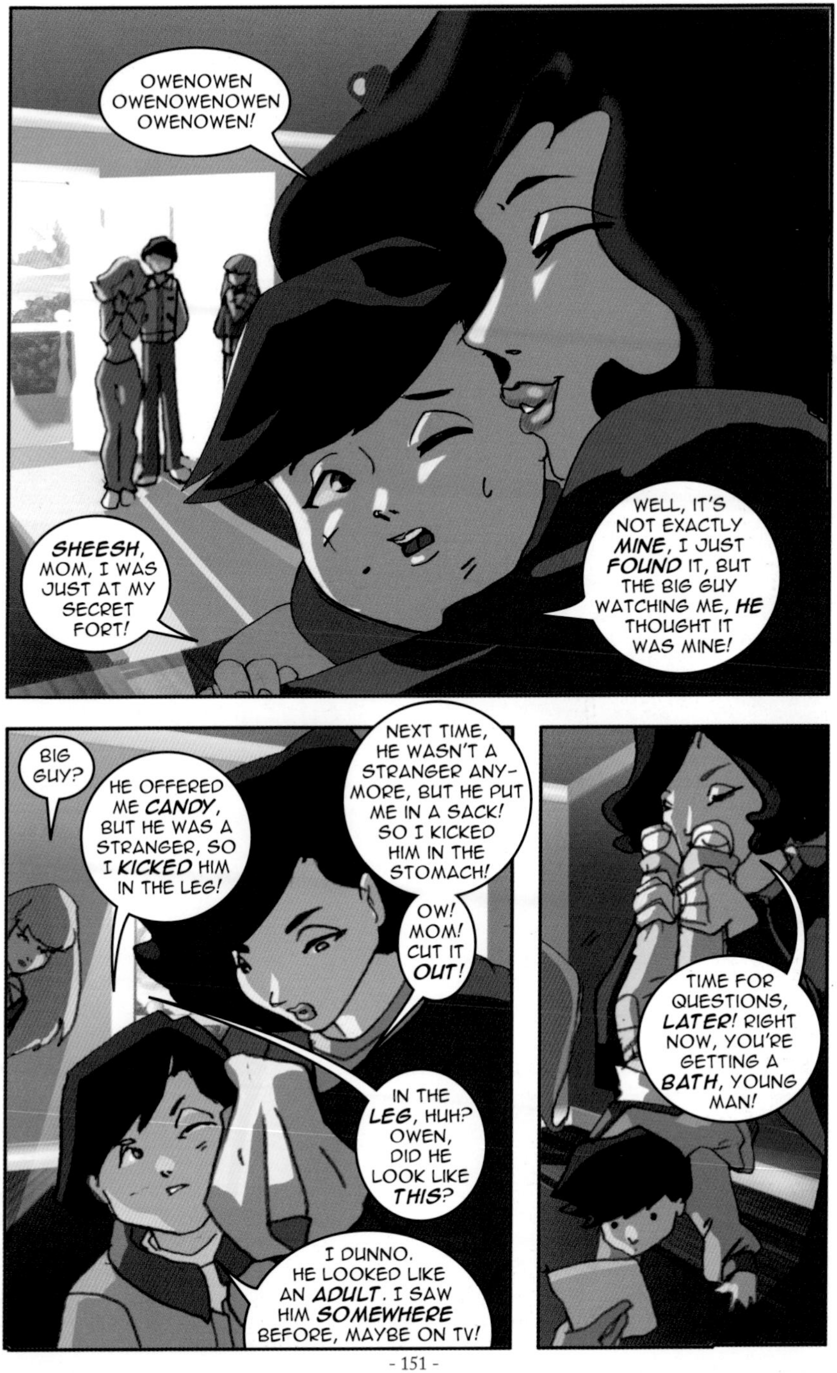
OWENOWEN OWENOWENOWEN OWENOWEN!
SHEESH, MOM, I WAS JUST AT MY SECRET FORT!
WELL, IT'S NOT EXACTLY MINE, I JUST FOUND IT, BUT THE BIG GUY WATCHING ME, HE THOUGHT IT WAS MINE!
BIG GUY?
HE OFFERED ME CANDY, BUT HE WAS A STRANGER, SO I KICKED HIM IN THE LEG!
NEXT TIME, HE WASN'T A STRANGER ANY-MORE, BUT HE PUT ME IN A SACK! SO I KICKED HIM IN THE STOMACH!
OW! MOM! CUT IT OUT!
IN THE LEG, HUH? OWEN, DID HE LOOK LIKE THIS?
I DUNNO. HE LOOKED LIKE AN ADULT. I SAW HIM SOMEWHERE BEFORE, MAYBE ON TV!
TIME FOR QUESTIONS, LATER! RIGHT NOW, YOU'RE GETTING A BATH, YOUNG MAN!

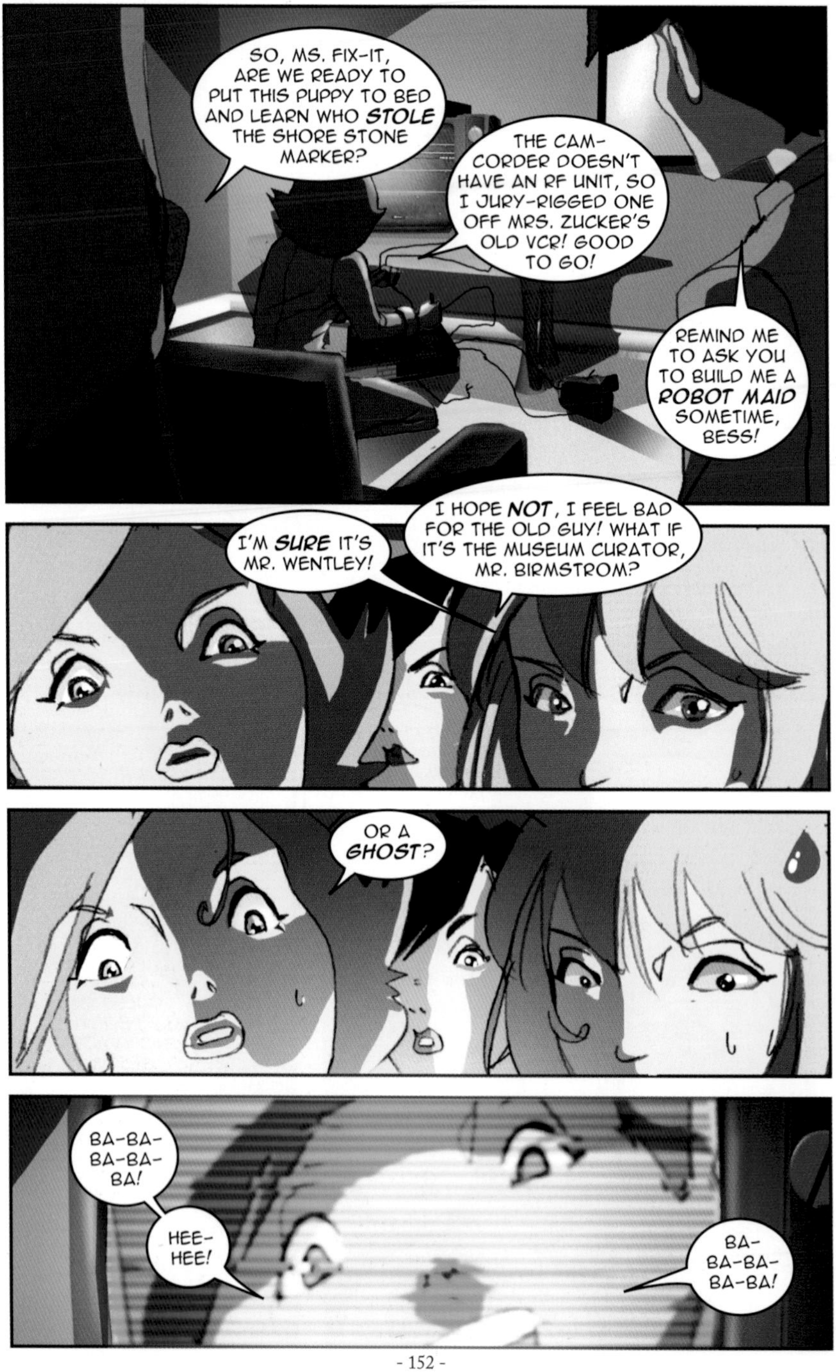
SO, MS. FIX-IT, ARE WE READY TO PUT THIS PUPPY TO BED AND LEARN WHO STOLE THE SHORE STONE MARKER?
THE CAM-CORDER DOESN'T HAVE AN RF UNIT, SO I JURY-RIGGED ONE OFF MRS. ZUCKER'S OLD VCR! GOOD TO GO!
REMIND ME TO ASK YOU TO BUILD ME A ROBOT MAID SOMETIME, BESS!
I'M SURE IT'S MR. WENTLEY!
I HOPE NOT, I FEEL BAD FOR THE OLD GUY! WHAT IF IT'S THE MUSEUM CURATOR, MR. BIRMSTROM?
OR A GHOST?
BA-BA-BA-BA-BA!
HEE-HEE!
BA-BA-BA-BA-BA!

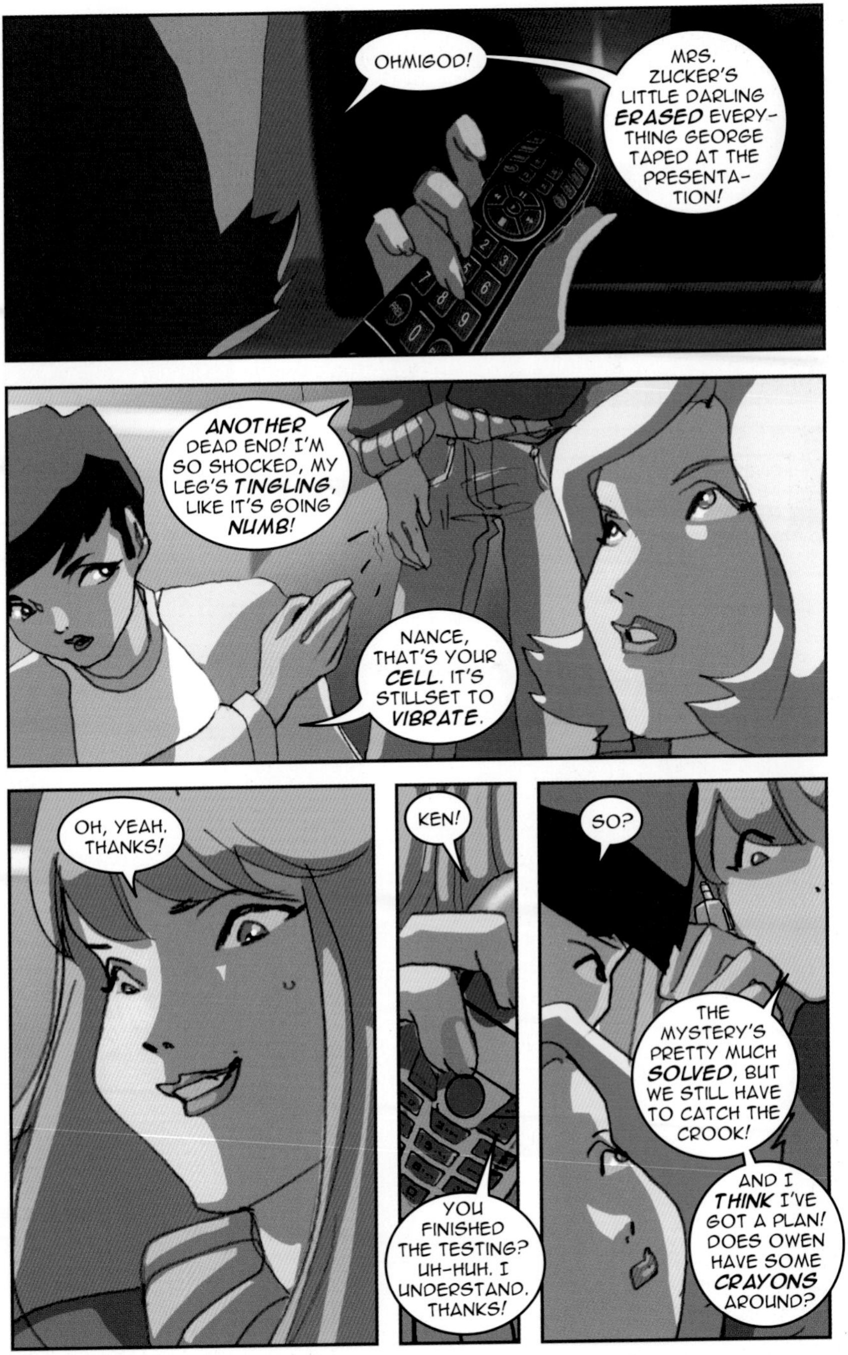
OHMIGOD!
MRS. ZUCKER'S LITTLE DARLING ERASED EVERY-THING GEORGE TAPED AT THE PRESENTA-TION!
ANOTHER DEAD END! I'M SO SHOCKED, MY LEG'S TINGLING, LIKE IT'S GOING NUMB!
NANCE, THAT'S YOUR CELL. IT'S STILLSET TO VIBRATE.
OH, YEAH. THANKS!
KEN!
YOU FINISHED THE TESTING? UH-HUH. I UNDERSTAND. THANKS!
SO?
THE MYSTERY'S PRETTY MUCH SOLVED, BUT WE STILL HAVE TO CATCH THE CROOK!
AND I THINK I'VE GOT A PLAN! DOES OWEN HAVE SOME CRAYONS AROUND?

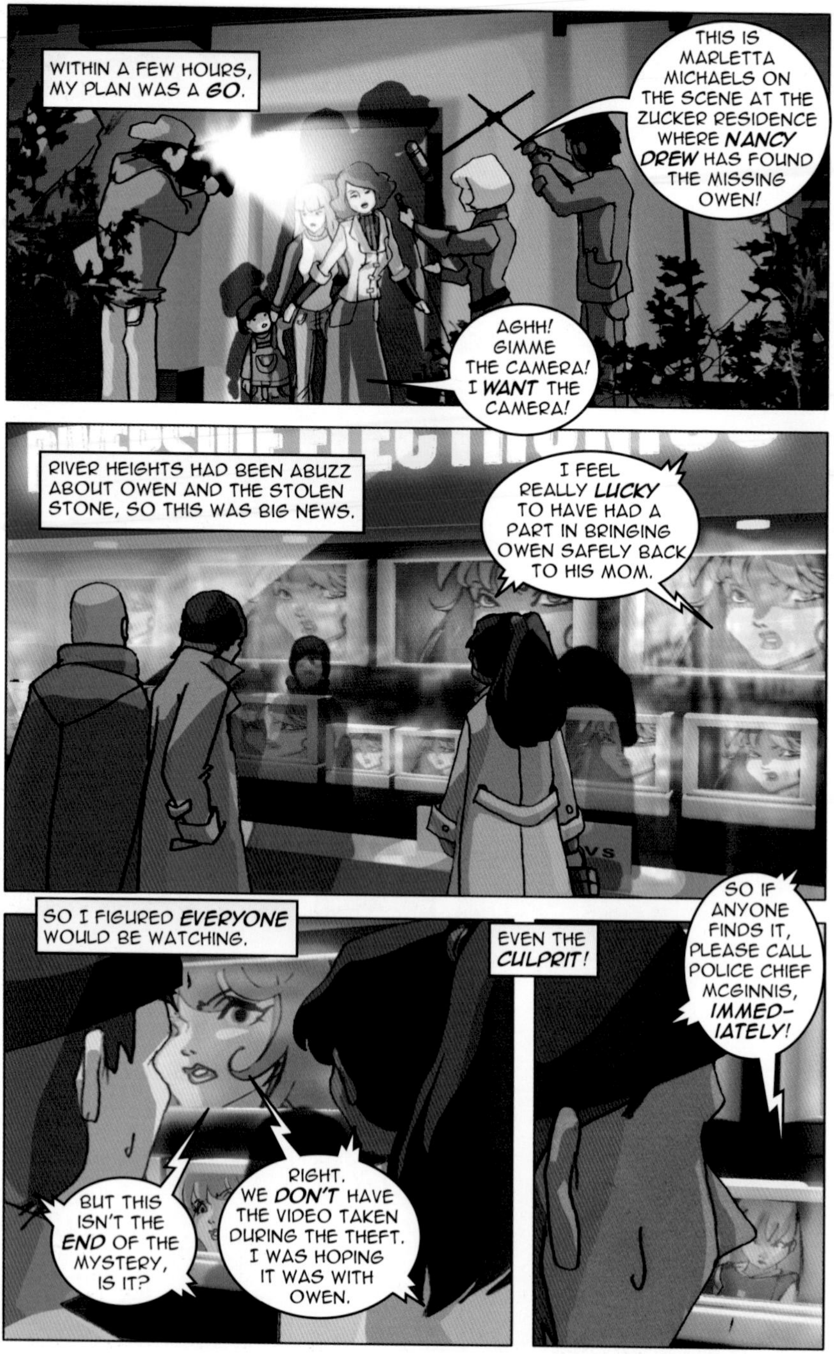

WITHIN A FEW HOURS, MY PLAN WAS A GO.
THIS IS MARLETTA MICHAELS ON THE SCENE AT THE ZUCKER RESIDENCE WHERE NANCY DREW HAS FOUND THE MISSING OWEN!
AGHH! GIMME THE CAMERA! I WANT THE CAMERA!
RIVER HEIGHTS HAD BEEN ABUZZ ABOUT OWEN AND THE STOLEN STONE, SO THIS WAS BIG NEWS.
I FEEL REALLY LUCKY TO HAVE HAD A PART IN BRINGING OWEN SAFELY BACK TO HIS MOM.
SO I FIGURED EVERYONE WOULD BE WATCHING.
BUT THIS ISN'T THE END OF THE MYSTERY, IS IT?
RIGHT. WE DON'T HAVE THE VIDEO TAKEN DURING THE THEFT. I WAS HOPING IT WAS WITH OWEN.
EVEN THE CULPRIT!
SO IF ANYONE FINDS IT, PLEASE CALL POLICE CHIEF MCGINNIS, IMMEDIATELY!

Y'KNOW, MY BEING A *VEGETARIAN* REALLY HONES MY INVESTIGATIVE INTUITION, AND I SMELL SOME-THING'S *UP!*

THERE ISN'T ANY-THING YOU'RE *NOT* TELLING ME, RIGHT?

MARLETTA, EVERYTHING I SAID IS *ABSOLUTELY* TRUE!

YEAH, BUT WHAT I SAID *WASN'T* ABSOLUTELY *EVERYTHING* THAT WAS TRUE. LIKE, I FAILED TO MENTION THE *REASON* WE DIDN'T HAVE THE TAPE WAS BECAUSE IT WAS *ERASED.*

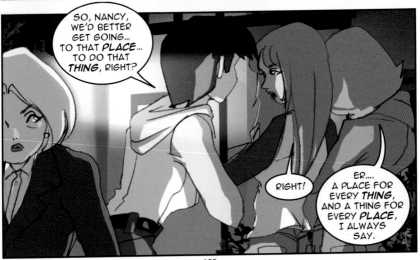

SO, NANCY, WE'D BETTER GET GOING... TO THAT *PLACE*... TO DO THAT *THING*, RIGHT?

RIGHT!

ER.... A PLACE FOR EVERY *THING*, AND A THING FOR EVERY *PLACE*, I ALWAYS SAY.

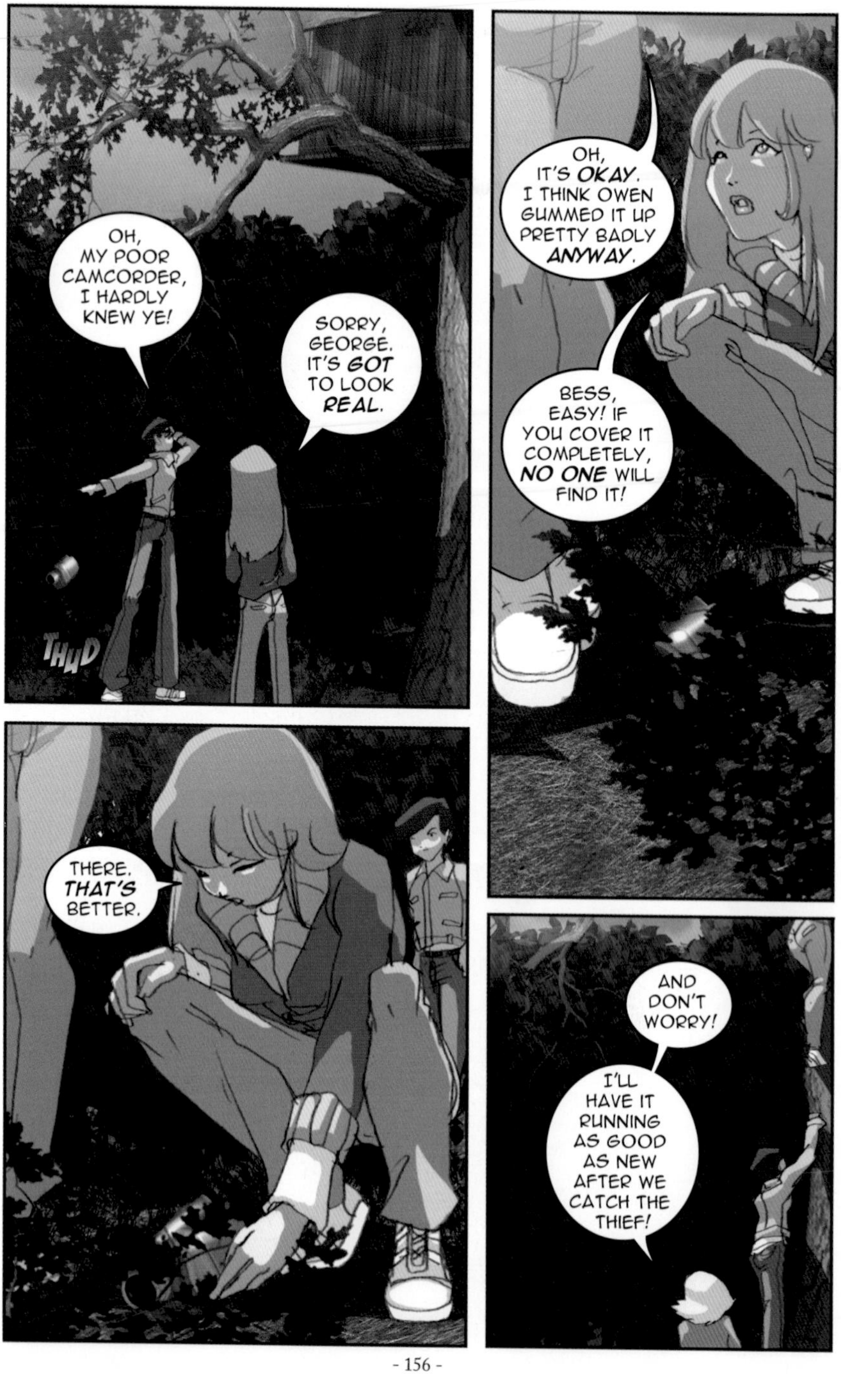
OH, MY POOR CAMCORDER, I HARDLY KNEW YE!
SORRY, GEORGE. IT'S **GOT** TO LOOK **REAL**.
THUD
OH, IT'S **OKAY**. I THINK OWEN GUMMED IT UP PRETTY BADLY **ANYWAY**.
BESS, EASY! IF YOU COVER IT COMPLETELY, **NO ONE** WILL FIND IT!
THERE. **THAT'S** BETTER.
AND DON'T WORRY!
I'LL HAVE IT RUNNING AS GOOD AS NEW AFTER WE CATCH THE THIEF!

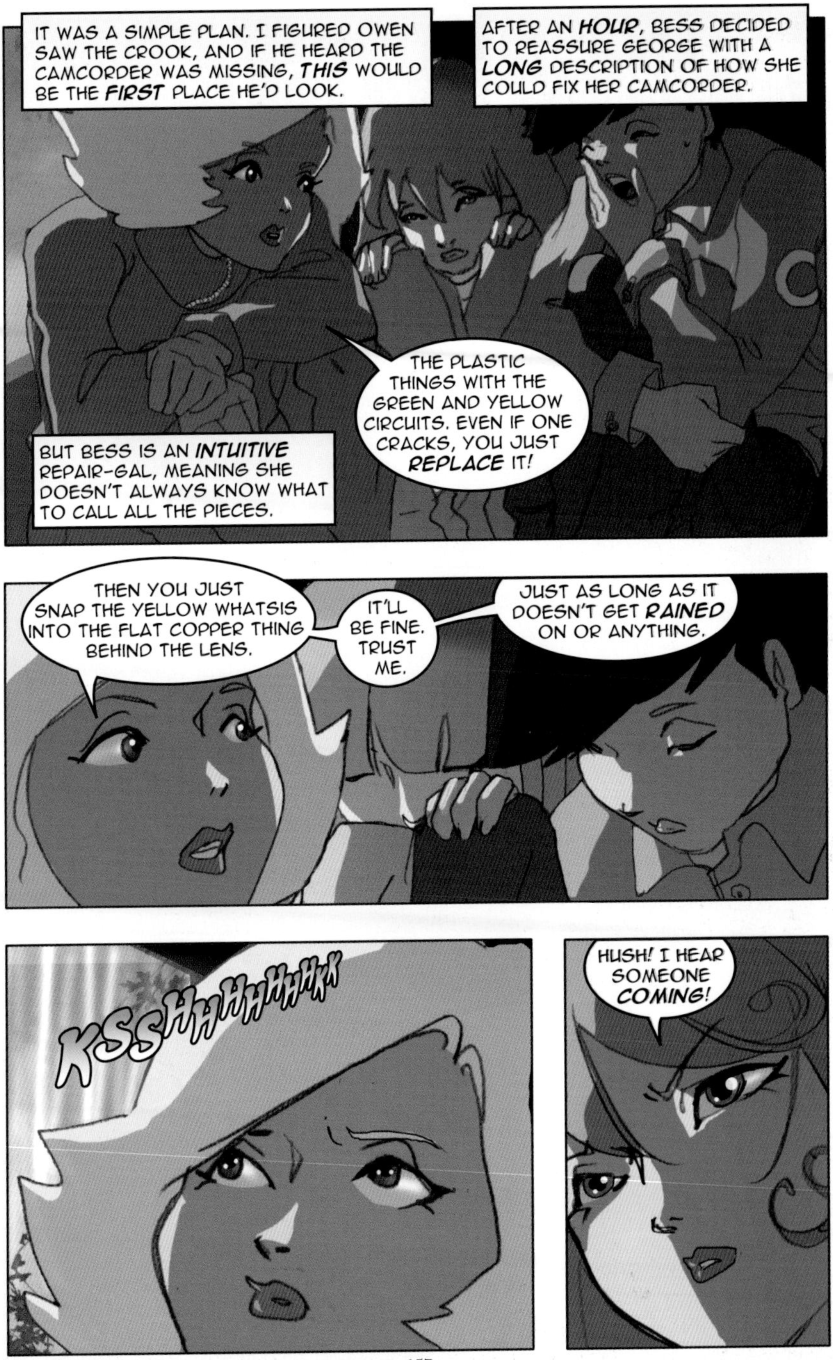
IT WAS A SIMPLE PLAN. I FIGURED OWEN SAW THE CROOK, AND IF HE HEARD THE CAMCORDER WAS MISSING, THIS WOULD BE THE FIRST PLACE HE'D LOOK.
AFTER AN HOUR, BESS DECIDED TO REASSURE GEORGE WITH A LONG DESCRIPTION OF HOW SHE COULD FIX HER CAMCORDER.
THE PLASTIC THINGS WITH THE GREEN AND YELLOW CIRCUITS. EVEN IF ONE CRACKS, YOU JUST REPLACE IT!
BUT BESS IS AN INTUITIVE REPAIR-GAL, MEANING SHE DOESN'T ALWAYS KNOW WHAT TO CALL ALL THE PIECES.
THEN YOU JUST SNAP THE YELLOW WHATSIS INTO THE FLAT COPPER THING BEHIND THE LENS.
IT'LL BE FINE. TRUST ME.
JUST AS LONG AS IT DOESN'T GET RAINED ON OR ANYTHING.
KSSHHHHHHKK
HUSH! I HEAR SOMEONE COMING!

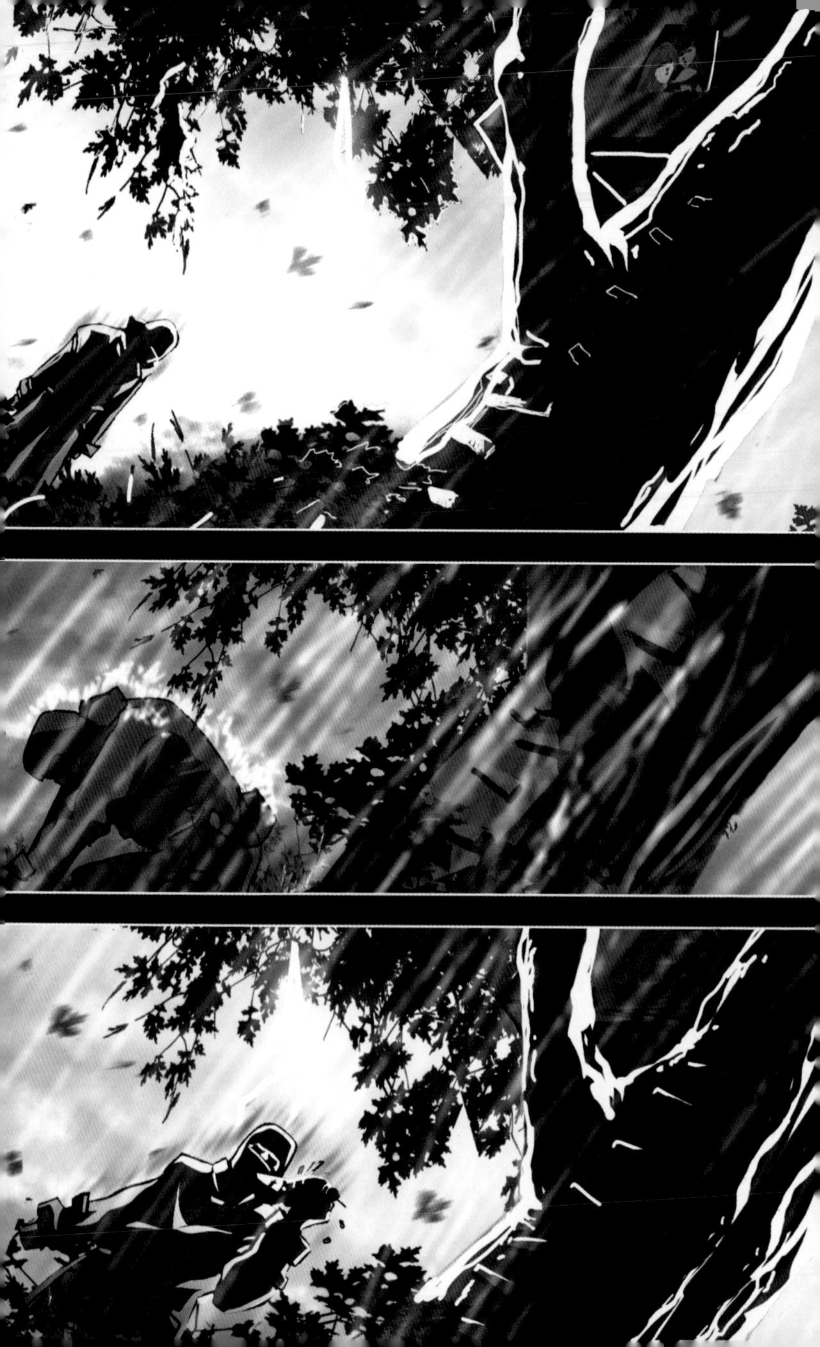

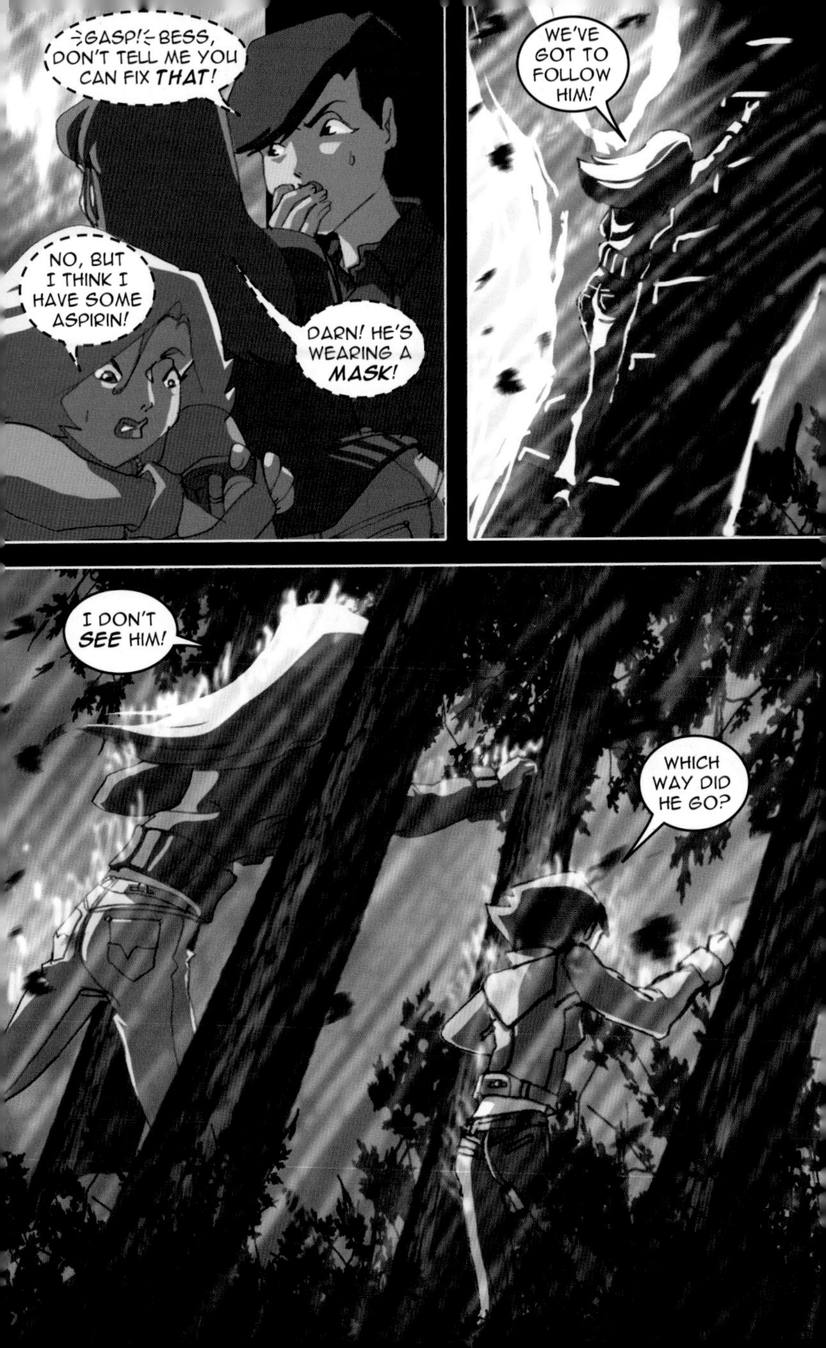

GASP! BESS, DON'T TELL ME YOU CAN FIX THAT!
NO, BUT I THINK I HAVE SOME ASPIRIN!
DARN! HE'S WEARING A MASK!
WE'VE GOT TO FOLLOW HIM!
I DON'T SEE HIM!
WHICH WAY DID HE GO?

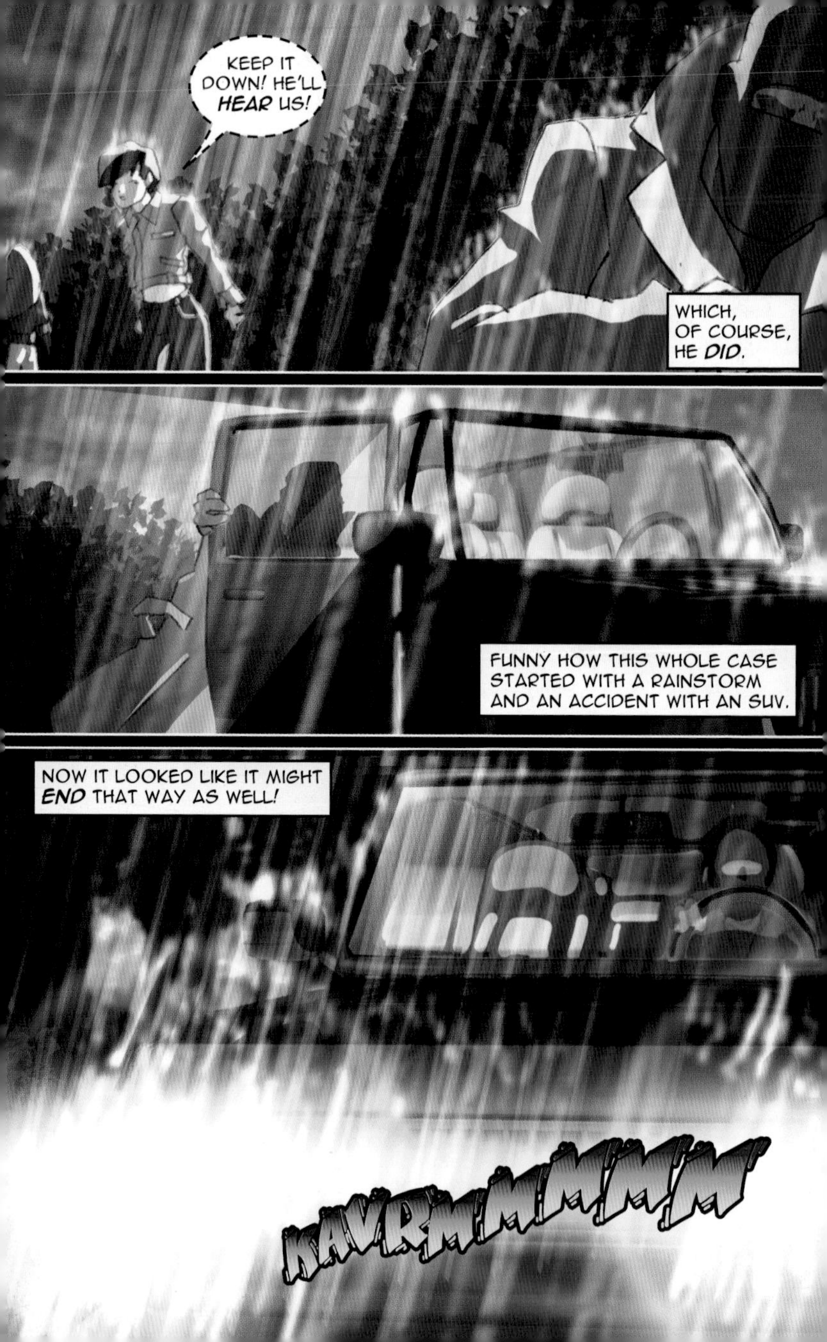
KEEP IT DOWN! HE'LL *HEAR* US!
WHICH, OF COURSE, HE *DID*.
FUNNY HOW THIS WHOLE CASE STARTED WITH A RAINSTORM AND AN ACCIDENT WITH AN SUV.
NOW IT LOOKED LIKE IT MIGHT *END* THAT WAY AS WELL!
KAVRMMMMMM

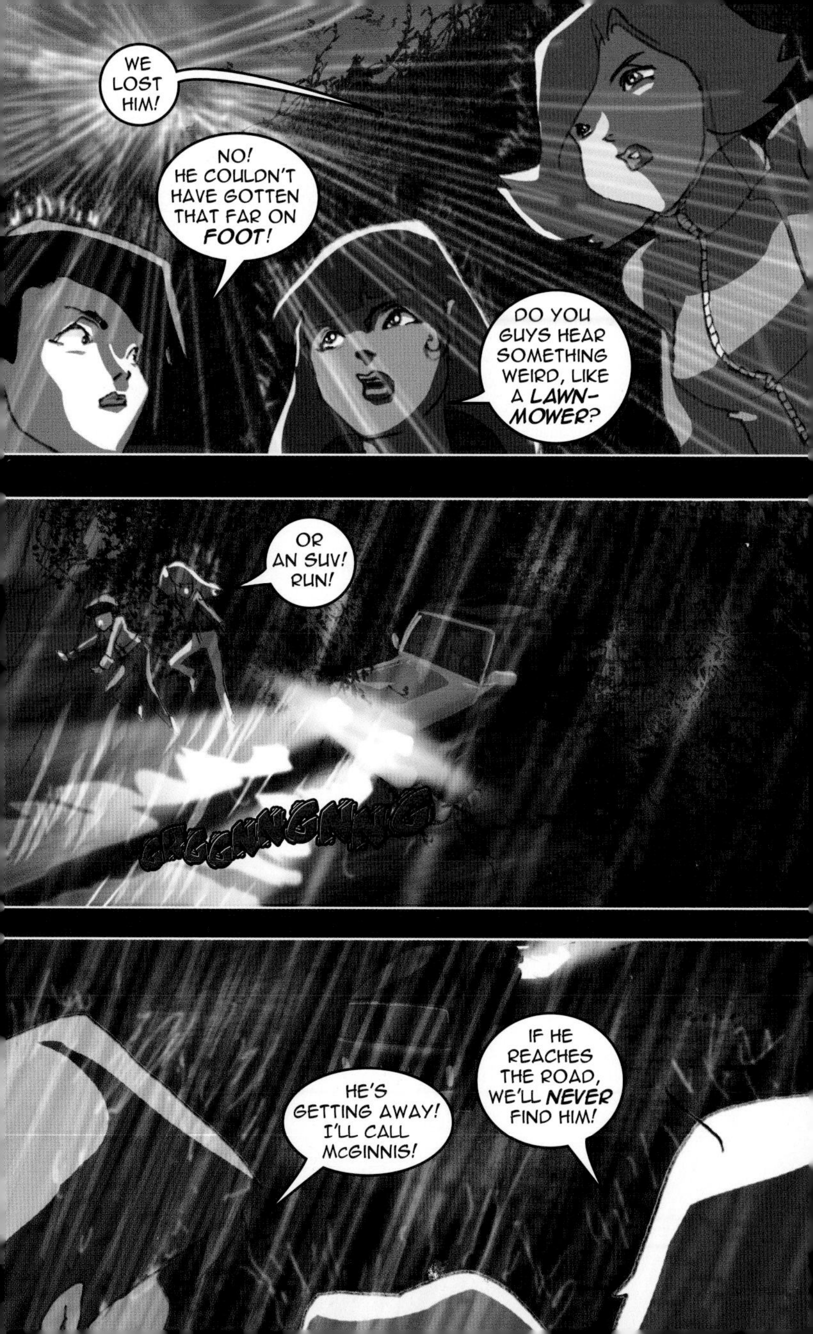
WE LOST HIM!
NO! HE COULDN'T HAVE GOTTEN THAT FAR ON *FOOT*!
DO YOU GUYS HEAR SOMETHING WEIRD, LIKE A *LAWN-MOWER*?
OR AN SUV! RUN!
HE'S GETTING AWAY! I'LL CALL McGINNIS!
IF HE REACHES THE ROAD, WE'LL *NEVER* FIND HIM!

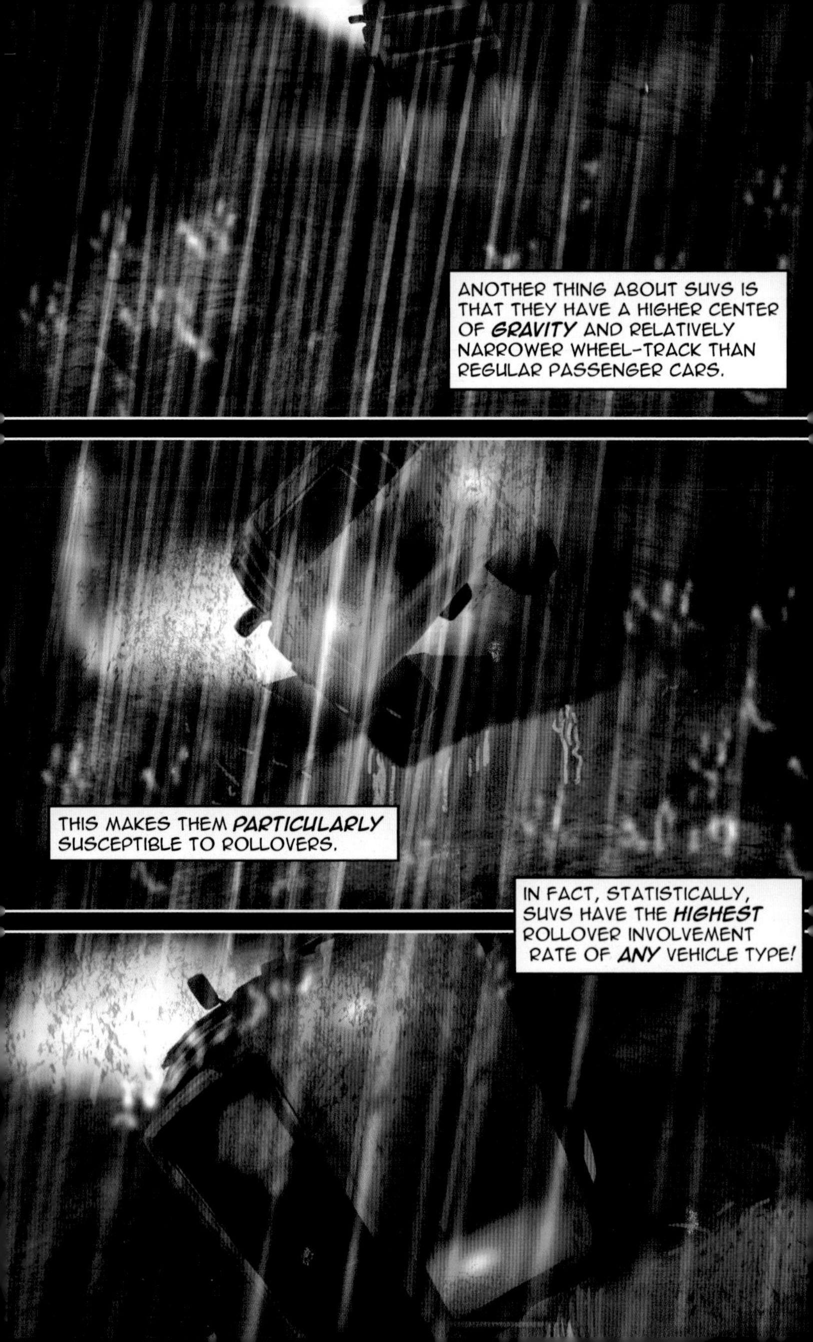
ANOTHER THING ABOUT SUVS IS THAT THEY HAVE A HIGHER CENTER OF GRAVITY AND RELATIVELY NARROWER WHEEL-TRACK THAN REGULAR PASSENGER CARS.
THIS MAKES THEM PARTICULARLY SUSCEPTIBLE TO ROLLOVERS.
IN FACT, STATISTICALLY, SUVS HAVE THE HIGHEST ROLLOVER INVOLVEMENT RATE OF ANY VEHICLE TYPE!

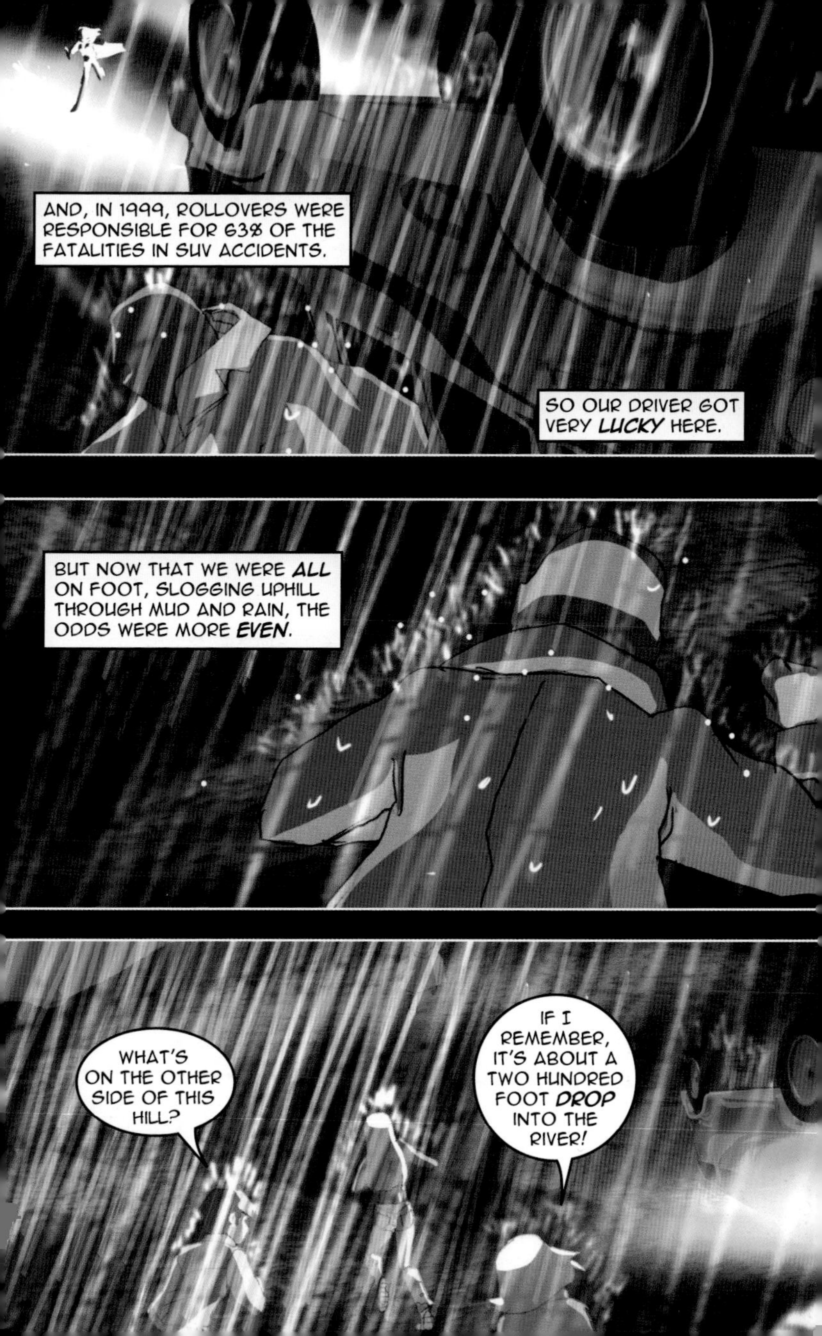
AND, IN 1999, ROLLOVERS WERE RESPONSIBLE FOR 63% OF THE FATALITIES IN SUV ACCIDENTS.
SO OUR DRIVER GOT VERY LUCKY HERE.
BUT NOW THAT WE WERE ALL ON FOOT, SLOGGING UPHILL THROUGH MUD AND RAIN, THE ODDS WERE MORE EVEN.
WHAT'S ON THE OTHER SIDE OF THIS HILL?
IF I REMEMBER, IT'S ABOUT A TWO HUNDRED FOOT DROP INTO THE RIVER!

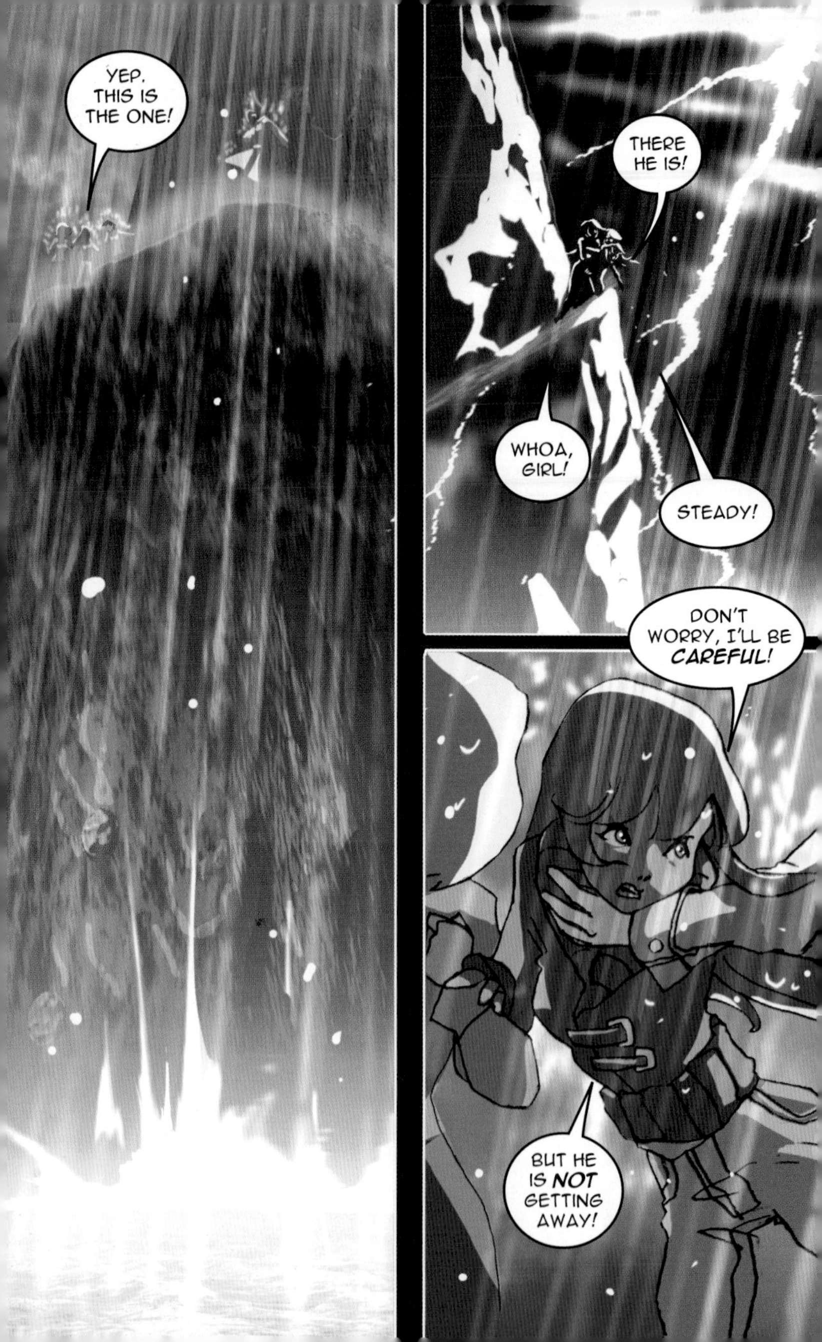
YEP. THIS IS THE ONE!
THERE HE IS!
WHOA, GIRL!
STEADY!
DON'T WORRY, I'LL BE CAREFUL!
BUT HE IS NOT GETTING AWAY!

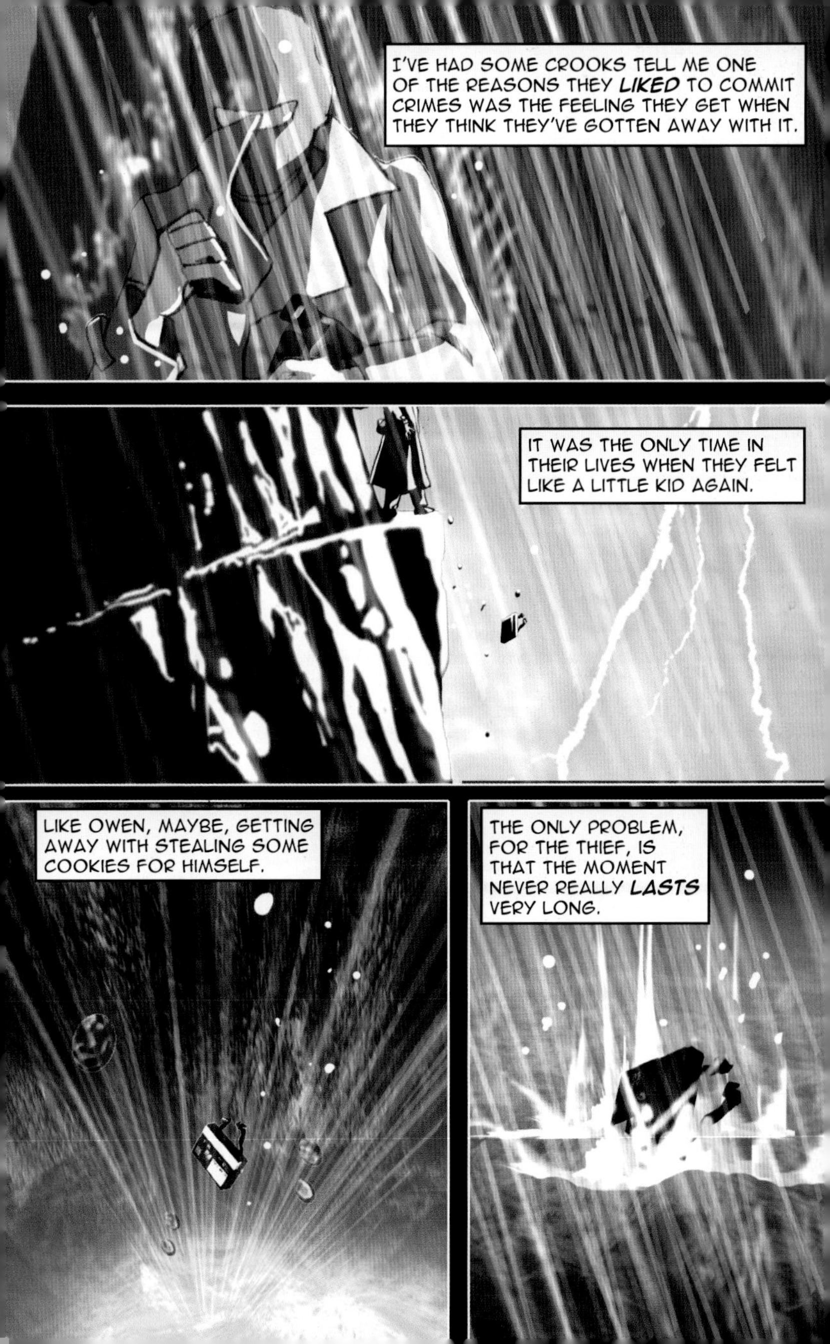
I'VE HAD SOME CROOKS TELL ME ONE OF THE REASONS THEY *LIKED* TO COMMIT CRIMES WAS THE FEELING THEY GET WHEN THEY THINK THEY'VE GOTTEN AWAY WITH IT.
IT WAS THE ONLY TIME IN THEIR LIVES WHEN THEY FELT LIKE A LITTLE KID AGAIN.
LIKE OWEN, MAYBE, GETTING AWAY WITH STEALING SOME COOKIES FOR HIMSELF.
THE ONLY PROBLEM, FOR THE THIEF, IS THAT THE MOMENT NEVER REALLY *LASTS* VERY LONG.

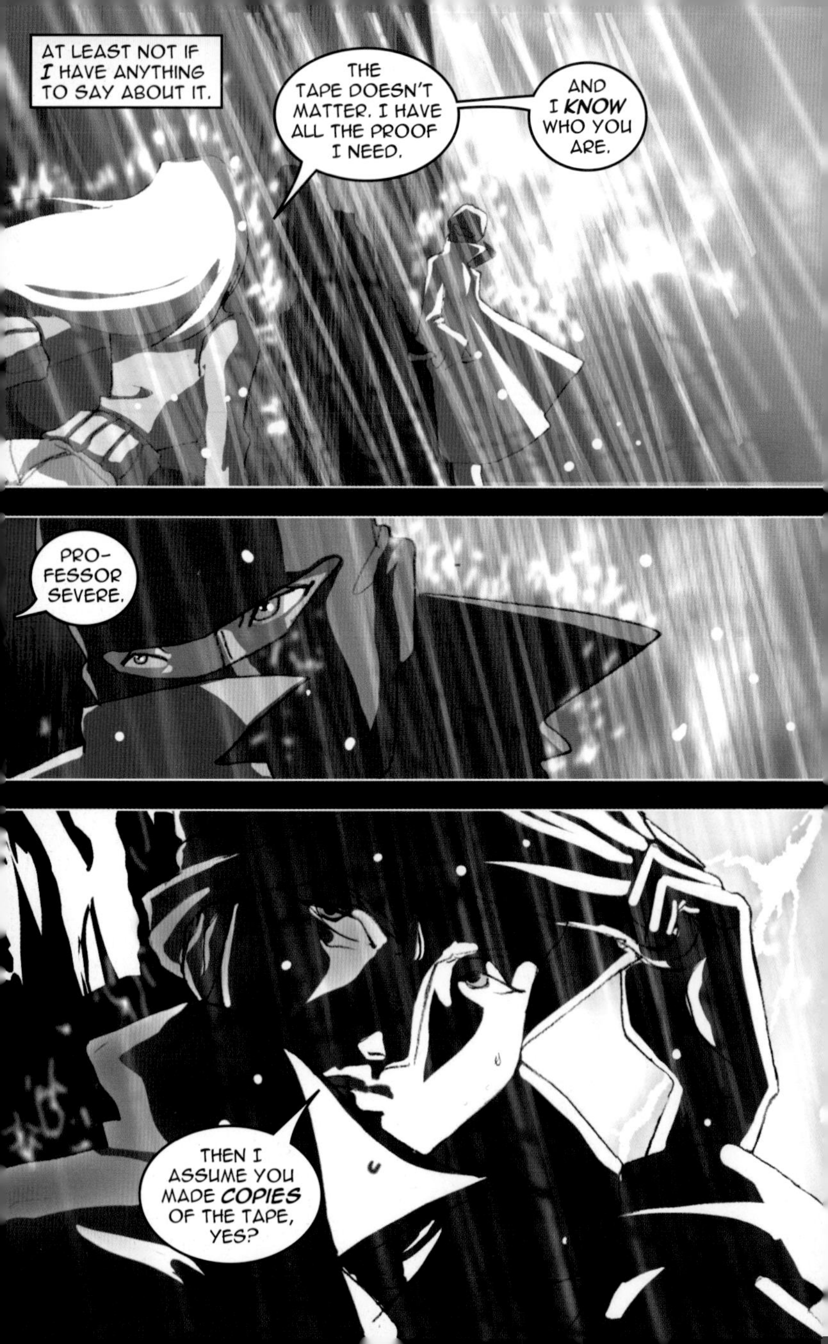
AT LEAST NOT IF I HAVE ANYTHING TO SAY ABOUT IT.
THE TAPE DOESN'T MATTER. I HAVE ALL THE PROOF I NEED.
AND I KNOW WHO YOU ARE.
PRO-FESSOR SEVERE.
THEN I ASSUME YOU MADE COPIES OF THE TAPE, YES?

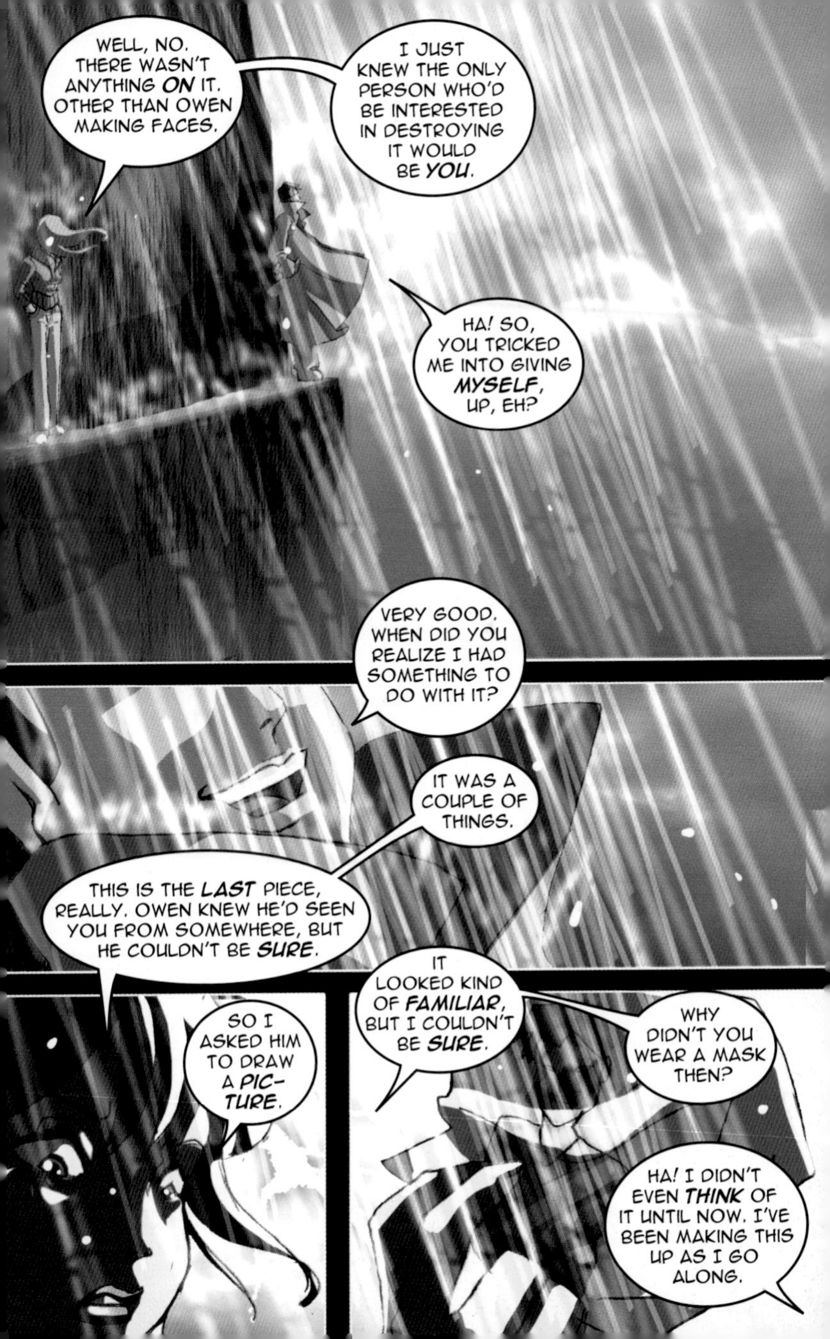
WELL, NO. THERE WASN'T ANYTHING ON IT. OTHER THAN OWEN MAKING FACES.
I JUST KNEW THE ONLY PERSON WHO'D BE INTERESTED IN DESTROYING IT WOULD BE YOU.
HA! SO, YOU TRICKED ME INTO GIVING MYSELF, UP, EH?
VERY GOOD. WHEN DID YOU REALIZE I HAD SOMETHING TO DO WITH IT?
IT WAS A COUPLE OF THINGS.
THIS IS THE LAST PIECE, REALLY. OWEN KNEW HE'D SEEN YOU FROM SOMEWHERE, BUT HE COULDN'T BE SURE.
SO I ASKED HIM TO DRAW A PIC-TURE.
IT LOOKED KIND OF FAMILIAR, BUT I COULDN'T BE SURE.
WHY DIDN'T YOU WEAR A MASK THEN?
HA! I DIDN'T EVEN THINK OF IT UNTIL NOW. I'VE BEEN MAKING THIS UP AS I GO ALONG.

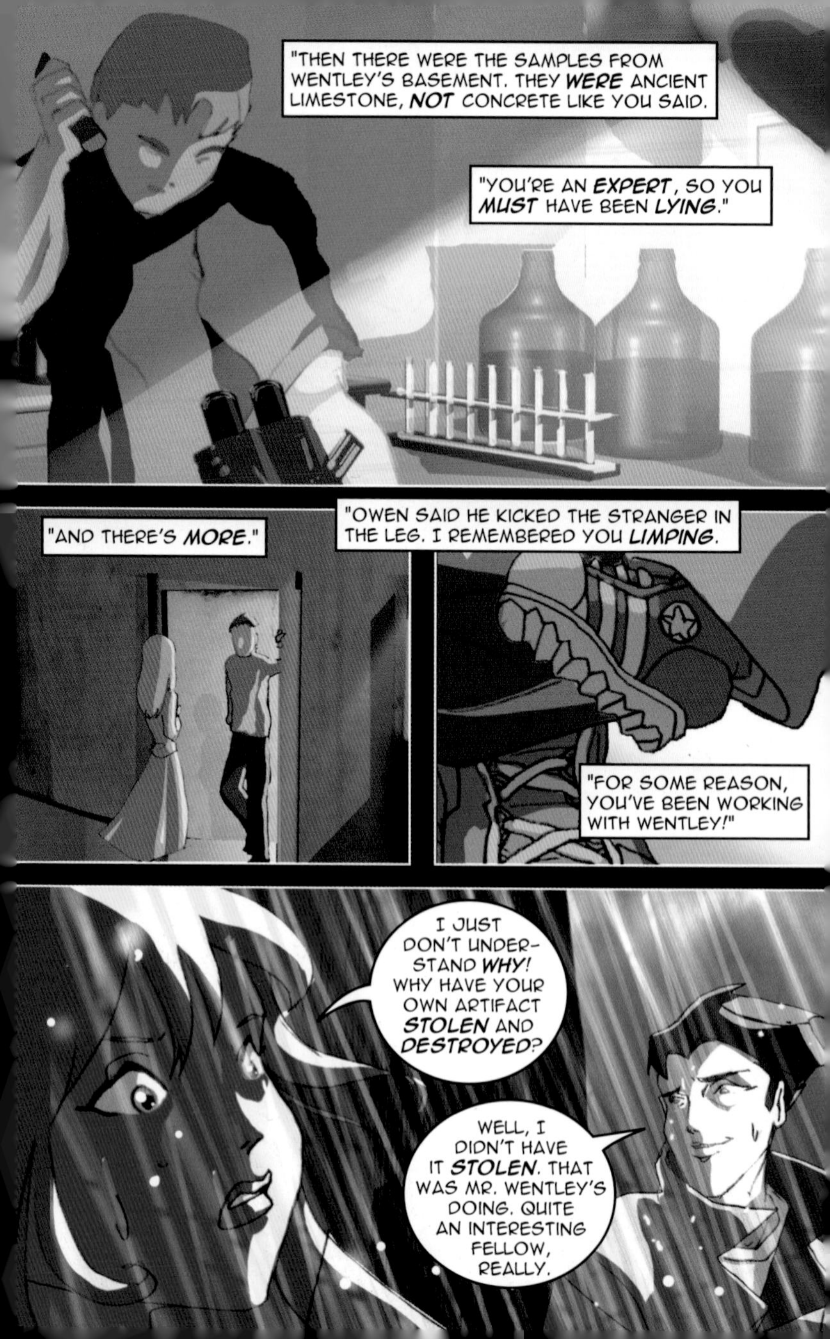
"THEN THERE WERE THE SAMPLES FROM WENTLEY'S BASEMENT. THEY *WERE* ANCIENT LIMESTONE, *NOT* CONCRETE LIKE YOU SAID.
"YOU'RE AN *EXPERT*, SO YOU *MUST* HAVE BEEN *LYING*."
"AND THERE'S *MORE*."
"OWEN SAID HE KICKED THE STRANGER IN THE LEG. I REMEMBERED YOU *LIMPING*.
"FOR SOME REASON, YOU'VE BEEN WORKING WITH WENTLEY!"
I JUST DON'T UNDER-STAND *WHY*! WHY HAVE YOUR OWN ARTIFACT *STOLEN* AND *DESTROYED*?
WELL, I DIDN'T HAVE IT *STOLEN*. THAT WAS MR. WENTLEY'S DOING. QUITE AN INTERESTING FELLOW, REALLY.

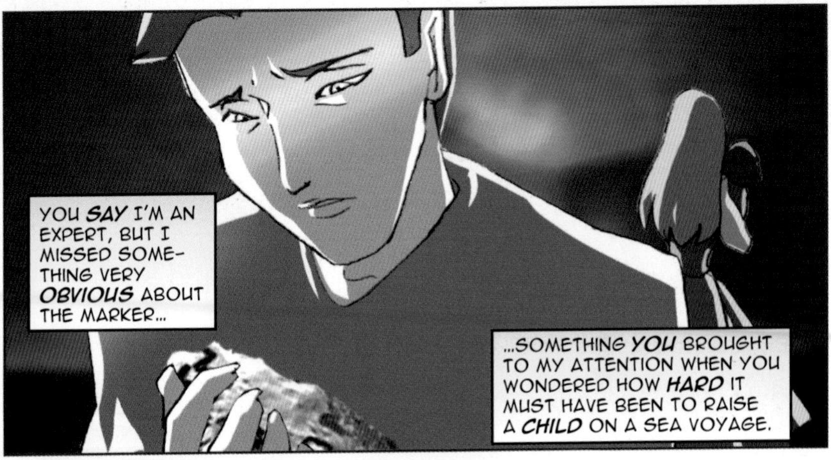
YOU SAY I'M AN EXPERT, BUT I MISSED SOME-THING VERY OBVIOUS ABOUT THE MARKER...
...SOMETHING YOU BROUGHT TO MY ATTENTION WHEN YOU WONDERED HOW HARD IT MUST HAVE BEEN TO RAISE A CHILD ON A SEA VOYAGE.

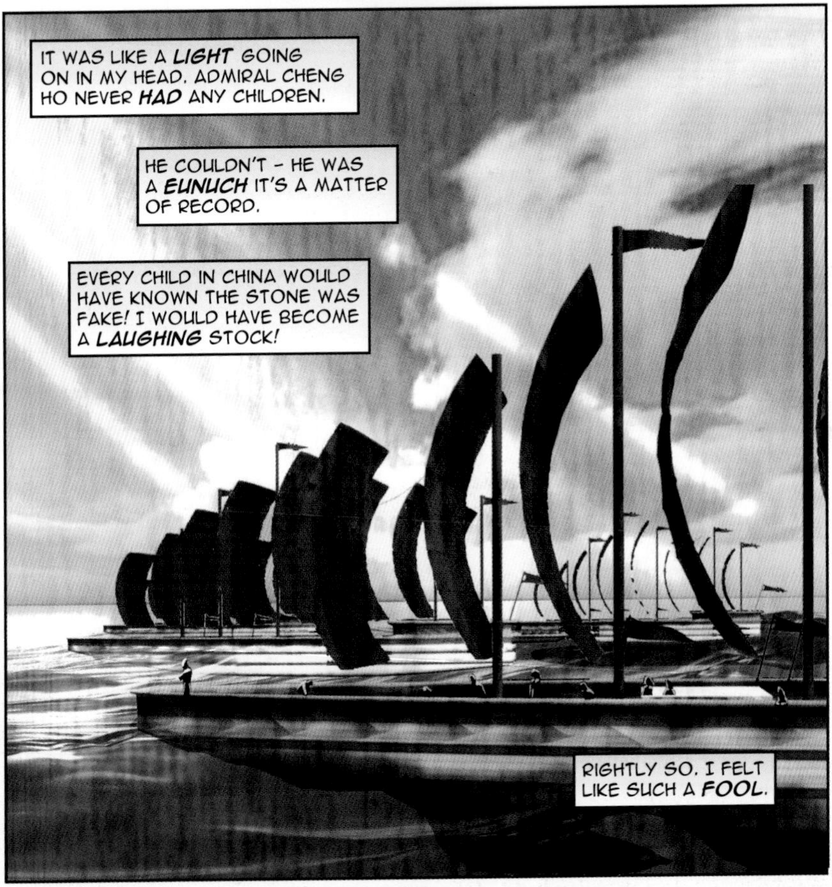
IT WAS LIKE A LIGHT GOING ON IN MY HEAD. ADMIRAL CHENG HO NEVER HAD ANY CHILDREN.
HE COULDN'T - HE WAS A EUNUCH IT'S A MATTER OF RECORD.
EVERY CHILD IN CHINA WOULD HAVE KNOWN THE STONE WAS FAKE! I WOULD HAVE BECOME A LAUGHING STOCK!
RIGHTLY SO. I FELT LIKE SUCH A FOOL.

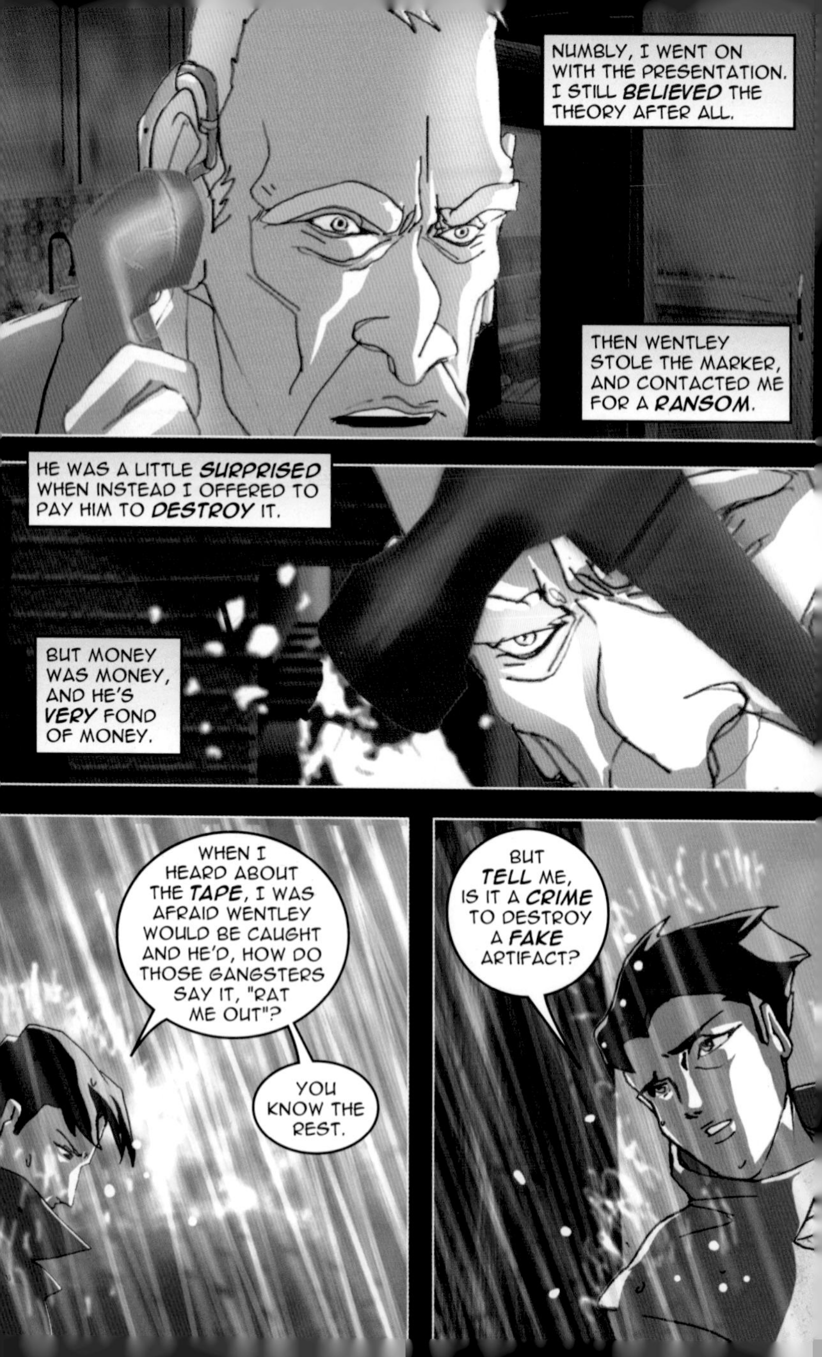
NUMBLY, I WENT ON WITH THE PRESENTATION. I STILL BELIEVED THE THEORY AFTER ALL.
THEN WENTLEY STOLE THE MARKER, AND CONTACTED ME FOR A RANSOM.
HE WAS A LITTLE SURPRISED WHEN INSTEAD I OFFERED TO PAY HIM TO DESTROY IT.
BUT MONEY WAS MONEY, AND HE'S VERY FOND OF MONEY.
WHEN I HEARD ABOUT THE TAPE, I WAS AFRAID WENTLEY WOULD BE CAUGHT AND HE'D, HOW DO THOSE GANGSTERS SAY IT, "RAT ME OUT"?
YOU KNOW THE REST.
BUT TELL ME, IS IT A CRIME TO DESTROY A FAKE ARTIFACT?

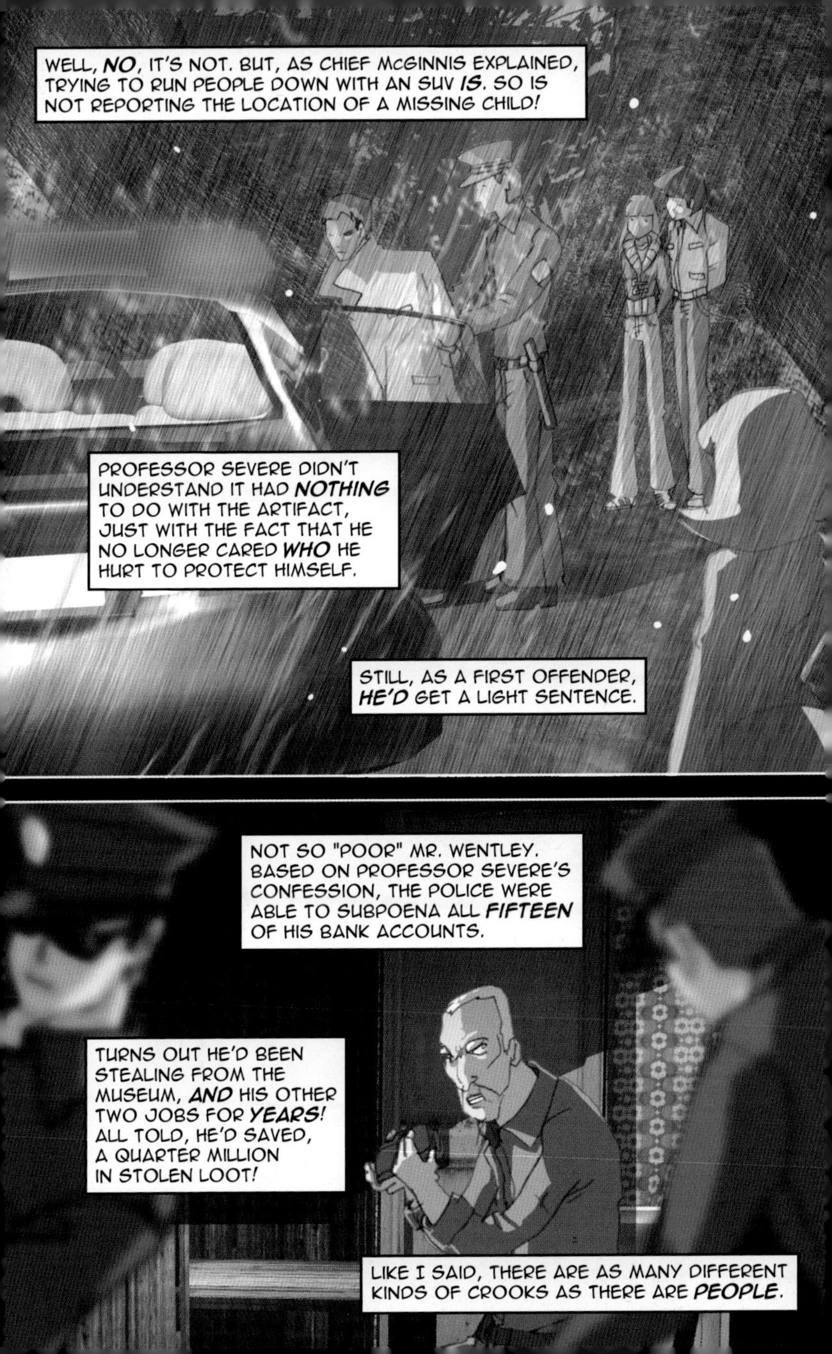
WELL, NO, IT'S NOT. BUT, AS CHIEF McGINNIS EXPLAINED, TRYING TO RUN PEOPLE DOWN WITH AN SUV IS. SO IS NOT REPORTING THE LOCATION OF A MISSING CHILD!
PROFESSOR SEVERE DIDN'T UNDERSTAND IT HAD NOTHING TO DO WITH THE ARTIFACT, JUST WITH THE FACT THAT HE NO LONGER CARED WHO HE HURT TO PROTECT HIMSELF.
STILL, AS A FIRST OFFENDER, HE'D GET A LIGHT SENTENCE.
NOT SO "POOR" MR. WENTLEY. BASED ON PROFESSOR SEVERE'S CONFESSION, THE POLICE WERE ABLE TO SUBPOENA ALL FIFTEEN OF HIS BANK ACCOUNTS.
TURNS OUT HE'D BEEN STEALING FROM THE MUSEUM, AND HIS OTHER TWO JOBS FOR YEARS! ALL TOLD, HE'D SAVED, A QUARTER MILLION IN STOLEN LOOT!
LIKE I SAID, THERE ARE AS MANY DIFFERENT KINDS OF CROOKS AS THERE ARE PEOPLE.

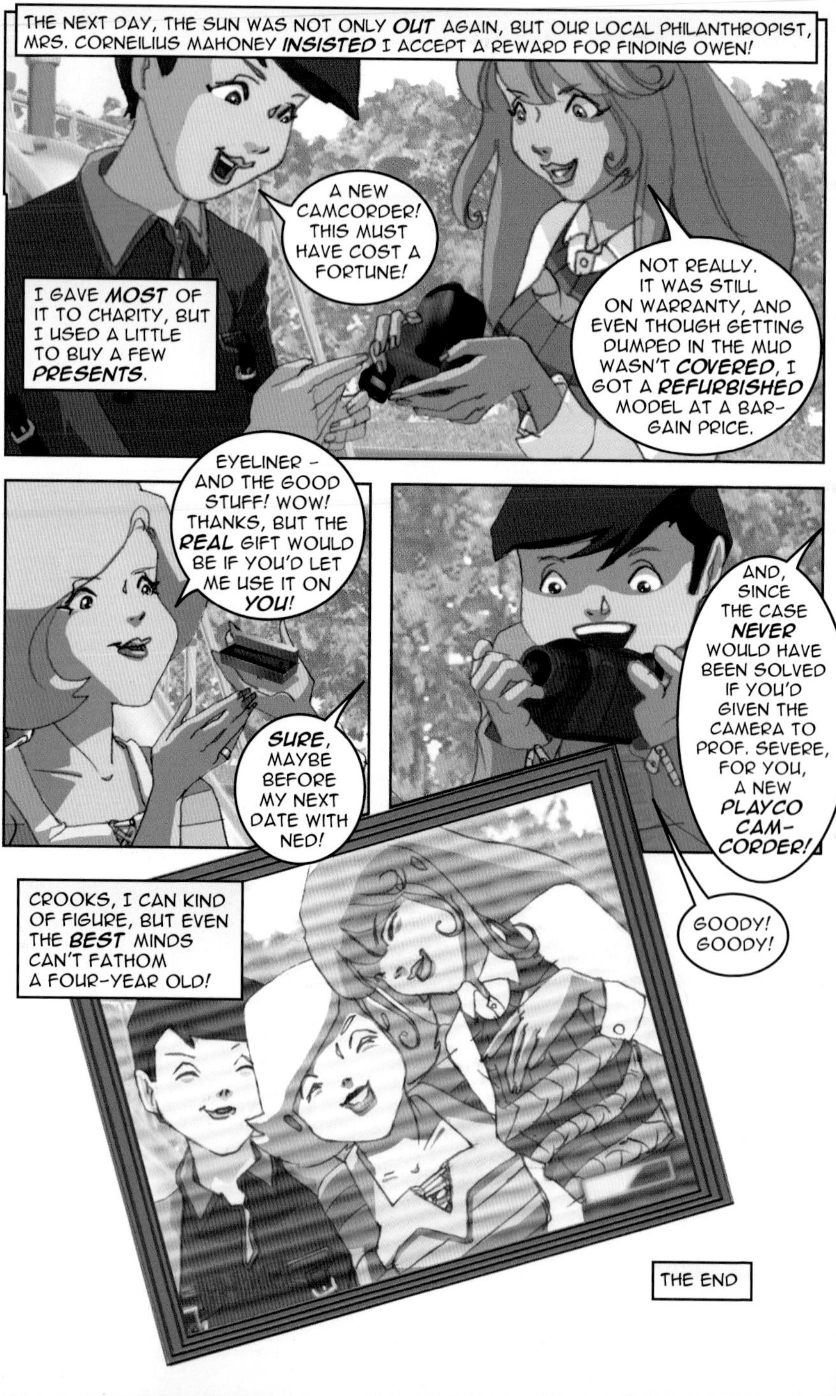

THE NEXT DAY, THE SUN WAS NOT ONLY **OUT** AGAIN, BUT OUR LOCAL PHILANTHROPIST, MRS. CORNEILIUS MAHONEY **INSISTED** I ACCEPT A REWARD FOR FINDING OWEN!
A NEW CAMCORDER! THIS MUST HAVE COST A FORTUNE!
I GAVE **MOST** OF IT TO CHARITY, BUT I USED A LITTLE TO BUY A FEW **PRESENTS**.
NOT REALLY. IT WAS STILL ON WARRANTY, AND EVEN THOUGH GETTING DUMPED IN THE MUD WASN'T **COVERED**, I GOT A **REFURBISHED** MODEL AT A BAR-GAIN PRICE.
EYELINER - AND THE GOOD STUFF! WOW! THANKS, BUT THE **REAL** GIFT WOULD BE IF YOU'D LET ME USE IT ON **YOU**!
SURE, MAYBE BEFORE MY NEXT DATE WITH NED!
AND, SINCE THE CASE **NEVER** WOULD HAVE BEEN SOLVED IF YOU'D GIVEN THE CAMERA TO PROF. SEVERE, FOR YOU, A NEW **PLAYCO CAM-CORDER!**
GOODY! GOODY!
CROOKS, I CAN KIND OF FIGURE, BUT EVEN THE **BEST** MINDS CAN'T FATHOM A FOUR-YEAR OLD!
THE END

WATCH OUT FOR PAPERCUTZ

Welcome to the fraud-filled, first NANCY DREW DIARIES graphic novel from Papercutz, the fascinating folks dedicated to publishing great graphic novels for all ages. I'm Jim Salicrup, the Editor-in-Chief and River Heights Demon stand-in, and I'm somewhat sentimental because you picked up this particular graphic novel.

You see, when Papercutz publisher Terry Nantier and I started this whole Papercutz publishing enterprise back in 2005, not too many folks believed that a graphic novel publisher devoted to publishing comics for children, especially for girls, could possibly succeed. Well, here we are, almost ten years later, and we're still publishing titles such as NANCY DREW DIARIES, which features two of the very first graphic novels Papercutz published. Be it luck, the enduring popularity of Carolyn Keene's Nancy Drew, or the combined talents of Stefan Petrucha, writer, and Sho Murase, artist, or whatever it was, we're thrilled to still be here publishing the adventures of everyone's favorite Girl Detective!

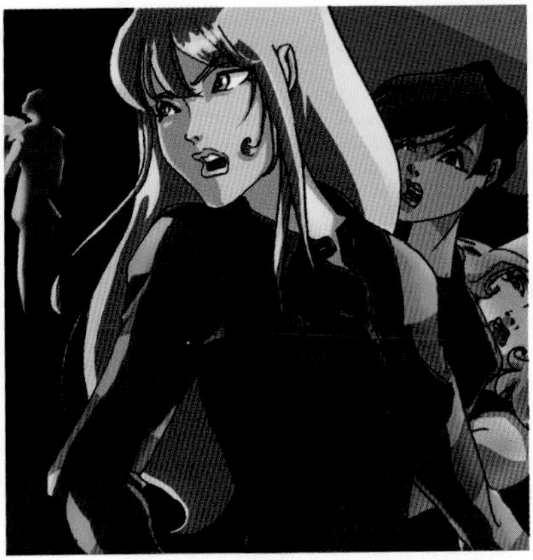

As we start out on our fourth NANCY DREW series, we must thank some of the wonderful people that helped make it possible in the first place. First up, Nellie Kurtzman and Robb Pearlman, two of the folks back at Simon & Schuster that had the faith that we could bring Nancy Drew and The Hardy Boys to life in the comics format. We must also thank Laurie Becker and Arlene Scanlon of Moxie & Company, for their continued support and never-ending efforts on Nancy's behalf. Thanks to everyone at Simon & Schuster for continually keeping Nancy in print in new exciting series. And to our distributor, Macmillan, for believing in Papercutz from the start. And of course, to Stefan Petrucha and Sho Murase, for always doing their very best work on this series and caring so much about the teen sleuth and all her friends.

But most of all, to YOU, the true Nancy Drew fans! Thanks to you for keeping the Mistress of Mystery alive for over 80 years! Whether this is your very first NANCY DREW book or you've been reading NANCY DREW since the very start (Bless you!), we thank you for your support and love of the top teen sleuth—Miss Nancy Drew!

Thanks,

Jim

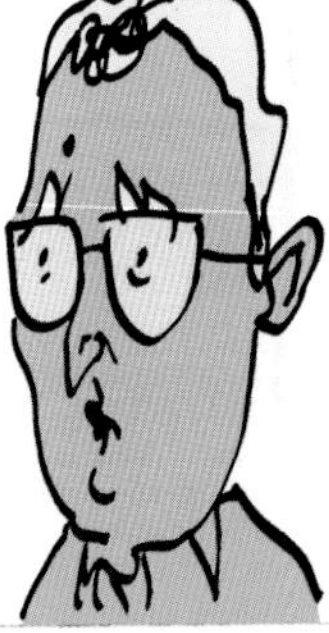

STAY IN TOUCH!

EMAIL:	salicrup@papercutz.com
WEB:	www.papercutz.com
TWITTER:	@papercutzgn
FACEBOOK:	PAPERCUTZGRAPHICNOVELS
REGULAR MAIL:	Papercutz, 160 Broadway, Suite 700, East Wing, New York, NY 10038

NANCY DREW GRAPHIC NOVELS AVAILABLE FROM PAPERCUTZ

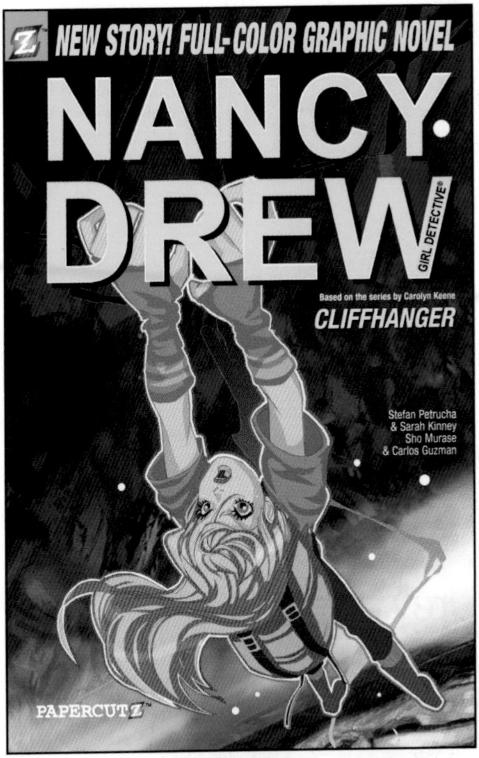
NEW STORY! FULL-COLOR GRAPHIC NOVEL
NANCY DREW
GIRL DETECTIVE®
Based on the series by Carolyn Keene
CLIFFHANGER
Stefan Petrucha
& Sarah Kinney
Sho Murase
& Carlos Guzman
PAPERCUTZ

#19 "Cliffhanger"

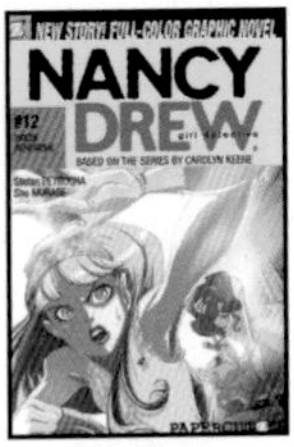
NEW STORY! FULL-COLOR GRAPHIC NOVEL
NANCY DREW
BASED ON THE SERIES BY CAROLYN KEENE
PAPERCUTZ

#12 "Dress Reversal"

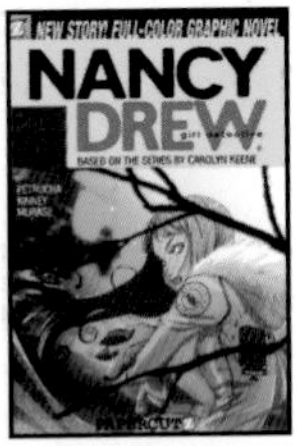
NEW STORY! FULL-COLOR GRAPHIC NOVEL
NANCY DREW
BASED ON THE SERIES BY CAROLYN KEENE
PAPERCUTZ

#13 "Doggone Town"

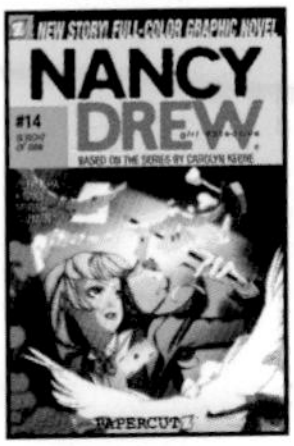
NEW STORY! FULL-COLOR GRAPHIC NOVEL
NANCY DREW
BASED ON THE SERIES BY CAROLYN KEENE
PAPERCUTZ

#14 "Sleight of Dan"

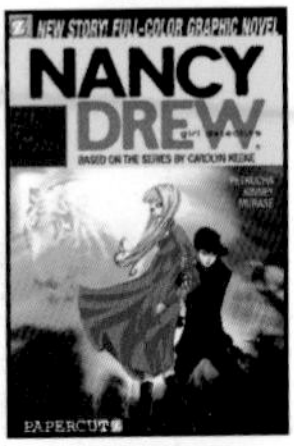
NEW STORY! FULL-COLOR GRAPHIC NOVEL
NANCY DREW
BASED ON THE SERIES BY CAROLYN KEENE
PAPERCUTZ

#15 "Tiger Counter"

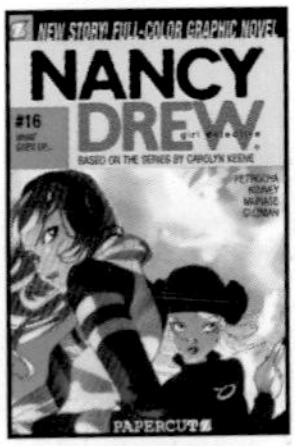
NEW STORY! FULL-COLOR GRAPHIC NOVEL
NANCY DREW
BASED ON THE SERIES BY CAROLYN KEENE
PAPERCUTZ

#16 "What Goes Up..."

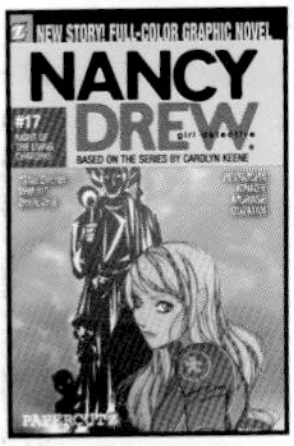
NEW STORY! FULL-COLOR GRAPHIC NOVEL
NANCY DREW
BASED ON THE SERIES BY CAROLYN KEENE
PAPERCUTZ

#17 "Night of the Living Chatchke"

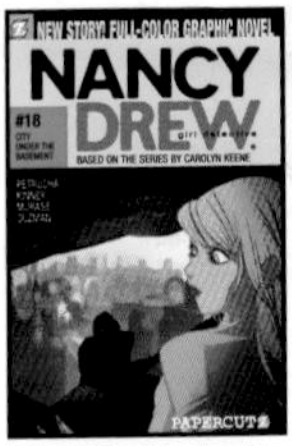
NEW STORY! FULL-COLOR GRAPHIC NOVEL
NANCY DREW
BASED ON THE SERIES BY CAROLYN KEENE
PAPERCUTZ

#18 "City Under the Basement"

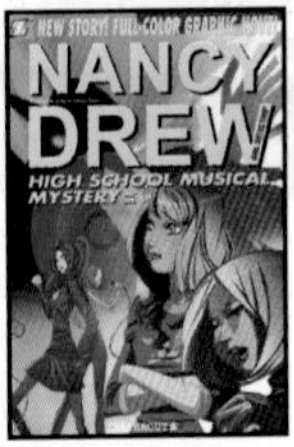
NEW STORY! FULL-COLOR GRAPHIC NOVEL
NANCY DREW
HIGH SCHOOL MUSICAL MYSTERY

#20 "High School Musical Mystery" 1

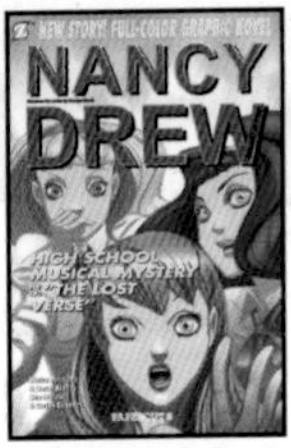
NEW STORY! FULL-COLOR GRAPHIC NOVEL
NANCY DREW
HIGH SCHOOL MUSICAL MYSTERY
THE LOST VERSE

#21 "High School Musical Mystery" 2

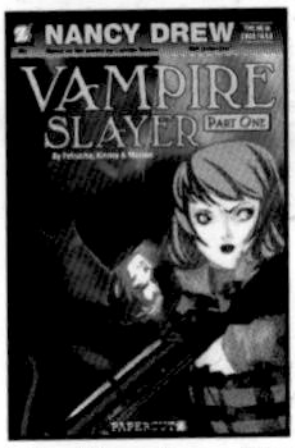
NANCY DREW
VAMPIRE SLAYER PART ONE
PAPERCUTZ

The New Case Files #1 "Vampire Slayer" Part 1

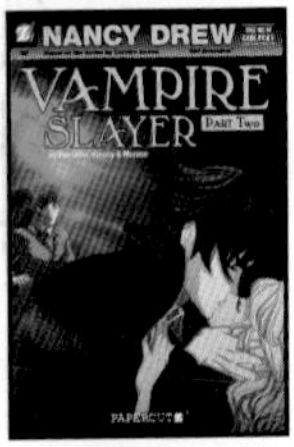
NANCY DREW
VAMPIRE SLAYER PART TWO
PAPERCUTZ

The New Case Files #2 "Vampire Slayer" Part 2

NANCY DREW Graphic Novels #12-19 are $7.95 in paperback, $12.95 hardcover. Graphic Novels #20 and #21 are $8.99 paperback, $13.99 hardcover. NANCY DREW The New Case Files #1 and #2 are $6.99 paperback, $10.99 hardcover. Available at booksellers everywhere.

Or order from us. Make check payable to NBM Publishing.
Please add $4.00 for postage and handling for the first book, add $1.00 for each additional book.
Send to: Papercutz, 160 Broadway, Suite 700, East Wing, New York, NY 10038
Or call 800 886 1223 (9-6 EST M-F) MC, Visa, Amex accepted.

papercutz.com

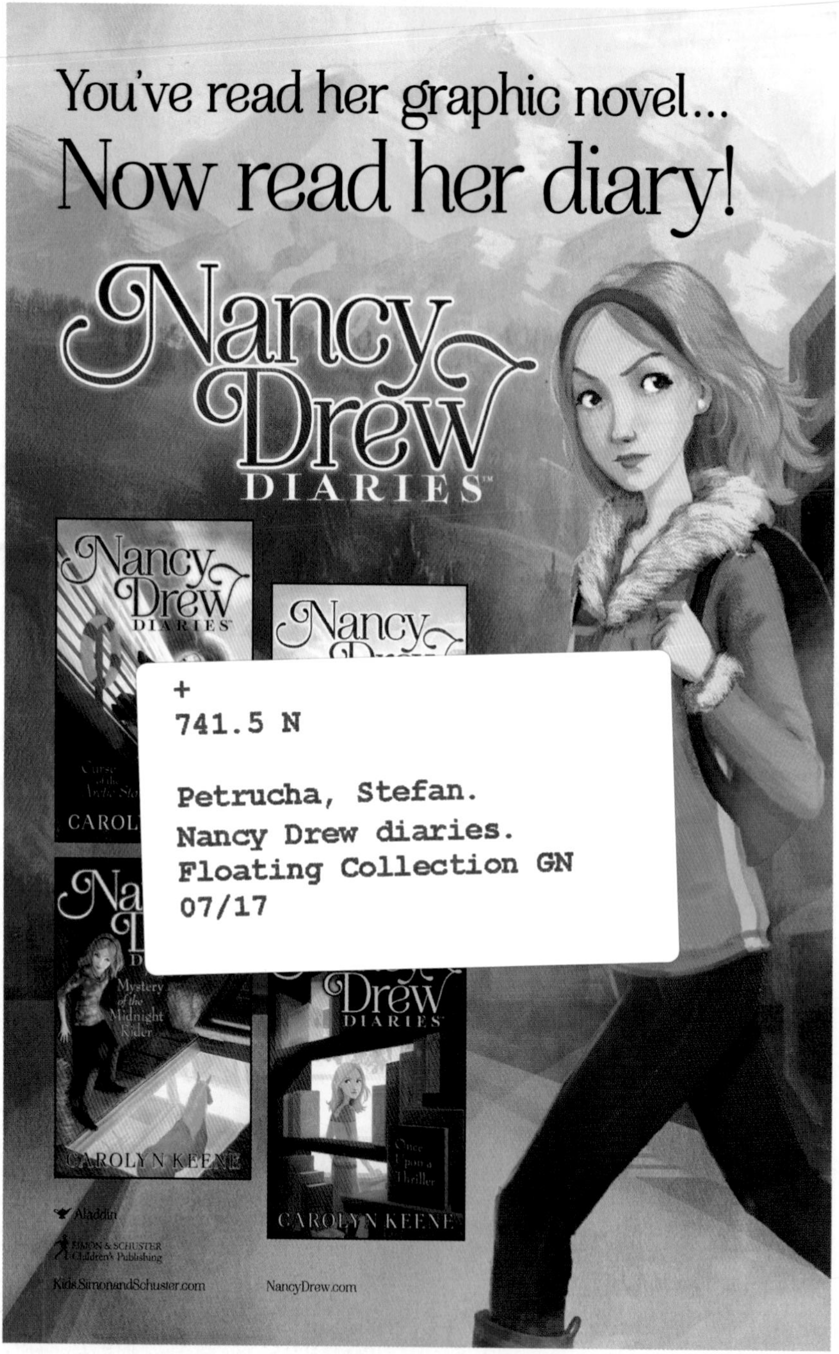
You've read her graphic novel...
Now read her diary!
Nancy Drew DIARIES™
Nancy Drew DIARIES™
Curse of the Arctic Star
CAROLYN KEENE
Nancy Drew DIARIES™
Mystery of the Midnight Rider
CAROLYN KEENE
Nancy Drew DIARIES™
Once Upon a Thriller
CAROLYN KEENE
Aladdin
SIMON & SCHUSTER Children's Publishing
KidsSimonandSchuster.com
NancyDrew.com